Praise for *THE NEW GIRLS* by Beth Gutcheon

"Gutcheon has an impeccable fix on time, place, and native customs—and...pathos of a vanished youth."

—*Kirkus Reviews*

"This is the story of those crucial relationships and of a harrowing loss of innocence."

—*Library Journal*

"There is a Fitzgeraldian quality in Gutcheon's portrayal of the space and beauty and order that money can buy....What we do come to understand—or rather, to feel—is what it was like to be among the young girls at this bastion of tradition and propriety in the early '60s."

—*Newsday*

"Gutcheon...is able to capture...a time and place."

—*Washington Post*

"The author moves in and knows the world about which she writes. Good entertaining reading."

—*Pensacola News*

"Well-written and always interesting."

—*Reader's Syndicate*

Also by Beth Gutcheon

Saying Grace
Domestic Pleasures
Still Missing

The New Girls

by
Beth Gutcheon

Harper Perennial
A Division of HarperCollinsPublishers

This book was originally published in 1979 by G. P. Putnam's Sons. It is here reprinted by arrangement with the author.

First Harper Perennial edition published 1996.

ISBN 0-06-097702-7

00 01 02 RRD 20 19 18 17 16 15 14 13 12

For their generous actions and reactions, I want to thank Robbie Fanning, William Ray, Ann Boyd, Joy Richardson, Ethelbook Nevin, R. Todd (Pine Tree Lodge, Prop.), Michael Cooper, David Gutcheon, and my lucky stars for my agent, Wendy Weil, for Diane Matthews, the editor you dream of and never get, and for the material assistance of David Taylor, my friend.

Contents

The New Girls

Fifteen Years Out

A hundred years ago, Miss Pratt's School for Young Ladies was a finishing school. Girls were sent there to be finished, in the sense that an end table is finished by a glossy coat of varnish. Finished also in the sense of completed; once Miss Pratt had pried their minds open and sorted and labeled the contents, she closed them up again, the lids nailed tight. In Miss Pratt's day there were only a very few things a well-bred lady ought to know, and all of them could be mastered before the age of eighteen.

By 1959 Miss Pratt's had long since given up the trade of finishing and had taken up instead preparing girls, presumably for college. If anything, its reputation was more illustrious than in Miss Pratt's day. For a school like Miss Pratt's, reputation becomes a self-fulfilling prophecy: the best school attracts the brightest girls with the greatest worldly and personal advantages, fills them with a sense of the school's consequence and their own, and in time collects the most promising of their daughters, as if in ransom.

Every October, for over a hundred years, when the dazzling blaze of autumn fails to heat the thrilling chill of New England air, graduates of Miss Pratt's flock back to the town of Lakebury to celebrate their fifth, their fifteenth, their twenty-fifth reunions. Their mode of travel has changed. In Miss Pratt's day they arrived sitting bolt upright in their carriages, since no lady would be seen in public lounging with her spine against the back

11

of her seat. But their motives have not. They come to revise the past. For of course it's not true that what's done is done and can't be changed. The present is constantly shifting the weight and meaning of events that lead up to it. Time isolates patterns in the rubble of remembered detail. Time is what separates meaningless moments from those that link into chains of cause and effect, joining the girls they were and the women they became. Miss Pratt's girls come back to reunion for the comfort of sharing common history, but also to seek consensus as to what the history was, since no one sees anyone else's story whole, at the time, or ever, and since no one can tell what the beginnings mean until she has an idea of how the story ends.

In October of 1978, when Lisa Sutton, '63, reached the door of the bedroom she and Muffin had shared as new girls, Muffin was already there. Lisa was panting from running up two flights of stairs; Muffin was at the window, wrapped in sunlight, watching the street for returning friends. Her face glowed, and her hair, released from the giant rollers of their prep-school days, formed an unruly halo around her face. It gleamed with premature silver, and the shade became her. These days, Lisa had to admit, Muffin managed to carry her plumpness with a casual ease that was as sensual as it was unconscious.

"*Sweetie,* I'm so glad to see you!" Lisa rushed across the small room and swept Muffin into her arms with a clatter of gold bracelets. "God, you smell like a kennel!" She kissed Muffin grandly on both cheeks in the manner she'd lately adopted.

"You know, you're very fucking rude, Lisa," said Jenny from the bed in the corner. "Has that thought ever occurred to you?"

"JENNY! MY GOD, I DIDN'T THINK YOU'D COME!" Jenny stood up for a dramatic embrace, smiling over Lisa's shoulder at Muffin. They'd just been saying to each other that Lisa always talked in capital letters for the first half-hour at least.

"I *do* smell like a kennel," said Muffin proudly. "Our new bitch began to whelp at five this morning and Chip was still with her when I left. I almost didn't have time to stop and change, but there was afterbirth on my—"

"CHRIST, MUFFIN, I don't want to *hear* about it," said Lisa, fishing in her purse. "Listen, that's a really nice skirt you're wearing, though—here, let me put some perfume on you. It's Norell, it'll suit you, you should always wear it. Did you get it at Saks?"

"What?" said Muffin, sniffing in surprise at the cloud of perfume Lisa sprayed on her hair and clothes. "Oh, the skirt? I think so." Lisa rolled her eyes at Jenny as if to say: Isn't she unbelievable?

"Anyway, dearlings, you're both looking *gorgeous,*" said Lisa, curling her legs under her as she settled into the only armchair. She was wearing a long tweed skirt with a man's shirt and vest, a style of dress that emphasized her slender beauty, as she very well knew. Her blond hair was freshly streaked, and she had taken to wearing tinted aviator glasses since she met Gloria Steinem at a cocktail party.

Muffin let the remark pass. She had long since learned that you could count on Lisa to head for her own conversational high ground. You had to let her, otherwise she paced and fidgeted in and out of the talk, looking for a way to turn it to the subject of how she was looking. Lisa had been obsessive about looks since the time she got sick sophomore year. But Muffin had changed. She no longer agreed, as she had at fifteen, that you were guaranteed to die happy if only you were as beautiful as Lisa.

"*Jenny,*" Lisa rattled on, "I thought that picture of you on the cover of *People* was the pits, didn't you? I mean, they made you look so *tired.* . . ."

Muffin and Jenny looked at each other and laughed.

"What's funny?" Lisa smiled too. "What's the joke? Oh, God, I'm so glad to see you both, this is *just* divine. When is Ann getting here? Where's Sally? Jenny, I can't get over how fabulous you look. In all these years, you're the only person I ever saw with *gray* eyes and truly auburn hair—I have to tell my friends all the time that you don't dye it. And the cheekbones . . . how do you do it?"

"Exhaustion and dope," said Jenny.

"What?"

"Just a joke. Listen, I'm sorry I didn't get to call you the last time we were in New York—I would have liked to meet your husband."

"Would you?" she asked. "Really? That'd be *great*—I can't get

over it that you came, I read you were supposed to be in Europe
or something . . ."

"That's true, actually," said Jenny. "I was supposed to start
my next album in London this week, but I really didn't have
enough new material. Of course, that's not what you say to the
guy from *Rolling Stone.* You say 'Beautiful Girl Rock Star
Rushed to Hospital for Emergency Surgery.'"

"Oh, that's terrible—think how guilty you'll feel when ten
thousand sweet young things rush out and send you flowers."

"No, I actually do have to go in to have my polyps operated on.
It's just that it wasn't an emergency. The emergency is in my
brain, where there do not seem to be any new songs."

Muffin looked at her. Jenny was leaning against the iron bed-
stead, with her left hand twirling a lock of hair at the crown of
her head, exactly as she used to when she felt under pressure.
"But there were new songs on your last album . . ."

"Yeah, John Prine's and Anna McGarrigle's. If it weren't for
my productive friends, I'd have recorded 'Melancholy Baby.' I'm
sick of thinking about it, anyway. Right now, I'm looking forward to a weekend in bed in a nice white room with cable TV
and a remote-control channel-switcher."

"What are polyps, though?" asked Lisa.

"I don't know—things on your vocal cords. Singers get polyps
and dancers break their knees and Margot Fonteyn has a husband in a wheelchair and Beverly Sills has a deaf daughter.
Maybe we should ask the Lord to let us all sit in a circle and
move the burdens one place to the left . . . let the dancers get
polyps and the singers break their knees."

"They're going to cut things off your vocal cords!" cried Lisa.
"What if they slip?"

"Lisa, for Christ's sake!" said Muffin.

"I'll be delighted. I'll retire to Mendocino and raise sheep and
babies and write my memoirs."

"You don't mean it!"

"That's true, I don't. Do you mind if we change the subject?"

"Ann! Ann!" Muffin leaned out the window, suddenly hopping
with excitement.

"A lady does *not* howl out the window, dear," said Jenny.
"They can probably still put you on bounds." Nevertheless, both

she and Lisa crowded to the other window to catch their first glimpse of Ann in years. She was smiling up at them from the sidewalk, her teeth, all of them it seemed, flashing white and even, her smile so broad that they felt she was embracing them from two stories below. Then she disappeared onto the front porch, on her way up to them.

"But Muffin," said Lisa, "didn't you know she was coming? I mean, sisters-in-law, at least—doesn't that family talk to each other?"

"She sent me a postcard from L.A. last week, and she didn't say a thing about coming, the fox! Ohmigod, ohmigod, I'm so excited!" Muffin jiggled with delight and listened for Ann's feet on the stairs.

"She sure looked chic as all get-out," said Lisa. "Beverly Dust told me she'd become an absolute hippie. I've been dying to have her call me in New York, it would be such a scream to bring in this hippie with sandals and the whole bit right past the doorman and say to my husband, 'This is Chip *Lacey's* sister Ann, my friend from Miss Pratt's.' I mean, you don't know Harvey, but he'd . . ."

Ann was there. She was hugging Muffin and kissing Jenny and giggling the wry giggle they remembered from when she was overjoyed, or when something struck her as particularly foolish, or both. Her sleek dark hair was in a knot at the back of her neck, already beginning to tumble. Though she wore no makeup that Lisa could tell, her eyes looked larger and deeper blue than ever, and one noticed with particular clarity her beautifully drawn mouth. Lisa hugged and kissed her warmly, checking almost automatically to see if Ann was wearing a bra.

"God, let me look at you," she said, holding Ann at arm's length by both shoulders and gazing up and down. "Incredible—still the hipless wonder—I swear you're looking better now than when we were fifteen!"

"We *all* are looking better, honey—except you."

"*And that's only because no one could look better than you did at fifteen,*" Ann and Muffin finished together in almost the same words. Lisa blushed with pleasure.

"Where have you been? Where are you going? How did you get here? How long can you stay?" Muffin and Jenny were peppering

Ann with questions. Ann was on her way home to Boston, and finished with road assignments for a couple of months. She'd been in Los Angeles doing a piece for *Esquire* "on the new baby movie moguls, or some stupid thing," she said. Actually she'd interviewed one of their classmates who was now a casting director with Paramount. "She's just lovely," said Ann. "*Exactly* the same. She hates California and sends you all love. And she has a new baby and a boy the same age as Sammy."

"How is Sammy?" asked Muffin. "How's Stu holding up?"

"I must say," Ann said, settling down on the bed opposite Jenny, "that Stu is a prince among husbands. I really think Sammy likes it when I go away. He comes home from kindergarten and puts his feet up on the coffee table and sits around with his daddy drinking sarsaparilla and not shaving and saying dirty words like 'underpants.' Just a couple of bachelors. I'm the one who gets homesick and misses *them* . . . they get along fine unless I'm gone so long they run out of clean clothes."

"But what about Stu's practice?" asked Lisa, whose husband, like Stu, was a lawyer, but whose workload was such, according to him, that he could not be expected to commit any time to family except by way of recreation when he felt like it.

"I don't know," said Ann. "He manages. Goes back to the office after Sammy's in bed or works around the clock for a few days when I get home. It all gets done." She looked around the room and smiled at the others. "Well"—she giggled—"here we are again."

"Oh, *where* is Sally?" Muffin was craning excitedly out the window. Having them all show up as she'd always pictured they would had her very keyed up. Now only Sally was missing, and though she'd never have said so, it was Sally that Muffin looked forward to most, because she'd dropped the farthest out of their lives. Sally, the fey, fearless Sally, who always screwed up, who had made them laugh till they cried on a hundred illegal midnights, their faces stuffed with blankets to avoid arousing the housemother. Sally, who always ended up herself being led off in disgrace. God, the illicit howls of laughter as Sally's solemn attempt at contrition erupted in helpless giggling far down the hall. The housemother's outraged bedroom slippers—flap, flap, flap.

Fifteen years ago, the week they graduated from Miss Pratt's, Muffin, Lisa, Ann, Jenny, and Sally had made a solemn promise to meet again at this reunion no matter what had happened to them all in between. None of them had ever mentioned the pact to each other again; it was understood that part of what mattered was proving that a single promise could carry across time, that words said fifteen years ago could bind the future with as much force as they had the day they were spoken.

And Muffin believed that although she'd been the worst scapegrace of all of them, Miss Pratt's meant more to Sally than to the rest. For one thing, since she hadn't gone on to college—hadn't been able to, as things worked out—Miss Pratt's had been Sally's whole education. But there was more to it than that. For some people (fish out of water at Miss Pratt's, God knew), the most deeply held feelings were the hardest to express. Muffin knew that Sally loved them all. And even though she hadn't heard from her in over a year, Muffin was more sure than ever that Sally would be here. Silence was just how she *would* set them up.

Jenny and Ann were lounging on the two narrow beds. Lisa sat on the armchair, and Muffin perched on the radiator by the window.

"Feels like the same mattress," said Ann, bouncing.

"I'm sure it is," said Muffin. "*Plus ça change . . .*" And she pointed to the ancient felt banner above Ann's head, covered with inscriptions from old girls to new girls and to their new girls in turn; it read: "When Better Women Are Made, Yale Men Will Make Them." They all giggled.

"Just goes to show you," said Ann, "that *here* is the true bosom of the male conspiracy . . ."

"It just goes to show you," said Jenny, "that no matter how much hipper these kids look, they're just as absurd as we were at fifteen."

"Speak for yourself. I'm sure *I* was never absurd," said Ann.

"I have a letter you wrote me from Florence one summer . . . a tightly reasoned explanation of the importance of your virginity . . . as I recall, you had just been to see Masaccio's *Expulsion of Adam and Eve from the Garden* . . ."

"Go home and burn it, or I'll kill you."

"Speaking of letters," said Lisa, "has anyone had any documentary proof lately that Sally can still hold a pencil?"

"She's so bad," said Muffin fondly.

"You know, I haven't really heard from Sally in about four years," said Ann.

"I think seeing your name in print made her feel shy," said Muffin.

"I suppose. But the dumb thing is, that when I used to think about having some success, I looked forward to having people I'd lost, like Sally, feel proud of me and want to get back in touch with me."

"Doesn't work like that, does it?" said Jenny.

"Nope."

The long slant of the afternoon sun was beginning to chill the air, as it always did in October in Lakebury. In an hour the reuning class would be gathered in Antique House for sherry (at Miss Pratt's, alumnae were known as Antiques). In the street below, the current Pratt students in blue jeans and Adidas were wandering in groups from dorm to classrooms, collecting books, packing their clothes, getting ready to take off for the weekend.

"God, can you believe it?" said Ann, watching them. "And we got out, what was it? One weekend a year? In our little skirts and knee socks?"

"Oh, but, *Ann*," said Lisa, "think of how close we were, being here all the time. I can't believe it's the same for these girls, going home to their families and their boyfriends every weekend."

"But there's a difference between intimacy and friendship, Lisa," said Jenny.

"What?"

"Nothing . . ." She smiled. "Wasn't it always you who used to moan about being in jail all year and why couldn't we get out more often to see our boyfriends?"

"I was sixteen," said Lisa. "What did I know?" They all laughed.

"The good thing about being sixteen," said Ann, "is that things are so *simple*. Did you notice that? When I was sixteen, in a chronic state of moral outrage, I thought that every estate in Greenwich should be dismantled stone by stone to make way for tract housing—Equality For All, to cure the world's pain. Now

I've begun to suspect that curing the world may take a more complex solution, and that in the meantime, human variety is a good thing and maybe Greenwich should be a landmark district."

"So embarrassing for you, dear," said Jenny.

"I'll say. And after all those years of indignation at Mrs. Umbrage, did I tell you, Muffin? About last year in Boston, I was supposed to get out to Needham for a talk show to promote my book during the worst snowstorm in twenty years? I had to get up at five in the morning to do it, but I got there on time; even the station manager was late. It never occurred to me to cancel; I just kept hearing Mrs. Umbrage saying serenely, 'If there is a storm, a Pratt girl leaves earlier, but a Pratt girl arrives on time.'" They all laughed.

"Well, I'm overcome," said Muffin. "Does Mrs. Umbrage know about this change of heart?"

"On the other hand," said Ann, "you don't have to keep a dog chained for three years just to teach him not to piss on the rug. The old bat."

"Oh, come on," said Lisa brightly. "It wasn't that bad; we all *lived*, didn't we?"

"Beverly!" Muffin yelled out the window. "Beverly Titsworth . . . Look up! Hi! Hi! We're all in my new-girl room—come on up! Oh, great," she said, pulling her head back in the window. "Beverly's coming up."

"Oh, *great?*" said Ann.

"She couldn't wait to rush up to me in New York and tell me Ann Lacey'd become a hippie," added Jenny. Ann laughed.

"She married Sally's brother Ralph. She'll know when Sally's coming," Muffin cried.

"What, Ralph the wild man?"

"Some wild man . . . I saw him last year at a charity ball. He hurried up to me and announced he was on the water wagon. 'I'm a two-fisted drinker—H_2 in one hand and O in the other!' Then I asked him how Sally was, and he said fine, and spent the next hour and a half trying to sell me life insurance." They all groaned.

Beverly bustled in, crying greetings, and kissed them each in turn. Never one to be tyrannized by fashion, she was wearing a

knee-length wool skirt and cashmere sweater with a string of
pearls—the same costume she had worn to church every Sunday
when they were in school. They all said how great it was to see
each other.

"Jenny," she cried, "my kids were so impressed when I said I
knew the gal on the cover of *People*! I went right out and bought
them one of your records."

"Which one?"

"I don't remember, but they just *loved* it, and my six-year-old
is dying for your autograph."

"You already have my autograph. I signed your yearbook
fifteen years ago."

"Oh, but come on, you weren't *Jenny Rose* then."

"I beg your pardon?" said Jenny, starting to laugh.

"Beverly," Muffin said, "we all made this pact with Sally that
we'd meet at this reunion. She said she'd come with stale cigarettes and a flask of bourbon for old times' sake. We're just waiting for her to get here so we can sneak into the woods and live
through it all over again."

"But, my God," shrieked Beverly. "My God—haven't you
heard?"

Heard what? Heard what? Oh, hooray, what's she done this
time? She's eloped again . . . she's had twins . . . she's racing
formula-one cars in Europe . . . she's skiing in the Buga-
boos . . . she's been blackballed from the Garden Club
. . . she's head of the PTA . . .

"Heard what?" they cried happily. "Where is she? What's she
done now?"

"She's killed herself," said Beverly.

CHAPTER 1

New Girls

When Muffin's grandmother arrived at Miss Pratt's in 1903, she took the train up from New York, along with two other girls, three trunks, seven hatboxes, twelve suitcases, and a chaperon sent by the school to escort them from Grand Central. They were met at the station by the school stagecoach, and at the gate of Pratt Hall by the maid who was to help them unpack their things and redo their hair before dinner. When Muffin's mother arrived in September of '32, she took the train from Boston to Hartford in the company of her three best friends and her brother, who was on his way to Yale. Her friend Grace smoked a cigarette after lunch in the dining car. When Muffin arrived in the fall of 1960, the first thing she did was to search out the bedroom on the third floor of Pratt Hall where her grandmother had scratched her initials in the window glass with her diamond ring. Muffin wished she could put her initials in the glass there beside them, but she didn't have a diamond.

Muffin had two secret sorrows in life. The first was her nickname; she would have preferred to be called Margaret or Meg. "Muffin" made her sound small and furry, or like something to eat. At Miss Pratt's she soon discovered that everyone named Margaret was called Muffy, and all Sandras were Sandy, Louises were Wheezy (except for one Lou), and there was one girl each called Cibby, Gub-gub, and Peaches.

Her other sorrow was that she thought she was fat. She

wasn't, particularly. Her mother, after six children, still wore
the same size eight she had at boarding school, and clearly
thought an ounce of extra fat a character flaw. While Muffin had
gained four or five pounds when she reached puberty, the truth
was, most of the extra weight was in her bust. Muffin took to
wearing Bermuda-length cut-off jeans and her father's old shirts
with the tails hanging out, and when she looked in the mirror
she saw a strange glob of a torso supported on slim strong legs.
She mourned the bony body she had lived in for three-quarters
of her life, and instinctively fell into the habit of keeping the
new one under wraps.

Muffin wanted anxiously to be popular—went on wanting it
and working for it, despite all the evidence that she already was.
Up until she was thirteen, she had been lithe and strong as any
boy, and because she was quick-witted and a natural athlete,
had always been much in demand with both girls and boys. Now
she felt with despair that no affection her friends had felt for the
coltish sprite she had been could extend to the unfamiliar thing
she had become. When the boys with whom she had caught tadpoles offered shyly to hold her hand in the balcony of the Sweetwater Movie Theater, she pretended to be eating popcorn. Everyone knew that the fattest girl in the ninth grade, Peggy
Higgins, had let Bim Burney kiss her breasts—everyone knew
because he had told everyone practically as soon as the lights
went on. Later, Peggy was hit by a bus and lay near death for almost two weeks, and the doctors said that her mountains of fat
were all that had prevented her breaking every bone in her body.
When that got around, it was the joke of the upper school.

Muffin went to parties, but only to dance fast to the Buddy
Holly records. When the night wore on and her friends began to
dance cheek to cheek and blow into each other's ears, which they
had heard was very exciting, she would slip outside by herself.
To the night sky, while the honeysuckle night breeze turned the
maple leaves till their backs showed silver in the moonlight, she
spoke poetry.

> What lips my lips have kissed, and where and why,
> I have forgotten, and what arms have lain under
>   my head till morning; but the rain

Is full of ghosts tonight that tap and sigh
Upon the glass and listen for reply;
And in my heart there stirs a quiet pain . . .

Songs of experience remembered, quiet pains suffered in silence, appealed to her quite a lot. She also went in for long nar-
rative poems about valor, sacrifice, and heroic accomplishments,
mostly ending with the line "Smiling, the boy fell dead."

She nurtured a fierce conviction that someday life would give
her a chance to show her own unusual mettle. Of course the dramatic circumstances in her case were always translated by her
from shipwreck or battlefield to the sphere of romantic love,
since the question of whom she would marry, and when and
how, was really the only wild card showing in the apparent
straight flush life had dealt her. *That* she would marry, and that
she would marry someone very much like herself and live the
rest of her life in Sweetwater or someplace like it, was of course
taken for granted. You would have to be deranged not to see that
the life that was her birthright was the best America had to
offer.

The life in Sweetwater was a life of financial and emotional
security, a life in which health, leisure, and proficiency at games
were the real and the ideal, and where good manners mattered
more than good ideas. The depression had come and gone, barely
noticed in the blue-chip preserves of Sweetwater Heights. The
war was over and there would never be another; the president
was one of their own, a good soldier and a Republican. There was
little reason to suppose anything would change very much ever
again. The only really devastating possibility that was given
any serious credence was the threat of the Bomb. It was mostly
joked about; no one in Sweetwater would be so patently elitist
and unsporting as to build a private bomb shelter. No, if the
Russians chose to bomb Pittsburgh, the members of the Sweetwater Country Club would take their medicine along with everyone else, content to know that when the dust cleared, God
would find them in dignified positions and clean underwear.

Although her parents did all they could to prevent the children perceiving themselves as different from anyone else,
Muffin could not help feeling that she belonged to Sweetwater in

the way that a young earl belongs to the country that gives him
his title. In a town famous for "old money," the Bundle money
was older, and they had more of it, than practically anyone else
in the Allegheny Valley. In the 1880s Sweetwater had been a
vacation resort, providing refuge from the crushing heat of the
Pittsburgh summer for the wives and children of the steel and
coal and catsup millionaires. But by the turn of the century,
when the mills had made the city's air unfit to breathe, the millionaires began to desert the North Side town houses for the
comforts of country living all year round. They built vast estates, put in indoor swimming pools, got up a fox hunt. But the
saying in Sweetwater was "Shirtsleeves to shirtsleeves in three
generations." A pattern was said to emerge, wherein some up-
start immigrant, a Frick or a Carnegie, made a fortune, raised a
son in his image to take over the company, and lived to see it all
lost by a grandson brought up to drink champagne from slippers, who unaccountably lacked the shrewdness to manage his
own checking account. At a time when other estates were being
sold or torn down—Sweetwater had a ten-acre zoning law, so
there was no danger of tract developments as yet—the Bundle
family was planning a new parquet floor for the ballroom in anticipation of Muffin's debut party.

Muffin more and more was looking forward to the time when
she would be fifteen and old enough to go to Miss Pratt's. She
liked school, she wanted to go to college, and she thought it
would be a great relief to be in an atmosphere where people
would care less about her looks—it was just girls, after all—and
more about *her.* Her mother had taken pains to paint pictures
for her of the bright crisp fall afternoons in Lakebury, how she
would walk with a few close chums to the old orchard to buy apples and cider, how she would share these treats with her roommates after lights-out, how she and her friends would laugh
together and care for each other. She had good friends in Sweetwater, but it wasn't the same. They had grown up with her and
they knew who she was; at Miss Pratt's she would have a fresh
start, her friends would choose her for her high spirits and her
able mind, and she would choose *them.*

She supposed she would miss her mother, though. Annette
Bundle and Muffin had been almost like sisters when Muffin was

growing up. It was Annette who had chosen her nickname—such a cute name for a cute little girl.

When Muffin was small, they often wore matching mother-daughter outfits to St. Stephen's on Sundays; Annette got them at Best & Co.—such a shame when Best's went out of business. Later, she would write solemn notes on her elegant notepaper, cream-colored with a blue border and AHB embossed at the top, to tell the school that little Muffin had swollen glands and would have to be excused, and then they would go off together for a week of skiing at Seven Springs. On weekdays they had the slopes all to themselves and there were no lift lines or "snow bunnies"—those ridiculous tubby young women who had spent a fortune on their pink parkas and tight stretch pants and then fell off the rope tow right in front of you and lay there whimpering with their ankles twisted and mascara all over their cheeks.

Annette was determined to be a pal to her daughter; she even insisted on telling her about the curse herself, though Dr. Balche would have been glad to do it. It really almost choked her, and of course she glossed over the part about the mess and the smell and the cramps—God, the cramps. She was also a little hazy in her own mind about what, biologically, the curse was for, so she glossed over that part too, and in the end simply explained as tastefully as she could that now that Muffin was getting older, if any of her friends said they couldn't go swimming one day she must not push them in, and that when the time came she was to come straight to Annette and she would be given a box of "napkins" and a collection of little paper bags to keep in her bathroom, in which she would conceal each napkin after it was soiled, so the servants wouldn't have to look at it when they emptied the wastebasket.

Close as they'd been, Muffin's mother, like a child who can't keep her fingers out of the fire, somehow couldn't resist badgering Muffin about dieting.

"For heaven's sake, she looks fine to me—why don't you let up on her?" said Jack Bundle to his wife in private.

"I'm trying to *help* her," said his wife indignantly. "The time to help is before it becomes a problem!" At dinner the last night before Muffin left for school, Annette tried to give her plenty of help to start the school year with by more or less vocally monitoring every mouthful Muffin ate. To her astonishment, Muffin for the first time in her life flared back at her.

"Look, it's *my* body, not yours!" she cried hotly. "And it's my life, and for your information, there are plenty of people who will value me for my mind and not care if I have a perfect figure!"

Her father completely agreed with her, but it was not his policy to allow his children to talk back to their mother, so he said, "Baloney, young lady. There are too many women who have both."

Oddly enough, that was pretty much what Lisa said during their first week as roommates at Miss Pratt's, when Muffin suggested shyly they should splurge on their diets a little, sharing apples and cider in the dark after lights-out.

Muffin didn't know it, but it was no accident that Lisa Sutton had been chosen for her roommate. When Lisa's letter of acceptance to Miss Pratt's had arrived at the Sutton's neo-Tudor house in Pittsburgh's East End, the first thing Miriam Sutton did was to place a call, person to person, to the headmistress, Mrs. Umbrage. They were so thrilled and grateful, she said, that Miss Pratt's had accepted Lisa. But there was something she just wanted to discuss with her. Lisa—Lisa was just so *thrilled,* by the way—Lisa apparently had her heart set on rooming with Muffin Bundle. Was there anything at all Mrs. Umbrage could do about that?

Mrs. Umbrage demurred. She could not approve. Miss *Pratt* would not have approved. Every year, of course, they had requests of this kind, but the school's policy was to separate girls who had known each other before their arrival in Lakebury. They were there to make contacts, not to form cliques. But Miriam persisted, and *it* occurred to Mrs. Umbrage that when Lisa's brother's grades had not been quite up to the mark for admission to Choate two years ago, the Suttons had all unexpectedly donated a new wing for the school science building, and she understood that Buddy Sutton was doing very decently at Choate after all. And so, it was arranged.

As a matter of fact, it was not Lisa who had her heart set, it was Mr. Sutton. Muffin and Lisa knew each other by sight, but

Miriam Sutton knew that Jack Bundle was the paradigm of the sort of fellow whose respect her husband longed for. She had reason to suspect that after the fox-hunting episode, it may have been Jack Bundle who blackballed Mort at the Ducat Club.

The Suttons had moved to Pittsburgh when Lisa was in fifth grade. Though they clearly had loads of dough, no one knew who they *were*. That might not have made so much difference—after all, things had changed since Mother's day—but there were other little things. First, they got off on the wrong foot by giving a series of lavish parties and inviting people who had not yet invited them. Then there was Miriam's jewelry. She had a great deal of it, most of it large, flashy, and real, and she tended to wear diamonds with street clothes. And Mort—well, the thing about Mort Sutton was, he tried too hard: he was overeager, in a way that wasn't quite . . . and of course he was always taking one step forward and two steps back. There was the time he learned that the Jupiter Island Club in Hobe Sound, Florida, was absolutely *the* place for the *crème de la crème*, so he pulled strings and got his family in one Easter vacation on *very* short notice, which impressed everybody because the Bakers had been trying for months to get reservations. But then he turned up at the beach club wearing these simply garish flowered shirts. *He* didn't know. All the right people seemed to wear them in Hawaii, where they had been the year before. Not that it was a *crime* to bring the wrong clothes, but it was that *kind* of thing.

Actually, they might have slowly made their way in spite of all. Miriam, one noticed, seemed to have gotten the word from somewhere that a well-cut suit from the local Band Box went down better on most occasions than a lot of imported designer clothes. (Miriam was paying a blue-blooded widow, whose husband had left her less well fixed than everyone thought, to advise her, but neither lady let on about that.) Besides, Miriam turned out to play a crackerjack game of bridge. But then Mort decided to take up fox hunting.

Fox hunting, he had discovered, was "the ticket" with the men he wanted to know in Pittsburgh. So he enrolled for riding lessons at the Allegheny Country Club Stables. Every afternoon he would appear dressed to the nines in ratcatcher tweeds, jodhpurs, and a bowler hat, and jog docilely around the show ring among the six-year-olds, with no apparent understanding of the absurd appearance he presented. Mr. Chubb, the riding master, complained to the directors that he was a dangerously slow learner. In fact, he had to be kept on the lead line after the rest of the class mastered posting to the trot. Whenever the children broke their ponies out of a walk, Mort dropped his reins and clung to the pommel of his saddle. His horse would take off clumsily after the others, crowding up on the ponies' heels and usually getting himself kicked, or one of the children bucked off.

Mort was undaunted by the overt discouragement of Mr. Chubb or by the subtle disapproval of the golfing ladies who could see him flapping about the ring from the back nine on weekday afternoons. He was determined to be ready to begin the hunting season in the fall. In June he made a special trip to Ireland, accompanied by an expensive "track consultant" he'd picked up who-knows-where. He returned with an enormous thoroughbred Irish hunter with expensive bloodlines, disgraceful confirmation, and a wild yellow glint in his eye. "He's a beauty, isn't he, Chubb?" cried Mort the day the van arrived. The first time Mr. Chubb schooled him over fences, the horse rushed his fences so badly that Mr. Chubb missed his timing and wound up with a bloody nose.

At the opening meet of the hunting season, Mort had his horse, whom he called Bellerophon, vanned to the meet instead of riding there from the stable like everyone else, because he wished to make a spectacular impression his first day out. He arrived in a limousine just as the hounds were about to be cast for the first run, and his appearance caused a most satisfying sensation. He was dressed in a scarlet coat adorned with the gray collar and engraved brass buttons of the Sewickley Hunt—the collar and buttons which can only.be awarded by the officers of the hunt as an emblem of membership—and instead of a bowler, a hard velvet cap, which may only be worn by the whips, the huntsman, and the master of the hunt. He mounted amid silence which he took for awe, as the hounds circled off seeking the scent. Soon the pack gave tongue and sped off across the meadow; the huntsman leaped after them, his horn throbbing "Gone Away." Bellerophon gave a mighty lunge, and Mort fell off, breaking both his arms.

* * *

Whatever the opinions of Pittsburgh society concerning the elder Suttons, everyone agreed that Lisa was a perfect beauty and a charming girl. "Unspoiled" was the word used most often about her; she had a freshness and a sweetness that could not be ignored, and all agreed that in this case the sins of the parents must not be visited upon the child. Lisa went to private day school in town and was admitted in spite of a long waiting list to an exclusive dancing school. There were several of these in the area, one each in Sweetwater, Ligonier, Pittsburgh, and Sewickley. When the children were in seventh grade, the dancing schools would meet jointly several times a year at one country club or another for a dinner dance. The children were driven long distances between communities of their peers in charter buses, the girls wearing taffeta dresses, their first stockings, and flat-heeled Capezio shoes, the boys in Brylcreem, blue suits, and shiny black shoes, everyone wearing spotless white cotton gloves. On the buses they sang camp songs like "One Hundred Bottles of Beer on the Wall" and threw spitballs. At dinner they sat in tortured silence or made stilted conversation in imitation of their parents, then for several hours box-stepped hopelessly around the ballroom. Sometimes the committee also provided entertainment. Muffin particularly remembered the time an animal trainer led a mangy bear onto the dance floor at the end of a stout chain. When the trainer cracked his whip, the bear would rear sadly up on his hind legs and give a feeble imitation of a waltz. Muffin knew just how the bear felt.

Muffin had seen Lisa at these dances and envied her apparent ease and the fact that once or twice she was actually cut in on. Once they had been seated across from each other, and when Muffin said to her dinner partner that she was going to go to Miss Pratt's, Lisa leaned across the table and said she had never heard of it.

The day the new girls arrived at Miss Pratt's, the entire senior class assembled on the porch of Pratt Hall to greet them. Each senior wore a gray skirt, a red sweater and knee socks, sturdy brown walking shoes known as Abercrombies because they were purchased at Abercrombie and Fitch, and a name tag. There was no compulsory uniform at Miss Pratt's, except for the Abercrombies, since Miss Pratt had considered that learning to dress competitively was an integral part of becoming finished. However, the combination of red and gray was a badge of seniority, of one's status as an Old Girl. Each new girl had been sent a suggested list of suitable wardrobe, and it specified that she must bring a gray skirt and red sweater and red knee socks, and that she was on no account to wear them together until she was an Old Girl. When that would be, and how the status would be conveyed, were deliberately not revealed. This was one of the famous "traditions" of Miss Pratt's School, and it operated much like the theory that in a classless, propertyless society, people will compete for blue ribbons instead of money if they are simply told that blue ribbons represent honor and glory. At Miss Pratt's every new girl yearned to become an old girl, without ever knowing what in real terms that could possibly signify. Most of all, she yearned for the right to the old-girl ring, a gold sealing ring with a picture of a mink engraved on it. If you wanted to wear the ring your mother wore when she was at Miss Pratt's, you brought it with you and handed it over to your old girl on the first day, and immediately became obsessed with curiosity about when you would get it back.

Every new girl had her own old girl to lead her to her room, help her adjust, and explain the rules to her, which were far too numerous to be absorbed in any way except through individual tutorial. Lisa's old girl was a small mousey creature who was obviously intimidated by Lisa's confidence and beauty, and Muffin's was the daughter of the vice-president of the United States.

Muffin arrived first. She unpacked her suitcases while her old girl sat on the bed swinging her feet and talking about the boy she had met in Bar Harbor that summer. "Are you an Episcopalian?" she asked as Muffin unpacked and carefully hung in her closet three wool dresses from Saks with the tags still dangling from the sleeves. "Three wool dresses, suitable for church," said the wardrobe list.

"You'll go to Pisco—that's the darling little stone church you can see up there beside the science house. The other girls go to Congo—that's the Congregational Church down Main Street;

you can see the steeple. I'm in the choir at Pisco. Oh, there's a Catholic church, too. Catho. You can't see it from here."

Downstairs on the porch below the window there was a flurry and a chorus of squeals from the old girls. Muffin went to the window and looked out; on the sidewalk a knot of girls was clinging together in a frenzy and bouncing up and down in their Abercrombies while around them half the class surged and reached to pat, shouting glad cries of welcome.

"Oh, Beryl Trimble is back. She's always late," said Muffin's old girl calmly, craning from the other window. "I guess I better go down and say hi." And she wandered out of the room. A moment later Muffin saw her old girl appear on the sidewalk, and she and Beryl Trimble flung themselves upon each other, warbling an ecstasy of greeting. They danced in lockstep on the sidewalk, screaming into each other's ears something about Teddy and summer and Bar Harbor; later it transpired that they had spent the month of August living a half-mile apart, seen each other only twice, the last time one week ago.

By lunchtime, about half the new girls had arrived. Some were to live in the bedrooms on the two upper floors of Pratt Hall. The rest lived in a long white building called Dorm.

Muffin had a front room on the third floor of Pratt, and after she finished unpacking she sat at the window watching the new arrivals pull up to the porch of Pratt Hall in taxis, hired cars, and limousines. She could hear the doors up and down the hall opening and slamming closed as the new arrivals on her floor began their unpacking, changed from their travel clothes to their skirts and blouses and Abercrombies, and pranced in and out of one another's rooms introducing or reacquainting themselves. It seemed from the cries along the corridor that many had met before, at summer camps or at Southampton, Fishers Island, Nantucket, and Northeast Harbor. Muffin didn't know anyone. Pittsburgh, it seemed, was not a natural part of the East Coast social cluster, as she had always assumed from Annette's Boston-bred chatter, but the Midwest.

Muffin's old girl had wandered off somewhere, so she was alone when the door burst open and Lisa Sutton swept in, followed by Tina Bell, her tiny old girl, and Mort and Miriam Sutton. "Oh, Muffin!" Lisa gasped with pleasure. "We're *roommates!*

Oh, I'm so *glad!*" She flung her arms around Muffin and hugged her as no one in her life had done before except her mother the day Muffin got home from Camp Onaway.

Lisa had been driven to school all the way from Pittsburgh because otherwise her parents didn't see how she was going to manage all her luggage and her records and stereo and her collection of stuffed animals, her Head skis, and her golf clubs. This morning at the hotel in Hartford she had dressed in her school clothes instead of a traveling outfit, so that when she arrived in her charcoal skirt, teal-blue sweater and knee socks, and trim little oxfords, she already looked more like an old girl than her old girl.

"Now, Muffin," said Lisa, plunking down on the bed beside her and hugging her once more, "tell me all about your summer."

"Lisa," her father interrupted, "you can put a lid on that girl chat for just a minute, can't you? Mort Sutton, a friend of your dad's." He crossed the room beaming to shake Muffin's hand. "Just wanted to introduce myself when I heard Lisa was rooming with Jack Bundle's daughter. Quite a coincidence! I think the world of your dad, you know, he's a great fella. Not many fellas in his position would give the kind of time he does to the Watson Home that way, or the Child Health. Keeps it quiet, too, doesn't do it just to get his name in the paper. I admire that." All the while he was talking, he held Muffin's hand between his and gazed at her in happy wonder. Muffin was mystified, as she had never heard her father speak of the Watson Home, or of the Child Health, or of Mort Sutton, so she smiled back and said, "Thank you."

"Well, I'll run along downstairs now. Miss Bell here didn't want me to come up at all, y'know. Said it was against the rules even for an old dog like me to be up here. Guess they don't want me to see you girls running down the hall in your skivvies. Ha, ha! Eh, Tina Bell? You didn't want to let me up at all? But I told her I was coming on my own. Couldn't go away without greeting Jack Bundle's daughter. All right, ha, ha, I'm going, I'm going." And after saying good-bye to Lisa and having a few more mild jokes at Tina Bell's expense about her strictness, he toddled off to wait for Mrs. Sutton in the car. In fairness, it must be said that when Tina was put on bounds for the rest of the term because she had failed to prevail over him, he sent her a handsome present.

While Mrs. Sutton unpacked Lisa's suitcases, Lisa had stationed herself at the open window overlooking the street. All at once she cried, "Mummy, come here, quick!" Mrs. Sutton and Muffin both joined her craning out the window to see where she was pointing.

"Oh, my Gawd," cried Miriam, genuinely excited, "it's Clifton Rose!" On the sidewalk, Muffin saw a tall, graceful man with a lined face and graying hair exchange a look with his daughter.

"Shush, Mummy!"

"Clifton Rose!" said Miriam again, pulling herself back inside the room. "I'd have died for Clifton Rose when I was your age—I remember him on Broadway, when Pop and I were courting! Gee, he's even handsomer as an older man!"

"He looks like a homo," said Lisa.

"Ohhh, no . . . do you think so?" Miriam seemed deflated. "No, honey, all those theater people look like that. I'm not kidding, I'd have died for him."

When Clifton Rose's daughter Jenny appeared in their hallway a few minutes later and was installed by her old girl in the room directly across from them, Lisa noticed that she pointedly failed to make any gesture of greeting toward her and Muffin.

"God, that poor Rose girl," said Lisa when her mother had finally gone. "As if it wasn't enough to show up in that blouse, she had to have big Mim yelling at her in front of all the old girls. She'll be weeks living that down. Don't your parents just drive you *crazy*?"

"Absolutely," said Muffin, who adored her father and assumed that her recent differences with her mother were probably her own fault.

"Mine too," said Lisa. "Absolutely bats."

Muffin sat at the window watching the street. The house was quiet now, for the bell had rung for lunch and everyone else had gone. On the street, Merton, the school patrolman who everyone thought was so dear, stood twiddling his tall white Stop/Go sign. Merton, as Muffin's mother often told her, was another Pratt

School tradition. He had been at Miss Pratt's since 1918. All day
long he stood on Main Street, stopping traffic when the girls
streamed back and forth across the street between classes and
before and after meals. During classes, when there was no one
about, he simply stood there in his huge blue uniform gazing at
the sky.

On Saturday afternoons, when the girls were permitted callers, Merton spent the afternoon cruising solemnly around the
loops in his car. Loops were specific walks the girls were allowed
to take with their beaux—up Main Street, down South Street,
around and back up to Main, or up High Street, down Lakebury
Avenue and home again on Main. All afternoon the girls and
their callers paced around and around these circles, and all afternoon Merton patrolled to see what they were doing. At four
o'clock he began to nudge the stragglers, reminding them they
were due at Mrs. Umbrage's for tea. It was said that Merton never forgot a caller. He forgot the girls, all right; they all looked
alike to him. But the callers were his business; he knew which
ones came again and again, and which ones parked politely
when and where he told them with no back talk.

Presently Muffin saw a huge gray limousine draw up at the
door of Pratt Hall. In the quiet of the September noon, she heard
Merton say without ever changing his expression, "Good afternoon, Mr. Lacey." A tall man with a noseful of purple veins got
out and went over to shake Merton's hand.

"Well, Merton, I'll be damned," he declared. "I haven't been
here since . . ."

"Nineteen-thirty-one," Merton supplied.

"Nineteen-thirty-one!" said Charles Lacey.

"Still have that Bugatti you used to drive, sir?" asked Merton.

"By God, I do! If you're going to ask me about the girl I came
courting, she married someone else." But Merton was not going
to ask that; he was not interested in girls, except insofar as to
see they were not run over.

Muffin watched with interest because an Ann Lacey was
meant to room across the hall with Jenny Rose and some girl
named Sally from Rochester who hadn't arrived yet. Soon
Muffin saw a tall elegant woman get out of the limousine, followed by a slender girl with straight dark hair and a narrow

handsome face. Muffin watched as the mother and daughter walked into the building, leaving Charles Lacey to follow with the baggage.

Ann Lacey was at that moment feeling very grateful that they had managed to arrive at lunchtime, when there was no one to see them. She had grown up a very private person in a community that seemed to feel that children neither needed nor deserved any privacy, and Ann had heard everything from her father's idleness to her grandmother's fortune to the inadequacy of her own backhand discussed in front of her as if she were a lamp-post, since she was old enough to remember. She wanted no more. She wanted no talk about who she was, or where she came from, or where she was going, or whether she'd get there; she just wanted to be. That was why, when she came upstairs and the girl came across the hall to greet her, to tell her the tales her mother had told of Merton's remarkable memory and ask, "Did your mother go to Miss Pratt's too?" Ann answered shortly, "No, my father did."

Later she was sorry and apologized to Muffin for her curtness. The silly part was that within weeks Muffin and the others knew as much about her as she knew about herself.

Ann's father did not work; he never had, as far as Ann knew. To outsiders Ann's mother explained bluntly that Charles was "not well"; she would never be led further than that into falsehood. To Ann, too, she had offered this euphemism, but only until she was eight. Then she let her know very frankly that her father was not ill, but drunk. "Would you rather she heard it from the children at school?" she demanded of Charles. He would not, but he had rather she had not heard it at all. Madelon Lacey suggested that if he felt that, then he had better give up drinking, but Charles never considered this alternative very seriously.

Ann had already begun dimly to realize that on some level the bargain between her mother and father, whatever it was, suited both of them very well. Her father, for all his vagueness, took careful note of all sorts of things you would expect him to miss. (He never seemed to know what grade Ann was in, or to remember that it was reading she was good at, not riding, or anything of that kind.) But he noticed if his valet had failed to tighten a loose button on his jacket, or if there were no flowers in the fingerbowls, or if the breakfast plates had not been warmed. But he hated managing servants, preferring to suppose that they managed themselves out of a wholehearted desire to please him. Madelon enjoyed managing people very much—or felt it was her duty, which came to the same thing. She managed Charles and Ann and Ann's brother, Chip, and of course, although it was still her mother-in-law's house, she had the whole running of the establishment at Greenwich as well.

Apart from the time Ann spent with her grandmother, whom she adored, or playing sports with her brother, Chip, Ann liked best to be alone. She was thought of at school as a "brain," a mixed blessing in any children's popularity contest. She was also intense and often overserious about the ideas she came across in her reading, large ideas about Art and God and Justice that may have been old to the world but were, after all, new to her. Her classmates in Greenwich thought this earnestness bewildering, and her mother called it "affected." In fact, Ann's behavior for the last couple of years was simply a mystery to Madelon. All of a sudden Ann wouldn't have even Coco Compton over to play anymore, and *what* was Madelon supposed to say to Coco's mother? That Ann thought Coco was a jerk and would rather read a book? Honestly, how a daughter of hers could ever turn up so snobbish and hypercritical was a complete mystery to her.

Both Ann and Madelon had been secretly looking forward to the day when Ann would leave for Miss Pratt's. Ann, because she believed that there, in a cloistered scholastic environment, she would at last find some kindred spirits to match her intellectual passions; Madelon, because she believed Miss Pratt's would deliver to Ann a well-deserved comeuppance. It was remarkable to Madelon that a girl with Ann's intellectual pretensions did not in any way seem to grasp the delicacy of her own situation.

It was important for a girl like Ann to be popular and develop the social graces, for inevitably she must marry, and of course she must marry well. To be specific, she must marry a man who had more money than she had, and in Ann's case, that wasn't going to be easy. A girl who had had Ann's advantages could only

be truly happy with a man of the same background, Madelon explained.

Yes, but there were plenty of talented, intelligent people in
the world who didn't happen to be rich, Ann had argued once. It
would be such a joy to find an honest, sensitive, but poor man
and reward him for loving her by making him wildly wealthy.

"Yes," said Madelon, "and then you could spend the rest of
your life trying to decide if he married you or your money." No,
money carried with it grave responsibilities and grave risks, and
only another wealthy person could ever really share or understand that. Like must marry like.

A girl preparing to take her place in Madelon's society must
go to boarding school; Ann granted that. A girl who was to meet
only the brightest girls from the best families, to be introduced
to their brothers and invited home to their house parties and
debutante balls, was best advised to go to Miss Pratt's.

Before her old girl was summoned from lunch to show her her
room, Ann registered at the school office while Madelon flipped
thoughtfully through the social register on the office desk.
"Would you like me to come upstairs with you?"

"No, thank you, Mother," said Ann.

"Very well," said Madelon, approving. "Good-bye, dear, I'm
sure you'll have a lovely time. Mrs. Compton told me that Carey
will be coming down to call on you—oh, for heaven's sake, *don't*
make that prissy face!"

Charles took her hand and kissed her cheek. "Well, now, good-
bye, honey," he said firmly, with an air of having rehearsed his
remarks. "We'll miss you."

"Yes, Daddy," said Ann. He hurried away toward the front
door, following Madelon.

Ann was so difficult to gossip and coo over that her old girl left
her alone, which was fine with Ann. She was sorry, though, that
her roommate Jenny Rose had gone out so quickly, when she
found Ann there after lunch. Ann was arrested by Jenny's looks
alone—her wide-set gray eyes and especially the waist-long
rust-red hair. Ann had practically never seen anyone her own
age before who didn't have a pageboy or a bubblecut.

Left alone, she set about transferring her knee socks and
McMullen blouses and Fair Isle sweaters from the sleek suit-

cases to one white-painted, battered dresser. She hung her Lanz and Cos Cob dresses in the closet, where she noticed that Jenny's skirts and dresses, like the style of her hair, were unlike any she'd seen before. Ann's ski pants and sweaters, long underwear, mittens, and hats went in the chest at the foot of her bed. ("Not chest, *coffin*," whinnied her old girl.) Ann had spent some time contemplating the two white-painted iron bedsteads that remained, trying to decide whether to choose the one by the window as her right of first arrival, or to leave it for the latecomer as a gesture of friendship. At last she decided to leave it.

At midafternoon, the last limousine arrived from Bradley Field, bringing the girls from Buffalo and Rochester and one freshman from Detroit who had been sick on the plane. Ann and Jenny's third roommate, Sally Titsworth, was expected with this group. Alone in their room, Ann listened with something like apprehension when at last she heard the click of the new girl's pumps and the clatter of old-girl Abercrombies thundering toward her room. What if I don't like her? What if she doesn't like me? But she needn't have worried.

Sally barged in laughing and dropping the stuffed Kanga with Baby Roo in its pocket that had been tucked under her arm, just as she got through the door with her suitcases. She was wearing a well-cut gray wool suit with a circle pin on the lapel and a linen blouse coming out of her waistband at the back. For as long as Ann knew her, Sally always had the slightly disheveled look of one who is without personal vanity, a trait Ann found instantly endearing. Sally was flat-chested and a tiny bit broad abeam, with sandy-colored hair, thin lips, and tortoise-shell glasses she called her "specs." Her grin was wide and warm.

"Well, what the fuck is *this*," she demanded, "the maid's room?" (As a matter of fact, it was; Pratt Hall had once been a popular way-station on the stagecoach route from Boston to New York, and the top floor was designed to accommodate the servants of well-heeled travelers.)

Sally's friends streamed in and out of the room without ceremony all afternoon.

"Damnit, Sal, I'm not even in your dorm," one wailed. "I'm all the way down by the infirmary!"

"Oh, no!" cried Sally, stuffing her sweaters into the same

drawer into which she had just put her underwear. "I bet Mr. Rebahr wrote and told them to separate us. . . . I wonder if he told them just to put me straight on probation before classes start too. Save wear and tear on everybody . . . what's your roomie like?"

"She had this pile of *True Confessions* magazines," said Sally's friend morosely.

"Oh . . . well, then I can cancel the subscription I was going to give you for your birthday."

"I can't believe you flew the whole way up sitting with that priest," said someone else.

"Oh dear," Sally explained to Ann. "When I got off the plane in New York to make a phone call, it seems I forgot to put down my Occupado sign on my chair—"

"And when we got back on, it seems there was only one seat left, by this priest or something, with the little collar," said the others.

"He said I was a very nice young lady," said Sally. "When we got off in Hartford, he even shook my little paw and God-blessed me." Her friends howled. It seemed that Sally had some special rank with them. A senior from Rochester who wasn't even Sally's old girl came over for an hour just to keep her company.

Sally, Ann learned, partly that afternoon and partly in bits and pieces through the long afternoons and nights to come, had grown up in Rochester, the daughter of an executive of some kind with Eastman Kodak, and of a plump, conventional society matron. Sally and her two brothers, Ralph and Pierpont (called Pepper), had each had a sum of money shrewdly invested for them by their maternal grandmother at the time of their parents' divorce, which happened when Sally was about eight. This event had broken over Sally's heedless head like a tornado, ripping across the landscape, uprooting favorite trees while leaving others untouched. It came quite without warning, for at that time it was considered unseemly to expose children to the causes of adult turmoil, however deeply they would be affected by the results. At any rate, it was announced one morning that Mr. Titsworth would henceforth no longer be married to Mummy, but to Aunt Hester, Mummy's old friend and favorite brides-maid; and that Mummy would now be married to Mr. Humph-

ries, a man with very loud taste in ties and socks and with two
small children who were coming to live with Sally and Ralph
and Pepper; wasn't that nice?

As the people involved were all quite prominent and as the
foreplay of this cataclysm must have been conducted semipub-
licly at the endless cocktail parties and club dances and card and
swimming parties of the community, the resulting shock waves
were felt throughout the little world the children inhabited. It
was, and continued to be, a source of annoyance in that one
could no longer invite the Humphrieses if the Titsworths were to
be present, or vice versa, nor could one invite the ex-Mrs.
Humphries with either, though that didn't matter much, because after she lost custody of the children, she got drunk one
day and set fire to the poolhouse and shortly after left town.

It was moreover a source of deep spiritual discomfort; for the
rearranged couples persisted as a reminder that not every harm-
less country-club flirtation dissipated the morning after; they
could ignite, and even explode, a thing no one cared to contemplate. Divorce in that place and time was still rare and much
stigmatized. In the midst of all, the three Titsworth children became displaced persons. No one knew any longer what status to
attach to them, their father's or their mother's (she was thought
privately to have asked for everything she got). To further com-
plicate matters, Clara Titsworth Humphries' mother, old Mrs.
Kellog, took a very strong attitude to the whole thing. She refused to hear details but announced that whatever had happened, it was disgusting; to teach her daughter a lesson, she
chose to virtually disinherit her and to make her three grand-
children financially independent instead. This certainly did
teach Clara a lesson, for it was observed that with his new wife's
altered expectations, so also did Mr. Humphries' attitude toward
her alter. He was frequently abusive of her, particularly before
her children, and sometimes in public. It also taught the children a lesson, one which Mrs. Kellog perhaps ought to have fore-
seen, but had not: with their mother more or less discredited as a
moral authority and their father largely absent, and quite a lot
of money at their disposal, they no longer had any particular
reason to consult anyone's opinions but their own. So far Ralph

and Pepper had been expelled from five different schools between them, and totally destroyed six expensive cars. Sally's position was slightly different in that she was younger than her brothers, and a girl. She was impressed and attracted by her brothers' picaresque behavior, yet she felt also what she sensed in her mother, a longing to be accepted and respected. Perhaps it was a matter of wanting to have her cake and eat it, too; perhaps a sense that a man may regain his equilibrium at any point, merely by mending his ways, but that a woman, once lost, is lost forever.

Suppertime. In the four-room of Green House, Libby Lanyard finished giving her classmates a perfectly *hysterical* description of the clothes her new girl, Jenny Rose, had brought. The only regulation item in the bunch was a pair of Abercrombies, Libby told the girls. Probably she had gotten those right because she'd been told what store to buy them in. Jenny had pullover turtleneck polo shirts and these weird sort of ethnic blouses covered with this embroidery, and *tights* instead of knee socks. "My God, tights! What is she, a beatnik?"

In a back room in Wood House, Leith Greenleaf, arrived back this afternoon with the rest of the junior class, lay on her bed in a cold sweat. Her head ached. She had always had headaches, but this year they were worse than ever. All summer her father, a pediatrician, had given her some kind of gray-and-red capsules whenever she wasn't well. But at school you couldn't have your own medicine in your room. If she wanted aspirin, she would have to go to the housemother, who kept everyone's pills in a shelf in her closet. But she didn't want an aspirin, she wanted her daddy; she wanted a red-and-gray capsule. Now she would have to go to dinner and sit upright at the table with the nausea boiling in her stomach and sweat rolling down her back, drenching her new Liberty print blouse.

In the three-room in Cabell House three popular juniors swore mightily and told each other how much they wanted a cigarette. "Oh, I need a weed," moaned Jane Lockwood, rolling her eyes.

"Christ, me too," said Pam Taylor. "I musta smoked a pack today already."

"Oh, I'm sick," howled Buffy Briggs. "Puffing up a storm right up to the Lakebury line. I'm having withdrawal—call Dr. Livewright!"

No girl was ever allowed to smoke a cigarette within the Lakebury town lines. If your parents came to take you out to lunch, you had to drive over to one of the restaurants in Avon or Simsbury to smoke. Neither could you have a drink, of course. The Coachhouse restaurant in the town of Lakebury would not even serve a Pratt girl a mint parfait because there was créme de menthe in the syrup.

In the front rooms at the top of Pratt Hall, Muffin sat in silence on her bed while Lisa rattled happily about her boyfriend, George Tyler. Muffin knew him slightly from the dinner dances; he was a senior at Hotchkiss and supposed to be the best dancer in Pittsburgh. Muffin wouldn't know about that; the only time he had danced with her, he had gotten rid of her by double-cutting with Howard Slugg before they had taken three steps. Howard Slugg was short with sweating palms, and he grunted audibly as he waded around the dance floor.

When the warning bell for dinner rang at 6:25, every girl was meant to be in her place ready to enter the dining hall. At the 6:30 dingle, strict silence settled quickly over the student body. All eyes turned toward the central corridor, and when the last whisper died, Mrs. Umbrage appeared in the doorway of her study, where she had crowded with the faculty like guests hiding at a surprise party. They marched in triumphant silence two by two down to the dining room, the faculty followed by the housemothers, a gaggle of blue-haired spinsters and widows in reduced circumstances, some of whom had been Miss Pratt's girls themselves.

Silence was kept until the last embarrassed new girl, scurrying from table to table with all eyes upon her, had located her assigned seat; then Mrs. Umbrage asked the Lord's blessing, and the room was suddenly filled with the scraping of chairs and the clatter of conversation.

Skipping a meal was not permitted; hungry or not, every girl was expected to come to table three times a day and sit politely from grace through dessert, in preparation for a lifetime of gracious attendance at meals she didn't want with company she hadn't chosen. At Miss Purse's table the first night, the absence of a new girl, Jenny Rose, was duly noted and reported. The next morning after prayers, Jenny was summoned to Mrs. Umbrage's study and put on bounds for the first six weeks of term.

There was one more day before classes convened and the term began in earnest. The new girls spent the morning with their old girls, learning their way around campus, discussing the rules, memorizing their schedules, buying their notebooks and pencils, and opening checking accounts at the bank on Lakebury Avenue. All necessities from razor blades to monogrammed school stationery were purchased at the school store in the basement of Logan House, although there was a perfectly respectable drug and stationery store on Lakebury Avenue, three blocks from Pratt Hall. The only public places in town the girls were permitted to enter were the churches, the library, and the bank.

Muffin learned that you could buy candy bars at the school store if you ate them on the premises. No food of any kind could be kept in the girls' bedrooms. If parents sent cookies and cakes from home, they were to be turned over to the housemother and shared with the entire dorm. Foods like fruit and cheese were not permitted at any time, because to eat them sometimes required the use of knives and spoons and it was felt that the girls would surely leave unwashed utensils on their dressers to attract bugs and mice. It was true that many Miss Pratt girls were unaccustomed to cleaning up after themselves; still, many felt that at sixteen or seventeen they were ready to shoulder this responsibility. The rules concerning what, when, how, and where girls could eat were so numerous and so arbitrary that the getting and sharing of illegal provender soon assumed a ritual significance. An unexpected parcel of cookies, for example, or a special layer cake tenderly baked by the family cook became a poignant symbol of the comforts and freedoms of home. Rather than surrender such an icon when it appeared on the mail table with the letters after lunch, a girl would generally eat the whole thing herself before the two-o'clock bell for athletics.

Muffin and Lisa spent much of the afternoon of their free day walking the loops with a junior Lisa knew from Hobe Sound called Beetle Blake. Jenny lay on her bed reading; Ann crept off to the swan pond beside the lower hockey field and tried to write a poem. Sally was off somewhere with her friends.

At the end of the afternoon, Lisa offered to treat Muffin and Beetle at the Pantry. The Pantry was a little shop operated by the school; it consisted of a tiny cottage on High Street where the girls could buy expensive stale cookies and English muffins and ice-cream sundaes from a bad-tempered old lady called Missy. On weekends and free afternoons the Pantry was packed with girls, laughing and shouting to make themselves heard, sitting on benches and each other's laps as they ate, lolling about on the porch afterward singing school songs. The Pantry was a cherished Pratt's School tradition.

"Isn't it *dear*?" shrieked Lisa as they elbowed their way in the door. "I've been dying to come here. The girls at Ethel Walker's don't have anything like this—isn't it *fun*?"

Lisa ordered sundaes for all of them, then insisted that Muffin have a brownie as well. "We'll start our diets together tomorrow," she said, giving Muffin a wink. "Come on—you hardly ate any lunch. Oh, look, there's Kathy Franklin and Audrey What's-her-name—I met them in Bermuda this spring. Kathy, Kathy, may we sit with you?" And she shoved off through the crowd, leaving Muffin and Beetle to follow as best they could. Muffin watched Lisa as she plunked herself down among the seniors, laughing and talking with breezy confidence of her welcome, making the other girls laugh in turn. Once she looked up at Muffin and gestured to her to join them, but there was clearly no room, so Muffin ate her ice cream standing up. Muffin felt envious and very drawn to Lisa; she felt if she stayed near her she might acquire some of the brittle grace that made Lisa so popular. Perhaps if people saw that Lisa was her friend, they would talk and listen to Muffin now and then, and learn to like her, too.

After supper there was eight-o'clock study hall, as there would be every night from now on except Saturday and Sunday. At evening study hall, their old girls explained, you were allowed to work in your room, but you could not talk and you had to sit at your desk—no lolling on the bed reading novels or knitting. The housemother patrolled up and down the halls listening at the half-open doors (closing doors was not permitted). If she heard conversation or found you reading a book not assigned in one of your courses, you had to report to Mrs. Umbrage at nine o'clock and were generally put on bounds. This evening, since no one yet had any work assigned, the old girls wrote to boyfriends and brothers and friends at other boarding schools. The new girls had spent two days acting as friendly and relaxed and cheerful as they could, and the effort had exhausted them. They accepted the enforced silence of study hall gratefully, each convinced that every other member of the class had settled in with ease and grace while she alone wanted to lock herself in a hot bath and burst into tears. Most of the new girls wrote a lot of letters to their parents the first few weeks.

Muffin to Jack and Annette:

Dear Mummy and Daddy:

Hi—this is your bona fide Miss Pratt's girl, speaking to you from Pratt Hall. I can't believe I'm really here! So far I love it— the girls are really cool, and my roommate is Lisa Sutton. Do you know her parents? She's from Pittsburgh and her parents say they're friends of yours. Lisa is *really* cool. She's the very beautiful blond girl I told you I met at the Fox Chapel dance—the one everyone cut in on. I guess she's a really good dancer. She seems to know a lot of people here.

How are you? Is everything all right? Daddy, did you remember to tell Neddy about exercising Mistress Moon? Please don't let him forget. You don't believe me, but he's really lazy. If you don't watch him, he'll let her just stand in her stall and eat corn till she founders. Also, she was favoring her right fore when I brought her in from cub hunting last week. If she isn't sound by now, will you call the vet? And give her an apple and a kiss from me.

I found out that some girls brought their horses here with them. I sort of thought of asking you to ship Mistress Moon, but then I decided that's silly. I'm here to study and make new friends, and if she was here I'd just want to ride all the time. But I think I will take riding as a sport this fall—you have to do sports for an hour every afternoon, and I don't want to play hockey anymore, and the new girls never get to take tennis, because there aren't enough courts.

We don't get to come home for Thanksgiving—we have to stay here and have intramural sports or something. Everyone is on either the Mink Team or the Peccary Team—M and P for *Miss Pratt's*. I'm a Mink.

Well, I have to go now. I'm disappointed about Thanksgiving. I love the holiday hunts and the family dinner and everything. But the food is pretty good here. Write soon. I miss you.

Love,
Muffin

Lisa to George Tyler:

Darling George,

Two Whole Days Since I've Seen You! You can't believe what the drive up here was like—Mummy blabbering the whole way about how snotty and exclusive Miss Pratt's is, how I'll meet all the *best people*. God, you know how she is. All the best people's chinless pimply millionaire brothers, she means. Oh, George, I miss you so much! Mother would absolutely cream in her pants if she knew about what happened that last night, but I'm *so glad*. Honestly, I dreamed about it the whole way up here. I feel as if we're married. Do you too?

You wouldn't believe this place—it's like a prison! Nothing but *girls* for three solid months—I swear, I'm going to go out of my squash. Do you know what? My roommate has never even been *kissed*. Isn't that unbelievable? She's not really so bad, but she will be if she doesn't stop stuffing herself. You should have seen what she ate at the Pantry this afternoon. Honestly, practically everyone here seems to think about nothing but food. Haven't any of them ever heard about sex, or what?

The girl across the hall is Ann Lacey, the department-store people. I think she's kind of stuck-up. Her roomate is Clifton Rose's daughter. Do you know who he is? He was a big musical-comedy star in the forties. Big Miriam was snowed over him. When she saw him coming up the street she absolutely leaned out the window and screamed at him. God, she embarrasses me so much I wish I'd pushed her out.

George, sweetheart, I miss you so much I could cry. Will you come to visit me? We can have callers Saturday afternoons, but you have to sign them up in Mrs. Umbrage's book a week in advance, so let me know. And we can't get phone calls except from relatives, so if you call me, say you're my brother—7:15 is the best time to call, that's between dinner and study hall.

I only get one weekend away the whole year! I think I should save it till winter term, so we'll have something to look forward to, but I just don't know if I can wait that long. What do you think?

Please, please, write to me *soon*. And send me a picture of you, a big *sexy* one. All the girls here are so impressed I have a *beau*—and a senior at that! Hah—if they only knew!

Good night, my darling. I kiss your eyes and nose, and *so on*.

All my love,
Lisa

Ann to Charles, Madelon, and Maude:

Hello, dear people!

I hope you all are well. I'm fine.

I've worked out my schedule so I can take third-year Latin. That's all right, isn't it? I'll take French, too. I think I'll be in third-year French, but I haven't heard the results of my comprehension test. My roommate Jenny is taking advanced Latin, too, and I'm glad, because I like her.

We begin classes tomorrow. I've met most of my teachers. I'm surprised, some of them are so old. The girl across the hall's mother was here twenty-five years ago and the teachers all remember her—the mother, I mean. Miss Pratt's is supposed to be very excellent scholastically, isn't it?

There are only three young teachers here. One is a math teacher called Mrs. Weinstein, but I haven't met her yet because she commutes from W. Hartford and doesn't eat here or anything. The others are a French teacher whose table I sit at. She has a beau finishing his Ph.D. at Princeton, though, so she'll only be here one year probably before she gets married. The last one is a Latin teacher. The French teacher says he studied to be a priest and he's qualified to teach college-level, so we're very lucky to have him. (The last Latin teacher died last month.)

That's about all. I'll write more about my subjects after classes begin. Mother, please don't say anything to Carey about me going there for a weekend. Sophomore girls can't go to men's colleges anyway. If he wants to see me, he can come to call. I hope you're all well. I miss you.

Love,
Ann

Sally to Clara Humphries:

Dear Mummy,

Well, we got here all right. I guess it's okay. My roommates are

Jenny Rose and Ann Lacey and she's from Grenitch, which isn't that far, so maybe her parents can come up and take us out sometimes. She said she'd ask.

My room's pretty nice and everything. I was right about the record player, we don't have one, so will you send mine please? And send some *food*.

Would it be all right if I come home for my weekend soon?

Love,
Sally

By return mail she received this letter from her mother:

Dear Sally,

I'm so glad you arrived safely and that you like your roommates so much. Isn't it nice that her people will be able to take you out sometimes, it sounds like *such fun*. You're a very *lucky girl* to be at Miss Pratt's. As you know, Mr. Rebahr wasn't *at all sure* you'd get in. And of course I know that now that you're there, you'll buckle down and enjoy yourself.

I am sending your record player by Railway Express tonight. Lester has it all packed, and will drive it into the station himself especially. He said to say howdy. By the way, his wife died two days ago. (As you know, she hadn't been at all well.) It would be sweet if you sent him a note.

The dogs seem quite dejected now that you are away. Ginger has been stealing dog dishes again. He stole one from Mrs. Philborne's back porch and the first I knew about it, she had sent her chauffeur over with a bill for a new one. Honestly, it *was* funny.

Your brothers are both off at last. Pepper had to buy a new car because the garage man said the Corvette was beyond repair. He bought a Jaguar, which I gather is very fast. I certainly hope he doesn't kill himself. I was looking at the atlas with the "littles" to show them where each of the "bigs" had gone, and was surprised to find that Hartford is really right next to Lakebury, so I guess you and Pepper will be able to see each other sometimes. I hope he likes Trinity better than Ralph did.

Dad Humphries thinks it's not wise for you to take your one weekend so soon. Besides, I've already let little Sharon move into your room.

Must dash, Lester has just brought Sharon and Bunky home from school.

XXXXXXXOOOOO,
Mummy

Sally to Pepper:

Pepper—
   Thanks a lot for letting little Sharon-poo get moved into my room. I bet the little bugger wets the bed. What am I supposed to do at Christmas, sleep with Dad Humphries?
   Mumsy tells me you bought a Jag. If you can remember where you parked it, why don't you come over to visit. I'll see if I can get you a date with my housemother.

Love,
Sally

Jenny Rose had gotten off on the wrong foot. Her clothes were obviously all wrong—if she hadn't known that from the way her old girl stared, she certainly did by the time her roomate, the skinny one, Ann, offered to lend her some little blouses with Peter Pan collars. And she was finding it bitterly difficult to adjust to the lack of privacy. Girls lined up three deep at the sinks babbling nonstop while brushing their teeth, waiting in line for the tubs and the shower, and always having to rush, knowing that others were standing outside the stall with their soap and their towels, and their razors, waiting their turns. She was keenly aware of what it was costing her father to send her here, and surprised to find that she had to share a room with two other girls. There were only two single rooms in the entire school, she had learned, and when she asked how it was decided who could have them, her old girl had shrieked with mirth. No one *wanted* a single. That meant you were a creep and no one would room with you. No, the best fun, really, the rooms people fought and died for, were the four-rooms. Jenny's old girl was in a four-room.
   The whole first week, Jenny spoke as little as possible and bided her time, waiting to hear from her father. On Monday, finally his letter arrived.
   Clifton Rose to Jenny:

Dear Jenny,
   I'm sorry I didn't answer your telegram right away, but it took me a day or two to decide what I wanted to say. I knew you would have some trouble adjusting, after the Village School, but it never

occurred to me you'd want to leave. I'm sure it is complete baloney, if you say it is, but quitting isn't like you.

Here are a couple of things I've decided not to say. I decided not to point out that going to Miss Pratt's instead of to Friends or Music and Art was your choice. Although we never discussed it, I assume you made the choice with the idea of being closer to your mother. A girl of your age must miss a mother very much, and a community of women and girls must have seemed like a good idea on that account. It might even *be* a good idea, if you give it a chance—a welcome change from Malcolm and me.

I also thought of pointing out that putting up with nonsense can be a constructive experience. Real life is not without its frustrations and dead ends, you know—Miss Pratt's doesn't hold a monopoly on that. Any number of Malcolm's mystics seem to base their philosophies on the concept of struggle as a positive good—because it teaches you that you can stretch yourself much further than you thought you could, and when you meet a barrier you cannot overcome, it teaches you to accept your limitation with dignity. Those are Malcolm's messages to you for the moment. I would add that there are some lessons that cost more in pain than they turn out to be worth, but it's much too soon to tell if this is one of them.

You can see where this is leading—I really can't let you come home now. I could give you philosophical reasons, but the truth is logistic. I'm leaving next week to do *The Mousetrap* in Florida for six weeks, and Malcolm just got a call to direct a light-opera company in Boston starting the first of October. They're doing *Mignon*, and you know how he loves it—he's been dancing around the house for two days warbling the Rondo Gavotte. I can't ask him to give that up and I can't break my contract and I can't take you with me. So I'm afraid you'll have to stay put.

I'll make you a deal—if you try as hard as you can for six weeks to settle in, I'll come up to see you when I get back from Florida and we'll talk about what to do. In the meantime, I want you to go out and see your grandmother as soon as you can—just have Mrs. Umbrage order a car for you and put it on your bill. Grandmother's only about an hour from you. I'm ashamed that we've seen so little of her since she moved up to the Fairmont. After all, she's missed your mother as much as you and I have—maybe more. Please write me and tell me how you find her. She's a grand old bird. I think your mother would have been like her, if she'd lived.

By the way, I got a pompous note from Mrs. Umbrage—where

did she get that handwriting?—saying that you've been put on bounds, whatever that means. She seemed to be saying you didn't eat your dinner, but it can't have been that, can it? She seems to expect me to cut off your allowance or something.

Bless you, dearest girl. If you need anything, Malcolm will be at home for another week, and I'll write you from Florida as soon as I know where I'm staying. My love to your grandmother.

Clif

CHAPTER 2

First Fall

There was no such thing as a minor infraction of the rules at Miss Pratt's. All rules were to be obeyed absolutely. The punishments for breaking them were deliberately unstated, for the trustees did not want Mrs. Umbrage hamstrung by the need to conform to precedents. Thus, one girl might be put on bounds briefly for smoking cigarettes in her closet, while the next girl caught would be suspended or expelled. Similarly, the rulebook stated that there would be no exceptions whatever to the meager list of "privileges" allowed the members of each class. Girls who believed what they read spent September to June virtually confined to campus, though in fact Mrs. Umbrage frequently excused girls for days, to attend their fathers' opening nights or campaign in their elections, depending upon whether the request appealed to her. This system of selective enforcement sacrificed the notion of equal justice for all to the higher lesson, that of the absolute and arbitrary nature of authority. This, Mrs. Umbrage felt, was the truly valuable preparation for what life held in store for Miss Pratt's girls.

When Jenny Rose came to ask for her permission to visit her grandmother who was ill in a nursing home near Hartford, Mrs. Umbrage said, "But of course not, dear. You're on bounds, you know." Jenny pointed out that it was hardly fair to penalize an elderly lady for something Jenny had done.

"And where *is* your grandmother, dear?" asked Mrs. Umbrage, absently taking mental inventory of Jenny's peculiar

clothes. "Oh, the Fairmont? Do you mean the *Fairmont,* on
Rindgely Road? Lovely gardens, I'm told. Quite a few of our Antiques there, you know, I notice when we send out the alumnae
bulletin.

"Well, my dear, suppose we leave it like this. You may go to
the Fairmont on Saturday afternoon, but you are to *consider*
yourself on bounds the entire time. I cannot make exceptions to
my rules just for you, you know, or soon every girl in the school
will be believing that hers is a special case. So you must not
smoke in the limousine, or stop at the drugstore, or make a telephone call or do anything that you could not do if you were in
Pratt Hall. I believe that solves things nicely, don't you?"

When the limousine arrived for Jenny at one on Saturday afternoon, the entire school was gathering at Pratt Hall for lunch
and everyone saw Jenny Rose, the first new girl on bounds, get
in. Lisa Sutton rushed over and slapped wildly at the window before the chauffeur could pull away. "Jenny!" she howled through
the glass. "*Where* are you going? I thought you were on bounds!
Listen, will you stop in a drugstore and get me aspirin and chewing gum? Muffin! Muffin! Jenny Rose is getting sprung—do you
want her to get you anything?"

"I don't think I'll be near a drugstore, Lisa," said Jenny.

"Well, then have a ciggy for me! Have two! Listen, where are
you going?"

"My grandmother's sick and I'm going to see her."

"Lucky stiff!" screamed Lisa at Jenny's receding back as the
car moved off down Main Street.

Jenny looked forward to seeing her grandmother again. She
was an elegant, well-read woman who had loved to talk and to
dance, and who told Jenny marvelous stories. She had been wid-
owed young and never remarried. She said that one marriage
was enough if it was a happy one, and she liked living alone. She
had had a cataract operation on one eye shortly after Jenny's
mother died, and her vision deteriorated further after that. As
she wrote, almost gaily, to Clifton and Jenny: "When I found
myself knocking on neighbors' doors to ask them to tell me if my
pilot light was on, I knew it was time to check myself into a
home."

At first when she went to the Fairmont she wrote long, amusing letters about the queer people there, the things she was doing, and the plays Clifton was in; she loved getting the Playbills. Once she had said, "Isn't it odd; so many of the people here are ashamed to be In An Institution, as they put it. They think it would be more dignified to be tyrannizing the household of some hapless son or daughter. I had far rather pay a stranger to do my dirty work for me. They get to support their families, and I get my independence. Very symbiotic." Lately the letters had been much shorter and less frequent, and they were no longer in Grandmother's handwriting.

The director was expecting Jenny. He told her her grandmother was waiting for her, and showed her on a map the location of her bungalow. She had evidently been moved much closer to the main building than the last time Jenny had visited.

The chauffeur left Jenny and arranged to be back for her at three o'clock. As Jenny walked up the path, she could see her grandmother through the window. She was sitting in a wheelchair facing the front door; her hands were folded in her lap and she was absolutely still, her whole body in an attitude of waiting.

Jenny let herself in. She saw her grandmother sigh and suddenly beam a smile of welcome. She held out her arms toward the noise of Jenny's footsteps, and Jenny rushed to hug her and kiss her on each cheek. "Well, Jenny dear, it's a pleasure to have you here. I've missed you," said Grandmother.

"I've missed you!" said Jenny. At that moment she felt that she had been missing her terribly for years. She couldn't understand how she could have stayed away so long.

"I know, dear," said Grandmother. "Tell me. That Admirable Crichton of a director informs me that you're at Miss Pratt's. I was awfully surprised to hear of you looking at boarding schools; somehow I never thought you were the type."

"Well, I don't think I am; I'm in trouble already. I got put on bounds the first day."

"Good for you! I never understood how your mother could bear it—it seemed like so much smug hoohah to me. She said it was worth it because she made so many good friends, but I told her she'd have made friends anyplace she went to school."

Jenny laughed. "You seem fine, Grandmother."

"Yes, I'm fine. How are you, darling . . . really? I'd tell you how well you're looking, but I can't really see you well enough to know." She looked at Jenny, her eyes blue and flat as marble.

"Your eyes are worse?"

"Yes, my eyes are worse. I can see you a little, but it's like looking at you from ten feet underwater. Lord, I wish I were ten feet underwater; I'd like to be skin-diving in the Bahamas right now. That's one of the things I always meant to do and never got around to. They say the fish are perfectly indescribable."

They sat in silence for a moment. "You see, they've moved me to a new *bungalow*—isn't that the most awful name for it? It always makes me think of Uncle Wiggily living in a bungalow with Nurse Jane Fuzzy-Wuzzy." Jenny looked around her carefully for the first time. The room they were sitting in was almost completely bare. There was no carpet and almost no furniture except the sofa Jenny was sitting on, and Grandmother's wheelchair. There were no paintings on the wall—what had happened to her beloved Mary Cassatts? Her cabinet of Chinese porcelain was not in the corner, as it had been in the old cottage; and most noticeable of all, there were no books anywhere. There were tables with a few magazines, and a television in one corner.

"They've had me give up what they call my 'knickknacks,' too much trouble for the girls to dust them—I can't do it myself, they say. And they've given me this kiddie car to wheel around in." She slapped the arm of the wheelchair. "I'm as fit as I ever was, or I would be if I ever got any exercise. But they don't want me tottering around here by myself because they're afraid I'll walk into a wall." She laughed. "Jenny, tell me. Are you reading as much as ever? I've been hearing so much about this man Updike. Have you read him?"

"Not yet," said Jenny, "but I want to. They never heard of him at the school library, but if I ever get off bounds I'll be able to use the library in Lakebury. Have you . . . read Updike?"

"Well, no. I've read the reviews, though. I get a large-print edition of the *Times* once a week, and it keeps me up-to-date. I get *The Reader's Digest,* too."

"*The Reader's Digest!* Oh, Grandmother!"

"Yes, I know. But beggars can't be choosers. There's a very

bright colored girl who slips in sometimes to read me *The New Yorker* or *Saturday Review. And, my dear,"* she said, making a pompous face, "it's not as if the old ducks were *bored!* Why, they all have television! I'd rather stare at the wall—if I could see the wall.

"Jenny, dear," she went on in a moment, "I really think I am getting a bit dotty after all. I've been talking about myself since you got here, and all morning I looked forward to hearing about you. Tell me something—tell me what it's like to be you. Give me something fresh to think about in the evenings."

Jenny told her about the last few years at the Village School, the progressive school she'd attended because it was right around the corner from their house. Last year, the principal class activity was operating the school's printing press. Printing-press year was always a difficult year for the Village kids, because when they were required to set type it was learned that at fourteen about half of them still couldn't read or write. "Ah," said her grandmother, "I'm beginning to see what attracted you to Miss Pratt's."

"I suppose I expected something like Eton or Harrow."

"Imagine your surprise. Though quite possibly Eton or Harrow would surprise you too. Evelyn Waugh said that no man could be truly uncomfortable in prison after the experience of an English boarding school. And, of course, you wanted to give your father and Malcolm some privacy. Oh, dear . . ." she said. "I've shocked you. Were you guarding my innocence? Darling, I may be nearly blind, but I *can* make out something that's six feet tall if it's right under my nose. Twelve feet tall, counting both of them. And besides, love is what interests me; conventions and categories do not interest me. Now, what else did you do when you weren't setting type?"

As young children they composed and directed their own plays nearly every day; lately in class they'd been giving more and more concerts on strange instruments they built in the school shop. Folk music was in the air in hip sectors of Greenwich Village. People were tracking down and recording the most amazing authentic American musicians, singing ancient blues and Elizabethan ballads and playing bottleneck guitar or mandolins or dulcimers. Small labels were reissuing early jazz and blues recorded decades ago on wax cylinders by brilliant long-lost musicians, some who were years dead, some who were now being rediscovered, still alive, sweeping floors for a living. Jenny's best friend, Solange, loved mountain music and was learning to play the banjo; every Tuesday night the two of them went clog dancing in a roach-ridden folk club uptown. Jenny was most drawn to Bessie Smith and Ma Rainey and the delta blues players. She sang a lot at school and was learning to play the guitar.

"Well, perhaps the printing-press people haven't done so badly by you after all—it's no small thing to have found something you love to do, and that you do well."

"How do you know I do it well?"

"Oh, my dear . . . I remember you singing when you were six years old. You had a three-octave range and a tone like a Stradivarius. Haven't you learned that about yourself yet?"

It was three o'clock. The car had come to the door; Jenny rose to go. As the intimacy of their conversation was interrupted, the mood between them changed abruptly. Grandmother became brisk and formal, preoccupied with the small business of saying the prescribed farewells, of sending messages to Clif and wheeling along to see her guest to the door. Jenny kissed her and said a last good-bye, but Grandmother didn't answer. Jenny stood awkwardly, still holding her hand, feeling as if she had overstayed her welcome and were being sent away, and yet not quite sure after all that she had been dismissed. Just as she was about to turn away, her grandmother said in quite a different tone than any Jenny heard her use before or since, "You know . . . growing old is so much worse than I thought it was going to be."

Jenny got home in plenty of time to prepare for Saturday night, date night at Miss Pratt's School. All the new girls were assigned dates with all the seniors. In the afternoons they usually washed and set their hair; at six o'clock the new girls put on their wool dresses, their nylons, and spike-heeled pumps, their pearls and a touch of blue-pink lipstick, generally Cherries in the Snow. Then they walked across the street to the senior houses and parted, each to knock timidly on the door of the old girl with whom she was doomed to spend the evening.

Together the couples attended Saturday-night supper. On Saturday night the faculty ate on card tables in Mrs. Umbrage's study and the girls dined in irreverent splendor in the dining hall, sitting together in cliques instead of at assigned tables, calling on their friends to get up and sing or tell funny stories. After dinner the couples would stroll about the grounds exchanging confidences by the swan pond, or in cold weather chattering in the seniors' rooms. At eight there was an entertainment, at which attendance was compulsory; generally it consisted of an overblown, out-of-work soprano singing German lieder or a lecturer showing time-lapse slides of his night-blooming cereus. But a clever lecturer could do with his audience what he liked; it was captive, it was eager, and it was in a state of unnatural excitability. Once when William Sloane Coffin, the chaplain of Yale, came with two handsome divinity students and spoke movingly on the need for willing social workers in West Africa, virtually half the school crowded into Mrs. Umbrage's study after the talk and attempted to sign up for missionary work in Ghana.

Jenny's date for this evening was Tina Bell, Lisa's old girl, whom Lisa kept calling Tinabel, thereby robbing her of whatever dignity she might otherwise have had in the new girl's eyes. She was a rather silly girl with sallow skin and large gaps between her teeth. Since she and Jenny had nothing in common beyond the fact that they were both on bounds, the evening progressed much like most blind dates. Tina and her two roommates chatted in a jolly, self-conscious way to each other, while Jenny and two other new girls sat in silence, first at supper and then on the step in the sweet autumn evening, fixed smiles on their faces, their eyes glazed with boredom. It was not until the entertainment began that Jenny had any privacy to think about her grandmother.

The program was a series of madrigals sung by a very good amateur group from West Hartford. Jenny knew most of the music well. In fact, she smiled slightly as it began, remembering Malcolm on a summer morning with the windows wide and the record player blasting, when he said, "Darling, aren't you just *prostrated* to think Palestrina never dreamed of such a place as New York City? And yet the music goes so beautifully with traffic!" Lost in the intricate counterpoint now, without Malcolm

to make her lean out the window and feel the sun on her face
and pretend the buses were adding a basso melody line, she
found a darker beauty in it. Hearing this music four hundred
years old, she felt that she understood the importance of form.
In four hundred years many thousands of voices had sung these
lines and then ceased to sing them, and all that mattered was
that the form—the song itself—survived. If one accepted with
equanimity the dying of voices one hundred years past, one logi-
cally accepted the future dying of one's own. It didn't matter,
wouldn't matter, the passing of any given person. What mattered was not *who* one was but *what* one was. What mattered
about Grandmother, for instance, was that she was a lady. Not
just a woman, but a very particular form of woman with a style
as complex and lovely as a motet's. And when she was gone,
what would live on beyond her would be not the personal details,
peculiar to herself, but the form, the idea of what a lady was.

Jenny thought of what she'd been taught this afternoon about
frustration, about humiliation, about institutions, and about
how a lady behaves. And she felt her eyes fill with tears of
shame at herself, and also of sorrow.

During the first weeks in term there were tryouts for the new
girls for the clubs. These were theoretically voluntary, but it
soon became clear to Muffin that a girl who didn't join as many
clubs as possible was assumed to have nothing to offer. There
was Glee Club, Drama Club, Mandolin Club (for musicians), and
the newspaper, the yearbook, current-events clubs for those who
read newspapers and *Time* magazine, Library Club for those
who read books, and the Welfare Club, which supported a
French foster child and spent Saturday afternoons at a local hospital acting as nurse's aides. All of these organizations had special rights and privileges.

Muffin would have liked to join everything. For Lisa there was
no question about it; she had already discovered that the fall-
term Glee Club dance would be held with Hotchkiss, and George
Tyler sang baritone with the Hotchkiss Glee. Ann and Jenny decided to try out for Glee together, because they found they had to
join something, and both liked to sing.

Sally surprised them all by announcing she was going to join the Welfare Club. "But why?" cried Lisa. "All you ever get to do is go to this hospital and read to kids in wheelchairs! My date last Saturday said their tongues loll out like this, and they piss on themselves!"

Sally just shrugged. "Maybe you can smoke in the car on the way over to the hospital. Besides, the tryouts are easy—all you have to be able to do is this." She crossed her eyes and stuck out her tongue at Lisa, her neck and arms imitating palsy. Lisa made a disgusted face and left the room.

The tryouts for Glee were surprisingly difficult. Many girls came out of the music bungalow crying after being told sharply that there was more to choral singing than picking out harmony to "Old Black Joe." The music master was a bit of a sadist, and he despised these soft, spoiled children for their scrubbed, silly faces, the sharp sweet smell of their hair, and the fact that they called him "Miss" Moltke, and not always out of his hearing.

For the tryout Moltke would play a chord and ask the girl to pick out the middle note. Then she had to sight-read the second-soprano part from a line of a Bach chorale. When Jenny had completed her tryout, Moltke said, "That's not at all bad, Jenny." She looked at him coolly. When she had gone, Moltke plumped into his chair and silently addressed the ceiling: "At last, Mrs. Umbrage, you tone-deaf martinet, out of all the brainless ninnies you have to choose from, you've *finally* sent me *one* with perfect pitch."

All the rest of the week there was avid speculation over who would be taken by the major clubs, when they would be told, and how they would be told. "They'll post a list, won't they?" asked Jenny one day at lunch. The older girls at the table, including several members of Glee, simply smiled secretly at each other and went on eating.

After lunch Lisa Sutton darted into Jenny's room from across the hall. "Girls! Have you heard anything about when we'll be tapped for Glee?"

"Oh, God, *tapped*," said Jenny. "I should have known—another frigging tradition!"

That night at ten o'clock the last bell rang in the senior houses for lights-out. In Pratt Hall Muffin turned over and muttered; she always went to sleep at 9:30. Lisa was just putting the last giant roller into her hair, stabbing around searching bobby pins in the dark. Ann and Sally were lying awake composing alternate lines of off-color limericks, and Jenny was crouched on the floor in the closet working on her Latin.

Suddenly out in the hall they heard a measured, resounding tramping. Clump, clump, clump, up and down the hall like the Gestapo; then hammering on each bedroom door as the clumping passed. The new girls got up and rushed to the doors; in the hall they found a procession of forty girls marching two by two; they were wearing Abercrombies, funny hats, and tan raincoats; for a moment Ann had the wild notion that they were naked under the coats and at a given moment they would flash them open like prostitutes on the Rheiperbahn. At last the tramping procession came to a halt outside Ann and Jenny's room. Lisa and Muffin were in the doorway opposite, Lisa with rollers and Clearasil on her chin, Muffin looking sleepy and scared to death. A small pale girl with bad complexion stepped out of ranks and gazed up and down the hall looking solemn and displeased. Then she wheeled around and pounced on Lisa, screaming, "Lisa Sutton—would *you* like to be a member of Glee?" Lisa gave a most satisfying howl and swept the girl into her arms. They staggered around the hall together, Lisa laughing and crying and shrieking, "Oh, yes! Oh, thank you!" When the commotion died down, the procession moved off and tapped a girl up the hall named Ruth George. Altogether it took them twenty minutes to tap six girls; Ann and Jenny were chosen, too. Ann beamed quietly and Jenny confined herself to a dignified thank-you, while Sally was so excited for them both that she bounced up and down on her bed in her shorty pajamas, squeaking, until she accidentally bounced on and broke her glasses. When the procession tromped out of the hall and down the stairs, Lisa scooted across the hall and settled herself on Ann's bed.

"Oh, God, girls, wasn't that just *fantastic*! I don't know when I've been so excited—I really thought I hadn't made it! Oh, we're going to have so much *fun* . . . honestly, I think I'd have *died* if I hadn't gotten in; I was sure that Miss Moltke would flunk me, the flit. I think I'll be a soprano. What are you, Jenny? Oh, wouldn't you just *hate* not to have gotten in? By the way, do you know the name of the girl who tapped me?"

"Lisa, your roommate's crying," said Sally.

Lisa clapped her hands over her mouth in a pose of horror. "Oh, no! Oh, I'm awful! I forgot all about her. Oh, I know how much she wanted to get in!" whispered Lisa. She made no move to leave, but went on chattering about how *terrible* she felt. Sally and Ann exchanged a look. Ann had tried to talk Sally into going out for Glee, since she could carry a tune as well as anyone, but Sally had been strangely dogged in her refusal. When Ann realized how afraid Sally was of failing, she'd dropped the subject. But Muffin, whose bright enthusiasm supported them all . . .

Jenny got up quietly and checked the hall for Mrs. Birch. In a moment she darted across to Muffin's room. Muffin was sobbing painfully. Jenny tried to comfort her, but it was difficult, because she was disgusted. The excitement of tapping, she felt, was of a false and humiliating kind, like something you'd see on *The Price Is Right*. But the pain it caused was real. "I'm sorry to be such an ass," Muffin wailed into her pillow, "but it was just so awful to see them walk back and forth, back and forth, looking right at me, but never stopping! The way they stared into my eyes, I kept thinking it's *got* to be me next, they'll stop in front of me next—and then, they were gone. . . ."

They could hear the screams of triumph on the floor below now as more new girls were tapped. Muffin began to weep again, still mumbling a bitter mixture of misery and apology. Jenny brought her a box of Kleenex. This was still going on when the clanging footsteps ascended to their floor again and proceeded resolutely straight toward Muffin's room, through the door, and right to the bed. She was tapped by a figure she never saw, who pounced on her on the bed where she lay prone; in retrospect, she regretted most deeply that she couldn't leap up and squeal and hug, because her eyes were red and swollen and her nose was running.

Muffin to Annette and Jack Bundle:

Dear Mummy and Daddy,
   Guess what—I got into Glee Club! So did Lisa and the girls across the hall, Ann Lacey and Jenny Rose. And, Mummy, guess

what? I was tapped by the head of Glee! It's a *very* big deal; everyone made a big fuss over me at breakfast the next morning. I'm so glad Jenny and Ann got in. I really like them both. Ann's very quiet and very smart, supposedly, but she doesn't show off or anything.

The horses here are pretty good, and Miss Von Riehban, the riding mistress, is very impressed that I have my colors. She says in Virginia they don't give you your colors till you've been hunting about ten years. Yesterday at the stable when we were cleaning our tack, she told us a story about the first year she was in charge of the horses here. One of the horses had colic, and she was afraid he had a fever, so she found the horse thermometer, which is about a foot long, and lifted up the horse's tail and stuck the thermometer in, and it went all the way in and disappeared. It's supposed to have a thong tied to the end for when that happens, but this one didn't, and she stood there for about ten minutes peering at the hole and trying to figure out what to do. Finally the horse passed wind and the thermometer slid back out again.

I'm taking French II, English, ancient history, and geometry. The math teacher's name is Mrs. Weinstein; isn't that a Jewish name? My geometry teacher is Miss Purse, who says she remembers you, Mother. Did you like her? Ann says she is crazy.

Almost time for lights-out; I have to go see if there's a shower free yet.

Lots of love,
Muffin

Lisa to Miriam and Mort Sutton:

Dear Mother and Dad,

Guess what—I got into Glee Club! I was so excited I almost died! It's really the best club in school. All the prettiest girls belong, and we have dances and concerts with boys' schools. The first one is with Hotchkiss. Too bad it's not Choate—it would be such fun to see Buddy!

Muffin and Ann Lacey and Jenny Rose got into Glee Club too. It's going to be such fun; I'm getting to be great pals with Ann and Muffin. Oh, Daddy—they have the sweetest gold Glee Club charms to go on your bracelet. I'd love to have one; if it's all right with you, would you drop a note to Miss Bird about it? Thank you—you're an angel.

Well, I have to go now—the bell for lights-out has already rung and I'm writing this in the closet, if you must know! I know it's naughty, but I couldn't wait to tell you about Glee. I'll write a longer letter *the minute* I have time.

Hugs and kisses,
Lisa

Lisa to George Tyler:

Darling,

Actually, I'm a little cross with you for not answering my last letter yet, but I know you're busy. Anyway, I have some news—I got into Glee Club! As I'm sure you know, we have a dance with you in October, which is why I decided to join. I really wanted to join the Drama Club, but maybe after the dance I'll quit Glee and switch over.

Muffin Bundle got into Glee too. Maybe if you're good I'll get you on her dance card—that should give you a thrill. Actually, I'm being very nice to her because Mighty Mort wants to get in good with her father, and, my dear, she thinks I'm the cat's ass. Which I am, of course.

Speaking of asses, I have a hysterical story to tell you. On Saturday night we have *dates* with the old girls. We get all dressed up and go and pick them up and go to dinner and entertainment with them. You can imagine the fun when we kiss good night at the door. Anyway, my date was some drip who lives in a single, which means she's a lunch, so I decided to pretend I'd gotten confused, and I went with Kathy Franklin instead. She's that very popular girl I told you I met in Bermuda. Well, she told us this story about a dance she went to in Nantucket this summer at some yacht club or something. Apparently there's this hysterical boy whose family owns half the town who goes around all summer getting drunk and taking his pants off.

So she went to this dance and this boy was there and she was dancing with him and she said, "I hear you go around everywhere getting drunk and taking your pants off," and he said, "Sometimes I don't even bother to get drunk," and she said, "Well, I've never seen anybody throw a Gotcha, and I'd be thrilled and delighted if you'd be sure to do it tonight." So he leaped onto a table, and apparently the commodore of the yacht club was still sitting there finishing her coffee, and he pulls down his pants and throws a moon right in her face. Well, of course he was hauled away and thrown out and all of it, but that's not the funny part. Kathy was

standing in front of him, not behind, when he did it, and apparently he had the most colossal hard-on, and she had never seen it before and she told us it was the ugliest sight she ever saw in her
life! All red and swollen up like an inflamed cucumber, with an
awful little blind eye staring right at her. She went on and on
about it, and I thought I was going to split a gut laughing, and she
didn't even know what I was laughing at!

Honestly, darling, I miss you more than I can tell you. Do you
miss me too? When are you going to write to me? I enclose the picture you asked for; just don't draw a mustache on it. Sleep with it
close to your heart, as you are close to mine. I'm living to hear
from you, seriously. Write soon and tell me you can come to call
some Saturday.

All my love,
Lisa

Ann to Charles, Madelon, and Maude:

Hello all,

How are you? I'm really fine, enjoying my classes a lot and really liking my roommates. I am taking French III, English, Latin
III, and geometry. I like Latin best. We're reading the *Aeneid*. It's
a very small class because Latin is only compulsory through Latin
II and most girls drop it after that. Yesterday one of the juniors
said she couldn't believe Latin had ever really been spoken because the syntax is so illogical from our point of view and Mr.
O'Neill and Jenny had a whole conversation in Latin, completely
unrehearsed. She has read the whole Gallic Wars and some Cicero
on her own, and she says Cicero's letters are really a lot like conversation.

Guess what, I got into Glee Club. So did Muffin and Lisa and
Jenny.

I miss you all. Mother, Carey tried to call me but I wasn't
allowed to speak to him because you can only get calls from your
family. Please explain to his mother if you see her. And, yes,
Mother, of course I'm making other friends. I just mention Jenny
the most because she's my roommate.

Love to all,
Ann

Jenny to Clifton Rose:

Dear Clif,

This will not be the long letter you asked for, because I miss you, and if I run on too long I'll start complaining, which would bore even me.

I saw Grandmother. A brief and humiliating crash course in dignity. She sends you her love and said to tell you she's fine, although at the moment the Fairmont is furious with her—she's organized about twelve of her neighbors to demand lessons in braille instead of Thursday bingo. Do *all* institutions react to the notion of change as if it threatened the moral fiber of the country?

When you talk to Malcolm, would you ask him please to send me some McMullen blouses? And some knee socks? Thanks. He knows my size, and I'm sure he'll know exactly what I need. I should have asked him in the first place. And give him my love.

You're a peach, old man. Write me how the show is going. Classes are fine. I got into Glee Club and I have a crush on my Latin teacher. Just your nifty little prep-school sweetie, here.

I miss and love you.

Jenny

Muffin to Mr. Sutton:

Dear Mr. Sutton,

Thank you so much for the lovely Glee Club charm! That was a lovely thing for you to do, and such a surprise! I have a charm bracelet my mother started for me last year, and it only has about two things on it, so you can imagine how proud and pleased I am to add this one! Thanks loads! I look forward to seeing you soon again.

Yours truly,
Muffin

Lisa to Mort:

Dear Daddy,

We just got the charms! Thanks so much, that was a perfectly sweet thing to do, sending them to the other girls too. I'm sure Jenny couldn't have afforded one, and Ann and Muffin were simply thrilled. More later!

Hugs and Kisses,
Lisa

Ann to Mort Sutton:

Dear Mr. Sutton,

Thank you very much for sending me a Glee Club charm. It was extremely thoughtful, and I appreciate it very much. We have all been enjoying Glee Club and I'm especially glad it's given me a chance to know Lisa better. I look forward to meeting you and Mrs. Sutton.

Sincerely,
Ann Lacey

One Saturday afternoon when Lisa had a caller and Ann and Jenny were in the library working, Sally came into Muffin's room and said, "Muffin . . . how's this for an idea? How about if we walk up the hill to the top of Lake Road, creep into the woods, and smoke cigarettes till we puke."

Muffin considered. "A good plan, but flawed. If they catch us, they may put us on bounds, or lock us in the stocks, or cut off one of our hands."

"I've thought of that. We'll go wearing raccoon coats, and anyone who sees us will think we are dancing bears. Just two bears, out for a smoke. We could dance a little."

"All right," said Muffin. "But where are we going to get cigarettes?"

"Mrs. Birch has a pack of mine, which I surrendered, when I was more naive, on the shelf in her closet. I propose to sneak in and steal them back."

"But if we go disguised as bears, what about the hunters? The radio says that all over Connecticut fearless woodsmen are stalking about shooting each other in the fanny."

"Oh, that's all right," said Sally. "We'll wear red hats."

That was the afternoon Muffin and Sally began to be friends. The cigarettes were stale and did in fact make them quite sick; they had been unable to get more than a few matches, so they sat on a log lighting each new cigarette from the butt of the last until the whole pack was gone. It was a pure, cloudless autumn day, with that peculiar golden quality of light which gives a feeling of evening all day long. The air had a dry, clean chill, and they sat huddled in their grizzly coats plucking burrs from their knee socks, smoking and talking about themselves.

"So you're big on fox hunting?" said Sally. "Do you actually kill a fox twice a week?"

"Oh, of course not," said Muffin. "Our hounds wouldn't recognize a fox if they fell over one. Though sometimes they go off on deer or rabbit. Almost all the hunts in Pennsylvania are drag hunts. Once my father went down to Virginia to hunt live fox with some friends, and he said he's never been so bored. When you hunt drag, you're always sure of a good run."

"What gets dragged, the dogs?"

"*Hounds.* No, they keep one fox in a cage at the hunt club, and twice a week the dragman collects his droppings in a bag and he drags that around the countryside wherever the master has decided the hunt should go."

"Oh, I *see.* They gallop around chasing a bag of foxshit. Then what happens at the end—do the dogs kill the dragman?"

"Not usually, but once when he got a late start the hounds caught him and chased him up a tree. Usually he hangs a bag of meat in a tree wherever the kill is meant to be, and then drives away in a jeep. Then we gallop up and the huntsman gets off and feeds the meat to the hounds and we all have a cigarette. Have a cigarette?"

"Don't mind if I do."

"In the old days when there were still foxes, and the country was all open, you could gallop around all day going wherever the hounds went; but now the place is getting built up, with trailers and pink ranch houses, so the master has to plan the hunt very carefully. Most of the people in Sweetwater Heights let us hunt through their estates, and the farmers let us hunt through as long as we don't trample the winter wheat. In return we give them a box of chocolates every Christmas, and we always let them know in advance when we're coming through their property so all the neighbors can set up on the lawn in folding chairs and have a good laugh."

"Why, is it funny?"

"They seem to like it, especially when someone gets hurt."

"Do they get hurt often?"

"Oh, yes, pretty often. If the hounds go through somebody's barnyard, where you have to jump in over a rail fence and out over some bloody big chicken coop three strides later, a lot of people jump in and their horses balk and they can't get out again. Then they mill around shouting and getting in each other's way, and in the end somebody usually falls off and gets trampled on."

"That doesn't sound very funny."

"Well, it depends on your point of view. It's usually the same people who fall off over and over again; they're good sports about it and usually come to the hunt tea straight from the hospital to show us their new casts. Of course, some people are killed. But in a way, that's the whole point. People who go fox hunting are usually people who have a great deal of everything, and since they don't particularly deserve it more than anybody else, they feel they have to be more gallant and reckless than everyone else. It's the high-risk theory of showing good form. If you have something that is so precious to you that you're constantly afraid of losing it, then you don't *have* it, it has you. Nothing should be so precious that you're afraid to risk it, not even your life."

They smoked in silence for a while.

"Boy," said Sally, "my mother would have driven you crazy."

"Probably—*my* mother does. But how do you mean?"

"Oh, you know—she's the type who jumps on a chair and screams if she sees a mouse. She wouldn't even let me have a two-wheeler till I was nine. Let alone getting on a horse—for*get* it. All the other kids had two-wheelers and I had this enormous tricycle. The only thing nice about it was when my brothers painted it green for me—the seat, the tires, the spokes—all green."

"That does sound nice."

"Yes, it was. Green handlebars—everything. We had just moved to my stepfather's house on a steep hill, and one day I just took my feet off the pedals and zoomed all the way down till I hit the wall at the bottom. It was neat. I got a concussion."

"Wow! Weren't you scared? Didn't it hurt?"

Sally considered. "I don't remember it hurting. I just remember waking up and hearing my brothers singing 'All the king's horses and all the king's men couldn't put Sally together again.' They were so proud of me. Some other kid had to go up and tell Mother I'd fallen down and gone to sleep and wouldn't wake up."

"Did you get to go in an ambulance? My best friend, Nancy, fell off her horse on the road and hit her head—*she* went in an ambulance. I rode with her."

"I think I went in a car—I don't really remember. I did get a two-wheeler, though, after that. My mother couldn't get a tricycle that had hand brakes."

"But weren't you afraid to ride on that hill?"

"Oh, no—I don't think so. The only time I can really remember being afraid was when we climbed the fire tower at some national park. I was afraid of being up so high, but not really afraid of falling—I was more worried that I'd jump."

"Exactly! Exactly, that's what I'm afraid of too. That, and I used to be afraid of the dark in my room because my nurse's bathrobe on the closet door turned into a witch hanging by the neck."

"Well," said Sally, "there was a crocodile under my bed, and I had to get up in the dark and jump way out from the foot of the bed toward the bathroom so it wouldn't bite my feet off."

"Those nice juicy little ankles."

"Yes."

They had finished the cigarettes. Muffin had a small atomizer of Lavoris, which they sprayed in their mouths and on their hair and their fingers. Then they clomped home down the steep country road, their hands in their pockets to protect against the chill of early dusk, their Abercrombies slipping now and then on the slick silver hardtop.

Jenny got off bounds the third Sunday in October, and the Laceys drove up from Greenwich to take Ann and Jenny and Sally out to Sunday lunch. They drove to a restaurant that was filled with boys from Avon Old Farms and girls from Farmington and Ethel Walker, all dining with their parents and smoking Marlboro cigarettes. There was a certain stir among the patrons when the group walked in, for Ann's grandmother Maude was dressed very much as she had when she was a debutante and looked like a tiny old Gibson Girl.

Sally and Jenny were extremely pleased about this. Ann had described her grandmother in glowing detail, and they were hoping that the day they met her would be one of her good days.

Ann's grandmother had been the most famous debutante of her decade. In 1905 she had married Theodore Lacey, the son of Isaac Lacey, who, as everyone knew, had arrived in New Jersey in 1874 with a peddler's pack and fourteen dollars in his pocket, and in twenty years had become one of the richest men in America. For years Maude and Teddy Lacey were the darlings of the society writers on two continents. They had been friends of Gerald and Sara Murphy and all that crowd of expatriate artists in the '20s, and the house in Greenwich where Ann grew up was hung with early Picassos (gifts of the artist), the library filled with first editions signed with love from Scott or Ernest or Gertrude, the walls hung with photographs of Maude with people like Diaghilev in places like Monte Carlo.

When Theodore Lacey died in 1941, Ann's father had already been sodden for years, so there was no question of his taking over the business. The family stock was sold, and Maude retired from public life to live "quite simply" on her two hundred acres in Greenwich, keeping just the one house on the Riviera for vacations. (Ann was delighted, in the telling, to hear Sally and Jenny hoot with laughter. In Greenwich this story was taken very seriously.) Charles and Madelon lived with Maude; she liked the company, and Charles and Madelon had already long outgrown any appetite they may have had for privacy.

If Maude regretted or resented the comparative quiet of the life she led in Greenwich, she certainly never complained. On the other hand, there came a day in 1953 when Ann came into the solarium to find her grandmother, quite alone, having tea with F. Scott Fitzgerald. She invited eight-year-old Ann to join them and was particularly pleased when Dorothy Parker and Alexander Woollcott stopped in as well.

The next day Maude dressed herself in the costume that had been her trademark in the '20s—a picture hat, feather boa, and a gold-headed cane—and ordered the chauffeur to drive her into New York. She pulled up in front of Lacey's Department Store, which had been in the hands of a British conglomerate for twelve years, and told the chauffeur to wait. Then she paraded into the store, nodding grandly to salespersons and floorwalkers, who turned to gape at her. (She and Teddy felt it was good for

morale to let the employees see the Laceys in person.) As was
her custom, she stopped now and then in her promenade to
choose an expensive item of merchandise from the counters and
present it graciously to a customer. When the manager came to
have her arrested, she selected for him a handsome silver cigarette case.

Chip found his grandmother embarrassing, but Ann enjoyed
her company very much. To Maude a woman's highest duty was
to be attractive and amusing, and Ann found her to be both. The
two of them would often have tea together, sometimes by themselves or sometimes with a few of Maude's oldest absent friends.
Or they would have long games of chess or backgammon; they
had had to give up bridge because if someone bid diamonds,
Maude was apt to counter with a bid of emeralds or her rare
black pearls, and she grew quite indignant if the bid was refused.

At lunch, the first thing Maude said to Jenny was, "Well, my
dear, I'm delighted to meet you at last. You know, I knew your
father."

"Now, Maude . . ." said Madelon.

"Now, Madelon!" Maude mimicked tartly. "I know what you
think . . . you think I've taken her for Margaret Truman.
Well, I haven't. I know Margaret well, and what's more, I don't
like her. This is Clifton Rose's girl; she has his eyes. I knew your
father, dear, the first year he was such a hit on Broadway. I believe it was in *South Pacific*, or was that Ezio Pinza? He was a
very distinguished man, dear, quite the rage among the ladies. I
tried several times to get him for house parties, but he would
never come, and to tell you the truth, I liked him the better for
it. So many of those show-business people like to come and parade around playing the artiste. They come down to dinner in as-
cot ties and they call attention to themselves all evening, claiming that they know nothing of haute cuisine or fine wines, but
care only for Art, and then when they've gone, you find they've
taken the Napoleon brandy."

"Are you sure Charles hadn't drunk it?" asked Madelon.

"Of course not. Charles only drinks Scotch."

"Well, now, how are your courses, uh, Ann?" asked Charles.

"Fine, thank you, Daddy. We're reading the *Aeneid*."

"Oh, are you?" And after a long pause he added, "Well, that must really be something."

"Jenny," said Madelon suddenly, "that dress is very becoming."

"It's Ann's," said Jenny.

"Oh, I see. Well, it looks very well on you." Madelon turned to Ann. "And how is the math going, now that you and Miss Purse have gotten to know each other?"

Ann made a wry face. "Miss Purse is unbelievable," said Sally.

"She really is," said Ann. "Something funny happened last week. It was so typical. Miss Purse was correcting a practice college-board test she gave us, and she had marked something wrong on all the papers that was really right. So I asked if we could discuss it, and practically the whole class agreed with me, so she got furious and called in Mr. Oliver from the next room and asked him which he thought was right. And *he* said—"

"Ann," Madelon suddenly burst out with irritation, "why must you *always* be so critical? And take your soup spoon out of your cup."

Later that night Ann told them that the whole meal pretty well summed up Life with the Laceys. "Jeez Louise," said Sally.

In the darkness, in her bed in the corner, Ann felt a glow of gratitude toward Sally and Jenny. It was the first time in her life anyone had taken the measure of her family together and not suggested it was she, Ann, who was obstinate, rude, and crazy. She had almost drifted happily to sleep when she heard Jenny say, "Besides, it's the dress looks *good* on you."

"What?" Sally mumbled.

"The dress looks *good*, not the dress looks *well*. Unless she was talking about its health."

That year, the last Tuesday in October was Antique Day at Miss Pratt's. From Boston and the North Shore, from New York and Cedarhurst, Bryn Mawr, Sewickley, Grosse Pointe, and Lake Forest, alumnae converged upon Miss Pratt's for their twenty-fifth reunion. They were trim and tan, far more fit than the lumpish pasty daughters they came to meet. All morning the

Main Street of Lakebury was filled with the honking of enormous station wagons, like the clacking of migratory geese, as the new arrivals greeted their classmates. The sidewalks and classrooms were crowded with sleek women dressed as if for golf, whinnying at one another in the clear October air.

By evening the Antiques were full of sentiment and sherry, and many became mournfully confidential over the beef pie. At Jenny's table, a plump matron from Winnetka announced solemnly that she felt there was something magic about Miss Pratt's. Not simply marvelous, you know, but literally magic. She invited them to contemplate her left hand, which beside a dazzling wedding band still boasted her Miss Pratt's ring.

"When I was a bride," she began in a quavering voice, "my husband took me to a lake in the mountains for our honeymoon. We went swimming every day, and one day I lost my Miss Pratt's ring. Well, I *wept*. My husband hired two skin divers and they spent the whole day looking for it. Then we had to go home, because of the horse show.

"Twenty years later we went back to the same resort for a sort of a second honeymoon." She smiled coyly. "And while we were standing in the lobby, a man dressed in flippers and a rubber suit, and still dripping, paddled up to the hotel desk and said, 'I've just found this ring on the bottom of the lake; it has initials inside and may belong to one of the guests.'" The woman gestured eloquently toward the ring stuffed on her pinky finger, but spoke no more; her eyes stood full of tears.

She gazed around the table taking each girl in turn, and each one murmured "Marvelous" or simply gazed in wonder.

Jenny considered her earnestly, and then remarked, "Nooo shit." That night she was put on bounds for the remainder of the term.

CHAPTER 3

The Glee Club Dance

*E*arly in October Ann and Jenny had decided they better have a grand passion for the new Latin teacher, Mr. O'Neill. It was Sally who actually started it, the day her section got back the results of their first quiz on the Gallic Wars. She showed them her paper, marked in red at the top: "D—see me. J.O'N."

"I didn't really fail," she explained sadly, "he just wants my body."

Jenny and Ann looked at each other with a flash of delight. "God, the cad!" cried Ann.

"No, no," said Jenny. "More to be pitied than censured! Overcome with passion, he lures her to him . . ."

"To the classroom, hung with its lascivious trappings . . ."

"Right, its inflammatory posters of the Roman Colosseum . . ."

"And he edges up to her talking about the correct use of the ablative . . ."

"But his voice grows husky! His hands are trembling!"

"And suddenly with a tortured cry he plants a tender kiss on her ruby reds!"

"Because I'm his favorite kind," said Sally. "He loves us ones with no tits, and glasses."

After a week or two Sally dropped out of the game, because she remained unable to master enough idiom to make the switch from textbook Latin to even the mildly colloquial prose of Julius Caesar; yet Mr. O'Neill was patient and reassuring with her, and even gave her some extra time in the afternoons for private coaching. She was embarrassed that he seemed to have faith in her when she knew perfectly well she'd never get it, and yet she was grateful. So, as usual with her when something became important, she refused to talk any more about him. But Ann and Jenny had kept it up with great enjoyment and invention. They liked to weave for each other highly colored semipornographic tales of the secret romances Mr. O'Neill carried on at his room in Mrs. Simpson's boardinghouse, sometimes featuring themselves, or sometimes Mrs. Umbrage or Miss Von Riehban, the riding mistress. At one point they even suspected him of an understanding with Miss Purse, but gave that up as too grotesque even for them.

They weren't the only ones, of course. Mrs. Umbrage had warned Mr. O'Neill that he would most likely have to put up with a fair amount of nonsense when she offered him the post. There weren't many young teachers at Miss Pratt's; they would like to have more, she said, but young men with families to support seemed to prefer the higher salaries in the public schools. And the young women—so many of them married after a year or two and left. No, for one reason or another, Mr. O'Neill would find that by far the largest part of the faculty at a school like Miss Pratt's would consist of women like the one he was replacing. Dear fluffy Miss Purblind, who had taught Latin at Miss Pratt's for nearly fifty years. An excellent mind, and yet she had been apparently content just to teach and live in comparative retirement with her roommate Miss Bird, the school registrar, almost like a sweet old married couple. Mrs. Umbrage wondered why.

Most of the new girls made a point of giggling and teasing each other when they found themselves assigned to Mr. O'Neill's table. Sandy and Linda, two girls who lived down the hall, whom Jenny could hardly tell apart, tended to pant and fall about when they saw him coming and to go around singing "Born Too Late." They had already reached the state of boredom with the term when practically any diversion was welcome. But for Jenny and Ann their crush mattered in a different way. First, because there had been a lingering stiffness between them from almost the first day of school. Or, to be precise, from the moment when Ann had mortally offended Jenny by offering to lend her some clothes. Neither was the sort to apologize, but both knew that the coldness between them had passed forever the Sunday Jenny helped herself to one of Ann's dresses without asking permission and wore it to church.

The other thing was that by the middle of October Jenny had begun to realize that she wasn't kidding. She and Ann would lie awake in the dark telling each other, giggling, that as soon as one was asleep the other would slip down the fire escape in her hooded cloak of midnight blue and dart unseen through the night up High Street to Mrs. Simpson's and in at O'Neill's waiting window. Never mind that High Street was brightly lit by streetlamps or that watchmen patrolled it continually till midnight, and never mind that O'Neill's window was on the second floor. And yet sometimes Jenny would find herself half-awake long after Sally and Ann were asleep, with a longing so vivid that she almost imagined it had come true. That she was in the dark beside him; that his arms were around her, his mouth wordlessly welcoming her; that his warm, lean body felt just so to her hands . . .

Jenny's awareness of Mr. O'Neill had actually begun almost from the first day of class. At first she simply observed, with almost mechanical sympathy, how shy he seemed. It was his first year of teaching anywhere, let alone at Miss Pratt's, and she liked him—all his students did—for his willingness to listen, his desire to please them as well as his requirement that they please him. It was a pleasure to work hard for him because he loved the language so much. Usually when the advanced class read their day's translations of the *Aeneid* aloud he would correct them as they went along, explaining things with such enthusiasm that he made being wrong as interesting as being right. But once in a while someone would read her lines without interruption, the English flowing like the poetry of the original. He would sit looking down at his desk for a moment afterward, silent, Jenny realized suddenly, because he was too moved to speak. The first time this happened, it went straight to her heart. The first time, it was she who stirred him that way, and she never forgot the answering feeling in herself.

Lately, she had begun to imagine that her feeling had com-

municated itself to him. Sometimes she would look up from her
work and find him watching her, his deep-set eyes so still and
thoughtful that she couldn't be sure if he was actually seeing
her or deep in thought about something else. One day, when she
was reciting Dido's plea to Aeneas to stay with her and love her,
he got up from his desk and stood beside it facing her. He was
scarcely taller than she was, and he stood with his hands in his
pockets like a boy, his dark eyes looking directly into hers, until
she felt that the words Vergil had written were her own, and
that she was speaking them to him and for him. When she had
finished, he just went on studying her. And then, although it
was a few minutes early, he dismissed the class.

Now when he walked around the room while they were working, her nerves quivered so with the sense of his presence that
she could tell where he was without looking at him. Sometimes
when he stopped by her chair she felt sure that his hip or his
hand had deliberately brushed her shoulder. In normal circumstances she would most likely have forgotten about it, having
never before been one to live in fantasy. But the idea of him became a real, if secret, comfort to her, something to wrap around
herself when other comforts failed. She let herself believe that
in some way she had become special to him, that he would listen
with attention if ever she chose to talk, as so far she had not really talked to anyone here. She believed she was significant to
him, and except for Ann and Sally, she was significant to no one
else at Miss Pratt's.

In his bedroom at Mrs. Simpson's boardinghouse on High
Street, John O'Neill, the new Latin teacher, awoke these mornings to the first feeling of peace he had known for some weeks.
He had at last achieved the simple conviction that he was losing
his mind. A year ago he had expected to be Father O'Neill by
this time. In the spring, when he announced quite suddenly that
he was leaving the church, his mother said that he was dead to
her and had Masses said for the repose of his soul at the Church
of the Precious Blood in Somerville, Massachusetts.

Shattering as his sudden change of plans had been, girls had
nothing to do with it. He was so sure of this that he had made a
silent agreement with God to hold to his vow of celibacy; in ex-

change he hoped that God would see fit to clarify for him certain of the matters of doctrine that were troubling him.

But since early October—and it was strange that he could not remember how it began—he had slowly become possessed by Jenny Rose. At first his possession took the form of a series of intense, inexplicable visions. She would be standing before him in class, reciting in her melodic, slightly wry voice her day's translation of Dido's plea to Aeneas to stay and be her lover, and suddenly he would see her stark naked. Or he would see her approach him after class with a questioning look and suddenly imagine that she was going to beg him to leave the building with her, to go and make wild love in a secret spot she would know, and feel a sag of disappointment when he heard her offer to bring him some milk and biscuits from the table in the hall before she went to her next class.

Soon he was forced to acknowledge to himself that these visions were no longer inexplicable or involuntary. He began to follow her with his eyes, in the classroom, in the dining hall. He saw her, in unguarded moments, touched by a passage of poetry, allow her eyes an expression of deep, sweet sadness. Sometimes, if the class was writing a quiz or a sight translation, he would get up and walk around the room, stopping behind each girl to glance at her paper. When he came to Jenny he would stop very near her chair, sometimes letting his hand brush against her shoulder. She gave no sign that she was aware of this, but at other times he would look up from a book and find her watching him with a curious, intent expression.

He took to having long walks through the fields and woods on weekend afternoons. At first he told himself this was purely in the interest of keeping fit, but always in his mind was the hope of somehow meeting Jenny, of finding her walking alone or sitting by herself. He could not bring himself to imagine what exactly would take place if they should meet, but somehow he felt that they would simply come together, tenderly and wordlessly. When he finally did catch sight of her, walking quickly late one Saturday afternoon with a girl whom he didn't know, she was laughing and never even saw him. He was ridiculously disappointed.

Concluding that he was mentally deranged brought him immense relief. He felt that under the circumstances he could not be responsible for his longings, and he gave himself up completely to a series of the first wholehearted Technicolor romantic fantasies he had ever had in his life. He imagined himself clumping manfully along the Mountain Road through huge drifts some snowbound day, coming upon Jenny lying with her leg twisted under her, half-unconscious with cold and pain. He saw himself lifting her, gently comforting her, Jenny burrowing against him with helpless, grateful tears, himself bearing her tenderly down the mountain, surefooted on the snowshoes with which he happened to be equipped. Or he imagined Field Day, the school holiday declared each spring when the entire school adjourned to some nearby parkland for a few hours of merry recreation. He saw Jenny tumbling into the Farmington River, himself recklessly braving the current to pull her out, the mouth-to-mouth resuscitation artfully administered, and the expression of dawning love in her eyes when at last her long wet lashes stirred and she recognized her savior.

They were boyish dreams, even he would have admitted, had he not been in such deadly earnest. As a Latin master, "puerile" is the word he would have used. But this passion had struck him with all the desperate intensity of first love. And it had its darker side. Sometimes he would wake in the night with a longing so vivid he imagined at first that it had come true—that Jenny was there beside him, that her lips were shyly grazing his, then seeking his mouth again, her long red hair writhing like living silk against his neck, and her firm breasts pressing against him, the nipples erect and hard as diamonds beneath his wandering fingers. He was not entirely naive. He *had* read *Peyton Place*.

When the Glee Club dance was only two weeks away, Lisa still had not heard from George Tyler. Ruth George was in Lisa's room talking about the music they were going to sing at the concert when Lisa suddenly burst into tears.

"Lisa . . . what's the matter?" Ruth didn't really care, but she certainly wanted to know why, if confidences were forthcoming, Lisa should choose to confide in her. Lisa had barely spoken to her since they arrived, except to borrow some shampoo and lately to chat about Glee Club. They were both first sopranos, and Ruth had to sing in Lisa's ear to make sure she stayed on pitch.

"Oh, Ruth . . . oh, forgive me for imposing on you like this—it's just that I'm so in love, I don't know what to *do!* Do you ever feel like that—just missing someone so much you want to die?"

"Gee, I don't know. I miss John, but I couldn't say I miss him that much."

Lisa gave her a teary, ingenuous smile. "Don't you just want to hear his voice sometimes, though? Sometimes I feel I could just melt, just to hear his voice. You know what I think about sometimes? You have a brother at Hotchkiss who probably talks to George all the time. He hears his voice all the time, and he doesn't even care! Sometimes I pretend that George will call you, pretending to be your brother, and then I come by and talk to him."

"Well, that hardly seems likely," said Ruth. "But if you're so desperate to talk to him, why don't you sneak into Catho some afternoon and call him yourself? I noticed last week there's a pay phone in the basement."

"Oh! I couldn't do that! That's illegal!"

"Suit yourself. I doubt if it's more illegal than for your boyfriend to call me pretending to be my brother."

That evening Lisa was late for supper. She waited upstairs till everyone else had gone; then she went from room to room searching closets for purses, collecting change until she had enough for a pay call to Hotchkiss.

"Yes, hello . . . hello? This is George Tyler."

Lisa had been standing in the dank hall in the basement of the Catholic church for almost ten minutes while the school operators got word that there was an emergency call for George Tyler.

"Darling," she whispered, "it's Lisa."

"Lisa! Oh, Christ, you scared the piss out of me! They had to get me out of soccer practice—I thought my father had had another heart attack!"

"Oh, darling, I've been worried about you! Didn't you get my letters? I thought something must have happened to you and nobody let me know."

"Your letters. Christ." She could hear him panting on the other end; he had run all the way from the athletic field. "Letters. No, Lisa. I haven't gotten any letters at all from you. I tell you what, there's a kid in the third form called George V. Tyler—he must have gotten them. What did the letters say, honey?"

"Oh, George, I'm so relieved! I thought . . . Well, never mind, I thought a lot of silly things. But listen, if somebody else really got the letters, you better get them back." She started to giggle.

"Dirty, huh?"

"Well . . . personal. George, listen, I wanted you to know, I got into the Glee Club here!" She waited for his elation, but he said nothing. "You are coming to the dance, aren't you? I mean, you haven't given up Glee, have you?"

"I'm coming," said George.

"Well . . . will you be my date? I have to let the officers of the club know if I want someone special."

There was a long pause. "Well, Lisa, I didn't know you were going to join Glee. Angie Plummer asked me if I'd take her— we've known each other forever. We showed each other our things when we were ten."

"Can't you get out of it? I mean, since you've known each other so long, couldn't you just explain that you're in love with me?"

"Oh, I couldn't do that. She's a great kid. I never stand up a friend—you know that. I wish you'd let me know."

"But I did!" Lisa wailed.

"Well, come on, it won't make any difference. We can dance together. Listen, honey, it's great to hear your voice, really. I've thought a lot about you. Thanks for calling. 'Bye."

That night at dinner, table assignments changed, and Lisa found herself seated beside Miss Pratt's most redoubtable symptom of cloistered virtue, the geometry teacher, Miss Purse. She was one of those rare women whom life has suited for absolutely nothing. She had neither looks, good temper, charity, nor intelligence, and she had been teaching math to sophomore girls at Miss Pratt's for forty-two years.

Dinner was a glutinous affair known as chicken fricassee, and Lisa found herself utterly unable to swallow a bite of it. She listened in dumb misery to the general conversation about food, courses, and football weekends. Then Miss Purse leaned forward and placed a hand lumpen with arthritic knuckles in a girlish pose at her throat, saying, "Girls . . . girls!" until she had the attention of the table. Lisa noticed that Miss Purse's pink linen bosom was seeping toward the smear of gravy on her plate. "Girls," said Miss Purse again, with a simper which Lisa suddenly found unbearable, "the most amusing thing happened to me this evening. You know my Budgie?" Everyone knew Miss Purse's Budgie. "Well," she trilled, "this evening I was having my bath, and Budgie was having his daily constitutional—you know, I let him out of the cage every afternoon, so he may taste the sweets of freedom. Well, I was having my bath, and Budgie suddenly flew near to me. And do you know, he settled right down on my chest and began to hop around! Why, it gave me the strangest *tingling* feeling!" The table was in perfect silence. Lisa watched, mesmerized, as the gnarled hand fluttered at the linen breast; for one horrible moment it seemed Miss Purse was going to caress herself. Then Miss Purse turned a bland smile on Lisa and said, "Now, do eat your dinner, Lisa. Beaux prefer a girl to be rosy and plump, dear."

Muffin didn't tell anybody, but she really was thinking about the Glee Club dance a lot. After lights-out she would sometimes lie in the dark and make up a picture of a boy she would meet there, a sort of unconscious composite of her father, Lisa's boyfriend George Tyler, and Howard Keel, whom she'd adored since she saw *Seven Brides for Seven Brothers*. This boy was shy and kind and apparently unaware that there was any girl in the room except Muffin. It was a warm, serious dream in which she took scrupulous care to be exactly as wise and gay as she meant to be. In this dream she was quite unselfconscious, thinking only of how to convey both self-possession and an unalloyed wish to please. Plenty difficult enough to express the person she hoped to be, without having to do it in the context of who all the other available girls apparently were and whether they were more or less than she. She and this boy danced as effortlessly as George and Lisa did, and sometimes understood each other so well that they kissed good night. She'd heard that sometimes happened,

so fleeting you thought you'd dreamed it, on the dark sidewalk
as the boys stood to file back into the buses.

"You awake?" Muffin whispered to Lisa one night.

"Mmmf . . . oh . . . yes."

"You had a date with the head of Glee on Saturday . . ."

"Second head."

"Oh, yeah, second head. Well, did she talk about the dance at
all?"

"Some, why?"

"I was just thinking about it."

"Oh, yes? Why?"

"You know . . . just trying to picture it. For instance," she
said, thinking privately of her dream boy, "if you don't want to
follow your dance card, do they make you? I mean, say if you and
George wanted to dance together instead of with the people on
your dance card. Is that all right?"

"What are you talking about? Why would I want to dance with
George all evening?"

"Well . . . I thought . . . I don't know."

"Jesus, Muffin, what do you think, he owns me? You don't
want to dance with the hometown boys all night. What would be
the point?"

"Lisa, you *said*—"

"You don't understand anything! You don't know anything
about boys. Christ, who'd expect you to—here it is the best years
of your life and you're spending them majoring in dessert!"

Muffin said nothing, but turned over in the dark, her back to
Lisa, feeling bitterly chagrined.

On Tuesday afternoons Sally and Muffin had the same free period, and Sally often suggested they take a walk in the woods to
share a quick cigarette. Today she appeared at Muffin's door
straight from hockey, still wearing her red tunic and bloomers.

"Yoo-hoo—you up for a nature walk? Little hike to study the
weeds? Hey, what are you all dressed up for—a date with Mr.
Oliver?"

Muffin was wearing a slip and her velvet sheath skirt that
she'd bought at Saks two months ago. She was staring at her
body in profile in the mirror, especially at the place where the

velvet cupped in tightly over her bottom. "God, I'm a load. I can't wear this to the dance."

"Really? Why not?"

"Look—look at this!" Muffin slapped at her bottom and thighs. "I wonder if you *have* to go to the dance. I can't wear this."

"Sweetie, what *are* you talking about? Look, I'll be glad to go in your place. I'll put two grapefruit in my bra and run around going, 'Hi, I'm Muffin Bundle.' No one will suspect a thing."

"It's not funny," said Muffin.

"Want to wear my skirt? It's full, better for dancing anyway." Sally trotted across the hall and came back with her own brown velvet skirt. Muffin wriggled out of her skirt gloomily and stepped into Sally's. She had to strain a little to close the zipper, but otherwise it fit.

"Okay? Just don't spill tuna surprise on it, will you? I'm on a clothes allowance."

"I don't know—now it looks like I have a giant potbelly . . ."

"Oh, for God's sake, what are we running here, a modeling agency? I'll tell you what. Let's trade—you take the slim hips and I'll take the ten-pound bozoom."

"Oh, *look* at that." Muffin pointed at the mirror. "I'm a load."

"You're disturbed. Come on, hurry up and change. We can get around the mountain loop before study hall, if we sprint."

The night of the Glee Club dance, Lisa dressed herself with special care. She hadn't eaten in almost two weeks, and her eyes had an unnatural, feverish glow; there was a flush of high color at her cheekbones. She stood before the mirror smoothing the soft blue wool of her sheath over her hips and buttocks. Although her clothes were beginning to hang on her, her hands felt fat, fat everywhere; she seemed to herself to be entombed in fat. She had tried to starve it off, to scald it off in baths almost intolerably hot, to run it off in long, punishing heats around the hockey field before and after athletics and sometimes again after dinner. But it hadn't worked. She was fatter than ever. She imagined the Hotchkiss boys, sleek, cool, appraising, whispering behind their hands to each other that the famous Lisa Sutton had run to fat. George would have told them about her, bragged to them that she was a beauty, and now they would find her a pig, a tank. She felt greasy with fat, as if it were oozing out her pores. She wished she could broil herself like the pig she was, like a rasher of bacon, till all the fat was rendered and nothing remained but lean, sensuous meat.

The night of a concert, the rest of the school dined on paper plates in the gym, leaving the Glee Club to entertain the visiting boys in the dining hall. The boys from Hotchkiss were assembling downstairs now. Ann and Muffin were dressed; Ruth had just run in to borrow a pair of dress shields. They would have to come down the stairs into the waiting crowd of boys; the boys would see her ankles before she could see the boys, and they would begin to whisper and giggle among themselves, then stop in amazement when they saw that the swollen piano legs belonged to Lisa Sutton.

She thought of how often before she had relished a moment like this one. How often she had waited upstairs in the dressing room at one country club or another, fiddling with her hair, adjusting her makeup till she sensed the right moment, when the boys would have finished hanging up their Chesterfields but not yet dispersed to the bar, when her date would begin to be anxious for her appearance but not yet irritated with waiting. Then she would descend slowly, usually at the side of some carefully chosen, less attractive girl, and hear the conversation falter, sometimes even get a whistle or two. She could assess her effect on every man present without appearing to look, then bestow herself on her waiting escort as if he were the only man in the room.

Now, descending the stairs, she was terrified. She felt lightheaded, and there was a buzzing in her ears, so in the end she noticed nothing and was introduced to someone and led to the dining hall almost before she knew where she was. The first thing she was fully aware of was her date—tall, pale, with a lantern jaw—asking if she would like him to bring her some milk. She shook her head, her hand against her clenched lips. On a plate before her was a quivering white lump of something with noodles in it. It looked like a mass of congealed fat, and out of it, staring directly at her, were two unnaturally bright green peas.

As soon as she was able to swallow, testing her tightened throat to be sure she could speak without gagging, her only thought was to so dazzle the young man beside her that he would not notice she was not eating. She turned on him the full radiance of her smile and began to talk. She told him bright, stylish anecdotes, gave him sudden breathless confidences, danced, leaped, and feinted, all the time in terror that if she gave him a pause, he would suggest that she touch that stuff with a fork, even carry it toward her mouth. By the time the plates were cleared and she dared to wind down the offense, the young man was so startled, so utterly disarmed, that he thought seriously of asking her to marry him.

All over the dining hall the girls squirmed in their panty girdles and pecked at their food. Whether the girls or the boys were the hosts at these affairs, it nearly always worked out that the boys settled themselves at a table full of their friends, and their hapless dates consented to join them willy-nilly. Thus the boys spoke nonchalantly to each other in loud voices, and the girls spoke very little and tried not to spill their food in their laps. Muffin found herself at the same table as Angie Plummer, whom she knew not at all, and George Tyler, who recognized her at once. Muffin's date was apparently a friend of George's, and Angie told her in the ladies' room that they were the two biggest snowmen at Hotchkiss. Angie considered this very funny. She thought George was a young ass herself, but had asked her to be his date, and she hadn't known anyone she liked better.

During the ice cream George suddenly clapped his hand over Muffin's milk glass and said ominously to her escort, "No more for her, Baker, she's a known tippler. Disgraceful reputation back home; many's the time I've rescued her from the gutter, one step ahead of the gendarmes."

"Oh, it's true, then, about the night she did a tassel dance on the piano at the Longview Country Club?"

"Perfectly true. Stay off the sauce, kid, that's my advice," said George to Muffin. Muffin was thoroughly confused. She could think of no reason why George should select her for attention unless he intended a double entendre at her expense. She looked unhappily at the chocolate sauce in her plate.

"You're a lucky man, Baker. Muffin here's the biggest thing on the Pittsburgh scene." Baker chuckled and finished his milk. George put his arm around Muffin's shoulders and snapped,

"Come to think of it, Baker, you've had quite enough to drink yourself. You stick with me, Muffin."

What is going on? Muffin wondered miserably.

After dinner the girls adjourned to the upstairs bathrooms. Pressed three deep before the bathroom mirrors, they jostled to get a last look at themselves before they went onstage.

"God, Marilyn, why didn't you tell me I had lipstick on my teeth? I'm going to die of embarrassment."

"Come on, look out. I'm trying to fix the back of my hair."

"Jenny, don't *you* have a pair of dress shields you could lend me? Oh, never mind, you wouldn't."

"Oh, Suzanne, let me have some of that powder. These lights make you look green. Do you suppose they do that on purpose?"

"*Christ!* I've got the curse! Look at the back of my dress!"

"Put cold water on it."

"No, don't. It'll smear."

"It'll be dry by the time the dance begins. Just say you sat on some chocolate sauce."

"Muffin, I saw George and Allan laughing with you. Were they talking about me?"

"They were just telling me a joke."

"Why would they tell you a joke? I know they were talking about me."

"George never told me he knew you, Lisa. Lend me a bobby pin, will you?"

"I can't walk around like this—I'm going back to the house to change."

"You'll be late for the concert."

"Miss Moltke will hit you with his purse."

"Jenny Rose's date is the coolest thing I ever saw. Jenny, what's your date like?"

"He wants to know why I don't cut my hair."

"Are you nervous about your solo, Jenny?"

"No."

"I would be. I'm so nervous as it is, I'm afraid I'll pee in my pants."

"God, I do that all the time."

"Do you think anyone can tell I've got Kleenex in my bra?"

"Everyone in your dorm, dear."
"Come on, we're going to be late!"

The concert went off very well. First the boys sang several Renaissance pieces, then the girls sang a series of Caucasian folk songs about tending goats, and together the two glee clubs did a long chorale that they had been separately rehearsing for weeks. After intermission each group sang a series of popular show tunes, and the girls finished with a very dissonant modern piece by a composer named MacLennan; only Moltke and Jenny seemed to realize that the second sopranos had completely lost the pitch after the seventh bar. For a finale, the girls' glee club had prepared a song described on the program as "American Trad. Ballad."

No one in the audience expected much of this. In their experience American Trad. amounted to "Oh, Susannah" and "She'll Be Comin' Round the Mountain." Gospel music was what Mummy's cook sang at the Baptist Church on Sundays, and the blues, as far as any of them knew, were periodic and subject to cure with Midol. The lights dimmed; the audience settled themselves for a raucous few minutes dealing with banjos or little dogies.

Jenny walked to the center of the stage. The spotlight shone in her eyes so that she could not see the audience. She could feel prickles of perspiration forming at her temples, and her long hair, hanging in a mass to her waist, seemed unusually heavy, slightly drawing her head back and forcing her to lift her chin. She began to sing *a cappella*. Her voice—clear, deep, astoundingly pure—soared through the dark space with startling power.

> Sometimes . . . I feel like a motherless child,
> Sometimes I feel like a motherless child,
> Sometimes I feel . . . like a motherless child,
> A long way from home . . .
> A long way from home.

At the last line, her voice held the hall so completely that not a breath was drawn. Then the chorus clattered in, bright shrill voices asserting in harmony that sometimes they felt they had never been born. Jenny sang a third verse, and the song was over. The lights went up, and the audience shook itself, roaring and cheering, as if to escape the embarrassment of having been touched.

The performance changed Jenny Rose's career at Miss Pratt's School. For the swains of Hotchkiss, the evening belonged to her. In the milling talk backstage after the concert, her date was besieged with boys wanting to be written onto her dance card. The girls crowded around her, hugging her, congratulating. They had heard her sing the solo *pro forma* in rehearsal, but they had never heard her stretch and bend a vocal line with such emotion or authority. It just went to show you, really, that you never knew what a person had in her. Ann embraced her, and Jenny was amazed to see tears in her eyes. Lisa, a strange hectic flush on her cheeks, pushed through the throng around her to kiss her on the cheek. John O'Neill sat alone in the last row of seats, watching without seeing the last girls straggle chattering up the aisles, the last housemothers bidding Mrs. Umbrage good night.

"Good night, good night, such a lovely concert."

"Yes indeed, so surprised, at first, that Mr. Moltke had given a solo to a new girl, but . . ."

"Quite right, sometimes an artist like Mr. Moltke simply *knows* . . ."

"And *hasn't* she a lovely instrument! Why, I wouldn't be a bit surprised if we were to hear from that young lady."

"Wouldn't be the first time the world had heard from a Miss Pratt's girl . . ."

"No, indeed; why, not ten years ago Fredericka Beinecke gave her own piano recital at Carnegie Hall."

"Good night."

"Good night."

Mr. O'Neill was filled with exultation and despair.

In the dining hall the floor had been cleared for the Glee Club dance. The tables had been pushed to the sides of the room, stacked on top of one another, with their white linen skirts gone and their legs in the air. A record player had been set up in one corner, a punch bowl in another. Mr. Oliver, the French teacher, Mrs. Oliver, Moltke, and John O'Neill had been drafted into acting chaperons. Moltke, in his ill-cut gray suit, was chosen to man the record player. Mrs. Oliver, in pearls and green taffeta, poured punch into glass cups, and Mr. Oliver, short and self-important, strode around and around the dance floor alternately clasping and releasing his hands behind his back.

The couples drifted in from the auditorium across the lawn. Hah, good, no smeared lipstick yet. Must watch these little pussies. *In Loco Parentis,* hah. If their parents only knew what he knew. He had seen the hot lust in their eyes. He had seen the lascivious titters when he read them Rabelais. Mr. Oliver frequently read them Rabelais to gauge the depth of their depravity.

O'Neill stood in the corner near Moltke. He was wearing dark slacks and a tweed jacket, bought in Harvard Square in September after careful study of the offhand elegance of the Harvard boys he had envied as a Somerville "townie." With his smooth face, his square Irish jaw, and long dark forelock sloping over his eyes, he looked much like one of the Hotchkiss seniors, though to him they seemed worlds apart. He almost hated them for their grace, their easy manners and light, confident banter; in the fall they would be going to Princeton and Dartmouth, and in a few years they would appear in the Sunday *Times,* engaged to postdebs from Briarcliff and Hollins. And he would be here— reading Vergil for the thousandth time with a handful of bright-eyed children, growing older, lying alone in his bed at Mrs. Simpson's with the curtains growing threadbare and the hot plate in the corner blowing the fuses, aching.

Jenny came in on the arm of a tall, handsome boy. Muffin came in with George Tyler; through some complex exchange of pledges, for reasons she hardly dared contemplate, he apparently had become her escort. (Why? Why was he paying her more attention than Lisa? Had Lisa hurt his feelings some way? What were the odds that he was actually choosing her over Lisa?) When the room was full, Moltke selected a Lester Lanin record, holding it disdainfully at the tips of his long fingers as if it were something he had found dead under the sink, and the dance began. At first, as instructed, O'Neill circled the dance floor, watching for daylight between the bodies of the swaying couples, catching snatches of conversation.

". . . decided where you'll apply?"

"I think Smith, for early admissions."

"Oh, a brain."

"Oh . . . you?"

"To hell, in a handbasket."

"Ha ha."

Twirl twirl twirl.

". . . and then we couldn't go to Rome because Daddy couldn't climb all those steps in the heat. He had a heart attack last . . ."

Twirl twirl twirl.

". . . raw fish and seaweed. I swear I ate cheese sandwiches at the Tokyo Hilton the whole time we were there."

". . . Maggie Lanier? She was my best friend at Sea Island last spring! Oh, give her my love!"

Twirl twirl twirl.

". . . score was tied, and the Kent goalie was out for a penalty, so I . . ."

Twirl twirl twirl.

When the song was over, Moltke lifted the needle and the girls consulted their dance cards, now hung from their wrists with braided silk thread.

"Jeffrey Baxter? I don't know him. We'll ask a freshman. Come on . . ."

"Ricky Partenheimer? Partenheimer? Oh, the soccer player. Over there, with the buck teeth."

"Ho, Tyler! This one's got you next?"

"Never mind, I know him."

Lisa threaded her way through the crowd at the punch table until she was standing before George.

"Hello there," she said gaily and too loudly.

"Well, Lisa! Is this one ours?"

He whirled away with her, two-stepping expertly.

"You smell wonderful. How've you been? Lost some weight, no?"

"No."

"Well, you're lovely, as always. Hey, you know? I'm so sorry I snapped when you called me. It was great to hear your voice. How's school?"

"Fine."

"You know what, I like your little roommate. She's very funny."

"Yes. I like her too," said Lisa, loathing her. She knew exactly what he was saying, exactly. He couldn't have found a clearer way of saying it. Muffin Bundle was exactly the kind of girl Lisa had always had contempt for. It was one of her tools of seduction, to make the kind of jokes about other girls that boys were said to make among themselves. It was her way of saying "I'm different from the others, I'm in another league." When George and others before him joined her in the game, she took it as their agreement—that she wasn't naive and soft like the girls, she was tough and wicked and grand, like one of them. If being Goody-Two-Shoes was as good as being Lisa, what would become of her? What would become of her? What would become of her?

"Lisa. Babe, pull yourself together." George stopped dancing, held her at arm's length, and looked at her. She was white, fighting hysteria. "Hey, babe, you're in tough shape." He chuckled uncomfortably and began to dance again; she stumbled a little as she tried to follow him. "You're too thin, babe. That's what's the matter. You're homesick. You know what, babe? You should talk to your roommate if you're unhappy. She wants to be your friend, really. She kept telling me how great she thinks you are."

Twirl twirl twirl.

"Thanks for the dance. Really, babe. Sure you're all right? Want some water? Atta girl. Take care. Chin up."

Twirl twirl twirl.

"Going to the Hols?"

"Sure, always."

"Good, I'll see you."

". . . at camp in the Grand Tetons."

"Catch any trout?"

"We *lived* on it."

". . . *hate* California. Daddy's skin's so sensitive the top of his head gets sunburned through his straw hat."

"What he needs is an indoor golf course."

Twirl twirl twirl.

"But, George, could I just ask you . . . ?"

"All ears, babe."

"I thought you and Lisa were sort of serious . . ."

"What, me and Lisa? Oh, hey, we had a couple of laughs this summer, but there's only one thing in the world Lisa Sutton's really serious about, and it ain't me, babe. So, want to learn to two-step? Hold on, here we go. . . ."

Twirl twirl twirl.

By the fifth or sixth dance, the dance cards were being discarded by the girls who had attracted enough of a stag line to choose their own partners. In the corners several daring couples were dancing cheek to cheek. Mrs. Oliver went on serving punch; Mr. Oliver, nearly beside himself, was partly concealed behind a curtain observing the shameless waltz of the little pussies.

Twirl twirl twirl.

". . . if we slip out before the last dance, can you meet me behind the bushes?"

"Shhh . . . Oliver."

Twirl twirl twirl.

"I can feel your heart beating."

"I can hear yours."

Twirl twirl twirl.

"What is that . . . a knife in your pocket? . . . Oh, God, sorry."

Twirl twirl twirl.

Jenny hadn't expected the dance to be particularly wonderful, but neither had she expected it to be a nightmare. Too late she discovered that ballroom dancing was a skill more specific than moving with grace, a skill that everyone else in the room had apparently been taught from birth. In Jane Austen novels when ladies did·not wish to dance they strolled with their sisters or asked their young men to bring them dishes of sherbet. No such luck here. There was no sherbet; Mr. O'Neill was guarding the door to the terrace to prevent any strolling, and the only girls sitting down were the ones who had been ditched. The only thing that prevented her going upstairs and not coming back was the thought of her grandmother. Once in the Andes her grandmother had smilingly eaten a roasted dog rather than show squeamishness. "I'd rather have eaten a dog, too," she looked forward to telling her grandmother later, but she would also be able to tell her that she'd stayed, and smiled.

She was getting a rush from two senior boys, the big-man-on-campus types to whom everything came so easily that they now vied for the sport of beating out one another much more than for the prize in question. They whirled her around the room in turns, their dancing needlessly flashy and hard to follow, she suspected. They wouldn't allow any of the other boys to dance with her, yet when one cut in, the other made an exaggerated show of disappointment that was nothing short of insult. "Oh, hey, *really?* Can't you give a guy a break?"

The one she was dancing with now, Kim Withington, had said as he claimed her, "Eat your heart out, fellah," then made a loud noise like a truck changing gears as he started to dance away with her. That left his friend laughing loudly. Kim was holding her hard against him, so tightly that it hurt; she was angrily aware of the large hard shape in his trousers, which he pressed insistently at her. Every time he turned her around he began to lift her so her feet left the floor altogether. This required him to hold her even tighter and was evidently a new form of joke, for she could see with each turn the other boy laughing and nodding his head at Kim.

"So," said Kim for the seventh time, "you went to Chapin, was it?"

"Right," said Jenny, smiling at him. He had the husky blond good looks of the prep-school athlete who in ten years would be trying to walk off a potbelly with a stag game of golf every weekend.

"How'd you like it?"

"Divine," said Jenny. "Tell me more about varsity soccer."

"I'm not on the soccer team, I'm on the football team," he said. "And I didn't go to Chapin."

He gave her a cold close look and tightened his hold on her. "You're almost as quick with your tongue as you are with your feet, aren't you?"

"Suppose you fuck off?" she said without thinking, mimicking his tone perfectly. Instantly she was sorry.

What happened next happened so fast that Jenny was never after able to sort it out clearly. Kim suddenly closed his grip around her with both arms, squeezing so viciously that she felt a sharp pain in one of her ribs. One hand took a tearing grip on a mass of her hair at the back of her skull, and through a rising, roaring blackness combined of fear and having the breath squeezed out of her, she could feel him still smoothly dancing and hear him hissing into her ear, "Dumb *bitch* . . . don't you *ever* . . . [squeeze] say *anything* . . . [squeeze] like that . . ."

Before he had finished the sentence, something forcibly broke his hold on her and she was set on her own feet, her head clearing quickly, but her ears still ringing. O'Neill steadied her with one hand at her elbow; he held Withington's upraised arm by the wrist. "That's enough," was all he said, softly, to Withington, but his eyes fixed him with such unmistakable challenge that in a moment Withington, flexing his shoulders and shaking his head angrily, dropped his arm and walked off the floor. Almost no one one else noticed the scuffle.

O'Neill turned back to Jenny. For a moment or two she stood perfectly still, feeling nothing. Then in a rush, feeling returned: humiliation, anger, fear, shame. Her lips began to tremble, and she hung her head; she shouldn't have to cry in public, not on top of the rest.

"Come here," said Mr. O'Neill, and he led her quickly out of the light, onto the terrace. "Take deep breaths," he said. The air was sharp and cold as he shut the doors carefully behind them. She inhaled deeply, hearing the breaths catch ragged in her throat. He said gently, "Don't let the bastards grind you down."

"No," she said, and began to sob. Which she should have done weeks before, with her heart so full of feeling lonely, and homesick, and sick of needing to seem proud of not knowing what everyone else seemed to know. She cried quietly and painfully, leaning against O'Neill's chest while he kindly patted her shoulder. When at last she felt calmer, she said unexpectedly, "No. Don't you let them grind you down, either." He smiled and held out a clean tissue he had found in his pocket. She straightened up and began to blow her nose and dry her eyes. When she was finished, she stood there staring down at the ragged paper ball in her hands. "Shit," she said, "I melted your heirloom hankie."

He started to laugh, and without thinking, held out his arms to her. But in the next instant the warmth of their bodies meeting in the icy darkness provided a sort of exquisite shock, with each sense suddenly aware of the heat of flesh, its delicate quivering smell, of their outlines melted into one shape vibrantly etched in cold. So in the end, unbeknownst to Mr. Oliver, it was one of Miss Pratt's own trusted lieutenants who was disarmed by surprise and gave in to his hopeless hunger, kissing Jenny in the cold dark shadow of the forsythia bush.

In the week following the Glee Club dance, John O'Neill would awaken some mornings and wonder if he was actually in love for the first time in his life.

Sometimes, alone in his room at night, he would open his text to prepare the next lesson and find a message from Jenny penciled in tiny letters between the lines. Sometimes just "hello," or sometimes "you've got a friend." He never knew how she managed to write them without being seen. Sometimes after class, when each girl filed by his desk to drop her homework or pick up an assignment, she might say softly, "I dreamed about you," with the same tone and expression the others used to say, "I'm sorry my assignment was late." Then she would be gone and he would stand grinning like a fool, wondering if they were ever going to exchange more than a sentence, so taut with pleasure that he almost didn't care.

One day as the girls were collecting their books to go, he said casually, "Oh, Jenny, could I see you for a moment?" She nodded brightly and called to Ann that she'd catch up with her. When they were alone, he could hardly look at her; at last he smiled helplessly and said, "You're driving me crazy."

"I know," she said.

"I don't know what we're doing. Help me."

"Talk to me."

"Where? When? I don't know what to do."

"Kiss me."

"Oh, *Jesus!*" They both began to giggle.

* * *

"What'd he want?" asked Ann as they walked up the hill together to math class.

"Wanted to know if I would please meet him in the stable tonight and make wild love to him, because otherwise he'll perish with passion for me."

"The stable! You could get up a threesome with one of the ponies!"

"Yes, that's probably just what he's thinking."

There was no place to meet. Literally none. The legal walks were patrolled by Merton; on the illegal ones you were all too likely to surprise secret smokers. There was one senior girl who was rumored to meet her boyfriend at night in the graveyard, but that seemed too morbid, and besides, the nights were too cold. All the school buildings were lighted and patrolled by watchmen round the clock, and being on bounds, Jenny couldn't safely so much as visit the town library, which was hardly more private than the school one in any case. Her best thought was to try the music bungalow during church, when everyone else might be hoped to be off campus. But she made a dry run there on Sunday, shut quietly into a little study room listening to *Cavalleria Rusticana* on earphones, so she could claim not to have heard the church bells, and was promptly discovered by Mr. Moltke. He declined to report her, fortunately, thinking Mascagni more uplifting than Reverend Upjohn, but still . . .

At last, when she was sitting bundled up by the swan pond one afternoon during her free athletic period, John O'Neill simply appeared and sat down beside her.

They were on opposite ends of the bench, looking at the pond, edged with bright dry leaves in crisp piles that were now and then lifted by the wind so they skittered along the water's edge.

"What are you doing?" he asked.

"Thinking about you."

"Oh." He took a deep breath, held it, finally let it out. "Let's start over again."

"Mr. O'Neill."

"Try John."

"John."

There was a silence. "So far, so good," she said.

"You stay so far away from me in class," she began again. "You used to touch me sometimes." He looked sheepish. "You did, didn't you?" He nodded. "Why?"

"Don't know." He looked intently at the pond. "Wanted you to feel someone caring for you . . . wanted to talk to you . . . wanted you to touch me."

"God . . . do you know there are probably beady eyes in at least four buildings around us watching us at this minute?"

"I know," he said sadly.

"I'd like to—"

"Don't say it. If I hear you say it, I might explode. Then again, I might not. How would I know? I never felt this before." They both smiled.

"How old are you?" she asked.

"Twenty-three. I know how old you are; I looked on your transcript."

"Sometimes, though, I feel older than you are."

"Sometimes I feel you are too. But I suppose that's not so strange . . . my sordid past, you know . . . *do* you know?"

Jenny nodded. She had in fact been passionately curious about his religious life. It seemed it must be intense and private, like any other passion, almost too intimate to talk about. But she needn't have been so scrupulous. He wanted to talk to her as he wanted her to talk to him.

A sudden gust of cold wind blew up and then sank again into the stillness of the November afternoon. Jenny looked at him, slouching with his hands in his pockets, wearing a light jacket and a muffler, and was filled with a tenderness as intense as any feeling she'd ever known. It was all she could do to keep from reaching out to touch him.

"I'm freezing, even in this huge coat . . . aren't you cold?"

"No," he said, "I don't feel it . . . I had a fairly ascetic period at one time and trained myself not to mind."

"Not hair shirts and everything?"

"No, but a vow of poverty . . . humble food and no over-coat . . . it sort of became a problem, because my bishop drove a Maserati."

"Why does everything you say make me want to laugh?" asked Jenny. "That's probably not funny at all. . . . John . . . ?"

"Yes?"

"I watch you all the time. I think about you all the time. I talk to you in my mind all the time. . . . John . . . ?" He jumped up suddenly and walked to the edge of the pond. Stooped, picked up a stone, and skipped it. Turned and looked at her, his face strained but his deep eyes glowing. A bell sounded in the hall of the nearest dormitory. In another minute a babble of voices announced that the hockey class was on the run from the practice field back to the dorms. As they came through the line of trees that edged the field, Jenny could hear Ann calling her. She stood up.

"Mr. O'Neill . . ." she said.

"Miss Rose . . ." he answered with a sudden smile. Then he walked off.

"Jenny, Jenny, Jenny." Ann was panting as she chugged up and fell onto the bench beside her. "Jenny . . . how thrilling. Tell all."

"Don't ask," said Jenny.

Ann studied her for a time and then said, "Okay. I won't. . . ."

"But just one more thing," Ann said later in the dorm. "You know what Elise said about Teddy Kennedy?" As election day drew near, they all talked a great deal about the Kennedys, with a sort of appalled fascination. In the entire student body, only six girls considered themselves Democrats, and only five counted, because the sixth was Jackie Kennedy's half-sister.

"She said that Teddy Kennedy has a face like a map of Ireland. Isn't that a great expression? Doesn't that just describe Mr. O'Neill? . . . Okay, I won't ask." And that was the end of that game.

CHAPTER 4

The Caller

In sophomore English class the girls of Miss Pratt's read Shakespeare's *Julius Caesar,* heavily annotated. They learned that in ancient Rome the priests practiced augury, a method of foreseeing the future by analyzing the entrails of a bird. In a world apparently controlled by omnipotent beings with practically no common sense, this must have seemed as good a system as any. The girls of Miss Pratt's, viewing their environment much the same way, devised a system of their own whereby they augured the future by analyzing the contents of their fruitcups. A cherry amid the canned peaches and grapefruit sections meant one would have a letter waiting on the mail table after lunch.

To most girls at Miss Pratt's, and indeed at similar boarding schools all over New England, there was nothing so thrilling, so tantalizing as the promise of a letter, unless it was the promise of a package which could conceivably contain cookies. Letters brought fond chatty gossip from Mummy, checks from Dad, news of the collegiate pranks of adored older brothers, and most of all, romance, in scrawled blue or gray envelopes from Wallingford, Deerfield, and New Haven. Nothing a girl could achieve at school, by way of scholarship, fellowship, or artistic achievement, mattered nearly as much as the fact that someone at Choate was thinking of her.

Ann Lacey may have been the only girl in school who dreaded the thought of the mail table. To her the mail brought rejection,

103

from *Poetry Magazine, The New Yorker,* even the *Ladies' Home Journal*—and from Madelon.

"Thank you so much for letting us see your manuscript. We are sorry it doesn't suit our present needs."

"Returning under separate cover."

"So sorry."

"Thank you so much, but . . ."

". . . suit our present needs."

". . . a little surprised not to have received the common courtesy of a bread-and-butter note from you *or* your little friends. After all, it's been three weeks since Charles and I drove all the way up to take you to lunch. . . ."

". . . don't think it wise for you to take your one weekend to come home this fall. You may receive a glamorous invitation over the Christmas holidays. Besides, I was thinking of going to the races that weekend. . . ."

"We think your allowance quite liberal. If you have spent it foolishly, you will simply have to make do. And for heaven's sake, I don't want to hear of you borrowing. There's no quicker way to lose friends than to borrow *or* lend. Particularly for a girl with your expectations. I don't mind telling you that I think it very unwise of you to lend your clothes about as you seem to do; you will soon find yourself being taken advantage of."

". . . think you're being very foolish about Carey Compton. He is a *very attractive* boy, as you would see yourself if you would get over this high-and-mighty phase of yours. The girl who gets him will be extremely lucky, in my opinion, and if you wake up one of these days and find that someone with a little more maturity and judgment has picked him off, you will be a very sorry young lady."

At last Ann had written to Carey inviting him to call, hoping that he would have the grace to read her diffidence correctly and make some excuse. However, she received his eager, cheerful, half-illiterate letter of acceptance almost by return mail.

"Oo, ah, who does Annie know at Yale?" cooed the circle around the mail table as she came up the stairs.

"Oh, just somebody from home," she said, reluctantly taking the letter. Which convinced them all at once that it was someone very special indeed.

Ann's objection to Carey was that he was an idiot, an objection Madelon dismissed as pretentious in the extreme. He was good-natured, reasonably presentable, and his mother was descended from two signers of the Declaration of Independence and was a good friend of Madelon's; his grandfather had amassed an enormous fortune in hair tonic. Furthermore, he was the first boy who had ever paid Ann serious attention, and Madelon strongly implied that in view of Ann's "attitude," he might well be the last. If his conversation was limited entirely to the performance of the Lawrenceville soccer team, it was up to Ann to study up on soccer so as to be able to share the discussion. Men liked a woman to be a good listener; a clever woman learned to listen attentively to anything.

Ann felt that Carey's courtship of her sprang not from any genuine affection, or even from any clear perception of any qualities that might distinguish her from any other reasonably pretty girl, but simply from a degree of self-absorption that prevented his even considering that she might not be thrilled with his attentions. But then, there was always the possibility—always a serious consideration with Ann—that she was wrong and her mother was right.

Perhaps her longing for a relationship with some intellectual content, based on mutual regard, was a willful affectation, an excuse she made to herself for a basically haughty, hypercritical nature. Besides, her mother made a persuasive case for the bird-in-the-hand theory of human relationships; Ann was a fool to snub Carey when she had no one else. A girl with any sense would string him along, and if something better came up, she could always drop Carey then, and no harm done.

Carey was coming the second Saturday in November. He was entered duly in the callers' book, and from time to time some of the older girls who were expecting callers the same day would single her out to exchange obscure pleasantries.

"Only eight more days, Ann—decided what to wear?"

"See you on the mountain loop—only six more days!"

"Is your caller driving down, Annie? Could he give my friend a ride?"

Ann was grateful for the attention, and as an act of good faith she set about arranging her feelings to give Carey proper credit as the author of it. Since the Glee Club dance there was nothing out of the ordinary to distinguish one week from another until Thanksgiving. The days were rigidly arranged to be as much like each other as possible; anything that broke the monotony took on the character of a boon of epic proportions. The coming of winter had settled in over the school like the closing of a door.

Ann began to look forward to Carey's visit. When the sophomores' lights went out at 9:30, she would often get up and sit in the dark at the window, looking out at the deserted street. Now and then a car passed, and she would watch the taillights recede into the darkness trying to imagine where it was going, wishing she were going too. The long, bare-fingered branches of the ancient elm tree sometimes tapped against her window when the wind was high, as if it wanted to come in; the sound seemed to her to be the sound of her spirit longing to get out. The radiators knocked; their heat subsided and the room became chilled. She would shiver in her nightgown, relishing the cold, filled with a sharp longing for experience, sensation, anything to break through the dull muffling boredom.

Perhaps Carey was not really a fool. His letters were affectionate; perhaps he was only shy, perhaps she intimidated him with her talk of art and poetry. One clear night as she sat in the dark at the window, she heard the senior girls who made up the octet singing group, the Daisies, leave the music bungalow after their late rehearsal. Their shoes clattered up the walk toward Pratt and stopped under Ann's window. They stood whispering; Ann heard the soft toot of a pitchpipe, then suddenly the night was filled with the sweet high lilt of their singing.

Bumbumbumbum   Somewhere there's music
Bum   How faint the tune
Somewhere there's heaven   Ba bum
How high the moon.
The darkest night would shine if you would come
     to me soon;
Until you will, how still my heart,
How high the moon.

They sang as they walked together back to their houses, and the music carried through the night, filling the cold November wind with the deep sweet sound of young girls' yearning. They were all waiting for love, living for love, and they believed in it as they believed in the moon—now as something promised them, owed them by the world; now as something eternally out of reach. Ann looked for a long time at the moon, nearly full, hanging just beyond the uppermost naked fingers of the elm; it had a warm, mellow radiance, like a pearl, not like the cold glitter of a diamond. The moon would be warm to the touch. She could see the moon; Carey could see the moon; the moon made them a triangle—Carey, the moon, and she. Silently, to the moon, she begged Carey's pardon for not having loved him before. She wanted love, so she would give it. She would kiss him warmly and willingly in the cold November afternoon, and he would know that he had a friend.

It was just as well that she couldn't know that so far from gazing at the moon, Carey had at that moment just won a beer-chugging contest at the Fence Club and was throwing up in the wastebasket behind the bar, to the delight of admiring cronies.

By the time the great Saturday arrived, Ann had worked herself into a state of heightened expectations that bore almost no resemblance to the real possibilities of the situation.

By this time she had allowed herself to be drawn into conversation about Carey, describing him in the best possible light, as she had come to see him, and in the best faith adding several totally imaginary qualities.

"He's not *that* handsome," she warned Muffin, "but he has these very soft brown eyes, and he's the kind of person who's much different when he's alone with you than he is in a group. I guess he's sort of a bad actor in a group." Muffin and Sally smiled and nodded. They all agreed that it mattered very little whether a boy was good or bad; what mattered was understanding *why,* so you could be his one true friend.

"A make-out artist?" asked Sally hopefully. She thought it would be flattering to be snowed by the type of stud who had a reputation as a seducer. There was always the chance that you'd be the one to trip him up and make him really care. . . .

"Not really," said Ann, stretching a point, "but I think he's basically very shy inside."

Several of her friends whose rooms did not look out on the

street had made arrangements for window seats in Jenny and Muffin's rooms for the early hours of the afternoon in order to witness Carey's arrival and the departure of the happy couple up the mountain loop.

Girls expecting callers generally ate very little at Saturday lunch, and they were excused before dessert so that they could change their clothes and put on their makeup by two o'clock. The eyes of the entire school followed them hungrily as they scurried out of the dining hall. Alone in her room, Ann felt tense, overexcited, and special as she tried on two blouses before finally choosing her black wool Lanz church dress and a gold circle pin. Downstairs, two hundred girls ate their way steadily through a mountain of Ritz crackers, cream cheese, and orange marmalade.

From her window she saw several callers arrive, stop to pay their obeisances to Merton, and proceed with easy confidence to Mrs. Umbrage's house; they knew the ropes, had done it all before. At last a taxi pulled up in front of Pratt, and Carey got out. Ann was watching from the window, and her heart misgave her. She wished he hadn't come in a taxi. It was so like one's maiden aunt to arrive in a taxi, not like the graceful mastery of the boys who sauntered up on foot or pulled up in their MGs. Her heart sank further as she watched him bumble into Pratt Hall; she pictured the scene below, Carey wandering foolishly into the study or the offices, while her friends streamed out of the dining hall. At last he reappeared and applied to Merton, who directed him to the headmistress's house. She sat tensely by the window waiting for the phone in the housemother's room to ring, announcing that her caller had arrived.

Carey stood up to greet her as she entered Mrs. Umbrage's parlor. He was much shorter than she remembered him. His short bristly hair had been freshly cut, and his ears looked enormous. He stood before her grinning his usual slack-jawed smile, and she noticed, though she tried not to, that his trousers were too short and his unpolished loafers were worn down at the outsides of the heels almost to the leather.

"Well," he said.

"Hello, Carey," said Ann.

"Well. Long time no see."

Ann smiled weakly. "It was nice of you to come."

"Oh, that's all right. I didn't have anything better to do."

Ann excused herself to pay her respects to Mrs. Umbrage, then they went out for their ritual walk. Ann's feelings were such a turmoil of despair and self-reproach for the distaste which overwhelmed her that she set a very brisk pace. By the time they were halfway up the mountain loop, Carey was puffing like an elderly carthorse.

"Got a letter from Coco," he panted at last. Coco was his sister, a freshman at St. Tim's this year.

"Oh . . . how is she?"

"Fine," said Carey.

When they neared the top of the Mountain Road, Ann asked Carey, "How's Yale this year?"

"Fine," said Carey. "I'm on probation," he added after a time.

"Oh, I'm sorry," said Ann. "What does that mean exactly, being on probation?"

"I don't know," said Carey.

They walked on in silence. Ann was in agony, feeling the silence bitterly as a sign of her failure. Meanwhile, Carey slouched along, apparently well contented, with his tweed jacket open in spite of the cold and his hands in his trouser pockets.

"Well," she said with an awkward laugh, "here we are."

"Oh," said Carey.

"Well. Shall we . . . um . . . go on along down, or . . ."

"Oh," said Carey again. "Oh, is this the top?"

"Yes."

"Oh, well, why don't we find a spot to sit down. A log or something. I brought some supplies."

Supplies, her brain echoed wildly. Those rubber things, what did you call them—Trojans?

"Supplies?" she asked.

"A little toddy for the body," he said wisely, showing a glimpse of a flask in his pocket.

Ann felt a queer rush of relief and disappointment; she laughed. Carey took this for assent and led her from the road into the woods, where eventually they found a large stump to sit on. The flask passed back and forth between them. Presently Carey became expansive and Ann learned quite a bit about how hard it is to make the varsity soccer team even though you were practically the best regular substitute on the whole frosh team last year. On the way back down the hill, at teatime, Carey fell down and got a bloody nose.

By the first week in December, Lisa was so thin that her skin had a queer translucent look, as if under bright lights you would be able to see through her. Girls in her dorm had begun to invite their friends to drop by to look at her bones when she was changing for athletics. Sally, whose stepfather had a leather-bound book of *Life* magazine photographs of World War II, declared that Lisa looked exactly like the people who had been found in the concentration camps—skeletons covered with parchment, stretched tight like the skin of a balloon. Lisa began to complain that there was something wrong with the bathtubs, that the school had deliberately installed supernaturally hard bathtubs that made her bones hurt when she sat down in them. At night Ann and Muffin would watch her standing before her mirror looking at herself with hollow eyes; again and again she would press her fingers to her cheekbones and then drag them down her cheeks to the jawbone, leaving red streaks against the yellow flesh, feeling for pockets of fat.

Muffin was baffled and terrified; she didn't know what to do for her. "Oh, my God, will you drop the subject?" Lisa demanded when Muffin expressed her worry. "I mean, you of all people," she added cruelly, pointedly eyeing Muffin's waistline.

"Have you just plain told her she looks like a dead lily on toast?" Ann asked Muffin. Muffin shrugged hopelessly. The truth was that sometimes when she looked in the mirror, she saw what Lisa saw. Sometimes she really did see herself as obscenely swollen with fat, and Lisa as elegantly slender. "That is the last straw," said Ann. "*You're* normal, she's a skeleton! She's got you as nuts as she is." She went to Mrs. Birch and demanded that something be done for Lisa.

Mrs. Birch spoke to Mrs. Umbrage, and Lisa was sent to the infirmary to be examined by Dr. Livewright. He announced that she was, in his estimation, extremely thin, and recommended that she take her meals in the infirmary, where she could be watched by the nurses. Lisa was highly indignant.

"Can you imagine that old quack telling *me* I'm too thin? What the hell business is it of his? Half the girls in this school will have heart attacks from overweight before they're forty, and *he* decides I'm too thin. Jesus!

"Then he gets out his ten-year-old insurance-company tables and announces that the average woman of my height weighs 123 pounds. The average American woman is twenty-five pounds overweight, for Christ's sake."

For the next three days Lisa ate her meals in the infirmary under the myopic gaze of Miss Detweiler. At first it was easy for her to conceal toast and string beans in her pockets or to drop a cutlet behind the radiator while Miss Detweiler was out of the room. But when Lisa's weight continued to drop, Miss Detweiler began dimly to entertain the notion that cunning was being practiced upon her, and thereafter did not leave the room when Lisa's tray arrived. Soon she was reduced to bargaining hopelessly, as if Lisa were a child: three bites of carrots and she could drink her coffee black; finish the chicken, and Miss Detweiler would personally account for the dessert. Lisa replied simply that if she were forced to eat, she would put her finger down her throat and vomit it all up again as soon as she left the infirmary; Miss Detweiler formed the alarming impression that she meant to do it on the steps.

Dr. Livewright was appealed to, and the next morning when she arrived for breakfast, Lisa found a new policy in force. Her tray as usual contained a bowl of oatmeal, four pieces of toast, milk, and coffee.

"Pure starch," she said scornfully. "I won't eat that—*nobody* should eat that."

"You don't have to eat it," said Miss Detweiler. "Just drink the milk."

"Well, it sounds as if you people are finally learning something about nutrition." Lisa picked up the glass and drained half of it. Her eyes widened with revulsion; then she hurled the glass against the wall with a howl of pure childish rage.

"It's *cream!*" she shrieked. Then she began to sob. "It's *disgusting!* Cream! Oh, God . . . oh, no . . . oh, God!" She was completely hysterical at last. She cried and cried and cried, bent over her tray like something broken. She got oatmeal in her hair, she knocked the tray on the floor, she spat to get the scum of butterfat out of her mouth, and she cried. Miss Detweiler was terrified and rang for the other nurses. At last Dr. Livewright arrived and gave Lisa a shot.

Before lunch, the word spread among the new girls crowded in the cloakroom that Lisa Sutton had been taken away.

"They got Muffin Bundle out of math class to pack a suitcase for her."

"What's the matter with her . . . is she sick?"

"I heard she was being thrown out."

"I was in the infirmary for a headache, and Miss Detweiler was in tears. Maybe she attacked Miss Detweiler."

"Well, somebody should."

"Where's Lisa gone? Did they catch her smoking?"

"Are you talking about Lisa? She's gone to a sanatarium!"

"Mrs. Birch drove her."

"Mrs. Birch? God, can you imagine Mrs. Birch driving?" General laughter.

"Do you think she's allowed to smoke at the sanatarium?"

"I bet she is—the lucky stiff."

On December 12 the temperature stood at eight degrees. There was not yet any snow. Girls were permitted to wear long pants when the mercury dropped below ten degrees, and many seniors appeared at breakfast in ski pants. However, Mrs. Umbrage announced at prayers that the thermometer outside her study window read eleven degrees, so the girls were sent back to the rooms to put on skirts.

Exams were scheduled for the last week before Christmas break. Seniors who had saved some of their late cuts were up every night till eleven, huddled in the study halls in flannel pajamas and hair curlers, drinking instant coffee, which they made in their mugs with tap water and electric heating coils that never quite brought the water to a boil. Juniors and sophomores, who were allowed to stay up only to ten o'clock and 9:30 respectively, appeared at breakfast stiff and hollow-eyed from hours spent cramming in the closet after the housemothers were asleep.

The night before the Latin III exam, Sally moved across the

hall to sleep in Lisa's empty bed, leaving the room for Ann and Jenny to study late. Ann and Jenny draped the windows with blankets so the lights would not be seen from the street. They moved the lamps to the floor beneath the desks and made a cave there out of bedspreads. Jenny had gotten from somewhere an electric percolator, a can of Medaglia d'Oro, and a block of gjetost, Norwegian goat cheese. Almost till dawn they crouched together, drinking steaming cups of fragrant coffee, cutting slivers of brown cheese as rich as chocolate, and read the *Aeneid*.

The term was almost over, and since the day at the pond, Jenny and John O'Neill had found no place to meet or talk. From being nearly sick with desire Jenny had retreated over the weeks to a feeling almost of anger at him that he didn't somehow find a way, although she knew there was no way. They talked with their eyes; once in a while they exchanged a few sentences walking from dorm to dining hall or passing on the street. She began to doubt that he had ever touched her.

When she was leaving the classroom the day after their final exams, he called her back.

"Jenny," he said, "you wrote a remarkable test."

"Yes, I know. For you."

He glanced at Ann, waiting for Jenny in the hall. "Well, I wanted to wish you a very happy Christmas. I know you'll be glad to get home—"

"John . . . come to New York."

His face closed. "Oh, I can't do that." He began to collect his papers briskly.

"You can."

"No." He stood up and walked to the door and held it open for her. She stayed where she was, looking at him, but his eyes never wavered as he gestured her to the door. She gave in, and he flipped off the lights as he left the room beside her. He hurried off down the hall. Walking with Ann, she saw him stride around the corner and heard his footsteps start up the metal stairwell; they stopped, turned, came back. He came around the corner and called to her, "I will." Then he took off up the stairs again.

CHAPTER 5

Christmas Break

On the evening of December 20 all exams were over, all suit-cases packed for Christmas vacation. At dinner the Daisies sang "Torches Here, Jeannette Isabella" and "Chestnuts Roasting on an Open Fire," and afterward the whole school sang Christmas carols, banging on their milk glasses with their knives between each song. After dinner, in the gym they were shown an actual Hollywood movie. As with all treats, attendance was compulso-ry. That night all over school girls lay sleepless, almost sick with anticipation. Those with edible plunder, bought illegally or stol-en from the dining hall, had parties for their friends, while the housemothers for once relaxed their vigilance, laid by their knitting, and drank sherry in each other's rooms. The next morning the fleet of buses and limousines arrived to carry the girls to the Hartford station and Bradley Field for their journeys home.

Almost nothing again in their lives compared with the licen-tious quality of the freedom experienced on that first day of their first vacation from boarding school. Girls who had never smoked before smoked incessantly from the time they crossed the town line till they reached the boarding area for their planes. On board they persuaded amused businessmen to order cocktails for them before lunch. They ate everything they were offered and bought candy and stale coffee cakes from vending machines to eat when the meals were gone. Once home in their own bedrooms they locked the doors, put on their oldest clothes,

115

took them off again, and went to take baths in their own bathrooms. For Muffin that was the ultimate luxury. She lay in her long pink tub, watching the steam cloud the mirrors and the window, thinking of what it meant to know she could take as long as she liked, and use as much hot water as she wanted, and no one would tap on the door wanting to know if she were almost finished. She lay in the tub for forty-five minutes, letting out tepid water and adding hot from time to time. She was reading *The Well of Loneliness*, a book about lesbians that had been circulating the school all term and had fallen to her just before exams. Presently her mother tapped on the door and called, "Muffin? Aren't you almost finished? You haven't even been to the kitchen to say hello to Bella yet, and she's so anxious to see you."

After that, Muffin put down her book, let all the water out of the tub, turned on the shower, and began slowly to wash her hair.

When Roberts drove Ann up the avenue of lindens and under the porte cochere, Maude, Madelon, Chip, and Charles were all waiting on the front step. They all laughed and kissed her, Chip picked her up in a bear hug, and Charles shook her hand and said how very, very glad he was to have her home. She spent the afternoon outdoors, by herself, shouting to the silence and running with the dogs till her feet and hands were frozen. Later she and Chip played tennis at the indoor court. At cocktails in the library Madelon offered her a glass of Dubonnet, and there was roast beef, Yorkshire pudding, and meringues glacées for dinner. After dinner Madelon, Charles, Ann, and Chip played bridge. Ann and Madelon won. Madelon told a funny story about taking old Mrs. Bibelot to Aunt Rachel's funeral. Old Mrs. Bibelot was senile and thought throughout the service that she was at a Colonial Dames meeting. Ann went to bed and sat up till past two, with pillows at her back and a silk coverlet pulled up around her, reading *Anna Karenina* for the first time and looking forward to sleeping all morning.

Sally was met at the airport by her brother, Ralph, and a friend of his from Lake Forest who was called the Pear.

"Christ, I'm glad you finally got here. We need you to line up some local talent for Pear," said Ralph.

"Yeah, Christ," said the Pear.

They went to the baggage room to get Sally's suitcase.

"I'll get a skycap," said Sally.

"Oh, hey, no, the car's right out front. I told the cop I was just coming to pick up my grandmother and her wheelchair and he said I could leave the car in front if I left the motor running."

So they waited inside the entrance till they saw the policeman walking away to ticket a double-parked car. Then they dashed for Ralph's Volvo.

"Peel out," yelled Pear, as Ralph lurched away from the curb.

"Hiyo, Silver," sang Ralph. "Give my granny a frosty." Pear reached into an ice bucket and produced a can of Ballantine ale for Sally, then handed one to Ralph and opened one for himself. They decided to go to the club to hoist a few before going home. "Dad Humphries and the Mère are going out for dinner, so if we take long enough we'll miss them completely."

"Drive on," said Sally.

They sat drinking in the bar of the club for a while. A bunch of Ralph's friends planned to show later on, he said. But they never did. After a while it was too late to go home for dinner, so they decided to go to Gregg Sandbach's house to play pool.

Most of Ralph's friends were already there.

"Sandbox!" cried Ralph, leading the way in.

"Titsworth! Pear!" cried Sandbach. He reached over and squeezed Sally's rear. "Where the fuck you guys been?" He dived into the ice-filled laundry tub on the floor and fished out three wet cans of ale.

"Been at the club, you asshole. Where were you? And what the fuck kind of way is that to talk in front of my sister?"

"Yeah," said Sally, opening her ale. "Watch your fucking language." They gave Sally a cue and Sandbach offered to bet any man in the room that she would clean him off the table. Porky Talbot's roommate from Loomis accepted, and the room filled with raucous cheers as he lost his money.

Sometime near midnight Sally lay down on the couch to clear her head and felt the couch plummet like an elevator that has snapped its cable. She gripped the slick leather with sweating hands, lifted her head, and stared at the wall till the swoon stopped. Then she said she thought she'd go on home. Somebody drove her. She didn't remember who, though she did remember that when he leaned across her to open her door he tried to kiss her and missed. Later she woke up in her room to find that Pear had passed out, fully clothed, on the bed beside her. Near morning she woke again with a raging thirst; Pear had thrown up. She went into the bathroom and drank several glasses of water, then went to find Ralph, who stumbled along the hall, cursing, and finally managed to haul Pear back to his room.

In the morning Ralph and Sally changed the sheets on Sally's bed and threw the old ones down the laundry chute before their mother discovered what had happened. Pear sat on the spare bed holding his head and trying to look contrite.

"Jeez, I'm really sorry, you guys. I'm really sorry."

"Sorry!" Ralph giggled. "*Sorry!* You barf all over my sister, and you say you're *sorry?*"

"Christ," said Sally, "I mean, what a sloppy houseguest."

They finally finished with the bed. It looked rather odd, but they decided to leave it and went off to find some orange juice.

On New Year's morning Muffin and her father went hunting. Her father wore scarlet tails and a top hat. Muffin wore her new bowler hat, which she had gotten for Christmas, and a pair of borrowed breeches, as she had been unable to fit into her own. As always on New Year's Day, the hunt met in the stableyard of Mrs. Alida B. Beebe's stud farm. (Mrs. Beebe, who was eighty-two, had been joint master, along with Muffin's father and grandfather before that.) This morning she was riding a new chestnut mare. The horse was green and fidgety and wore a red ribbon in her tail to warn that she was likely to kick. "'Ware hounds, goddammit!" Muffin could hear Mrs. Beebe yell as she hacked up the drive. In the stableyard, hounds and horses breathed white clouds of steam into the bitter air, prancing and sawing back and forth or around in circles, to keep their feet from freezing in the snow. The riders, red-faced with cold and anticipation, drank neat bourbon from the stirrup cups passed around by Mrs. Beebe's butler.

The hunt was long and strenuous. It began to snow during the second run, and by the kill the air was thick with white. Hacking home through the leafless woods, the hunters' sweat-drenched shirts began to freeze against their skin inside their coats. There was little talk. Slowly the brown-flecked lather on the horses' necks cooled, dried, and caked on their coats. Muffin's boots were tight, and her toes had frozen. The pain was excruciating.

Calmly and silently a voice inside her head repeated, "It cannot last forever. It cannot last forever. Home is before us, we will reach it sometime. Before dark I will be warm again, then I will remember that I was cold but I will not feel the pain. The pain will not seem real then, so it is not real now. This cannot last forever." Most hunts in the area ended their season at Thanksgiving, but the Sweetwater pack went out until the snows got too deep for the hounds to run; it was a point of pride with them all.

At last they did reach their home stable. One by one they tossed their reins to the waiting grooms; they dismounted briskly, smiling with clenched teeth to keep from wincing as their frozen feet seemed to shatter upon striking the hard ground.

The horses were untacked and covered with blankets; all but the most elderly riders walked their own horses to cool them, treading stiffly and gingerly, as if they were on stilts. When the horses were back in the stalls, Muffin and the others went to the tack room to wash the caked salt lather from their boots with dripping sponges and saddle soap. Then they rubbed Lexol into the clean leather with their fingers to prevent it from cracking as it dried. No matter how cold or fatigued he was, a proper sportsman took personal care to see that his horse and his gear were put to bed properly. Owing to this conservative policy, when Muffin's grandfather died at seventy-six he was wearing a pair of boots he'd bought when he was at Princeton.

It was late afternoon before Muffin reached the hunt tea. There she restored herself with hot tea laced with a whiff of bourbon, venison, Smithfield ham, turkey, and various hot and cold vegetables and salads. Happily she and the others sprawled on Mrs. Beebe's antique furniture, with their faces still streaked with sweat and dirt, creases lining their heads where their hard hats had been jammed on, the ladies wearing hair nets, the men highly aromatic. Maids in white uniforms passed among them offering canapés and clearing empty plates. More and more non-hunters arrived dressed for cocktails. At last Muffin found her mother and asked to be driven home.

She had had her bath and was in pajamas, eating supper on a tray in the TV room, when the phone rang. It was George Tyler.

"Did you have a big Eve?" he asked heartily.

Muffin, who had sat up with her sister, Merry, to watch the ball drop in Times Square, said not really.

"Well, we're having a little hair-of-the-dog party out at Burt Jones's house in East End. His parents have gone to Nassau. I thought maybe you'd like to come."

Muffin was speechless.

"We were coming out to Sweetwater anyway to get some other girls," said George. "I could pick you up in an hour."

"No," she said firmly. "I mean, I'd love to, it sounds great, but I don't think my mother would let me. I've been hunting all day and everything." An unchaperoned party? With George Tyler?

"Hey, no kidding. You're too much—I've hardly even gotten out of bed yet. Did you shoot anything?"

"I mean fox hunting."

"Christ, I've always wanted to do that. Would you take me sometime?"

"Sure," said Muffin miserably.

Muffin mentioned this call to her mother when she came in later that night.

"Why didn't you go?" Annette demanded. "It sounds like a fun party."

Two days later George called again. He wanted to take her into Pittsburgh to a hockey game. She said all right.

She expected another crowd of his friends, but he arrived in a large station wagon, quite alone. It was a snowy night. He chatted charmingly with her father before they drove off. On the boulevard, halfway to town, she discovered she had forgotten her cigarettes. She put her purse down on the floor of the car and watched the snow flurries over the river. "Watch out, this is a speed trap," she said when they got to Ben Avon. He slowed down till they were out of the township. She picked up her purse again and searched it thoroughly, then put it back on the floor.

When she picked it up a third time, he said, "What are you looking for?"

"Cigarettes. I guess I forgot them."

"Aw, you can live without them for an hour, can't you?"

"I can," she said angrily, "but I don't *want* to."

Lisa was allowed to leave the sanatorium the day before Christmas. She had her hair in a French twist and a dab of rouge in the hollow of each cheek. She wore her once-sleek-fitting black sheath cinched in at the waist with a gold chain belt, creating a nicely bloused effect in the bodice. At five-feet-eight she weighed ninety-three pounds. She knew she looked good; as she walked through the airport, carrying herself delicately as if she were a tray of dishes, literally everyone she passed turned to stare at her.

On the plane she did not refuse her lunch, although the food was remarkably vile. She not only took it, she ate at least half of it, and of this she was very proud. She knew she had surprised Dr. Ducie with her remarkable control, and she was not a child, to behave only because ordered to by some external authority. No, the control was within herself.

Dr. Ducie had turned out to be an extremely intelligent man. Unprejudiced, unhysterical. He was tall and ugly and thin as a stork, which she liked.

He'd come to her room the first night carrying her dinner tray. She had looked at it and at him with contempt: they were all so transparent, Dr. Livewright, Dr. Ducie, all of them.

"Oh, let *me*," she said acidly. "Isn't this how it goes? 'Miss Sutton, do eat your lovely dinner, see what delicious food we've brought you!' You can save your breath and from now on save your lambchops—I don't care if you bring me steak or Alpo. The idea of putting something in your mouth and chewing it and swallowing it for the incredibly irrelevant reason that you like the taste strikes me as pitiful. Imagine being a slave to these little cells on your tongue—it's depraved."

"I couldn't agree more," said Dr. Ducie.

He found Lisa a very interesting case. He followed everything she told him very intently; he was interested in the way she phrased things. She could see he was impressed. He did arrange for her to be served only a salad and some sort of meatcake that the two of them called Alpoburger. She didn't know what was in it exactly—meat mixed with some kind of health-food grains or something. She got the same thing every day, lunch and dinner. He knew it didn't matter to her. And as the days passed, they talked. It was a great relief to have such a thoughtful, clear-headed listener after the overwrought noncomprehension at school, especially Muffin's. Muffin's spontaneous kindness to her haunted her: how could Muffin *be* like that? How could someone dare to be like that? Could someone learn to be like that?

It had suddenly come to her one day, she explained to Dr. Ducie, that most people were slaves to their bodies. That practically everything they did, if you thought about it, was planned to win them some pointless, useless, totally temporary tickle in this stupid lump of meat that was their body. Eating, sleeping, sports, sex—just think about it. Well, she had suddenly realized that the body was just an envelope that the true person needed to live in, and it was insane, absolutely nuts, to allow the body to control the person. That was the day she took control. She would make her body a perfect machine, the perfect symbol of the clean, clear, perfect person she wished to be inside, and that was all it would be. But God it was strange to be the only person to understand such an obvious thing, to be surrounded by people who thought of nothing all day long except slopping this endless mush of food across their tongues for the inane reason that they liked the taste, which was nothing more than the tongue's way of feeling the food. Of feeling it. Of *feeling* it. It was like some kind of slavery, the things people did because they liked the way it felt. Well, she was a slave no longer. She was free and in control.

She explained to Dr. Ducie how her theory applied to sleep, to exercise, and to sex, as well as to food. He seemed particularly interested in sex, which bored her, because since starting her new regime she was so far from tolerating the sort of racking desire she used to feel at the touch of, say, George for example, that now she only remembered it intellectually, like a sort of contemptible thing that had once happened to someone else. But she explained it carefully anyway. She supposed he couldn't help but be interested; men did seem to be like that, but she couldn't help thinking how embarrassing it was for them.

But most of the time he was very sound, Dr. Ducie. He absolutely agreed with her that a rational person wished to eliminate the useless, the unnecessary, the storm of accidents and feelings that hailed so destructively into most lives. Of course the body was a tool, nothing more, and of course one's only obligation to it was to keep it in peak working order. Then he set up a series of tests, mental and physical, in which they charted exactly how much food her body needed in order to be efficient. It was terribly interesting, really. He showed her that at certain points in the day—late morning, late afternoon, mid-evening usually—she scored less well on certain kinds of tests if she hadn't eaten than she did if she shoved down X amount of the Alpoburger. They worked out all the things that she wanted her body to do: to think clearly, to function well for, say, an hour of tennis, to move bowels regularly, to be free of headaches. Then they tinkered with her food supply, as one might tinker with the richness of the mix of gas and oil in a temperamental motor, until both were satisfied.

What had particularly impressed Dr. Ducie, she thought with secret pride, as she handed the stewardess her tray, was the way she'd applied her concept of control to the necessity of eating— once she'd accepted that it was necessary. She decided deliberately to think of each mouthful of food as sawdust, and to challenge herself to control all outward signs of disgust. She would not only eat, she would eat with every appearance of enjoyment. In that way she controlled not only her own body, but the feelings of those around her, who watched her with pitifully anxious eyes, looking for a reason to interfere. Control of herself as a way to make other people treat her as she wanted them to. Thank you for that, Dr. Ducie.

She needed all the control she had that Christmas. Her mother and father met her at the airport, and she was interested to note that when he saw her emerge at the door of the plane, her father began to cry. Goodness, she thought, as if from a great distance while she hugged first him, then her mother. I wonder what it's like to be that glad to see someone?

She had to admit that there'd never been such a Christmas in their house, not even when they were children. Her father had elaborately researched every detail he could of a true Dickensian Christmas. There was a chain of sleighbells on the door; there were holly and mistletoe on every mantel and molding and stuck behind every picture frame. The tree was lit with candles in antique Victorian holders and strung with cranberries and popcorn and white velvet ribbons.

"We had Mr. Purnell in to do the decorations this year, honey," said Mort, beaming anxiously. "You always said he has the best taste in town. Ought to at those prices, ha-ha. Do you like it, honey?" She did, as a matter of fact. She liked it very much, now that she thought of it. And she was even very glad, she guessed, to be home.

Miriam had talked Mort out of his original plan—to have an old-fashioned wassail bowl and "a few friends" in to welcome her home. "We could ask that boy Tyler to bring her whole gang over, whadya say?" Miriam had said no. But he had been up half the night making eggnog with raw eggs, bourbon, and whipped cream—old Virginia recipe, he said eagerly. To Lisa it tasted exactly like shoe polish, but her father and brother, Buddy, drank a lot of it.

Christmas Day itself became something of a blur after a while. There were so many lights and so much noise, at least compared to what she was used to. She had trouble being more than listless over the perfume and jewelry in her stocking—somehow glitter and smells didn't interest her as they once had. She did revive a little when she opened her big present and found a deep lustrous sheared beaver coat. She was touched; she'd been so cold these last few weeks, and she knew her mother thought she was too young for fur. That unguarded moment of gratitude did much to make up to her parents for what they felt every time they looked at her.

The rest of vacation, she slept a lot. Muffin called her once but didn't mention whether she'd heard from George, which was really all Lisa wanted to know. It didn't matter, of course. She just wanted to know. Anyway, she was sure he'd call her himself sooner or later. She knew him. He couldn't stay away from her. She remembered his voice in the dark the moment he entered her. That cry, those words, his lips. She remembered feeling him give himself to her, for that moment at least. It was easy to remember, since she hadn't been similarly abandoned to him. She supposed he had sensed that; she supposed he regretted trusting her. Nevertheless, she believed he would call.

He dropped by without calling the day before she left for school. He looked more handsome than she remembered, with his cheeks flushed with cold and his blue eyes bright. His hair was tousled as usual. She wasn't really sure he'd been well, though. His smile changed to a strange sort of strained expression when she opened the door to him. She could tell by the way he studied her that her looks were deeply compelling to him. And no wonder; let Muffin Bundle try to look like this. She invited him into the den and closed the door, as she had so often before. He began a little of his old teasing banter at first, but she didn't bother to respond. She was just thinking of an interesting thing. She had played her hard-boiled sparring game with him because she felt being weak was a tactical error. Nobody liked it, nobody loved it. Now George loved to tease her, poking here and there for a unguarded spot, the way guys kidded each other. Wouldn't it be interesting if he actually believed she was tough? She had always assumed that if you showed you could be hurt, you lost the game. Now, suppose she had it backwards? Suppose that being allowed to find the tender spot was really what he wanted? You had to admit, that was an interesting thought.

She noticed that George had stopped in his halfhearted teasing. He had stopped talking, in fact, and was just sitting there, very still and very close to her, looking at her with these strange sad eyes. She looked back curiously, her own pale eyes sunk so deep in the sockets of her face that they looked like candles flickering in a cave. Almost as if it were happening in a dream, she saw that he was reaching for her, unbuttoning her blouse, almost in slow motion. She saw him free, then cup, her breast. She saw him touch the small soft nipple very gently with his fingertip, then repeat the gesture with the whisper of his lips. No response. She saw, rather than felt, him lean his head against her naked breast and start to cry. Jesus, people sure were a bundle of nerves these days.

Jenny and Clif and Malcolm had had a quiet Christmas together. They had celebrated a day early because on the actual night of Christmas Clif had to be in Boston to rehearse for the New Year's Day opening of a new musical. Their holiday ended with the midnight Christmas Eve carol service at the Church of the Ascension on lower Fifth Avenue. Clif and Malcolm wore the silk-lined mufflers that Jenny had given them; at home was her gift from them, a complete edition of the works of Charles Dickens, bound in soft blue calfskin. It had been a quiet, happy day. But after the holiday, time seemed to slow to a crawl.

The morning of New Year's Eve day, Jenny was home alone reading when the doorbell rang. She padded to the door in her stocking feet and opened it, and there stood John O'Neill.

Snow had been falling lightly since before dawn, and there were glitters of white in his dark hair and even gleaming like tears on his long eyelashes. It melted as they stood there. Jenny stared. All week she'd been making bargains with fortune (if a red car comes around the corner before I finish singing this verse, he'll come; if I don't answer the phone until the fourth ring, it will be John). Now that she had actually made him materialize, her heart gave a lurch and then seized up; for a moment she was seriously afraid it had stopped.

"Well," he said shyly.

"Mr. O'Neill." (Very small voice.)

"Try John."

She drew him inside and hugged him, and he held her so hard that his cold cheek scraped fiercely against her face. Finally she remembered what was supposed to come next, in her dream of having him there, and she led him into the sun-filled sitting room and made him take off his icy jacket and boots. Then she brought steaming cups of coffee, fragrant with cardamom, and sat down beside him on the couch.

For a long time they just smiled at each other, exchanging a soft word or two now and then, occasionally laughing. At last he put down his coffeecup and very softly kissed her. She hardly dared move, but she reached up to touch his cheek, and when at last his mouth opened against hers, she felt a great shudder go through him.

After a while he said, "Would you like to know how hard I tried not to come here?"

"No, I don't think so. Anyway, it's all right."

"To be here? Is it? I doubt it." He looked at her.

"On the other hand, I don't care." That made him laugh, which she hadn't expected but which she liked.

"I got you a present," she said.

"Did you really? What is it? But . . . did you know I'd come?"

"No, I thought you wouldn't. I just hoped."

She went to her room and brought back a little package, carefully wrapped. In it was a first edition of *Under Milkwood* by Dylan Thomas. She could see that he was pleased.

"I was surprised how hard it was to find a clean copy," she said. "I finally got it at the Gotham."

He opened it carefully in the middle of the book first, to ease the spine without breaking it, and read a page, smiling. She liked the careful way he touched the pages.

"Poetry seemed like the right sort of thing to give an Irishman," she said.

"Exactly the right thing."

"Even if you don't want to see me, you'll have something from me you can touch, to remind you."

"But it's hardly a matter of not *wanting* to see you . . . ."

"Yes, I know . . . but I don't care."

He shook his head. "You're braver than I am."

"Or have less to lose. In all fairness."

"Please don't think I don't want to."

"Okay. I won't now."

They were beginning to get used to the idea that they were together. John looked around the room and said suddenly, "Where's your father, for instance—how do I explain to him what I'm doing here? 'Good afternoon, Mr. Rose, my name is Mr. Chips and I've come to debauch your daughter'?"

"God, you're jumpy. In the first place, what you're doing is holding my hand. I doubt if even Mrs. Umbrage would call the vice squad. Second, my father isn't home and neither will anyone else be, at least for a few hours. Third, if they were, they would think you were some nice sophomore from Yale, a little young for his age. Fourth, why don't you shut up and lie here and I'll read to you."

She sat down on the carpet in her favorite reading place, propped with pillows against the window seat. He lay in a patch of sunlight beside her. She began *Under Milkwood* and read for the better part of an hour. It was fun to do the different parts in character, and she read well and with pleasure. She could see John luxuriating in the poetry like a cat stretching by a fire.

"I *love* your voice," he said when she paused for a moment.

"You do?"

"Yes—you knew that. I thought you could see me turn to jelly whenever you read aloud in class."

"You never told me any such thing, and you never turn a hair. You must think I'm a mind reader."

"Yes, I think I do, actually. I think everyone can read my mind when I think about you, and I go around surprised all day that they haven't had me arrested. More, please." She stroked his hair and went back to reading.

When they finally finished the book, they bundled up and went out into the glittering frigid afternoon. It seemed impossible to be other than open and overjoyed to be together under that brilliant sky, in all that perfect whiteness, and they marched through miles of fresh-packed snow. There was so little traffic that most of the time they walked side by side in the middle of the street. When their cheeks were chapped and their toes thoroughly frozen, they finally stopped at a little restaurant on Christopher Street and sat in the sunny front window eating hot thick soup and black bread. Then they set off again, plodding through the drifts, all the way to Gramercy Park to the apartment John had borrowed from an old friend from seminary.

It was growing dark as they arrived, but John did not turn on the lights. Instead they took off their boots and coats, and he led Jenny into the bedroom, where he lay down with his arms around her and just held her in silence for long minutes in the darkness. She felt as if every nerve in her body were quivering with awareness of him—the rich clean salty smell of his skin, the rough chin against her forehead, the smooth lean muscles of his back beneath her hands, the hard thigh that lay against hers. Even with her eyes closed, with every sense she was seeing every inch of him and she wanted him to stay exactly there, exactly still, forever. Some slight coil of tension in his body made her fear that if she jarred him he might spring away. She began to move her hands imperceptibly, willing them to be so soft and quiet that he would only feel the love from them, not even the palpable touch.

Minutes or hours passed. Their breathing changed. It grew deeper and slower, and Jenny knew that he could feel her hands, that he was allowing them and needing them. With one hand he touched her face; he lightly and slowly traced each feature with his fingertips. Then he kissed each eyelid, then her mouth; he kissed her as he had that morning, and she could feel the passion well up in him and into her, making a soft hungry sound in his throat, then hers, and leaving them both trembling. Finally he pulled a little away from her and lay with his hand on her breast, looking at her. She could feel her own nerves, so taut it seemed they were singing, and now and then a tremor would run through her. For a long time they lay in the near-darkness, their mouths almost touching.

"I'd like to go to sleep holding you," he whispered. "And wake up holding you and feel you here beside me all night."

"All right."

"And finally have you feel me loving you after wanting to for so long . . ."

"All right," she whispered.

"What?"

"All right."

"All right?"

"Yes."

"Oh . . ." They both began to laugh.

"What time is it, anyway?" She got up in the darkness and went out into the living room to find a lamp and a clock.

"Almost nine!" It seemed remarkable. It would have seemed equally remarkable if it had turned out to be seven, or midnight. She ran her hands through her hair, sat down, stood up, walked around, looked out the window, dazed with desire, and sat down again.

"What was I doing?" she asked. John was watching her from the bed, through the small doorway.

"What?"

"I said, what was I doing?"

"Oh." He smiled.

"Now I remember. The phone."

She called Malcolm. When he answered, she could tell from the chatter in the background that the room was full of people, and she remembered that it was New Year's Eve. "Oh, *good*, it's you, darling . . . hold on a minute while I take this in the other room, will you?" There was a silence and then he came on the line again, calling, "Hang up that other phone out there, would someone?"

"Hi, chum. What's going on?"

"Oh, just some neighborhood lowlife who didn't get asked to a big party anywhere else. We're making beef fondue, but Tony just curdled the béarnaise—there's lots for you. I was hoping you'd call so I could tell you."

"That's lovely of you, Malcolm. I'm sorry I didn't leave you a note, but I decided to come over and spend the evening with So-lange. We're going to watch Guy Lombarbell."

"I see. You sound a little distracted, by the by. Are you sure you're all right?"

"I'm very all right, Malcolm. Super all right."

"Not drunk?"

"No."

"Not raped or kidnapped?"

"No." She giggled.

"If you were a piece of music right now, what would you be?"

"Oh, Malcolm, you worrywart." She actually loved this game. "I guess I'd have to say . . . Franck's D-minor Symphony."

"Well!" said Malcolm. "*Well.* I guess all I can say, then, dear, is take care of yourself and I wish it were me, and I'll see you in the morning."

"Malcolm," she asked suddenly, "have there been any messages?"

"Two. Your father called to wish us Happy New Year, and So-lange called to say she was leaving for New Jersey with her parents and she'll see you at Easter. Good night, lamb." He hung up.

Jenny went back into the bedroom. "What are you laughing at?" John asked.

"Nothing, just happy." She sat down on the bed and began to kiss him. It *did* seem as if the happiness would well up in both of them and bubble over. She undid the buttons of his shirt one by one, then took the shirt off and examined the strong lines of his arms and chest with her lips and hands. She put a hand tentatively on his belt, but he said quickly, "No." She had never seen a man naked, at least not since she was six, and was not really sure she wanted to now, but she wanted to love him any way that would please him. "Please don't," he added more politely.

She said, "Okay."

He helped her take clothes off, and all the time he studied her and touched and kissed her, his eyes were wide and she thought he looked like a little boy. She shivered and he made her put on his shirt. Then they pulled up the quilt from the foot of the bed and lay down in each other's arms, to sleep and kiss and whisper through the night.

CHAPTER 6

Winter Term

According to Miss Pratt, there were two subjects upon which a lady was expected to be utterly uninformed. These were of course money and sex. Naturally, a lady had to know enough about bills and coins to deal competently with tradespeople and to know how much to tip (Miss Pratt's rule of thumb was "fifteen percent and a little extra, for who you are"). But as for what money is, how it works, and how people get it or keep it or lose it, it was felt the less said the better. Of course, nothing remotely like an economics course was offered; instead Mrs. Umbrage devoted one Sunday-morning prayer talk to the topic each winter. The talk was always the same; its message, that the only people who talk about money are those who don't have it.

As for sex, in the hundred and ten years that Miss Pratt's had been finishing young ladies, the subject had never come up. But in the winter term of 1960 an incident occurred that was to bring about a modest change. It was this.

A junior girl named Brooks Bundy returned from vacation with a copy of a recent best-selling book that her mother had lent her to read on the plane. The book was about a Jewish boy who went to Harvard and tried to pass for Episcopalian. Of course there was nothing remarkable in his doing that. However, another character in the book made fun of the boy, asking when he planned to have a monkey's foreskin grafted on. Brooks did not understand this remark, and since it seemed to be a literary puzzle, she took the book to Miss Smith and asked her what

133

it meant. Miss Smith became angry and told her to ask Mr. Oliver. He referred her to the biology teacher, who recommended that she take the matter to the minister at Pisco. By this time Brooks had finished the book and lost interest, but the matter did not rest there. It was discussed by the faculty, and then by the trustees. The idea was put forward that times were changing, and while this idea was not uncontested, the majority feeling was that it might become necessary to provide certain rudimentary facts about sex, if only to enable the girls to recognize an indelicacy when they saw one.

Someone suggested that an elective course in health and hygiene be offered by the biology teacher, but this was quickly voted down; the biology course was quite salty enough as it was. There were large, detailed charts of human anatomy in the science building to which each senior class was exposed in due time. Mr. Bonpane's lecture on the physiology of the male erection was so well known that the very phrase "spongy tissue" was enough to send any of his students into hysterics. It was also known that when he reached the subject of the respiratory system, Mr. Bonpane invariably called for volunteers with whom he would demonstrate mouth-to-mouth resuscitation. As for the mechanics of coitus, Mr. Bonpane chose to answer the inevitable questions by describing how Mrs. Bonpane had spent their wedding night locked in horrified tears in their bathroom at the St. Regis. Surely no more should be offered by way of specific detail.

At last someone mentioned having seen in the Hartford *Courant* a review of a book called *For Girls Only: An Expert Answers Teenagers' Questions about Life and Love.* The book was by a lady who wrote an advice column for a Boston newspaper; the review was most enthusiastic, and the book carried an effusive endorsement from Pat Boone. It was decided that a copy should be ordered for the school library, and this, it was hoped, would end the matter.

In the meantime, a highly comic account of Brooks's interview with Miss Smith had circulated throughout the student body. So many girls had gone to the library to look up "foreskin" that the dictionary now fell open to the page when it was picked up. Brooks had a long list of girls who had asked to borrow the book about the Jew, and Ann was one of the first on the list. Even before she read it she had been informed of the meaning of "foreskin" and of its hilarious synonym "prepuce," but still no one exactly understood the reference to grafting. Ann guessed that it was in some way connected with circumcision, which she believed occurred at a Jewish boy's bar mitzvah.

Ann read the book rapidly and solemnly, and afterward she thought about it a great deal. It made her feel restless and naive, a condition she particularly disliked. She had never met a Jew, to her knowledge. Her father had mentioned once that he knew some at Yale, but they were not gentlemen. Her mother had a childhood friend who had married one; the friend was now in a sanatorium near Boston, hopelessly insane. Beyond this she had never heard her parents mention Jews in any way; and this taboo was explained in terms of Christian charity. ("If you can't say something nice, say nothing at all.")

One Sunday afternoon Ann, Muffin, and Lisa and some others decided to go to the Pantry for tea and English muffins. Lisa had returned to school at the beginning of term. She was still grotesquely thin, and her hair looked dead and lusterless, like the undercoat a collie sheds in the spring. Otherwise she seemed nearly her old self.

The snow was deep; on the curbside the snowplows had piled it shoulder-high. The girls walked single file along the narrow shoveled path. There had been an hour of rain the night before, followed by a flash freeze; every twig and pine needle was glazed with a thin coat of crystal. Now and then wind stirred a branch; its icing cracked and slid suddenly to the ground, making a sound like shattering glass.

"Did you finish the Jew book?" Lisa asked Ann. Her fur-lined après-ski boots squeaked loudly in the snow.

"Yep. It was great."

"God, it will be fabulous to get to college, won't it? No more rules, no more housemothers, just Jews and pinko professors."

"Look out, world, here we come." Their breaths froze in the air as the cold stabbed their lungs.

"Did you ever know any Jews, Lisa?" Ann asked.

"Sure, there were a couple at Ellis last year. One was my best friend, in fact." She spoke very casually.

"Hey, we played hockey against Ellis last year," said Muffin.

"Ooo, I bet we played against each other. I was center forward."

"That's right! I remember!"

"Muffin, are there any Jews in Sweetwater?" Ann asked.

"No. But I met a man at lunch at the Ducat Club with Daddy, and he was one."

"They let Jews in the Ducat Club?" asked Lisa sharply. She was aware that her father had been blackballed twice.

"Oh, sure. Daddy says they'll take as many nice ones as there are."

"How many are in now?"

"Two."

They all laughed. Linda Hawley said, "My father says the thing is, he takes Jewish customers out to the theater and they have champagne and everything, and then in the morning the Jews turn around and buy their ore from somebody else for half a cent a carload cheaper."

They considered this. Ann said, "Maybe your father should stop entertaining and just sell his ore cheaper, too."

Linda said, "Yeah, I know, but . . . you know."

Ann said, "I suppose." And after a while she added, "I wonder if I could get into Radcliffe."

Ann couldn't stop thinking about the book. One night after lights-out, she asked Sally, "If you fell in love with a Jew, would you marry him?"

"Are you kidding? I wouldn't get a chance. Dad Humphries would make a lampshade out of him."

"I mean seriously."

Sally thought about it. At last she said, "No, I wouldn't. Because if I really loved one, it would be all right for me, but what would happen to the kids? I mean, they wouldn't be Jewish and they wouldn't be not. I don't think people have any right to just do whatever they want if it's going to fuck their kids up."

"Well, you could live someplace where it wouldn't make any difference."

"Oh, yeah? Where?"

"Maybe you wouldn't have kids. Anyway, parents have to

live, too; you can't do everything just because it's best for the kids."

"Jesus, you're so wrong!" said Sally. "People shouldn't be *allowed* to have kids if they feel that way. Nobody makes you have them. I didn't ask to be born. Parents do whatever the hell they want, and then everyone treats the kids as if they're fucking bad seeds or something. . . ."

"Keep your voice down!" They waited a moment, listening for Mrs. Birch.

"Anyway," Ann went on in a whisper, "you can't keep people from having kids."

"You should be able to. It's a hell of a lot better than having a bunch of little half-breed kikes, with everyone whispering behind their backs and leaving them out of things and pointing at their little hooked noses."

"Oh, come on . . . it wouldn't be that bad," said Ann doubtfully.

"You bet your ass it would."

The cold that winter in Lakebury was particularly intense. At afternoon athletics, some played basketball or did calisthenics in the gym; others bowled duck pins in the basement of the town firehouse. But most preferred to be outdoors. They skated on the swan pond, those with skis blundered up and down the slope of the meadow behind the stable. If the courts could be kept clear of snow, they played tennis, wearing scarves and sweaters over their gym suits, their naked thighs mottled an opalescent blue. In early February an outbreak of influenza swept the school. Green House had to be turned into an auxiliary infirmary, and so many were sick that classes were suspended for three days. Sally was particularly ill, and the girl in the next bed to hers was removed from the infirmary by ambulance in the middle of the night. She didn't come back to school, and it was presently learned that she had died.

Beyond that, there was little to break the monotony, except that in Pratt Hall a gold watch was stolen from Muffin Bundle and an antique cameo ring from Linda Hawley.

Bad weather kept most callers away. However, one Saturday

afternoon Jenny Rose's cousin Arthur arrived unannounced to visit her, and she could not be found. She had not signed out for a walk, a phone call ascertained that she was not at the Pantry, she was not in any of the study halls, nor anywhere else that anyone could see. The housemother was quite twittery over it. "There . . . mmm, there . . . She'll be so disappointed . . . here . . . there . . ." (Mrs. Birch muttered "here, there" almost constantly while walking or talking, as if she were always looking for something she had lost.) When Jenny reappeared at dinnertime, she was sent to see Mrs. Umbrage.

"Perhaps you will explain to me why you could not be found this afternoon," said Mrs. Umbrage.

Jenny replied that she had gone to the music bungalow to play the piano and fallen asleep.

"You know," said Mrs. Umbrage, "I doubt that very much."

Several more thefts occurred in Pratt Hall, and two were reported in Dorm I. Eventually news of these reached Mrs. Umbrage. Kleptomania was a common event at Miss Pratt's and other schools; Mrs. Umbrage had found that the best policy was to take no official notice, for once the news of a thief became general, the girls began laying traps for each other and sooner or later a great many people would be falsely accused. In the meantime, in Mrs. Umbrage's experience, the real thief was never caught until she decided she wanted to be. Therefore, she asked the housemothers to keep the losses as quiet as possible.

One morning in prayers Mrs. Umbrage made a rather cryptic speech to the effect that her years had given her wisdom to tolerate and forgive a great deal more than perhaps the girls gave her credit for, that her job as headmistress was, above all, to *understand* the problems and distresses of her girls, whatever they might be, and that if any girl had anything at all on her mind, any burden that Mrs. Umbrage could help her with, she was to step forward without fear of punishment or breach of privacy. The great thing, if something is troubling you, is to get it off your chest.

Winter dark settled early over Lakebury. At this time of year Mrs. Umbrage spent the late afternoons in her study in Pratt

Hall, where the dining-room servants could lay a fire for her and serve tea while she answered letters and returned the day's phone calls. Here, too, she could entertain the housemothers from time to time, and meet when necessary with disgruntled faculty members. It was preferable to her own little house in this season, for while the house was close by and much admired by students of Federalist architecture, it was very imperfectly heated and perennially cluttered with notes, books, and stacks of index cards comprising her life work, a critical biography of Bronson Alcott.

One evening shortly after the bell signaling the end of afternoon study hall, there came a knock on the study door.

"Walk in, please," called Mrs. Umbrage, just finishing a note and signing her name with a flourish. (She took pride in signing her name with enormous, florid capital initials.) The door opened and closed behind Ann Lacey.

Mrs. Umbrage betrayed no surprise at seeing her, and indeed she felt none, except perhaps that her message in prayers had borne fruit so soon. She observed Ann with a grave, rather gratified expression. "Well, Ann. What can I do for you?"

Ann was clearly nervous. She had trouble meeting Mrs. Umbrage's eye, and she gave the impression that she was going to deliver a prepared speech. First she said, "Mrs. Umbrage, I want to thank you for what you said in prayers on Tuesday." Mrs. Umbrage tipped her head slightly. "There *is* something that has been on my mind for some time now." She stopped again. Again Mrs. Umbrage waited.

"Mrs. Umbrage," Ann went on at last, "you often say that the friendships we make here will affect our whole lives. That . . . you know . . . that the girls we meet here are as much a part of the education as the classes. You say that it's important to meet girls from different places." This time she paused for so long that Mrs. Umbrage volunteered that that was true.

"Well, then, what I wanted to say was, I want to know why there are no Jews here."

Mrs. Umbrage nearly started, for this was not at all what she was expecting. Off her guard, she regarded Ann with momentary astonishment, and at last said archly, "How do you know that there are not?"

* * *

It took Ann the better part of the evening to work out exactly
how she had been outmaneuvered. "But my point was that we
ought to know Jews who are *Jews*, not Episcopalians," she raged
later at Jenny. "Every single one of us goes to church every Sunday. What does she do, only let them in if they convert?"

"She didn't say there *are* any," said Jenny.

"I mean, it's unconstitutional," Ann shouted, with more passion than accuracy. "For that matter, it's unconstitutional to
make *us* go to church if we don't want to! Christ, they even make
Mitsu Ashiko go, and she's a Buddhist!"

"Maybe it's not against the Japanese constitution."

Lisa, in a pink robe with a bag of curlers in one hand and a box
of bobby pins in the other, rushed in, slippers flapping, and settled on Jenny's bed.

"I could hear you yelling all the way in the bathroom. What's
happening?" Jenny told her what Ann had done.

"And you know what she said?" Ann demanded, interrupting.
She flared her nostrils and arched her brows and repeated in
fruity tones, "But my dear, how do you *know* there are not?"

Lisa took the pins from her mouth and stared, frankly
thrilled. "How fan*ta*stic!" she said. "Who do you suppose they
are?"

Jenny had caught the flu toward the end of the epidemic, and
she couldn't seem to shake it. She insisted she felt quite well,
but she didn't look it. Ann thought she was very pale, and she
hadn't been sleeping well. She began to break rules carelessly,
as if she wanted to be caught. She was often insolent to Mrs.
Birch, who twittered about her in a hurt, solicitous way that
seemed to infuriate Jenny. She was sharply rebuked by Mrs.
Umbrage for reading a book during Sunday-night hymns. Jenny
refused to apologize; Mrs. Umbrage threatened to report the incident to her father. "Oh, dear," Jenny replied, "do you suppose
he'll cut off my charge account at Bendel's?"

She read a great deal of poetry, English and Latin; much of it
made her cry. She seemed to be living on a knife edge; feelings
of joy or of sorrow sliced into her, exposing depths that embar-

rassed her and puzzled Ann and Sally. She often went off by herself to the music bungalow and didn't come back for hours.
There was a strange incident one morning in Latin class.

The class had finished its day's translation of the Georgics,
with a few minutes to spare before the bell. Jenny asked if the
class could look at a poem she was having trouble translating,
an ode from Catullus. O'Neill took the open volume she handed
him and copied onto the blackboard,

Ille mi par esse deo videtur
Ille si fas est superare divos
Qui sedens adversus identidem te
Spectat et audit
Dulce ridentem . . .

"All right. Can anyone translate? Jenny?"
She got up. "I think it says, 'He seems to me to be a god . . .'"

"He seems to me equal to a god
He, if possible seems to surpass the gods,
Who sitting before you like . . . as . . . I
  do . . .
Watches and listens
Sweetly laughing . . ."

"Softly laughing," O'Neill corrected.
"Softly laughing."
"Very good," he said, after a time.
"I'm not sure what it means."
"Anyone else? Page?"
"He thinks the gods are laughing at him . . . ?"
"Ann?"
"No, I'm not sure."
"Jenny, then," he said reluctantly. The expression on his face
was hard to analyze; it seemed almost stricken.

"I think he's saying, 'I don't know how anyone can just sit
there calmly and watch you, and listen to you . . .'" She
stopped.

Ann heard O'Neill say quietly, "Oh, God," and then he turned quickly and left the room.

When Jenny slipped into the dim stable and stopped, as always, to listen for sounds of any creature present except the horses, the building seemed so still that she was afraid he hadn't come. The building felt empty of human presence, and as she climbed to the hayloft, the soft scuff of her boots on the ladder made a sound that seemed to be heard by only her. However, as her eyes grew accustomed to the dimness, she saw him, lying very still against a bale of straw. His face was turned away, looking out the small round dust-webbed window.

"What if I'd been someone else?" she asked coldly. He didn't bother to answer. They'd long since worked out what each would do and say if anyone saw them coming or going. She sat down across from him on another bale and looked at him. She felt a hundred years older than the girl who had greeted him with such a rush of joy on New Year's Eve day.

He held his hand out to her. She softened, took it, and slipped down to sit curled against him as she always had at first, when it gave them such a sense of wonder just to be together.

"Please talk to me," he said now, keeping her hand in his as if he knew she wanted to take it back.

"I said it this morning."

"All right . . . I know." They sat in silence for a time.

"Do you have to make it hurt this much?" he asked her.

"It hurts me this much! I love you . . . I want to be with you . . . I want to make love with you." She said it relentlessly.

"We just can't."

"*You* can't."

"I can't. It's not safe. It's not right."

"Right!" she said bitterly. Then: "You're just afraid because you're a virgin."

"That's true," he said, his voice shaking, "but that's not why."

She was ashamed. There seemed to be no cruelty he wouldn't forgive in her. "I can't bear this. I'm going." She went quickly and noisily down the ladder and out into the frigid air, and immediately regretted it. She wanted only to be with him, on any terms, and needed the comfort they'd been to each other so many times before. But she felt too discouraged and sad to go back.

Sandy Gooch and Linda Hawley were roommates and soul-mates, one of the lucky pairs who are thrown together by chance and find all their tastes and inclinations affirmed in each other. They looked much alike, both slender, flat-chested, with blondish hair and open, good-natured expressions. Sandy's nose was long and arched, Linda's upturned at an improbable angle. The caption under her yearbook picture was to read, "The nose that says 'Why don't you?'" Also under her picture would be the oft-repeated "I'm not Sandy, I'm Linda," and under Sandy's, "I'm not Linda, I'm Sandy." They were always together, and nearly always laughing.

In spite of their high spirits, they both claimed to hate Miss Pratt's "with a passion." It was a fact that with the first shock of homesickness that engulfed Linda when she arrived in September, her reproductive system had suspended operations; as of February she had not had a menstrual period in seven months. She reported with great hilarity that her mother had rushed her to a gynecologist over Christmas to make sure "everything was all right." "Can you imagine? She thought I was *preggers!*" shrieked Linda. "Too much!"

Linda and Sandy had arranged their schedules so they could do everything together. Since they had the same free period in the afternoon, they often chose that time to take their baths. They would lie side by side in the tubs in the deserted bathroom, separated by the whitewashed walls of the tub stalls, their voices floating back and forth in the steam.

"Hell, I forgot my soap."

"Okay, just wait till I finish shaving my pits."

"Thanks."

"Here it comes—heads up," and a cake of soap sailed over the partition from one tub and plopped efficiently into the other.

"God, my thighs are flabby. I've got to go on a diet."

"Oh, have you noticed *Cindy's* thighs? She's got these little pillows blooming out at the tops of her stockings—they rub together when she walks."

They both crowed with laughter, for Cindy was a pet peeve of theirs and they had been encouraging her with treats from the Pantry all term.

"Do you think Cindy could be the klepto?"

"No, I *told* you. She was away on her weekend when my ring was stolen."

"Damn—I'd love it to be her. What do you think about Lisa Sutton, then?"

"Oh, no. I really like Lisa. Besides, she's too much of a brown-nose."

"Jesus, she really is bucking for Government, isn't she?"

"Well, she'd be good—I mean, she's friendly and pretty and she can really turn on the charm for the parents and everything."

"I guess."

"Who's that? Did someone just come in?"

"It's Jenny," replied a voice from one of the toilets.

"Hi," said Sandy.

"Hi," said Linda.

"Hi."

"Hey, Jenny, who do you think the klepto is?"

There was a pause.

"What klepto?"

"What klepto?" cried Linda and Sandy in unison. "Jenny, where have you been?"

"What do you mean?" Her voice sounded defensive. "I've been at the music bungalow."

"I mean, where have you been all term—didn't you hear someone's been sneaking all over the dorm lifting jewelry?"

"No," said Jenny. The toilet flushed, and they heard her footsteps leave the room and diminish in the hall.

"Do you believe that?" demanded Sandy.

"I don't believe it. Except she really has been pretty buggy this term. Hey—do you think it could be her?"

There was another long pause. At last Sandy said thoughtfully, "I don't think she's the klepto. But I had another thought—are you ready for this?"

"What? What?"

"I bet she's the Hebe."

CHAPTER 7

Grace Under Pressure

$\mathcal{M}$onotony has a way of reordering priorities. The regimental sameness of the days at Miss Pratt's gave life a rigid, calcified quality—a quality, in fact, so unlifelike that it gave one the sense, not of being, but of waiting. Every morning of the week the bells began to shriek at seven o'clock. At 7:30 every girl was in her place at breakfast; on every table was a bowl of dry cereal, another of apples, a pitcher each of skim and of whole milk, and one of juice. After grace the girl at the top-left corner of each table went to the kitchen for a large bowl of hot cereal and a tray of egg cups, big end up for soft-boiled eggs, small end up for hard-boiled, and a plate of toast. When the meal was finished the girl at the lower-right corner of the table cleared the plates away. Each morning the girls rotated their seats clockwise by one body, so that the server and the clearer changed once a day.

Everyone sat in her place until the last table had been cleared; when the head of the dining room rang her bell, all rose and stood in silence as the housemothers and teachers marched into the center aisle and out of the room two by two. Then each girl carried her chair into the front parlor of Pratt Hall, where she put it down and sat on it until after prayers, conducted by Mrs. Umbrage, which comprised a Bible reading, the day's announcements, and a hymn.

From 8:30 to 8:45 was free time; from 8:45 until 12:55 classes were held, each exactly forty-five minutes long, with a five-

145

minute break between each one to allow for getting from one
building to another. The bell rang at the beginning and ending
of each period. At five minutes to one came the bell ending the
last class; at one, each girl was in her place for lunch.

Lunch lasted forty-five minutes. Afterward one had fifteen
minutes to return to the house, heart in her mouth, to see if she
had received any mail. However, the mail itself, when it came,
was rarely so satisfying as the drama of expectation that preced-
ed it.

From two o'clock to three was the first athletic period, from
three to four the second. Each girl spent at least one of the periods in some form of prearranged activity; the other was at her
disposal. From 4:30 to six o'clock was study hall.

Dinner was at 6:30 every night. From eight to nine was evening study hall, and at 9:30 all sophomore and freshman girls
turned off their lights. On Saturday morning there were no
classes, but a two-hour study hall instead; and in the evening
there was layer cake for dinner. On Sunday, breakfast was a
half-hour later, prayers were considerably longer, everyone
went to church, and dinner was served at lunch. Another moment fraught with possibility occurred at the end of this meal,
when hopes and sometimes bets rested on whether there would
be chocolate sauce or butterscotch. Hershey's syrup was by far
the most common, but butterscotch sauce, when it appeared,
dense, turgid, almost unbearably sweet, was cause for rejoicing.
Sunday-night supper was thin soup and Euphrates sesame wafers, the balance of the cost of a normal supper being given to
charity in the name of Miss Pratt's girls (who had not been consulted).

Each morning when the bell began to drill without warning
into Muffin's consciousness, her first response was a great dull
wave of despair. Another day of suspension, a day of waste. Oh,
God, to waste time—to *waste* it, when time is all there is? What
if she died? She felt as if she were dying at that minute—lying,
listening, as doors began to open, footsteps began to pad down
the hall to the bathroom—dying slowly, her punishment, to
have to regret every second she had failed to live to the full.

The only possible way to endure this time was to view it as a
hostage of the future. To tolerate the tedium, to conform, to re-

spond, never to ordain or control, was a penance which would be rewarded in some time to come in some way not clearly imagined. She had to use it to prepare herself, and the way to do that was of course to get really beautifully thin. If she were thin, the future would be hers, her vengeance. Unfortunately, getting thin required negative action, *not* eating, while the fact of monotony demanded positive action, definitely taken. So every morning at breakfast Muffin aggressively ate a single apple and sat adamantly still for twenty-five minutes while the rest of the school sloshed through the Wheatena and the marmalade and toast. During this period she was visited by feelings of anger and resentment for the boredom and the waste of time of sitting when she might have been elsewhere.

By lunchtime she was generally exhausted and depressed as well as bored, and by her free athletic period she was so filled with despair that it became necessary to go to the school store and buy a Heath bar in order to reaffirm her sense of her own autonomy. This she would eat in her room, slowly, luxuriously sucking the chocolate, shaving off slivers of toffee with her front teeth, dissolving the succulent splinters in the womb formed by the tongue and the roof of her mouth. She experienced intensely the gratification of simply satisfying a simple desire. Afterward, she hid the wrapper.

One Thursday morning Mrs. Umbrage announced slyly that the following day would be Winter Free Day. Although the girls had been chafing over the lateness of this boon (it had been postponed because of the flu epidemic), they responded with a roar of appreciation such as they might have produced had Mrs. Umbrage parted the Red Sea. Buses would appear at eight o'clock sharp to carry the girls to Mount Tom for a day of winter fun.

Relief! Release! A chance to wear the new Bogner ski pants she got for Christmas! Muffin resolved to eat nothing for the rest of the day; perhaps she would lose ten pounds by morning.

The day dawned overcast and sullen. Everyone came to breakfast in ski clothes over layers of long johns. Muffin was crammed into her Austrian stretch pants like a sausage in elastic casing. It was not comfortable. Lisa was chic in the latest from Abercrombie and Fitch, corduroy knickers with heavy hand-knitted knee socks. (Lisa had methodically gained back almost half the weight she had lost, and lately had even seemed to Muffin to show an unguarded spark of appetite for an occasional piece of fruit or a sliver of Jenny's contraband cheese.) After grace the serving girls vanished into the kitchen and reappeared bearing trays of English muffins and large platters of bacon, insufficiently cooked; the noise in the dining room rose to a fervent hum, for this breakfast was another of the special treats granted only once a term, and many were confused and disappointed to have two special events on the same day, since it left one thing less to hope for, to get them through the rest of the term.

By the time the buses reached the mountain, winds were blowing gale force; the man at the lodge reported that effective temperature at the top of the mountain was minus forty degrees. Also, he said, there was no one else on the slope that day except another busload of kids "from one of them schools . . . uh, Millsex or whadyecall." Miss Crutpole, the athletics director, reminded all the girls to put Nivea cream on their cheeks before mounting the chair lift, to prevent the fluid in their cheeks from freezing.

Giddy with excitement, the girls split into gaggles and fanned out over the slopes.

("Gee, I wonder which cheeks the Crut means. Does she expect us to fall on our faces?")

Muffin and Lisa decided to go at once to the top of the mountain. In the chair on the lift behind them, two boys from Middlesex made sarcastic comments on the floundering figures below, in voices meant to be overheard. "I bet they try to pick us up," whispered Lisa. At the top of the lift a figure muffled to the eyes in a hooded sweatshirt with a filthy scarf wrapped around his nose and mouth held the chair for them to alight. Lisa led the way to a spot sheltered by trees and stood watching as the next chair arrived at the top. When she heard the attendant grunt at the boys and jerk his head in the girls' direction, she smiled to herself and bent to her bindings. Muffin, subtly thrilled, took care not to look in the direction of the boys' approach. Swiftly, with elaborate carelessness, she knelt to adjust her bindings, and as she did so, the back seam of her ski pants crashed open from the crotch to the waistband.

"Having trouble with your bindings?" asked a male voice from somewhere above her.

"No, thank you," she cried, edging sideways to keep her back to the trees. She pulled off one mitten and held it in her teeth, freezing naked fingers twisting the tension nut of her heel strap. Without further encouragement, the figure swooped off to join Lisa and the other boy. From beneath the brim of her hat she caught a glimpse of male perfection, dazzling long eyelashes with a pimple blooming beside its nose. She saw Lisa say something; the three glanced at her and laughed. Lisa shrugged and waved, then the three disappeared in quick succession over the lip of the mountain.

Muffin spent the rest of the day in the ladies' room. Miss Crutpole, with a contemptuous smirk, supplied some safety pins, but these were insufficient to repair the real damage. She was first onto the bus at the end of the day, and when Lisa joined her at last, she agreed with the rest that she had had a fabulous time. That night at supper she soothed and punished herself by consuming three desserts.

By the last two weeks of term, the new girls were not only sick of school, but of each other. Sally complained so monotonously about how hard the teachers graded her that Jenny told her to shut up, and for a week they didn't speak to each other. Ann grew closemouthed and snappish and spent all her time in the library, and Muffin talked so obsessively about home and her horse and what she would do in the vacation that other girls on the hall began to parody her conversation in the bathroom in the mornings.

Only Lisa seemed unaffected. No, she didn't think Miss Purse was *completely* bughouse; yes, she thought the kitchen was pretty fair about seconds on dessert. No, she wasn't going to die if they had calisthenics instead of skating one more time; no, she didn't think Mrs. Birch was the birdiest little twit. Actually, she'd have been a royal pain in the ass if she hadn't backed up the public sunshine with private acts of sweetness. If you were especially down, you might suddenly find a Swiss chocolate bar or some fragrant soap or a copy of *The Prophet* by Kahlil Gibran cunningly wrapped and hidden someplace like your socks drawer. Although she would smile and say, "My, how did that get there?" word got around, and most of the new girls felt more than ever that, really, Lisa was dear.

Spring vacation came at last, and not a moment too soon.

At home in Pittsburgh, Lisa waited to see what George would do. There were only two possibilities, she was pretty sure: either he would come straight to her the minute she got home, or he would stay completely away from her this vacation and the next and the next, until what had passed between them this year was so far in the past that it would never need to be discussed.

When he hadn't called by the third day, Lisa accepted an invitation to a party in Fox Chapel from a tall, stoop-shouldered boy with red hair she met at the club. The party was at Dana Linsey's house; George always said that Dana was "good people." "She's good people" meant a girl who was instinctively moral and ladylike in her own behavior, but full of fun and never shocked at "bad acting" in the boys. Lisa counted on George to be there, and he was.

It was the first party she'd been to since the sanatarium, and thank God it was Dana's—Lisa couldn't regain her status without the support of the girls, and if one of them showed suspicion or curiosity, the whole group would shy away from her like herd animals from the lame calf that could bring the wolves down on them all. But Dana never hesitated; she hugged Lisa and told her that she looked like hell, and soon the others came up in twos and threes to give her the big hello and welcome her back by ignoring the fact she'd been missing. Lisa settled back into her old groove of gossip with girls, suggestive teasing with the boys, and soon had drawn the usual circle of people who gravitate at parties toward sources of light and heat.

It was almost an hour before she felt a strong hand pinch her hard in the ribs. "Hey, bones," said George heartily. He was inching by her sideways through the crush, so that in case she greeted him coldly he could keep moving on to the bar. But her welcome was perfectly done. Eyes wide, beaming smile, loving kiss on the cheek. Squeal of delight, perfectly timed release of his eyes and his hand—a greeting of special warmth, but only enough to flatter, not enough to imply obligation. In her eyes George read nothing that the others could not read. She went back to her conversation, and he went on to the bar.

Late in the evening he finally came to dance with her.

"How lovely." She smiled at him, exactly as she had smiled at the last partner. After a few steps she added, "My dear, it must be a little drunk out."

"B'lieve so," he agreed. He hummed a little with the record. "Began drunking a little bit ago. Drunking cats and dogs. Oop, pardon me, that your foot?" She just smiled.

He began to hum again. "So, how you been?" he asked after a while. "How's Glee Club?" She was fairly sure from his expression that that was nearly the last thing he'd meant to bring up, but she smiled happily and began to answer. She just loved Glee Club, they were learning a piece by Ralph Vaughan Williams which they would give at the Bushnell Auditorium in Hartford in the spring, together with most of the other prep-school glee clubs. They had had a dance with Groton in February, and Groton was going to the Bushnell . . . was Hotchkiss? Wasn't that fun? Was George enjoying the baritone part? All the time she was talking, as if she were at tea with her housemother, George had his hand on one of her breasts and was squeezing the rigid nipple as if he'd forgotten it was attached to her.

The song ended. "More beer," he said. He took her hand and turned toward the bar.

"Are you sure more beer? You look a little sleepy," she said. It was the start of a secret signal, but she spoke with such a casual tone that it might have been a coincidence.

"*You* look sleepy," he said. "Your date looks sleepy."

"Golly, do you think so? Perhaps I best hurry home and catch some ZZZZ's." No coincidence.

He gave her an hour to get rid of her date. It was almost three in the morning when he walked up the Suttons' driveway and knocked softly on the French door to the den at the side of the house, so she could let him in without waking her parents.

Muffin found herself hoping that George Tyler would call her over the vacation, but he didn't. She had had several letters from him during the term, but she had a sinking feeling that her answers had been unsatisfactory; perhaps too eager, perhaps not encouraging enough—it was hard to tell. Anyway, he didn't call. However, one night she received a call from Lisa's mother.

"May I speak to Lisa?" Mrs. Sutton asked fondly.

"She isn't here," said Muffin, quite surprised, since she hadn't heard from Lisa all vacation.

"Oh, really? Well, when she gets back, would you remind her that she has a dentist appointment at eleven o'clock tomorrow? You make sure she gets up in time, the lazy thing. Thank you, dear."

"You're welcome," said Muffin. "Good-bye."

The night before she was to leave to go back to school, Muffin's father came to her room as she was dressing for bed and offered to buy her a fur coat of her choosing if she would lose ten pounds. This filled her with resentment and humiliation, and she made no answer.

Springtime in Lakebury, as elsewhere, was a time of extravagant buoyancy. The main street of town suddenly blossomed forth in clouds of dogwood and flowering cherry; sap ran freely in maple trees, and pretty freely in the girls as well.

Many mooned through classes deep in dreams of spring-vacation romances. On warm afternoons the lawns were dotted with young bodies, bare-legged in gym bloomers, caressing themselves with baby oil and nursing their infant suntans. On weekends they took to the woods singly and in pairs to write doggerel and talk of love.

"Don't Jill and Tony make the dearest couple?"

"She's so lucky."

"Do you think they do it?"

"Oh, no, do you?"

"No, I'm sure they're too much in love."

"Have you ever been French-kissed?"

"Have you?"

"Remember that guy Allan?"

"You did it with *him?* Was it . . . ?"

"Disgusting."

"Did he know you thought so?"

"I don't know how he could miss it, but he did. I was sort of embarrassed for him, actually."

"You know something I don't understand—how come boys get so excited just from doing things to you, you know? I mean, how come you're never supposed to do things to them?"

"Yeah, that's weird, isn't it?"

"Jesus, Terry gets so steamed up just from kissing me, it sounds like he's going to blow up. 'Oh, please, baby, just let me a little, ooo, aaaah, I can't stand it'—even if I just lie there. Like the whole thing is happening in his head. I feel like saying, 'Listen, I'll just sit out here and read a magazine, let me know when you're finished.' You know?"

"Really weird."

"I mean, he keeps going, 'I need you, I need you,' and all the time I get the feeling he's forgotten I'm there. Because why else does he get so fired up about doing things to me *I* don't even like?"

"Like what?"

"Like sticking his tongue in my ear. Who the hell wants a big wet tongue in their ear? All I can think is, oh, Christ, did I wash them? What if he gets a big mouthful of wax—*that'll* be nice."

"Gee—I read that was really exciting."

"Well, he read the same thing. It's foul."

"And he keeps on doing it?"

"Sure, *he* likes it; who cares if I do?"

"I don't get it."

"Me either."

"You know Sally Titsworth, that new girl, she had a really wild reputation in Bermuda this year. . . ."

"Ooo, like what? What's she do?"

"Well, I know she got asked to this beach party with all the college guys . . ."

"I heard Sally Titsworth was *wild* in Bermuda this spring . . ."

"What's that mean, she rode her motorbike on the wrong side of the road?"

"I heard that was the least of it. . . ."

"Meaning what, exactly?"

"Meaning I heard she was wild, that's all. What are you so touchy about?"

"She's my roommate," said Jenny.

"Well, pardon me for living."

The spring was a time for testing old friendships and forming new ones, for pairing and parting, and pairing again. As the days lengthened and grew warmer, an almost hectic air of courtship pervaded the atmosphere, and underneath it ran a thin current of hysteria, for the spring was also the time of choosing roommates for the coming year.

"Sandy and Linda have asked me to room with them next year," Lisa told Muffin one night.

"Oh. Well, could I borrow some shampoo?"

"Sure. I told them I was hoping you'd ask me."

"What did they say?"

"They said we could try for a four-room."

"Gee, that'd be great. Thanks for the shampoo."

One night shortly after, Muffin went to Mrs. Birch's room to ask for some aspirin.

As she stood at the open door, about to knock, she heard a startled cry from Mrs. Birch's lavatory.

"Mrs. Birch! It's Muffin. Is something wrong?"

"Oh, my dear . . . oh, dear, there, just a moment please." The door opened and Mrs. Birch appeared, drawing her long bathrobe away from her nightdress, with a stricken expression on her face. Her lips were trembling.

"Oh, Muffin, dear, excuse me, oh, dear, there, I'm afraid something odd has happened."

"Can I help you? Are you sick?"

"Oh, no, I . . . here there . . . I don't know what I ought to do."

Muffin followed her furtive glance toward the lavatory; through the half-opened door she could see a puddle on the floor at the base of the toilet.

"Something's leaking." Muffin went in and found the floor

slick with urine. Mrs. Birch was clutching helplessly at her
nightclothes, murmuring with distress. The ancient satin hem
of the nightgown showed a dark wet stain. Muffin lifted the seat
of the toilet. Wordlessly she removed a sheet of Saran wrap that
had been sealed smoothly over the mouth of the bowl. She deposited it in the wastebasket and set about mopping the puddle on
the floor with handfuls of toilet paper. Mrs. Birch was incoher-
ent with shame.

"Here, there, I don't understand. Has the plumber been here?
Nobody told me . . . there . . ."

"I think it was a joke, Mrs. Birch."

"What, a joke . . . here? Oh, you mean . . . ?"

"I think it must have been."

Mrs. Birch twittered doubtfully, miserably. "Oh, yes, I see
. . . there. Of course the plumber wouldn't do it, would he? No,
of course not. Yes, I see. Well, it is really very witty, I can see
that. Here, there. Ha, ha, here, here."

"I'm so sorry, Mrs. Birch."

"Not at all, dear, not at all. And now what can I help you with,
there? Some aspirin? Good night, dear. Sleep tight."

When she returned to her room, Muffin found Sandy and Linda waiting for her. They were wide-eyed and bouncing, stuffed
full of glee. "Oooo, was it a *scream*?" they cried. "Ooo, couldn't
you *die*? Oh, God, I wish I could have seen her face. Oh, what did
she do? Was it a panic?"

"Not really," said Muffin.

Sandy and Linda took Lisa aside later and told her the story;
they said they didn't want Muffin to room with them anymore.
Lisa replied that she agreed with Muffin completely. Sandy and
Linda announced that Muffin and Lisa were a couple of pricks,
and the union was annulled.

Muffin and Sally went to the school store together. Sally had
just failed a Latin quiz; Mr. O'Neill had written tersely at the
top of the paper, "F—No comment." Sally had been crying.

"Want to have a party tonight?" asked Muffin.

"Sure, what the fuck?" Muffin grandly ordered a tin of Almond Roca, and Sally asked for four quart bottles of Listerine.

"My God, what do you do with all that?"

"I drink it," said Sally. "It's twelve-proof."

At ten that night they met in Muffin and Lisa's room. The shades were drawn, and Lisa provided a candle, which they set on the floor, and seated themselves cross-legged around it, wrapped in blankets. Each drank off a tooth glass full of Listerine. Then Muffin and Sally began daintily and methodically to consume the tin of candy, while Lisa read aloud to them from e. e. cummings.

After a while they all had another glass of Listerine.

"Guess what I have," said Muffin.

"The trots."

"*For Girls Only: An Expert Answers Teenagers' Questions about Life and Love.* I took it out of the library."

"Well, good Lord, get it out here!"

"Absolutely! For heaven's sake, let's have an *expert* answer some questions for once." Mr. Cummings went back to the shelf; Miss Van Kleek was produced.

"Jesus—I'm almost sixteen. How have I lasted so long without an expert answering my questions?"

"I *am* sixteen; is it too late for me?"

"Never too late. Here, have another round first."

"I can't. I'd rather die."

"Does the expert answer our questions about death, too?"

"Come on, no pikers—one, two, three, drink!"

"Where do you want me to start?"

"Start with fucking."

"That's not in the index."

"Start anywhere."

Dear Miss Van Kleek,

I have a very embarrassing problem. I never thought I'd be writing to you, but I don't know where else to turn. You see, I'm a little heavy. My girlfriends say it doesn't matter and my Mom says it's just baby fat and I'll grow out of it, and she says I can carry it off because I have big bones. My problem is, does a heavy girl have a chance with boys?

Wondering

Dear Wondering:

Your girlfriends don't mind if you're fat (though they may wonder behind your back why you have so little self-control). But it doesn't matter how nice you are if the guys don't get close enough to get to know you (and no one wants to cuddle with a tubby!). There's nothing hard about losing those extra pounds once you make up your mind. Believe me, the first time that cute boy in the second row offers to carry your books for you, you'll know it was worth it!

"Dear Miss Van Kleek, it's not my books I want him to carry."

"Dear Miss Van Kleek, the cute boy in the second row is Mary Cartwright."

"Maybe if you go on a diet *she'll* carry your books for you."

"I never thought of that. Gee, I'll start tomorrow."

"Frankly, I bet she'd carry them for you anyway."

"Do you all wonder behind my back why I have so little self-control?"

"No, we wonder right to your face, sweetie."

"Fuck off. And pass the Almond Roca."

Dear Miss Van Kleek:

I know you hear from a lot of different people, but I bet you never heard of a problem like this before. Every single time I have a big date, it seems I get a pimple beside my nose. I use a nationally advertised acne product and wash my face three times a day, but it still happens every time. Don't tell me to ignore it, because I can't.

Embarrassed

Dear Embarrassed:

It is possible that this is your body's way of telling you that you are really not ready to date yet. This is nothing to be ashamed of, so consider giving up dating for a time. Then in a few months you can try again—your body will let you know when you're ready!

You don't say how old you are; in case you are over eighteen, we should consider another answer to your dilemma. Many girls have trouble with their complexions around the time of their monthly period. Could this be happening to you? I suggest you keep a chart, marking off the day your period comes and the days you get a pimple. Don't be surprised if you find a connection! If you do, then of course you can just tell your guy that you have to wash your hair if he asks you out during the week your period is due.

* * *

"Christ, you know what? That happens to me! Every single month I get a big zit right here!"

"Where?"

"Here. I thought it was teenage acne; now she tells me it's going to happen every month for the rest of my life."

"You can tell your husband you have to wash your hair for a week."

"Or I can have myself fixed."

"You know what? Chocolate and Listerine aren't too good together."

"No."

"I can't tell if I'm getting high or sick."

"Better have another round. Help clarify the situation."

"I think I'm beginning to get a buzz."

"Really? What does it feel like?"

"Feels like I'm hearing you from about ten feet underwater. Oh, bartender!"

"Guess another round won't kill us."

"You *guess*?"

"Lemme see the label. 'Thymol, benzoic acid, menthol, methyl salicylate, eucalyptol, alcohol twenty-five percent.' Sounds all right to me."

"What if we go blind or something?"

"We'll just drink it till we need glasses."

Dear Miss Van Kleek:

I heard that if you let a boy put his hand inside your pants you're not a virgin anymore. Is this true? Please answer by return mail.

Have to Know

Dear Have to Know:

Virginity is a two-pronged question. Technically, being a virgin means having your hymen—the precious membrane of flesh stretched across your vaginal orifice—intact. Ordinarily you retain this until your wedding night, when it is broken gently and lovingly by your husband's member. But occasionally the hymen is stretched or broken during strenuous exercise, especially excessive horseback riding.

* * *

"Pardon me. Wouldja mind defining 'excessive horseback riding'?"

"Oh, shush."

"I mean, what's excessive? For that matter, what's a vaginal orifice?"

"It's right next to the post orifice."

"Aaaaagggghhh."

"I thought that was the library."

"Oh, shut up."

Of course when the hymen has been broken by nonsexual activity, the girl is still a virgin.

However, there is another aspect of virginity which is far more important, and that is *purity*. It is possible to be a technical virgin and yet have lost your purity forever; this would be the case of a girl who let a boy put his hand in her panties. Purity is the bride's most precious gift to her husband. When a man takes your virginity, he takes your flower, in the truest sense. It is a moment a man treasures and remembers his whole life long, and in return for this gift he feels a love and protection toward his bride that will sustain you both through the most trying times. It is the foundation of a successful marriage. And when a husband is cheated of this gift he is often angry and bitter, and he has every right to be.

"Dear Miss Van Kleek, if we all retain our technical purity, how are our husbands going to find out what to do to our vaginal orifices?"

"They're supposed to practice on liver in milk bottles."

"Well. I must say, I am feeling very, very ill."

"Yes."

"I think I best say good night, all."

"Goodnightol."

"Good night."

"Good night."

Spring gushed on toward summer. When the temperature reached eighty degrees three days in a row, the girls were given permission to put away their woolen skirts and knee socks and to return to cotton clothes. Pitchers of iced tea, very sweet and

garnished with fresh mint, appeared at luncheon. On Saturday
nights everyone came to supper in the costume of Swiss milk-
maids, their modest dirndls displaying slender waists and small
swelling bosoms. Around their necks the girls wore identical
strings of dried colored beans, imported from the Caribbean.

As the end of term approached, the atmosphere grew feverish.
There were exams to prepare for, papers to write, applications to
fill out for jobs as mothers' helpers on the Cape or in Maine;
many hoped to be accepted to go to France with the Experiment
in International Living. (A few applied for other countries. Ally-
son Grosscup went to Copenhagen one year, but she complained
that the only Danish she learned in six weeks was how to say "I
love you" and "No, thanks, I'm on a diet.")

In prayers Mrs. Umbrage announced that Mr. Shaftoe of the
St. Margaret's School would once again be leading a group of
girls on his version of the Grand Tour of Europe. Everything
was to be first class; the group would sail from New York on the
twentieth of July on the *Mauretania,* sister ship of the *Lusi-
tania.* Notices of the trip had been sent out to all the parents.

"I love the idea," said Maude, who had called to tell Ann she
would like to give her the trip as a birthday present. "I remember my first trip to Europe with a maid and four steamer trunks,
and now all one hears is crossing the Atlantic in seven hours
with these little drip-dry suitcases. You should certainly go in
luxury once in your life, darling. You'll never forget it. And it's
so clever of Mr. Shaftoe to take you on the *Titanic—*"

"*Mauretania,* Maude," said Ann.

"Hmm? Oh, whatever—I knew it was something about sinking. Anyway, those Cunard liners have lovely appointments."

Ann was very pleased and wanted the others to try to come
with her. Lisa and Muffin thought it would be absolutely neat,
and to their great excitement, their parents did too.

Final choices had to be filed at the registrar's office as to next
year's roommates. Muffin, Sally, and Lisa decided to room
together. Ann was going to room with Jenny. When the dust
finally cleared, only poor Kathy Howard had no one to room
with; she had received a grateful pledge from Gigi Bacon weeks
earlier, but while Kathy was in the infirmary with impetigo,
Gigi defected to a girl from Antigua who promised to take her

home at Christmas vacation. This accident marked Kathy for the rest of her career at Miss Pratt's, and while she later became a prominent lawyer with a famous politician husband, no one who was at school with her ever thought of her except in terms of her dandruff and her loneliness.

The long fragrant evenings, the pressure of exams, and the thought of the summer vacation just ahead made the girls gay and wild and a little mad. The new girls, filled with undirected longings and insatiable expectations, expected daily to be made old girls and given their school rings, and daily they were disappointed. Tradition was that the greater the suspense that surrounded this event, the greater the sentiment and satisfaction; but the new girls of 1960 were oddly unlike those of 1920.

There began to be angry and mutinous rumblings. The old girls reported with displeasure that there was an unwonted amount of giggling and irreverence during singing in the garden, a cherished ceremony that took place under the willows every fine spring evening after dinner. News of this new and querulous mood eventually reached Mrs. Umbrage, and she found it disturbing.

It had begun to occur to Mrs. Umbrage, once or twice in the past few years, that girls were somehow not the same as they used to be, and she couldn't imagine why. The old rituals, beloved for decades, seemed to have lost some magic. The girls themselves seemed to have lost their simple-hearted passion for surprises, though what they might want instead, she couldn't bring herself to think. But she found the change disquieting; in fact, this spring she began to feel it had gone far enough. She decided to take action.

One Sunday morning after a lengthy Bible reading from the book of Job, Mrs. Umbrage announced that her talk for the morning was to deal with changing times. She began by reading a list of rules that were in force at Miss Pratt's at the turn of the century. "No card playing on Sundays. No student may receive newspapers, periodicals, or novels. No girl may bring novels to school. Students may dance together between tea and evening prayers, but Miss Pratt requires that there be no waltzing. No girl may leave her house without a hat. Each year one or two girls are bid to attend the Yale Junior Promenade. Permission will be given to attend this one event, but the girl must be older than seventeen years of age, and this is the only invitation she may accept. Nothing may be read on Sundays except the Bible. No diets will be permitted. No candy or other eatable may be brought to school, nor may any girl keep health biscuits or food tablets of any kind in her room." And so on. There was more, about decorum during tea, about the sort of needlework that might be done during the evening while Miss Pratt read aloud from Edith Wharton or George Eliot. (She didn't approve of Mr. Dickens; he was too sentimental.) The girls listened with close attention, giggling now and then and nudging each other.

"Clearly a great deal has changed since 1905. But what I wish to discuss this morning is not change, but constancy. As you all should know by now, the real challenge in a changing world is not to recognize the outmoded, but to preserve that which remains valid.

"Let me read to you what a great man once said about the girls of Miss Pratt's. This man was at the time the secretary of state of our nation. His wife was an Antique, and his daughter was a student here in 1948. The occasion was the one hundredth anniversary of the founding of Miss Pratt's. His speech read in part:

"'In the history of America I can think of no group of women who have contributed so unstintingly of themselves to the good of the community. They have volunteered their labor in the service of those less fortunate than themselves. They have done much to further the cause of culture and the arts, and most of all their patience, their faith, and their quiet courage have made the husbands and sons of Miss Pratt's girls the leaders of this great land.'

"Patience, faith, and quiet courage," intoned Mrs. Umbrage. "These are the qualities of a true Miss Pratt's girl, the qualities you will need in the years before you when you leave this school. Times have changed, yes; you need no longer wear a hat at all times. But the qualities expected in a lady remain the same.

"Some of you may feel that we at Miss Pratt's are unnecessarily strict about some things. You may think there is no good reason for some of the rules and traditions of this institution. But you are mistaken. For Miss Pratt's is more than just a school; it *is* an American institution. We do more here than simply give you a solid grounding in Latin and algebra.

"The rules of Miss Pratt's have each come into being for a reason. When you are older, you will understand this, and you will take pride in having lived up to them. As for the traditions—traditions invented and maintained over the decades by you girls yourselves—each has its function. Each in its way prepares you for the life which is ahead of you, a life that will make demands of you about which you know nothing." Here Mrs. Umbrage was, to her own amazement, overcome with emotion. She had to pause and breathe deeply to control the quavering in her voice.

"Patience," she continued, "patience, good humor, and above all, grace under pressure—these are the qualities you will take with you into the world. To learn to swallow disappointment, to put others before yourself, to offer love instead of criticism, all these are the qualities of a Christian and a lady. You may think you have been under pressure before. You may think, with exams before you, with the pain of parting from well-loved friends that happens here every June, that you are under pressure now. But these pressures are as nothing compared to the pressures that life has in store for you. You may feel keenly your disappointments and even frustrations during these days, but when you are older, the memory of them will fade and grow dim. What you will remember is the peace, the hope, and above all the friendship of these days, and in time you will come to see that these were the happiest days of your life." Here Mrs. Umbrage found it necessary to pause again; this time she sat silent for quite a long time.

"When you are young, it is easy to fall into the mistake of believing that you can force life to suit your requirements, to go at your pace and in the direction you choose. But life is not like that, and neither is Miss Pratt's. There will be a great many times in your life when you will have to wait, to be patient, even to be disappointed. At such times, a lady does not cavil or complain; she bows, she submits with grace. That is what distinguishes her from the less fortunate. To bow to the inevitable is the essence of good breeding; good breeding is something you all bring to Miss Pratt's. Otherwise you would not be here. To have the wisdom to recognize the inevitable is the something extra we endeavor to teach you while you are here.

"For all these reasons, to illustrate the difference between right and privilege, and above all to give you the pause some of you evidently need in which to contemplate the great good fortune which you already enjoy, I hereby declare that this term, there will be no Field Day at all. Mr. Moltke, hymn number thirty-seven."

A wave of sullen fury greeted this announcement and crested and broke in various places and ways throughout the school for the rest of the day. At church a number of girls who had never done so before declined to take Communion. At lunch some refused ostentatiously to eat anything; others ate startling amounts. By nightfall no fewer than seven delegations from all three classes had separately requested meetings with Mrs. Umbrage, at which they offered to report the real or imagined crimes of their friends, roommates, new girls, and old girls, if Mrs. Umbrage would agree to hang these scapegoats and let the rest of the school go free. Mrs. Umbrage reflected sadly to herself that the teenage girl was at bottom a vicious beast, and that the less scope given her natural instincts, the better.

In the privacy of the girls' rooms, the declaration had a variety of individual effects. Sally, closemouthed, expressionless, and angry, stole a pack of cigarettes from Mrs. Birch's closet and went off to the woods to smoke them all. Ann, naturally disposed to blame herself for everything, secretly believed that the whole school was being punished for her rudeness to Mrs. Umbrage over the Jewish question. Jenny declared that Mrs. Umbrage had won the Sophistry of the Year Award and professed to think the whole thing very funny. Lisa talked indignantly about it the whole afternoon; she demanded to know whose fault it was, since she was quite sure it was not hers.

Perhaps of all of them, Muffin was affected most deeply. She believed simply and miserably in Mrs. Umbrage's statement that these were the happiest days of her life. She knew she was not exhibiting grace under pressure, and she felt her failure bitterly. She resolved to keep a diary in which she would preserve these dear golden days for a mature time when the memory of them would be her joy and her solace.

The next day at dinner the kitchen produced the girls' favorite once-a-term dessert, an intensely sweet-and-sour confection called lemon heaven. Muffin ate eleven helpings, handsomely capping the previous record of nine. Her friends were horrified and impressed and made quite a fuss over her; her whole table was proud. Muffin herself was badly frightened. Her stomach felt so distended that she began to fear it would split like an overripe pumpkin, spilling its fetid contents into her abdomen. As soon as the girls were excused, she stepped gingerly upstairs to the bathroom and into a toilet stall, where she slid the bolt and bent over the bowl. She reached her longest finger deep into her mouth until it touched her epiglotis. Finally a small quantity of hot, sour liquid, thick with whitish clots, heaved stinging over her hand and into the open mouth of the toilet. It seemed a miserably small amount, considering the effort required to dredge it up, and unlike a normal vomiting, the first upheaval was not followed by others. Again she applied the finger, and again she gagged forth a thin bilious stream. She kept this up until the muscles of her rib cage ached painfully. She still felt stuffed and heavy, but apparently a fair portion of her meal had already escaped beyond her recall into the sanctuary of her intestines. Later she told Lisa what she had done, and Lisa told her it was the coolest idea she ever heard of. Soon the Muffin Bundle Diet was all over school.

After a time the outrage over Field Day was forgotten and the girls surrendered themselves to the enjoyment of the maudlin sentiment that was so carefully orchestrated to reach orgiastic proportions on graduation day, when the whole school would parade in white dresses through the garden carrying a chain of daisies, unless it rained. Every night now there was weeping at singing in the garden as the girls stood arm in arm in a grand circle singing bowdlerized versions of turn-of-the-century torch songs from books hand-copied by girls now gray or dead and handed down from generation to generation of Miss Pratt's girls. "In the gloaming, as we linger . . ." they would trill, each filled with romantic visions of all the other girls who had stood there singing the same songs from the same fading books, of how those girls were grown now, out in the world somewhere longing for their lost youth; of how they, too, would grow up and part and long one day for these golden moments themselves.

One night in the last week of term, Sally reported to Mrs. Birch that the toilet in the small bathroom was backing up all

over the floor. Satisfied that it was a genuine malfunction, Mrs.
Birch called the maintenance man, who arrived very much out
of temper with a box of plumber's tools. Sally and Mrs. Birch
stood around in their nightclothes supervising. The rest of the
girls had gone to bed. The maintenance man plunged away manfully with his plumber's helper, muttering dark things about
"yer girls and yer sanitary bandages and the sense God gave a
horse," demanding now and then to know if these girls didn't
know a thing at all about "yer plumbing, with their foul hair-
pins and their sanitary things." At last, fumbling with his thick
rubber glove in the trap, he brought forth an odd gelatinous
mass and held it up for their inspection. The thing had the
approximate volume of a grapefruit; it was grayish purple, shot
through with streaks that looked like blood.

"Well, here, 'at 'ere's about the most disgusting thing I've
seen."

"My word, here, there, what do you suppose . . . ?"

"One of yer sanitary . . . ?" said the man doubtfully.

"Looks like an abortion," said Sally, trying to be flip.

"Yeah," said the maintenance man. "'At's what it looks like to
me, too."

"Jesus Christ," whispered Sally to Jenny and Ann. "I mean, I
was just trying to be funny—*I* don't know what an abortion
looks like." They made her describe it twice more.

"I don't know what one looks like either," said Ann, "but what
else fits that description?" They stared at each other in the darkness, the whites of their eyes glimmering wide.

"My God—the poor girl." Jenny said what all were thinking.

"Who could it be? Who *could* it be?" Jenny suggested one
name; Ann thought of one other. They went over every girl on
the floor, room by room. In the end, they were still looking blank
and almost frightened.

"It couldn't be any of them . . . any of us. How could it happen? *When* could it happen? How could anyone go through that
alone and not turn a hair? I heard of a girl at Abbot who even
paid her friends to hit her in the stomach, and she still didn't
miscarry. . . ."

It was unthinkable, insoluble. They discussed whether to tell anyone, and agreed that they should not. "If it's true, whoever it is has been through enough," said Sally, "and maybe it was just some strange junk in the plumbing."

However, it was all over school by the following night, whether they told or not.

Lisa was one of the only new girls who had mastered the art of being excused from sports on the grounds of having her period. During winter term she had even managed to spend a day in the infirmary *between* periods, with a complaint known as Mittelschmerz, soon described throughout the school as "a severe pain in the abdomen, occurring at ovulation, usually on the day of your midterm geometry test." One secret of Lisa's success was to be so gung-ho about athletics three weeks out of four that Dr. Livewright was slow to suspect her of the sloth that seemed to infect the rest of the students. But this week he simply refused her, saying she was not pale, had no fever, and could in his opinion play softball perfectly well. Her retort was to faint during the second inning, a gesture which was greatly appreciated, since it had not had any serious practitioners at Miss Pratt's since the days of whalebone corsets. Dr. Livewright confined her to the infirmary for the rest of the day. However, he declined to examine her, a snub meant to convey his doubt that there was anything the matter with her at all.

Toward the end of the week there was finally answered the great question which had so burned in the new girls' imaginations during first term but which had really ceased to interest even them: when and how were they officially to become old girls, and be presented with the gold Miss Pratt's rings. The answer was that two nights before graduation they were suddenly and coyly informed that they should choose an old girl to wish on their rings. ("To do *what?*" asked Jenny.)

This tradition was actually left over from the turn of the century, when the "Miss Pratt's Crush" was a well-known phenomenon in schools and colleges, subject of high prose and low doggerel. The Miss Pratt's Crush was the love of a new girl for some elegant senior who was her date on Saturday nights, with whom she waltzed after holiday germans, and whose love in return she openly wept and wished for when the inevitable moment of parting came. Far from disapproving, Miss Pratt positively encouraged these passions, and thus the ritual pledge over the rings, for everybody, became the rule. The amorous nature of the friendships had largely died out by the '50s, although certainly not the taste for sentimentality. Everyone made themselves very miserable over the notion that they would never see so-and-so again, and they generally wept and had sweet, sad talks with each other, ending with the two solemnly begging each other to Be Happy.

CHAPTER 8

The Long Vac

Jenny, in rebellious exile at the home of her paternal grandmother in Peekskill, New York, and Sally at home in Rochester, together sent champagne to the sailing of the *Mauretania* on July 20 and separately looked forward to the postcards and flimsy blue aerograms packed with three different handwritings that arrived from various spots in Europe for the next six weeks.

("What a shame you couldn't go with them," said Gan-Gan to Jenny sweetly. Gan-Gan Rose had never concealed her irritation that her son had gone into the theater instead of becoming a banker like her husband, a real man. If his income fluctuated, that was an embarrassment she ignored. She was always piously ready to take Jenny herself, but she never suggested assisting financially, which would have been tantamount to subsidizing a grown man—he did seem to be having a run of luck at the moment, but not enough, apparently, to send his child to Europe with her little friends. Gan-Gan could never quite get used to seeing her son's presence in a play advertised in the paper, like so many yards of upholstery—she'd been brought up to feel that a gentleman's name appears in the press only three times: when he's born, when he marries, and when he dies. Well, enough said. It was just lucky the child had the lawns and woods around the house in Peekskill to go to in the summer, that was all. If she was bored, she certainly couldn't blame her Gan-Gan. That was something her father would have to answer for.)

Jenny and Sally took particular pleasure in forwarding to

each other any mail they got from Europe, along with elaborate messages.

Southampton

Dear Sal,

This is a picture of the boat. The group is great; our room is small; we have a cute steward.

Food fantastic; Shaftoe lets us order whatever we want. We try to eat only things that come to the table on fire. A. and L. send love and *thanks* for the bubbly!

XXXXX,
Muff

London

Dear Sally,

Yesterday Muffin and I got picked up in a very posh restaurant called Simpson's. So dissolute, speaking of which, how are you? Last night Mr. Shaftoe made us all eat snails for dinner and one of mine looked just like your brother, Ralph. (Pardon it, please, I'm a little tiddly.) *Write,* you illiterate bag.

XXXXX,
Annie

Rochester

Dear Jenny,

I have arranged to have these delivered to you by a messenger in a baggy blue outfit with a blue stripe on its leg. Do not be deceived. In reality this messenger is Ethel Merman. She thinks she is a mailman, but the doctor wants you to handcuff her to the piano leg and teach her to sing "Anything You Can Do, I Can Do Better." Please send us your report in triplicate by return mail.

Nurse Titsworth

Peekskill

Dear Nurse Titsworth:

That messenger couldn't sing a note. We left it chained to the piano leg all night and in the morning it had gnawed it almost all the way through. We had it taken out and shot, and I am now wearing the uniform myself. In the meantime, the water is rising, typhoid has broken out in the next village, and our food is almost gone. Last night we ate the last of the carrier pigeons, so I am having this delivered to you by a rough man who just arrived paddling his own canoe. (See illustration.) Send help immediately.

Your friend,
Jenny

encl.

London

Dear Jenny,

You were the only person who got mail to us in London! We *haunted* the American Express office, too. It is wet and we feel homesick, boo-hoo! Glad your summer is going well. This is a picture of the Tower of London, where we went this morning.

Love,
Lisa

Assmannshausen

Dear Jenny and Sally,

We have so much to catch you up on you'll have to share this letter, so Sally, if Jenny doesn't forward it to you, get mad at her, ha ha. Copenhagen was *heaven,* especially Hamlet's castle and the Little Mermaid. Shaftoe took us to meet a lenzbaron (sp?) which apparently means Superbaron, and he's the last lenzbaron in Denmark and also a hunchback! We had lunch at his castle and he gave us schnaps and beer and Muffin smoked a cigar.

XXXXX,
L.

I did not *smoke* it. He just offered it to me and I took it home. Anyway, we got to Assmannshausen this morning. The Rhine looks like a four-lane highway, all brown and full of barges. I have a cold and can't taste anything. We all have to check in and out with Shaftoe every time we leave the hotel now because in Copenhagen he caught Frannie (that's a girl from St. Mag's) coming in from a date with one of the waiters. Did we tell you Shaftoe wears a beret and shouts at everyone who doesn't understand English? He figures they'll understand if he says it louder. Nous sommes tristes a vous ne pas hear from. Write to us in Florence *please.* Très missing you.

XXXXX,
Muff

They didn't leave me much room, the witches. I'll write small.

Today we went to tour the wine cellars here (very famous). This was the guide's patter:

"We have wine stored here from many tens of years, beautiful wines. When we hear the American soldiers are coming, we build a phony wall here, and behind it we put all the worst wine, new and raw. The soldiers come and they find the wall, and they say, 'A new wall, we must break it down.' And they do. They drink all the wine that they find and break the bottles, saying, 'This is very good wine, their very best, which you know because they hid it from us.' Then they go away, and they never know that just here"—he points to a further arch—"was yet another new wall, and behind it the very finest wine the Rhine produced, for centuries famous among those who know. Ha ha!" the guide cried merrily.

"Ha ha ha," cried Mr. Shaftoe.

These people hate us for being American.

Miss you, write soon, or I won't give you your presents when I get back.

> XXXXX,
> Ann

> Florence

Dear One,

This is the Ponte Vecchio where I bought some gold earrings and Lisa got her ass pinched thirteen times.

> Love,
> Muff

> Venice

Dear Jenny,

We had white grapes and blue cheese by the Grand Canal tonight. (See picture, arrow shows our table.) Italian fluent—in Florence, mastered "Vat a via" (hit the road) and here we say "Jetsa in canal" (jump in the lake). This the extent of Lisa's conversation with the natives, who admire blonds.

> XXXXX,
> Muff

> En route

Dear Sally,

Adored Italy, except none of the Italian women shave their pits.

This is Lake Lucerne. Too much to tell you in a letter, are you coming to meet us? *Please* do.

Love,
Lisa

Paris

Dear Jenny,

At last Paris. I was afraid you hadn't gotten my letters from Florence. (We are given to believe that neither Italian trains nor post have worked since the loss of Mussolini.) Anyway, *hooray* that you can meet us. Sally is coming down too; she convinced her mother she needed to go to N.Y. to Saks before school anyway. We'll all go up to Greenwich for a couple of days. Maude especially asks for you.

Much to tell. Principal news at the moment: Eiffel Tower about as awful as one expected, and Muffin has stopped talking to Lisa, which makes it a real treat to go anywhere with both of them. Can't wait to see you.

Ann

Sally and Jenny were waiting for them at Idlewild, and the joyous babble of stories and interruptions went on all through the drive to Greenwich and erupted again as soon as they arrived and could open their suitcases to present their gifts. It wasn't till after dinner that Sally or Jenny could get much of a word in.

"Hey," said Sally to Muffin. "You haven't told us about the guy you picked up."

"What do you mean? What guy? Who told you about that?"

"The guy you picked up in Simpson's—*you* told me . . ."

"Oh, no, it was me!" cried Ann. "Oh, let me tell—wait till you meet him!"

One morning Ann and Muffin had walked from their hotel to Buckingham Palace to watch the changing of the guard, which as far as they could tell never happened. Then, because it began to rain, they got in a taxi and said to the man that they wanted to go someplace for lunch. They were hoping to be taken to some interesting tea shop where taxi drivers ate, but they were delivered instead to Simpson's in the Strand. This was very grand. So grand, in fact, that they wished very much for the taxi man to think it was just what they'd had in mind, so they went in and sat down and ordered. They asked for mutton because it seemed so Dickensian, and squirmed with pleasure when it proved to be an enormous joint under the ornate gleaming dome that rolled up on a linen-covered table and was carved with a flourish to their instructions. They had some peas and floury potatoes, too, and tucked their sandaled feet far beneath them under their chairs, hoping they wouldn't be noticed. All through the meal they were nudging each other and making mental notes for their diaries and letters home.

The attendant presented the check. It may seem surprising that the thought of the check had never entered the mind of either of them until that moment, but they were very unused to carrying money. They were not allowed to go into any shops while they were at school, and when at home, all meals and clothes and drink were either paid for by parents or signed for. They operated on a vague assumption that "lunch" as a genus cost about $1.35. However, when you changed the pounds to dollars it became apparent that this luncheon had cost a great deal more. They looked at each other blankly, took out their wallets, and counted the bills, looked at each other with bafflement, then alarm. Attempting to hide their actions behind coffeecups, they took out all their silver and began hopelessly adding up the coins.

Then they put their hands in their laps and sat staring at each other, not wanting to speak, hoping the other would have some idea of what, in dignity, they ought to do.

Ann looked up. A tall boy of perhaps eighteen had come up, not quite to the table, but near, as if asking still to be invited.

"Excuse me," he said very politely, "but I wondered if there's some way that I might help you." By his clothes he looked very English, but his voice was American. His eyes were large and blue, with beautiful lashes, and his face was very handsome, with an almost feminine beauty.

"Well . . ." said Ann.

"Um . . ." said Muffin.

He sat down beside Ann, took the check and rapidly checked the addition, figured the tip, and laid a five-pound note and several ones on the salver with the check. Then he wrote his name and an address on the back of a card he found in his pocket and handed it to Ann. Just as he rose to leave, he said, "Oh," and handed Ann one more note, saying softly, "Give this to Charles on your way out." They watched him return to his table across the room, where he apologized briefly to his companion, a very handsome woman of about fifty. They gathered their purses and raincoats, now rumpled from being sat on, and hurried out. Their fear that they would not know who Charles was was unfounded, for he materialized as they reached the door, bowing and wishing that they would return soon again.

There was no one at the hotel when they got back. They talked about what they ought to do. There was no phone number written with the address he had given them, but they felt that they should call and thank him. A maid answered the phone. Ann asked for Philip Sterret, but instead a lady came on the line who sounded not very cordial and who said at last that Philip could not come to the phone. When Mr. Shaftoe came in from shepherding a group through Mme. Tussaud's, they were waiting in the lobby to tell him the whole mystifying story. Mr. Shaftoe laughed loudly, demanded the number, and soon returned from telephoning to say that Mr. Sterret would be pleased to join them for dinner and hadn't these ninnies ever heard that a lady does not telephone a gentleman? He went away laughing all the way down the hall.

That evening began a friendship between Philip and the girls which was to last a lifetime. Philip was the son of an Englishman and an American woman, now divorced. He went to Andover in Massachusetts, where he was a senior. In the summer he visited his father in England. The girls came to call him the Man of Measured Merriment, because he was courtly, gentle, and endlessly generous to all of them and yet seemed without passion, either for serious ideas or for their persons. That is, he never got drunk and tore at their clothes or flung himself upon them in an attempt to stick his tongue down their throats, which was the usual form of courtship among the young men they knew. He invited Ann, Muffin, and Lisa down to the races at Goodwood.

They were terribly underdressed for luncheon at the pavilion, as they had not yet seen *My Fair Lady* and had no idea that people would wear pearls and feathers and morning clothes to a sporting event. They had dressed as if for Yankee Stadium, which Philip appeared not to notice. They ate smoked salmon and stared about; then Philip and his father took them to the Royal Enclosure. Muffin especially was nearly undone with delight at what she kept calling "the magnificent horseflesh." At one point in rapture she turned to Philip and jostled a small woman in a pink silk dress and hat, who turned out to be the queen. After that she was so overcome with excitement that she had to be removed.

Mr. Shaftoe had repaid Philip for the lunch at Simpson's, but by the time they left London, most of the group was in his debt for some special kindness or other. On the last night he invited Lisa to go to a nightclub with him and some friends. Lisa drank too much and got bored and was very rude to Philip, who only grew quiet and said gently that of course she was very tired and it was his fault. This made her even ruder. He came anyway to the hotel next morning to say good-bye to them all and to promise to come to call at Miss Pratt's in the autumn.

"A lady doesn't call a gentleman on the phone!" cried Sally.

"*Yes,* we were so embarrassed!"

"So we're going to meet this Philip?" asked Jenny.

"He promised . . ."

"But, Muffin, who did you think I meant when I asked about the boy you picked up?"

"What? Oh . . . well, it was really so hard to keep track, you know. At one point I was beating them off with a stick."

The last afternoon in Copenhagen Lisa and Muffin had gone to Tivoli together while the rest of the group went with Mr. Shaftoe to tour the Carlsberg beer factory. Resting on a bench in the gardens, a tall, stunningly handsome blond boy asked if they had a match. He told them his name was Kjeldt and asked theirs. Then he began to smoke and talk.

"I am very tired," he said. "I am meeting my brother and his girlfriend here yesterday, but they do not come. Since my brother is having money, I sleep on this bench." He laughed cheerful-

ly and drew on his cigarette. "My brother is selling for me my
motor bicycle. Motor bicycle? Yes, in Oslo, and bringing me
money. But he is somewhere and until he comes I wait here." He
laughed again.

"But have you had anything to eat?" asked Muffin.

"A little chocolate, a little beer. I have still some chocolate
here." He found a half bar of chocolate in his knapsack and
showed them.

"But you'll starve," said Muffin, admiring.

"Oh, no," he said. "Here, have some chocolate with me. I will
find something else before long."

"No, no, thank you. *Lisa,* we can get some meat pies—we'll
tell Shaftoe we didn't like lunch at the hotel. Okay?" She led
Lisa away.

"God, isn't he gorgeous? Wouldn't you love to do that, just take
off around Europe with a knapsack and just do whatever you
want?"

"Maybe," said Lisa. They bought meat pies and beer and
brought them to him, and Muffin chattered to him while he ate
them with a lack of ceremony that slightly surprised her. Lisa
didn't say much.

"Well, we have to go now," said Muffin. "We're leaving tomorrow, but if you want, we could smuggle you some breakfast."
She told him where their hotel was.

"Yes, I know it, it's near the big square," he said. "You know
the great bronze trumpeters there—they say if a virgin ever
crosses the square they will blow their trumpets . . . but it never happens." He grinned at them as they walked away.

That evening Mr. Shaftoe took the group to the Coq d'Or for
dinner and then back to Tivoli one last time for the fireworks.
They got in late and were told to go straight to bed so they would
be up early, packed and ready to take the train to Germany.
When Muffin and Lisa came into their room and turned on the
light, they found Kjeldt, apparently naked, stretched coolly in
Muffin's bed sound asleep.

"*What?*" shouted Muffin, dropping her voice in mid-shout to a
whisper as Lisa urgently shushed her. "How the hell did he get
in here?" she whispered loudly.

"Keep your voice down!" Lisa led her as far as possible from the door to the hall and to the next room. "Keep quiet! I don't know how he got in here, but for Christ's sake, if anyone else finds out, Shaftoe will send us home. You heard what he said to Mamie yesterday. God, can you imagine what Beverly would say?"

"But what'll we do?"

"We'll tell him he can sleep on the goddamned floor and get out of here before anyone wakes up in the morning." She woke him up and told him to get out of the bed and be quiet. He smiled and shrugged and unrolled his sleeping bag on the floor.

"Can I at least have a pillow?" he asked, grinning.

"It's not funny!" snapped Lisa.

"But if you don't give me a pillow, I might by mistake make a lot of noise," he said. She gave him a pillow. In a few minutes he seemed to be snoring slightly, comfortably. Lisa, too, was soon asleep. Muffin lay awake in the pale midnight light for a long time.

She must have dozed off at last, because when she opened her eyes it was darker, as in the earliest moment of dawn. She didn't know what had wakened her. But as her eyes gradually became accustomed to the darkness, she saw that the form on Lisa's bed was not one body, but two. Kjeldt was lying absolutely still beside Lisa, who was sleeping on her back, breathing deeply and evenly, cheek on the pillow and one arm flung above her head. The coverlet on the bed was turned back, and her nightgown was unbuttoned to her hips. The soft white cotton had been lifted aside, so that her left breast lay exposed. The moon gave a silver sheen to her skin, while the nipple of the breast lay dark and soft like a small round mouth. Muffin lay perfectly still, not even blinking. Moments passed. Then very softly Kjeldt reached his hand toward the breast and poised his palm above it, not touching it, but just hovering as if caressing it with the warmth of his flesh. At last, lightly as a breath, the hand brushed the nipple. Lisa didn't move, and her breathing remained deep and regular. Again he stroked the breast lightly, softly, then again, and again and again, in a slightly circular caress. He stopped. Lisa stirred slightly; he began again. He stopped. The nipple beneath his hand was stiff, reaching. The hand returned, closing softly over the whole breast, moving gently and ceaselessly. Muffin could see that his whole upper body was part of the rocking motion of the hand, and Lisa's breathing had changed slightly, too, to a deep rocking rhythm that seemed to follow the motion of the man. He stopped again, and Lisa shifted, making a small sound in her throat. For a moment her own left hand moved toward the breast; then she relaxed and her breathing grew more even. Kjeldt was very still. Then once again he began to stroke the breast, still softly as a fantasy but with a steady rhythm, and the nipple hardened once again, the breathing became again shorter, needier. He stroked and rocked, stroked and rocked, till Muffin heard his own breathing begin to quicken, like Lisa's. He lifted Lisa's hand where it lay against the pillow. With her own soft palm, he caressed the nipple, guiding it to make his own gliding, caressing rhythm.

He took his own hand away, and Lisa's own continued its stroke in obedient insistent motion against the nipple. Her lips parted slightly and her body reached slightly with the caress. Kjeldt's hand moved to her loins, and without ever breaking rhythm, he began the same feather-light rocking against her there. His upper body was supported on his elbow. In the dim light Muffin could see his eyes fixed on Lisa's face. Her eyes were closed; her whole body was moving ever so slightly now with the hand soft and ceaseless, hidden from Muffin by the coverlet. His hand gave a soft deep thrust; Lisa started and her legs moved apart. Her own hand moved still against her breast. His hand thrust again, and she lifted against it. Then suddenly, swiftly, he had swung himself above her. His knees were between hers and his hips thrust into her. He lunged convulsively once, twice, once again, then held for a long rigid shuddering moment. Then his head sank down on the pillow. Muffin lay, scarcely breathing, as she had from the moment she first opened her eyes. She felt that she lay that way all night, but at seven when the alarm rang, she had to shake herself awake, and Kjeldt was gone.

All day she was engorged with a hot heavy feeling of shame and loss. She watched Lisa intently, nodding, smiling, giggling, struggling sweetly with her German phrase book to talk to the conductor on the train. She studied to detect some difference in Lisa, but there was absolutely none.

CHAPTER 9

Juniors

*J*unior year at Miss Pratt's brought the thrill of coming into your own. The new girls had to stand when you entered a room, and to hold doors for you when you streamed in and out of the dining room. The senior class and the new girls were responsible to each other; for the most part, the juniors were allowed to cultivate themselves.

One night about two weeks into the term, Sally was late getting back to the dorm for evening study hall.

"Where *is* she?" whispered Lisa crossly when 8:30 had come and gone. "God, she's such a hacker—she'll get us *all* in trouble if she gets caught."

"She went to a special meeting of the Welfare Club after dinner," said Muffin, "but I don't know why it would last into . . . Wait a minute, here come feet up the stairs."

"Sally!"

"Sally!"

Sally came in flushed and smiling and closed the door behind her, although it was supposed to be ajar. "Don't panic—we're allowed . . . special dispensation from the pope."

"What's up? Where were you?"

"Bonnie Hazel just found out her family's going to the Philippines—her father's been made ambassador. She's leaving next week, so we had to elect a new second head of Welfare, to take her place."

"The Philippines!" cried Lisa. "That lucky dog—the Philippines!"

"Sally," cried Muffin, "why did it take so long? Who'd they elect? Not Jennifer Gamble? They elected *you*, didn't they? Oooooo, wow!" Sally grinned and her face got all pink; she reminded Muffin of a puppy wriggling with pleasure at being praised.

As soon as the nine-o'clock bell rang, the three of them streaked across Main Street to the school office to send the traditional telegram to Sally's mother. The school assumed that all parents were deeply interested in any honors paid to their daughters, and newly elected officers often did get telegrams and flowers from home in return the day after Tap Day. No one noticed that Sally's parents reacted in any way to her elevation, however unusual it was for a junior to be made a club officer, but about two weeks later a large package arrived from Pepper addressed to Nurse Titsworth, and it proved to contain a bedpan. Muffin and Sally were overjoyed with this, and they talked the school gardener into transplanting into it some geraniums from the school greenhouse. But apparently the maid who cleaned their rooms complained, because the next day it had been confiscated, flowers and all. Mrs. Umbrage gave Sally a good talking to about her appalling indelicacy, expecting to keep such an object on the windowsill when it should be hidden in the lavebo, and reminded her that she had only to land on academic probation, to which she was perilously close, and it would be Mrs. Umbrage's pleasure to strip her of her club affiliations. Muffin and Lisa were in tears of laughter before Sally had finished recreating this scene for them.

Club officers were busiest at the beginning of the year, and Sally gave a lot of time to meetings on tryouts, meetings on whom to accept, meetings on the club programs for the year. Then tapping began, Glee Club first, as always, then the others in close profusion. Welfare Club tapped in the dining room one morning after breakfast wearing nurses' hats fashioned of paper, with thermometers in their mouths. Clomp clomp clomp, would *you* like to be a member of the Welfare Club? A lot of people would, if only because social service looked terrific on college applications.

"Well, it's all over, girls," said Lisa after lights-out, the night the last club tapped its new members. "Next time they tap, it'll be *our* turn, to be heads of clubs and heads of school—ooo, I love it. You know, I think next year for Glee we should try for a really good-*looking* club, don't you, Muff? There's enough people who can carry a tune, I don't see any reason to have a bunch of lunch pails standing onstage, do you? Like Jilly Putnam? I'd be embarrassed, actually, to stand onstage and see real grossers representing Miss Pratt's. Jilly Putnam's at my table; you should have seen her face the night we tapped for Glee. She honestly thought she was going to get in. She must have tried out for about ten different clubs. She kept talking every meal about all the tryouts, and how *neat* all the clubs were, and how *neat* it would be to get in—where is she from, anyway? God, that voice—in the afternoons you can hear her on the hockey field all the way up here. Her laugh sounds like a donkey."

"She was very nervous at the newspaper tryout," said Muffin. Jilly was, at fifteen, about five-eleven and growing, and if anything her enthusiasm was more outsize than her person. It was all over school that she'd been first to the dorm on opening day, and had greeted the next arrivals by sliding down the banister bellowing, "Hi, I'm your new housemate!" Unfortunately, they thought she said "housemaid," and they gave her a very wide berth for the next few days; by the time they figured out who she really was, she had become a laughingstock.

"Nervous!" said Lisa. "That mess doesn't have any nerves. She's so crazy to be in on everything, she says 'yes' no matter what you ask her. She's always talking about Fishers Island, so tonight I asked her if she knew Al Vanderbilt from Fishers and she said 'Oh, sure, he was a doll.' I just made the name up; there isn't any Al Vanderbilt. Do you know, she didn't even get into the Library Club? She didn't even get into the *Welfare* Club? She didn't get into one club! Boy, I'll be glad when we switch tables this time!"

"She didn't get into *any* club?" asked Sally.

"None," said Lisa. "Zero."

One night about a week later there was a delay at the end of dinner. The dessert had been cleared and yet the head girl in charge gave no signal to rise. Then they heard the clump clump

of marching shoes, and out of the kitchen came the members of
the Welfare Club, looking very solemn and carrying books as if
ready to read aloud. Sally and the senior head of the club led the
procession with blood-pressure gauges strapped to their arms.
They marched a complete circle around the dining hall, while all
eyes followed them and a growing hum of whispers buzzed in the
room. "What are they doing? What are they doing? Who is it,
Welfare? They already tapped! They gave a special tryout—
some new girl had a special tryout. Their tryouts were really
hard this year. But they let my sister's roommate take it as a
written." At last, the twenty-some club members stopped in the
middle aisle. The student body was astonished to see the head of
the club step forward. She looked very stern and then she called
in a clear, resonant voice, "Jilly Putnam . . . would you be a
member of Welfare?" Jilly, her face paper-white with tension,
sank down, put her head on the table, and burst into loud sobs.

For a moment there was a buzz of amazement. Then Jilly's
roommate appeared beside her, beaming and squeaking and pat-
ting her on the back, and she was followed by another classmate,
and another. Muffin, her throat aching with tears, looked hard
at Sally, but Sally and the senior head looked blankly ahead of
them, as if unaware of the hum of suppressed excitement
around them. Then the two marched sternly off, with the rest of
the club behind them, and the signal was given allowing the student body to rise. Dozens of new girls crowded Jilly, pleased and
impressed with her drama; Muffin hurried out to the cloakroom,
where she found Sally looking nonchalant, and hugged her
hard. Muffin's eyes were brimming with pride. Lisa spoke not a
word to either of them the rest of the evening.

From time to time Mrs. Umbrage would single out one of the
students to give the brief inspirational talk in Sunday-morning
prayers instead of preaching herself. No one knew exactly how
she chose the speakers; sometimes they were the obvious school
leaders, but sometimes they were the opposite—the shyest, most
tongue-tied new girls—or simply unknown quantities, as if this
were the way Mrs. Umbrage chose to test their mettle. For the
last Sunday in fall term, she tapped Lisa.

All the new girls were thrilled for her; always "pretty," "friendly," and "dear" in public, she was one of their heroines. Her roommates felt sorry for her. They'd never seen her so nervous. "I have no idea what to say," she moaned. "I'm not a speaker . . . I'm not a writer . . . I've been sitting next to Sandy Gooch in English all week hoping I'll get her cold and have to go to the infirmary."

Sally and Muffin laughed. "Hey, you can do it. Just relax. Oh, good, there's the bell. Want milk and graham crackers, Sal? How many, three? How many for you, Lisa?"

"What? Oh, I don't want any."

"Yes you do, sweet pea, you're getting nutso about food again. I'll get 'em, and you'll eat 'em." Muffin went to the hall, where the housemother put out milk and crackers for them every night at bedtime, and brought back their share, plus Ann and Jenny.

"What would you do if you had to give the Sunday talk, Jenny?" Lisa pounced on her.

"I'd eat my crackers," said Jenny. Lisa obediently began to chew, swallowing mechanically as if she were eating paper. "I think I'd sing 'The Marseillaise,'" said Jenny, after thought.

"Oh, be *serious*."

"I am serious—haven't you ever listened to 'The Marseillaise'? That's what I call inspiration."

"I know exactly what I'd say," said Ann. "I wish she'd asked me."

"What? What would you say?"

"I'd say, 'Look, you people are living in a dream. You think that being rich and privileged is this adorable stroke of luck and that all you have to do about it is say "Ooooo, lucky me!" Well, baloney! It's not luck, it's responsibility! It's a big debt! It means you have to work your butt off, starting here and now, to deserve what you've got more than someone else, either that or you can go *join* the people starving in China, but you can't just . . .'" Ann's eyes flashed and her voice had grown more and more emphatic. "Excuse me just a moment while I climb off this soapbox," she added, and sat down.

"Would you really dare say that?" Lisa gazed at her, impressed. Most Sunday-morning papers dealt with the impor-

tance of prompt thank-you notes or with respecting your grand-
parents even if they were senile, because someday you might be
too.

"You bet." Ann was filled with zeal, and she shook her head
earnestly.

"Can I say it?"

"Absolutely. I wish you would!"

They saw very little of Lisa all the next day. She stayed in the
library, staring at her blue-lined paper, and wrote a sentence every half-hour or so. But late that night she had managed to neat-
ly recopy a page and a half of script, and her fingers were
stained with blue ink from her fountain pen. She was very quiet
and she didn't offer to let any of them read it.

The paper was not only a success, it was an event. Lisa took
her place at Mrs. Umbrage's table after the hymn, looking
scared to death. She cleared her throat several times, her eyes
firmly fixed on the paper. Then she began to read in a clear soft
voice that shook slightly:

"We are privileged children of the privileged class of the most
privileged nation in the world. Do you know what that makes
us? It makes us the most heavily obligated people on earth. If
you think the position you were born to means only that life is
going to be a lot easier for you than it is for the starving Chinese, you ought to think again.

"You haven't deserved to be what you are. So now you can
make a choice. You can give away what you have and move to
China to starve, or you can spend the rest of your life trying to
earn everything you were born with."

There was a startled hush in the room. Ann and Jenny looked
at each other with eyes wide, suppressing grins. From time to
time during the rest of the talk Ann would silently gesture with
her fist as if to say, "Go get 'em!"

"You have an obligation," Lisa went on, "to everyone in the
world who is hungry, or diseased, or illiterate, to deserve what
you have more than they do. And there is only one way you can
do that: make the best of yourself. Your life is *not* yours to live
as you like. It's one big debt, to individual people and to humani-
ty as a whole. We have an obligation to make the most of our op-
portunities, to do our best, to work when we don't feel like it, so

we will be the best prepared to repay the world for giving us the best. Don't let anyone tell you you're the luckiest kid alive. Your obligation is the heaviest cross in the world, and you have no right to unshoulder it for one minute, unless of course you are willing to surrender it completely and catch the next boat to China."

Lisa dared to raise her eyes at last, and actually trembled to see on every face that her audience was stirred, astonished, and deeply moved, with the possible exception of Cheryl Woo, the Chinese-American new girl whose father had made a killing in the restaurant business. But if applause were allowed at prayers, she would have gotten an ovation. The new girls felt her thought was original and profound. The older girls said, rightly, that this was a side of Lisa they'd never seen before. Faculty members commended her talk privately all the next week and viewed her with new respect, and Mrs. Umbrage held her hand an extra beat and looked at her extra thoughtfully when she thanked her for her effort. Ann and Jenny, full of pride, cut her out from her admirers like cowboys with a prize heifer and carried her off in triumph to the Pantry, where they made her eat a huge butterscotch sundae.

Winter term began on an upnote. The new girls who were living in Ann and Jenny's old room heard Mrs. Birch shrieking in her bathroom one night. They fell over themselves running to help her, and found her howling in the shower, her naked body streaming red with what she thought was blood but which was really red dye from the hat she was wearing. This story, all over school by the end of breakfast, gave no end of pleasure. The next night Mrs. Birch tried to put one of her girls on bounds because she found her entertaining her roommates by dancing around her room wearing only a half-slip and ski boots, crying, "Are you a Springmaid?" But Mrs. Umbrage vetoed the punishment for some reason. Poor Mrs. Birch. Even next spring, when it was learned that she had to have a breast removed, everyone's first reaction was to laugh.

Jenny was far happier this year than she had been before. She had the right clothes, for one thing. For another, Mr. Moltke was working with her on his own time, training her voice. She had solos at every Glee Club concert and was adored by the new girls. She had dropped Latin and had gotten special permission to take independent study in German and Italian so she could begin to sing opera. Mrs. Umbrage tutored her herself with the help of Berlitz records, since the school regularly offered only French and Spanish.

One evening when Jenny was monitoring study hall over in the new girls' dorm, Ann found she was out of lined paper and went to borrow some from Jenny's notebook. When she picked it up, several pages of expensive gray stationery, written over in a man's handwriting and obviously folded and unfolded many times, fell out of the back of the notebook. Ann read:

The hope I dreamed of was a dream,
Was but a dream; and now I wake
Exceeding comfortless, and worn and old,
For a dream's sake.
Lie still, lie still, my breaking heart,
My silent heart, lie still and break.
Life and the world and my own self are changed
For a dream's sake.

Be still, I am content.
Take back your poor compassion!

Joy was a flame in me too steady to destroy,
I thought; till I learned what destruction there
     can be in joy.

When I meet you, I greet you with a stare,
Wondering where a flame goes, when the candle
     isn't there.
I will not let you love me, yet I am weak;
I love you so intensely that I cannot speak,
When you left, I stood apart
And whispered to your image in my heart.

I looked at you with eyes grown bright with pain
Like some trapped thing's
And then you moved your head slowly from side to side
Slowly, as though the strain
Ached in your throat with anger and with dread.

And then you turned and left me, and I stood
With a queer sense of deadness over me,
And only wondered dully that you could
Fasten up the latch so carefully.
Till you were gone. Then all the air was quiet
With my last words that seemed to leap and quiver
And in my heart I heard the little click
Of a door that closes—quietly, forever.

"I borrowed some paper from your notebook," said Ann when Jenny came in.

"No, no, no, put it back. Neither a borrower nor a—" Ann held up the sheets of gray paper with the familiar handwriting. Their eyes met. Jenny took back the pages and put them quietly away in the back of the notebook. Neither mentioned them again.

Juniors were entitled to leave school for the weekend twice in the year. That winter Sally and Muffin and Sandy Gooch and Linda Hawley went with Sandy's mother to the Johnny Seesaw Ski Lodge in Vermont. The thermometer stood at twenty below when they arrived at the lodge in the dark. In the time it took them to go inside and ask for help unloading the car, the gas line froze, so they had to leave the car parked at the steps until the proprietor could find time to help them get it started Saturday afternoon. Sandy's mother kept calling the proprietor Mr. Seesaw for some reason, though he was actually a Mr. Roberts. They did miss the day's skiing, and the next day the effective temperature on the mountain, counting the wind, was such that you were in tears of pain after each run and had to go inside to recover feeling in your hands and feet. Still, they were welcomed as conquering heroes when they returned to school Sunday night and said it had been absolutely cool as a moose.

Lisa took her weekend to go to meet George Tyler in New York, chaperoned by her mother. Jenny spent her weekend at Mrs. Umbrage's, as girls sometimes did who couldn't afford to go anywhere else. She slept late and ate lots of English muffins, which she fixed for herself in Mrs. Umbrage's pantry, and had a glass of sherry in the evenings and said she had enjoyed it very much.

One of the new girls, not one anyone knew very well, didn't

come back from her weekend. She had gone to stay with her grandmother in New York, and on Sunday morning she got up, dressed herself for church, put on her gloves and coat, and jumped out the window. There was a note pinned to her body when she was found; it gave her mother's name and phone number in San Francisco and added, "You may definitely call collect."

CHAPTER 10

Sea Island

$\mathcal{A}$t the end of February, Miriam wrote to Lisa:

> Your father and I have decided to take a house in Sea Island this spring for the Easter vacation. The Snyders had it last year and there are lots of bedrooms and then a terribly cute sort of bachelor's dormitory over the garage. So why don't you invite Ann and Muffin and one or two others. Buddy will be bringing Maggy. You girls can each invite a young man—if we overflow, we can always rent cots from the hotel.

Lisa invited Jenny and Muffin and Ann and Sally. Jenny wrote for permission but found she couldn't come, which made them very indignant. (Years later it occurred to them that she couldn't afford the plane fare, but this never crossed their minds at the time.) Sally and Muffin were wild with excitement. Lisa invited George Tyler, and he said he had a friend named David Bell who would like to come, too, so that was a date for Muffin. Madelon wrote to Ann that she had always thought of Sea Island as a resort for the newlywed, the overfed, and the nearly dead, but it was very kind of the Suttons to include her, and why didn't she invite Carey Compton to go along. Ann wrote that she would like to invite Philip Sterret, and after consulting the *Social Register*, Madelon agreed that that would be all right. Sally invited her brother, Ralph, who decided to bring along Pear and another boy, who was so fat they called him the Algonquin Twins.

Mort met the girls at the Jacksonville airport to make the ninety-mile drive to St. Simon's and in to Sea Island. "How ya doin', how ya doin', how ya doin'?" he yelled proudly, shaking hands with them all around. Lisa's brother, Buddy, and Maggy were already at the house. The rest of the boys were due at various times tomorrow. Buddy would pick up all except watchacall—Sterret—who had written he would take a U-Wreck-It at the airport, sure that the Suttons could make use of an extra car with that gang. "Smart fella," said Mort. "I'd of gotten Buddy one, too, but he had his license suspended last week, ha, ha."

He talked nonstop along the long flat straight highway while the girls poked each other and giggled and said, "I can't believe it," over and over. The road was lined with scrub pine hung with Spanish moss and with billboards for Stuckey's, offering pralines, pecan rolls, fresh orange juice, and fireworks. Mort insisted on stopping to buy them firecrackers, if only because they were illegal everywhere else in the States.

The Suttons' house was built of cream-colored stucco with a roof of arched Moorish tiles in the transplant Spanish style of the Cloister Hotel itself. Inside it was lined with glass and mirrors and furnished as if from a Carole Lombard film. On one side of the vast two-story living room were the kitchen and dining room, with the master bedrooms above. On the other side of the house were the bedrooms for the girls. The boys slept in a long low room above the garage, which everyone called the slave quarters.

The first morning, over grits and ham biscuits, Mort made a little speech to the girls, saying that they were to conduct themselves as if they were his daughters, to sign his name for anything they wanted, and of course to let him know if there was any little thing at all he could do for them.

"You know where the bar is here, you just help yourselves, and if there's anything you want we don't have, you just ask Black John to order it for you.

"Say, we'll all go to the Cloister for dinner tonight, and, Lisa, I want you to take the girls into the shop there and you each get yourselves something pretty, some of those beaded sweaters or something. Just something to remember me by, ha, ha."

They spent the day at the beach club, lying by the pool. At midday, when the waves were highest, they rented inflated rafts and played in the surf, struggling through the cold brown sea to beyond the breaker line, then riding back in on a crest, only to be tumbled end over end against the sandy bottom. The surf swirled with silt from the narrow river that cut the island off from the rest of Georgia and opened into the sea just south of the beach, and the wind was cold still in early April. It was the Sunday before Easter, and the island was quivering with young people on spring vacation. (It was a family resort, and therefore a sort of prep-school haven, since the older crowd who vacationed without their parents were more likely to go off alone to Nassau.)

For the first few days their routine was sunbathing, listening to the transistor radio, and eyeing boys.

They skipped lunch, having only a Dusty Miller from the snack bar, which consisted of vanilla ice cream, malted-milk powder, and fudge sauce. (For variety, they sometimes ordered Goldbrick Sundaes instead, made with a kind of hot chocolate sauce that hardened as it hit the ice cream, forming a thick bittersweet shell around the melting white.) They ate these on the terrace at the edge of the beach, their oiled faces turned toward the sun between bites, sipping iced tea with lemon and afterward feeding the abandoned crusts of other people's club sandwiches to the grackles that flocked expectantly among the tables.

George's friend David Bell was supposed to be Muffin's date, but the first few days they saw very little of him. George admitted that David had a "friend here that he was spending time with." "Not very nice for Muffin, George," said Lisa when she found out.

"Sorry," said George. "I didn't expect him to spend all his time there."

They were lying in the hollow of some sand dunes, where they had slipped away after swimming and made love. Now, in the enervated aftermath, George was on his back with his head on Lisa's thigh, eyes closed. Lisa was keeping an eye out for any of the parties on horseback that sometimes appeared here suddenly, cantering down from the stables to the beach.

This week was the first time George and Lisa had made love outdoors, let alone in sunlight, and she was surprised and moved by the beauty of George's body. And by the extraordinary sensuality of the sun, like a witness and a third lover. As she closed her eyes and tipped her face upward, she felt its steady warmth as a caress, and in a moment her nipples tingled and stiffened, and the spot between her legs began to pulsate with the same flushed heat. She opened one eye a crack and looked at George. His whole body was limp and still. He might have been asleep. She thought for some minutes of guarding his sleep, but the deeper his breathing became, the more her own tension increased. Finally, on impulse, she bent over and whispered delicately into his ear, a light musical stream of words of lust and seduction, finding words and phrases that she scarcely knew she knew. The result surprised her. The novelty of hearing them on her own lips tapped a vein of passion in her that ran very wide and deep. As if in a trance, she automatically found more and more phrases and images that did to his flesh what she usually did with lips and hands, and as she watched, the still penis at the pivot of his motionless body swelled and stiffened until it stood straight and quivering. She had never felt such a wrenching swell of power. Or of weakness. She poured whispered words into his ear, never touching the flesh with her lips, no longer able to tell tenderness from filth, almost unbearably excited, pushing pushing pushing for an explosion. There was a sudden flurry of limbs in the shifting sand, and then their first point of contact, his penis slamming into her, once, twice, again, again— the sun beat against her eyelids, making lurid erotic shapes floating in blackness. Someone yelled; herself. Another second and he was finished. A short or long time later, coming back from far away in blackness, she felt him kissing her ears and neck with enormous gentleness. Her heart returned the tenderness with a great unreserved rush, and as she kissed him, she knew he felt it.

In the last week of sleeping and eating and living together, the group had grown in comfort and companionship, passing through stages of shyness and sparring and stiltedness to a kind of friendship that was almost familial. In all the relationships,

among and between the girls and the boys, there was new kindness and in some cases other new emotions as well.

Ann and Philip Sterret often played tennis together in the afternoons while the other girls were washing and setting their
hair. (Ann's was fine and straight and required little devotion.)
Ralph and Pear and the Algonquin Twins played golf most
mornings, and after a few days Sally and Muffin joined them.

"I haven't had much practice," Muffin said. "I never felt that
golf gave you enough exercise."

"Exercise!" said Pear.

"You don't want exercise; that stuff will kill you!"

"We come here because they make such a good planter's
punch."

"Speaking of which . . ." said the Algonquin Twins.

"Yes," said Pear. "Your turn to buy."

"At ten in the morning?" asked Muffin.

The Algonquin Twins soon returned to the first tee with a tray
full of drinks. The boys carried their own clubs and the girls' and
hired a caddy to carry the tray.

The more they drank, the better they seemed to play, and by
the end of the first nine Ralph had birdied three holes. Sally and
Muffin were so weak with laughter that Muffin had to crawl
down the fairway to the green. The Algonquin Twins decided
that Sally needed some assistance, so at every shot he would
stand behind her, and just as she began her swing he'd yell,
"Swing now!" He tried to help her by putting his arms around
her from behind, but his belly was so large that he couldn't
reach all the way down her arms to the club.

"I have an idea," said Ralph. "Better get a golf cart, that way
we won't have to pay this good man here to carry a tray of empty
glasses."

"Great idea," said the Algonquin Twins.

"We'll commute to the bar. Won't interrupt the game at all."

So Ralph and the caddy sprinted back to the golf shop and
soon returned in a golf cart, with Ralph driving at surprising
speed and the caddy carrying another tray of drinks.

They set off again, the Algonquin Twins shouting "Swing"
and "Steady, now" every time Sally addressed the ball. Ralph
and Pepper's game began to deteriorate, and on the fourteenth

hole they both lost their balls in a grove of scrub pine. A four-some of men in plaid slacks stood on the tee and watched them sourly as they scrambled back and forth across the fairway.

"You want to drink through?" yelled Pear. Ralph and the cad-dy went in the golf cart to refill the tray, while the others floun-dered around giggling, looking for balls. The Algonquin Twins tenderly draped Sally in Spanish moss. When Ralph returned, the play continued, but not until they had pressed several drinks on the caddy. Pear said he looked so sober, it was putting him off his game.

The course actually had a nineteenth hole, since it was a twenty-seven-hole course. When they got to it, Ralph said, "I have to play this hole. The nineteenth is my favorite hole. But I don't seem to have any balls." Howls of laughter. The caddy, who was now fairly looped himself, produced a ball from some-where, and Ralph and Sally and the Algonquin Twins teed off. The others said they couldn't see the flag.

"Don't see what difference that makes," said Ralph, and he swung wildly. First he took a huge divot which he was convinced was his ball as it sailed off. When they persuaded him that the white thing still at his feet was the ball, he swung again and drove it soundly into a large pond well off the left of the fairway.

"Keep your eye on it! Watch where it goes, caddy!" And he ran for the golf cart. They watched him tear off across the course af-ter the ball, and without a moment's hesitation he drove at full speed into the frog pond. He hit it with a tremendous spray on either side of the cart. Sally and the Algonquin Twins were clinging to each other screaming with mirth, the caddy giggling helplessly, and as the cart slowly sank, Ralph stayed at the wheel yelling, "I got it!" till the water was up to his neck.

When their laughter finally subsided to weak choking noises, Pear wiped his eyes and moaned from the grass where he lay, "Oh, Christ, I can't get up—I've pissed on myself."

After dinner in the evenings the air was sweet and heavy with the smell of tropical flowers and, depending on the wind di-rection, the scent of the pulp mill over in Brunswick. Sometimes they would dance on the terrace at the hotel or go to the movie in the lounge, or play bingo in the clubrooms. On Wednesday night all the young people would drive out to the Oasis, the local after-hours bar, where they drank gin-and-tonics at filthy crowded tables, elbow to elbow with the "local talent," and listened to the Washboard Band.

Usually the last thing before sleep, the girls would gather in Lisa's room to gossip.

"Are Buddy and Maggy still out? Where do you think they go?" asked Muffin.

"Do you think they're doing it?" asked Sally.

"I don't know," said Lisa, "but if they're not, somebody must have a hairy case of blue balls." Laughter. They didn't like Maggy.

"I don't know what to do about the Algonquin Twins," said Sally. "He keeps pawing me and inviting me to beach party."

"He's got a crush on you. . . ."

"Yeah, he'd crush me all right if he got on me. . . ."

"Sally!" They all knew that she liked to use language much coarser than what she felt. In return they pretended to be much more shocked than they ever were.

"But really," said Sally, "how do you keep them from putting their hands all over you without hurting their feelings?"

Lisa said, "I always say, 'That's no-man's-land,' when they go below the . . . chin." Everyone laughed again.

"I'd like to have the problem," said Ann. "Philip's so polite he may die a virgin."

"God, and he's so gorgeous!" said Lisa. "Are we quite sure he's a guy?"

"Oh, come on," said Muffin, "he's just shy."

"Well, you know what Mort says."

They all made disgusted faces. "Yes, spare us."

George's friend David Bell finally reentered their lives. He spent the whole day with the girls at the beach on Thursday, sitting a little apart, watching first one, then the other with brooding eyes. He didn't say where he'd been, and nobody asked him. Once in a while he'd gaze at a line of birds speeding for the horizon and say moodily something like, "Do you ever wish you could just fly to the edge of the world?" to no one in particular. The girls agreed that it was most arresting.

The next night, Good Friday, the hotel gave a fish fry down the island in a grove deep with Spanish moss and lit with torches. The guests of honor were the Baker's Dozen singing group from Yale, whose performance was always a highlight of spring vacation. The Sutton group had sour hour with Mort and Miriam, then drove down in three cars, all piled on each other's laps. At dozens of long wooden tables, people were eating and drinking. Men wearing white aprons and chef's hats served fried fish and spicy hush puppies, corn, rice, and barbecued beef from the steam tables that had been trucked out from the hotel.

"You get in line for the grunts," said Ralph to the girls, "and we'll belly up to the bar." While the girls got food and the boys ordered drinks, the steep cathedral space carved by the living gray-green stalactites of moss was filled with rich antiphonal gospel music by a group of black singers from St. Simon's.

After dinner in the flickering torchlight the Baker's Dozen stood in a half-circle in their white dinner jackets and sang. Their voices sounded from the edge of the grove like the distant honeyed drone of inebriated bees. Muffin fell in love with a short blond tenor with a dissolute face who gave a plaintive solo:

I'll be around . . .
No matter how
You treat me now . . .
I'll be around, when he's gone.

When the singing was over, the group dispersed into the crowd, greeting old friends, looking for new ones.

"Great solo," said Muffin shyly to the tenor as he passed.

To her amazement, he sat right down beside her and said, "Now, what makes you say that? 'Zat your favorite song?"

They fell into conversation, and she began to realize that he was extremely drunk. "Hey, have another, Boots," his friends would yell at him from time to time. "Yeah, tell her another, Boots."

"So where are you staying?" he asked, leaning close to her. "Hey, no kidding?" when she told him. "Hey, we stayed there last year, me and Briggs and Evans, or What's-his-name. Big house, sort of pink, with lots of mirrors? Yeah, they put us up last year there. We stayed over on the side, upstairs from the fireplace. What room you in? You in the yellow room? Hey, no kidding! My old room. Hey, I get homesick for my old room, what about a date? Huh? A late date?"

"No, really, I have a date," she said, looking around uncertainly. David Bell was sitting alone, watching her. "With him," she whispered to Boots, and jerked her head at David, to whom she had not spoken more than three words during the entire week.

"Oh, oh, oh, with him, eh? The big guy? You like big guys?" he asked sadly. Then he cheered up. "But you don't have to spend all night with him, right? You and me can have a late date. In my old room. Our room." He started to giggle, and then to hum. "You, you . . . yoooou, you liked my solo . . . ha, ha . . . you'd like to have a little date with me later. Later." He straightened up and looked very serious. He whispered very slowly and clearly, "I'll see . . . you . . . later." Then he went off giggling and snapping his fingers to take a leak in the woods.

"So what's going on?" said David Bell, sitting down beside her. She told him. "I see, I see," he said thoughtfully. "I see what we can do about that. Wait here a minute." He went off toward the bar and spoke to George, who sent him off toward the parking lot. Soon he was back.

"All taken care of," he announced. "It is under control and in the bag."

"What is? What did you do?"

"Just arranged a little surprise for Mr. Boot. And it's all clear with Lisa, so you've got nothing to worry about, except that you can't go back to your room tonight."

"Oh, swell! And where, exactly, do you suggest I spend the night?"

"Well," he said, "I suggest you spend it with me."

"The secret of building a fire in the wind," David said, "is to believe in it." He crouched on his heels over the small heap of driftwood chips and dried dune grass he'd collected, shielding it from the wind. "I've got two matches, or rather you've got two matches, but all we'll need is one. Now, watch. You concentrate on the heart of the fire, where you want the heat to be, and you will a flame to be there. Then, when you've got it good and ready,

you light your match . . . like this . . . shit . . . like this,
and . . . presto." The dune grass caught and crackled like fine
electric wires and held the heat long enough to ignite some
small sticks of driftwood. He tended them carefully, adding bits
of ever-larger size until he could lay a thick branch across and
then another to make a V-shaped trap for the heat. Soon he added a third and saw it take flame. Then he stretched out beside
Muffin on the blanket and said, "See? It's all the power of the
heart."

"I see. And do you do other tricks?"

"Of course I do. I've arranged a very good trick to amaze Mr.
Boot, for example."

"But you won't tell me what it is, so what else?"

"I make things materialize by the sea at night, when I need
them very much and have almost given up hope of finding them.
Don't light that cigarette."

"What? Why not?"

He didn't answer. He leaned on one elbow, looking at her, his
gray eyes almost yellow in the firelight. The wind stirred the
dark hair on his forehead. He reached to brush it from his eyes,
then reached to brush hers back from the temple. Then very
slowly, still thoughtfully, he leaned over and kissed her.

"Need another log," he said. "Don't move a muscle." He went
to the fire, blew on the ashes to raise a flame, added a larger log,
and came back to lie beside her, this time sliding his long lean
body close against her.

"What are you thinking?" he whispered.

"Well . . . doesn't that star up there look yellow?"

"Where?" He rolled onto his back.

"There . . . there." She pointed.

He turned back to her. "What are you thinking?"

"Well . . . do you believe in God?"

"Of course."

"You do?"

"Of course. Does that surprise you?"

"I don't know—you seem so moody and cynical. Why is that?"

"Hush a minute." He put his arms around her and kissed her
eyes and her nose and then her mouth. "Just hush," he whispered, rocking her. Then after a time he said, "See, now, you do

some tricks, too. You think to interest me you have to get me to talk about myself. Don't you?"

"Yes."

"Well, I'll talk about myself when I'm ready; we were talking about you. Tell about God."

"Well . . . I think that . . . there is a power that is truly greater than we are . . . that can do great miracles, the great miracles in the Bible . . . but I think the power is love." She looked at him with eyes wide. He looked very serious.

"So God is love," he said.

"No, love is God."

He looked at her for a moment, then bowed his head. The expression on his face, now in shadow, looked almost like pain. Then his eyes met hers again and his face opened into a deep glowing smile that warmed her through.

"God!" he said, hugging her. "Do you . . . what's your real name, by the way?"

"Margaret."

"I'll call you Meg. I can't call you that other stupid thing. Do you know, Meg, I want to be good to you? Do you know I never said that to any other girl in my life?" He began to kiss her. She put her arms around him tentatively and felt the great sleek muscles of his back quivering.

"You're cold," she mumbled against his mouth.

"Not cold. Never be cold again," and he kissed her and kissed her, rocking her, stroking until she felt she was dissolving, every nerve in her body following his fingers. He began to press against her insistently. He made a small noise in his throat, a pleading and yearning noise that almost seemed to come from somebody else. His hand was between her legs.

"David," she whispered, nearly beside herself.

"Hmmm?"

"David . . . I love you."

"Oh, God . . . God, I know. Love you, too."

"David . . . I can't sleep with you." She was aching with wanting him, and her whisper was choked.

"You what?" All motion crashed to a halt, as though the earth had stopped.

"I can't sleep with you." Her voice was small and terrified.

There was a long, long silence.

"You mean, you can't make love with me," he said.

"Yes."

"But you can sleep with me. You can sleep in my arms tonight?"

"Oh, yes."

"Well, then."

He held her against him, warm and still, shaking a little now and then. At last he got up to put the last log on the fire, wrapped the blanket around them both, and whispered, "Sleep."

The fire was out and the moon had set when they both woke up at the same instant. There was a commotion in the dunes, one voice howling and others chiming in the darkness. Soon they heard footsteps running, and then the Algonquin Twins, weaving horribly, lurched over the edge of the dunes and emerged shouting on the beach.

"Lea' me alone," he bellowed. "I wanna die an' it's none of your business!"

"Stop, stop," they heard Ralph yell, gasping with laughter between words. "Stop, Twins, don't do it!"

"Gonna cut my wrists, you murfucker. Yer fucking sister doesn't love me. Never will. *Never* will! She loves 'at shithole with the white suit—shitholes like that, *'at's* who she loves."

"Stop him, stop him," yelled Ralph, falling down. George and Philip ran past after the Algonquin Twins. "He's got a church key, he's gonna cut himself," Ralph yelled from the sand.

"Gotta *rusty* church key, you dumb twat, gonna kill myself *now!*" Then he fell down, too, and George and Philip caught up with him.

"No, no, lea' me alone!" yelled the Algonquin Twins as Philip disarmed him while George held him down. Then it sounded as if he had burst into tears.

"Hey," said David, "race you?"

They leaped up, grinning, and began to run, away from the fading voices. They ran and ran and ran until Muffin felt that her heart would burst. Then they pulled up, laughing and panting, and walked and walked and talked and talked a long way on down the beach, arms around each other, stopping often to kiss. It was remarkable, really, how much they had in common—almost unbelievable. Muffin told him about riding Mistress Moon, about how she only felt totally free, completely herself, when she was galloping alone across an open field, where she knew every trail and brook, knew how each meadow looked frozen in winter and deep in summer and at all the seasons between, when she knew that she was young and strong and good and that she was not safe, of course, not flying at breakneck speed, but that it didn't matter. No one was safe, and fear didn't matter. Only joy mattered.

He was stunned, he said. Because he knew, he knew. He knew exactly what she meant. He'd ridden every day of his life till he left home for college. He'd begun riding steeplechase when he was fifteen. In fact, it was almost certain he had a mount for the Carolina Cup in a few weeks. He stopped walking and turned her to face him.

"If I ride, will you come and watch me?"

"But . . . I don't . . ."

"Say yes."

"Yes."

He gave a whoop and picked her up and swung her around. They walked on in the sunrise. He was interested in theater, he said. Did she read Melville? He was going to play the lead in a stage adaptation of *Billy Budd* in the fall. In fact, all the secret, most important corners of herself seemed to find some answering voice in him, in the things he'd done, the things he wanted to do.

They walked till broad day; then, not wanting friends to break in on their joy, they decided to go to the hotel for breakfast. They had croissants and sweet butter and pots of strong coffee in a room full of flowers, with live canaries singing in vine-covered cages. Then Muffin signed Mr. Sutton's name to the check and they walked slowly back by the beach and parted to get some sleep.

When Muffin woke, it was nearly four. She had a date to meet David in the garden at the hotel. They would have tea and climb with it to a secret corner of the roof where you could see the ocean and the treetops. She waited in the lounge with the harps for an hour. At five George came in, looking around as if searching for someone. "Hey, Muffin," he said casually.

"Hey, George," she said.

"So, watcha doing?" He sat down beside her. "Hey, you looked pretty high when you came in this morning. You had a good time, huh?" He kept looking around, as if he were expecting somebody.

"Actually," said Muffin, "I'm just waiting for David. We were going to have tea."

"Oh, hey, I'm sorry. God, I'm an ass. I should have told you right away. I just got back from taking David to the airport. His father's very sick. He had to go home."

Muffin stared at him as if she had not heard. Inside she thought for a moment her heart had stopped. She felt a flash of cold, then a sudden great rush of pain.

"Yeah, he had to go. Gosh, I'm sorry, I didn't know you had a date with him. I hope you didn't wait long."

"But . . ." She was surprised to hear her voice quite calm. "Didn't he leave a message for me?"

"No. Well, he said to say good-bye to Lisa and all the girls, you know. Well, I gotta get back. Want a lift?" Muffin nodded. There would of course be a note for her at the house.

When she and George walked into the house, they were greeted by cheers and fanfare. The whole party was gathered in the living room, drinking and celebrating the success of the Boots affair. It had come off so smoothly and had caused such a riot that the whole island had been laughing about it all day, and Mort and Miriam had invited the Baker's Dozen for drinks to make the most of it. Boots arrived almost immediately behind them.

"Boots, darling!" shrieked Pear, and flew across the room to him.

"How I've longed for your body!" groaned Boots, sweeping Pear into his arms. "But, my dearest, why didn't you shave?" There was more, in the same vein, accompanied by hoots and cheering. Gradually the scenario emerged of Boots creeping softly up the stairs, Boots stealing into the darkened room to the sleeping form in Muffin's bed, Boots passionately turning the bedclothes back "with his lips all puckered up," screamed Pear, "going hhhhhhhhhaahhhh," panted Ralph, to find Pear in the bed, half comatose but waiting, and Lisa in the next bed primed to snap on the light at Pear's signal. Chip and Philip announced that against stiff competition—here Ralph got a round of applause—Muffin had definitely won first prize for the vacation, and that Boots would make a presentation as soon as a suitable prize was found. Boots offered to unscrew a fluted glass candle sconce from the wall, as being near to hand, but Mort, bellowing happily, ordered him to make himself a drink instead. Boots said to Muffin in a low voice as he passed her, "I don't like your little tricks at all." But publicly, though he was rather loud and red in the face the rest of the evening, he continued to take the joke over and over, the only way he could.

After dinner they all went to a dance at the beach club, where the Baker's Dozen sang again. Afterward each of them danced with Muffin at least once, full of congratulations. When Boots cut in to dance with her, they applauded. Then Pear rushed onto the floor and tapped Boots on the shoulder, saying, "May I?"

"Charmed," said Boots, and he waltzed smoothly away with Pear in his arms, to the huge delight of the party.

Philip asked Muffin to dance. "You've never looked prettier," he said softly.

"I've never been happier."

"I'm glad," he said.

"I'm in love," she said.

"On you it looks good."

George cut in. "How ya doin', chum?" He gave her a hug.

"Doin' great, chum. How's your act?"

"Up and down, up and down."

"Oh, ho, ho."

"Oh, ho, ho, yourself. Listen, did I ever tell you what happens if you push my nose?"

She pushed his nose, and he made a beep sound. She giggled. "Can I do it again?"

"Sure," beep. They both giggled.

"What if I pull your ear?" Honk.

"George?"

"Sir?"

"Could you give me a ride back to the house in a little while? I'm sort of expecting a phone call."

"Oh," he said. "Okay. Just let me tell Lisa where we're going."

Sally and Ralph were demonstrating the polka, which neither of them knew how to do. Sally fell down.

"Whoopsie," said Ralph, staggering. "Whoopsie." Before he could help her up, Philip stepped in and gave her a hand.

"My dear, they are playing our song."

"So they are, so they are," she said, clinging to him. He held her quite tight, supporting her.

"Are you sure this is our song?" she asked in a moment. "It doesn't usually make me sick."

"My mistake," he said. "They're playing the sick song. Let's sit it out."

"Let's," she said. "But why don't you carry me?"

So he picked her up and carried her off the floor and out the door to the silent terrace. He sat down in a chair with Sally on his lap. She began to cry. She sobbed for a long time, and when finally the sobs subsided, said, "Why don't I have a good cry?"

Philip laughed. His arms were strong around her, as if he could shield her from what she was feeling, as well as from the night wind. He'd been watching her all evening, afraid she was heading for a crash. The night before, one of the Baker's Dozen, a shy, good-looking chemistry major from Indiana who had scarcely heard of Miss Pratt's, let alone of Sally or her brothers or their money, had taken a shine to Sally. Philip had watched them dance together, and late in the evening he passed them sitting very close together on a couch, and overheard the Yalie describing in passionate tones the sheer physical splendor of the DNA molecule, while Sally, with flushed cheeks and pale eyes sparkling, gazed at his face as if her brain had just melted. But it was almost lunchtime before Sally appeared this morning, and when she did, her eyelids were swollen. She was wearing her glasses, which she rarely did when boys were around, although she was very nearsighted, and her thin lips were compressed into a line, an expression Philip had seen before when she was hurt, which reminded him of an empty teller's cage with the grille clamped shut. She had ordered a Bloody Mary for breakfast.

Sally said to Philip, "He didn't dance with me once tonight, the fucker. Didn't look at me while he sang. Didn't even talk to me. Oops, wait a minute. I might be going to throw up." She sat still for a minute or two, clutching the arms of the chair and taking deep breaths.

"What's the verdict?"

"Not going to. Oh, Philip."

"I know, I know," he said, stroking her hair.

"I really wanted him to like me," she said. Her breath still caught in her throat as she drew it in. "He talked to me for hours and he talked about asking me up to Yale. So I went out to the beach with him and we were making out, and he put his hand under my sweater, and I thought, would Lisa do this? I mean, I wanted to—what the fuck?—but I was afraid he'd just think I was . . . so I said, 'That's no-man's-land.' And he got this terrible look on his face, like he was terribly hurt, and then he said, 'That's the most vulgar remark I ever heard.' And he got up and left." Philip held her in silence and looked at the stars. "Well, I wonder if I can walk yet," she said after a while.

"Why? Where are you going?"

"To get another drink," she said, tottering off.

"No, you're *not*," and he picked her up and started toward the parking lot. She struggled at first, then began to tickle him. Laughing, he started to run, trying to get to the car before he dropped her.

Ann sat in the dark by the pool with the Algonquin Twins. He was morose. He just stared at the green underwater lights in the pool and said nobody loved him, nobody had ever loved him, and nobody would ever love him.

"See? You're laughing," he said. "I'm dying of unrequited love, and you're laughing."

"No I'm not." She giggled. "I swear I'm not. Oh, God, the coal's gone from the end of your cigarette. Where is it? I think your pants are on fire."

"Really?" he said. "Well, if I do happen to go up, I want to be

buried like a Viking, in this pool here, with a flaming pyre . . ."
He went on talking somberly while she slapped at his pants legs
with her hands, laughing loudly.

"Now, *look*"—she pointed—"there's a big hole in your cuff. I've
saved your life."

"My life's an empty shell. Sally doesn't love me, she's gone
home with Philip. She'd rather talk to Philip than me. She's in
love with him."

"He's taking her home to sleep it off," said Ann.

"Don't you believe it. They're in love, everyone's in love except
me. I mean, I'm in love, too, but nobody's in love with me."

"*I'm* in love with you," said Ann.

"You are not." He announced that he was just going to sit
where he was till he died, until Ralph came along and persuaded
him to come with them to blow up raw eggs on the beach with
Mort's firecrackers.

Between three and four o'clock in the morning, the house was
awakened by loud raps on the door. When Black John opened it,
there stood two of the Georgia highway patrol's finest, and in the
driveway was a patrol car with the light on the top still flashing.
Philip and Sally climbed out of the back, looking shaken and
very white. Mr. Sutton was called.

"This fella your houseguest?" demanded the officer. The other
drew Philip and Sally to the door. Mort asked what had happened.

"Speeding on a Georgia highway, killed a pig, ran into a telephone pole, and wrecked a car belonging to the Jacksonville,
Florida, Hertz you-drive-it company. And lucky he didn't kill
the young lady here." He jerked his head at Sally.

"Sally! Dear, are you all right?" cried Miriam, flinging herself
out the door in her dressing gown. Sally nodded dumbly and
allowed herself to be drawn inside.

"This young man's in serious trouble here, sir, speeding on a
Georgia highway, destroying a valuable animal . . ."

"What happened, Philip?" asked Mort.

"I can't say, sir. I just seemed to lose control of the car. I'm extremely sorry, sir, that it happened. I know you must have been
worried."

"Yes, we were," said Mort. "Mrs. Sutton and I were very concerned when you didn't return at the usual hour. Thank you, officer, for bringing them back. And thank God they weren't hurt. Now, sir, what exactly were the damages?"

"Well, he's not drunk. We took him right to the station and tested for that; but speeding, you know, and the pig."

"Well, officer," said Mort, "you see these kids, they have to be back up north tomorrow evening . . . Come in for a moment, won't you? Black John, bring some coffee, please. They have to be back up north tomorrow night to go back to school, you know—awful nice kids. I've known their parents for years. Now, what would you say a valuable pig is worth these days? I don't know much about these things. I'm a city man, but I wonder if you couldn't straighten this thing out some way, so the children can get back to school? What would a pig run, now? Three, four hundred? Thank you, John. Give the officer some cream, will you? Well, now, you just wait a moment, sir, and we'll see if we can't take care of this." He was soon back with a thick wad of bills, and the officers went away, having agreed to have the car towed back to Jacksonville and to square the owner of the pig. Miriam came down to say that Sally was all right—sound asleep, in fact. Philip saw Mort look sharply at Miriam when she reported this. She returned a slight expressive sign, something in the rise of the eyebrows. They both looked at Philip. Philip said he'd write Mr. Sutton a check in the morning, if that would suit him. A long look passed between them.

"Of course, I'm just guessing, son," said Mort finally, "but I believe we ought to thank God no one was hurt and forget it. You're guests in my house, both of you . . ."

Philip nodded once. "Then thank you, sir."

The two men shook hands. Then they parted and went to bed.

The next day, their last, was gray and quiet. The boys were too tired and hung-over to do much more than jibe rather cruelly at Philip about the accident. Sally was very quiet, Lisa and George were lovesick, and Muffin for the first time in her life was frankly eager to get back to school, for certainly *there* would be a letter or a phone call from David.

CHAPTER 11

Daisy Chains

Sandy and Linda were late getting back to school from spring vacation. They were late because on the flight back from Nassau their plane was disabled in a violent electrical storm and it crashed on landing at Idlewild airport. Several people were killed, including the copilot. People screamed and cried during the storm, as the plane rose and crashed through peaks and valleys of violent, invisible force in the hellishly crackling sky. A small child was torn from his mother's arms by one heart-stopping lurch and actually rolled the entire length of the aisle howling with terror. Linda caught the child on the bounce as he rocketed past her and strapped him into the seat with her. Everything in the overhead racks crashed out onto the floors, first from the starboard side of the plane, then the port. The mess added so much to the chaos, and thus terror, that many in the tourist cabin began to cry. Linda had one arm wrapped around the child's. Her other hand was in Sandy's.

"Hush, baby," she whispered over and over into its hair. "Hush, baby, it's all right, hush, baby. We'll be all right." Beside her she could hear Sandy chanting.

". . . maker of heaven and earth, and in Jesus Christ, his only Son, our Lord."

"Beautiful debutantes much mourned in fearful air crash," whispered Linda to her, nervously.

"Suffered under Pontius Pilate, was crucified, dead, and buried."

211

"Hush, baby, it's all right, baby."

"And sitteth on the right hand of God the Father Almighty." Linda could see the baby's mother, her eyes yellow with fear, straining to see around the edge of the seat to where the baby had gone. Linda kept calling to her, but in the weeping and the crashing of the storm, she couldn't make her hear. Then the plane struck the runway.

The worst injuries were among the first-class passengers. The tail only bounced hard enough to jam the rear door, so Linda and Sandy, far back in the smoking section, were among the last to be taken off. Anyway, they stayed on board to help those who were hurt or undone. Linda was still holding the baby, whose mother had been taken away on a stretcher crying terribly for the child. It was some time before they could make the emergency squad understand that the baby was not theirs. In the meantime, they were calm and helpful, gathering shattered belongings and making the stewardess give a bottle of brandy to an old woman who couldn't stop crying.

They had to walk a long way down the runway in the rain to the terminal building. Then they waited a long time to be told about their luggage. Eventually the airline said that the hold was crushed shut. They should leave their addresses, and the luggage, if any, would be sent on to them when the plane had been cut open. Then they found there were no more planes to Bradley Field that night from Idlewild. By taking a helicopter they managed to catch the last flight from La Guardia. This took all their money. At Hartford they had to borrow cash from the ticket agent to pay for a taxi back to school. They wrote down his name and address and gave their fathers' names to him for surety. They managed to get to school before midnight, just under six hours past the last acceptable minute for returning from vacation. Mrs. Umbrage put them on bounds for the term.

There would be a time later in her life when Ann would view her school years with ironic balance, but at the time she could see this event only in the flicker of a fine lambent rage.

"I'm rather impressed, actually," said Muffin. "Can you imagine *Sandy* and *Linda* handling all that?"

"Easily," said Ann fiercely. "You put people in a stupid situation, you get stupid behavior. You put them in a different situation, and you find they have something fine in them. I could absolutely spit."

Ann headed the small delegation sent by the junior class to protest to Mrs. Umbrage. She explained exactly why Sandy and Linda had been late, very coolly and carefully, as if Mrs. Umbrage could not have understood. Mrs. Umbrage listened with her usual courteous attention. "But you see, dear, the reason they were late has nothing to do with it," she said.

"How can reason have nothing to do with it?"

"The rule is that no student may be late for any reason. To make exceptions is to invite excuses. If there is a storm, a Miss Pratt's girl takes an earlier plane, but a Miss Pratt's girl arrives on time."

"But it was an act of God!"

"I'm sure, dear. But you'll find life is full of acts of God."

It was not an act of God that Muffin never heard from David Bell again. She never reproached him in her heart, and apart from one bewildered letter, which he didn't answer, she never tried to find out what had happened. She just assumed that in some profound way she had been at fault. She might never even have heard his name again except that one Saturday night a girl named Dede Bell who'd graduated the year before dropped in with her boyfriend to have supper at school and see her friends. It was a very hot night and they were allowed to take their plates out onto the lawn, where everyone grouped around Dede to watch her smoke a cigarette and to watch her beau eat the same food they were eating.

"We're on our way back to Northampton," said Dede. "We went to the Carolina Cup last weekend with my cousin David, and then we stopped in Philadelphia to see my mother."

"Oh! Is David Bell your cousin?" cried Lisa. "We met him this year in Sea Island."

"Lucky you," said Dede. "Hey, does anyone want that last piece of cake? Wanta split it, Mike?"

"Was he riding?" said Muffin in a small voice.

"What? No, here, you take the part with the icing."

"Did he ride in the Cup?" she repeated.

"Who? David? David on a horse? You must be kidding."

Spring term was an especially busy one, as the juniors prepared to take over the powers of the senior class. The only person who was really watching Muffin draw into herself was Sally.
She saw that where a few months ago she would have taken the
audacious course, Muffin grew hesitant now, conservative. She
grew self-protective for the first time in her life. Where she had
spoken with brimming assurance of David, now she spoke with
assurance of nothing, and her defection left Sally nervous and
lonely. Muffin didn't want to smoke in the woods with her, to
share the thrill of risk with her, or to be there to haul her back
when she went too far. It scared Sally to see Muffin so subdued,
and she missed her friend.

One Saturday when George had come up from Virginia to call
on Lisa, they heard Sally clatter along the sidewalk in her Abercrombies to join them as they strolled the town loop. Of course it
was illegal for her to speak to a boy not her own registered caller, but she didn't care.

"Sal!" George gave her a great bear hug.

"I'll buzz off in a minute, Lisa," said Sally, "but, George, I had
something special to ask you. . . . What happened to David
Bell?"

"What? What do you mean?" asked Lisa.

But George knew immediately. "Is she taking it hard?"

"What hard? What are you talking about?" said Lisa.

"Of *course* she's taking it hard—she hasn't even mentioned
his name, in fact. What the fuck went on?"

Lisa was fidgeting, her hand on George's arm, wanting either
to go or to be included. George looked at his shoe. But Sally ignored Lisa and she looked relentlessly at George.

"See," he said at last, "when she came in from the beach with
him that morning . . . she was glowing . . . you didn't see
her. . . . I thought, Jesus, the girl is *beautiful*. She looked like
she'd never been really happy before in her life. We talked for a
minute or two, and then after she went upstairs I went back over
to the slave quarters to get my sneakers because Lisa and I had

an early tennis court. On the stairs I could hear David, already up there. He was talking to Ralph about Muffin. . . ."

"Yes? And?"

"Well, I waited till Ralph came down to breakfast, and then I went up and told David that if he wasn't off the island in six hours, I'd break both his arms."

"*Jesus*, George!" cried Lisa. "What did he say?"

"Never mind."

"Well, what was the big idea of inviting him to be Muffin's date, then?"

"Look, I knew he was supposed to be a snowman, but I didn't know he was a cruel shit."

"First I've heard there's a difference," said Sally angrily.

It was the second week of May, a hot bright Thursday.

"We should go back," said John O'Neill. "They'll miss you.."

"I know." Jenny didn't stir. She lay on her back in the long grass watching a high thin cloud lay fingers across the sun. There was a drone of locusts, no other sound except for a far-distant shout from a new girls' game of Capture the Flag. The school was having its Field Day. Behind a screen of pines flowed the river, shallow and icy. Their bare feet were still bone-chilled from standing in the water, trousers rolled to the knee, waiting for the incautious movement of a crayfish. They had scooped two into a jar and held them up to the sun, then let them go again.

"Have you ever read the Tao?" she asked after a while.

"No. Should I?"

She closed her eyes and said, "In danger, if you are wise, you are like water in a ravine. It fills all the low places and doesn't halt where it must plunge downward. Nothing can make it lose its magic." In both minds was the image of the fresh stream standing in glistening crests as it flowed tireless and unscarred over rocks that had bruised their feet.

He rolled up onto his elbow and looked at her. At length she opened her eyes again. They were wide and pale, a complex dazzle of blue and violet with tiny shards of yellow. "Will I ever see you again?" he asked.

"No."

"If I'd known it was going to hurt this much, would I ever have started?"

"I thought I started. I'd do it again. You can't go through life saying, 'What is this going to cost?' You need what you need. There's not enough time in life to waste it being afraid."

"Maybe it hurt me more than it did you."

"John, don't start again." He sat up. She watched from the grass as he began absently to pull the field flowers that grew within reach.

"I loved him and there were times when he loved me," she said softly to his back. "He loved me, and there were times when I loved him."

"More quotes?"

"I've had lots of time to read lately."

He was silent awhile, working the flowers in his hands. He said without looking around, "I feel as if my heart is going to break if you don't want me to make love to you."

"But it's too late," she said. It wasn't clear if she meant late in the afternoon. They were silent.

"Well, here." He turned at last and handed her the chain of daisies he'd been making.

"A daisy chain? For graduation and parting? That's a bitter little present, isn't it?" She sat up. He looped the chain around her neck, gently lifting her long auburn hair free from the flowers. "I didn't mean it that way," he said. "I really didn't."

They sat looking at each other. They were very close together, but they didn't touch. At last she said, "I'll make a present for you. I'll make you something out of words."

He said, "Thank you."

"You leave first this time, all right? Go back by the river. I'll come around through the field in a few minutes." He looked back only once, when he was nearly out of sight. She was still sitting perfectly still, exactly as he had left her.

When they met in the halls or at meals after that, she was always wry and courteous. After about a week he received this in the mail:

If I wanted, I could catch the moon tonight.

＊　＊　＊

The moon is an evil lozenge
Which, once swallowed,
Lodges in the throat with a throbbing silver ache

Tonight, if I wanted, I'd
    hold it in my hand
And knead it with hard knuckles of revenge

But it could only end in sticky pain
And, underneath my nails,
    stale smell of cheese.

Perhaps, if you had helped me with it then,
The time we held it cupped between our eyes
We could have caught it there,
    as with our mouths,
We, half uncertain, trapped that first sad kiss.

Or if you asked, I still might reach it down
Although it well might splinter in my hands
And pierce the trusting bone with glassy pain

But never mind.

Oh, if I wanted, I could catch it still.
But what if, when I touched,
    it disappeared
And proved that it had never been at all?

I do not want it back
It's only that
Tonight
I feel that I could write
the saddest song.

There'd been some talk of Philip driving down from Andover to go home with Ann when she took her weekend. But he wrote to say that the state of Georgia had suspended his license for six months after all, and that he wouldn't be coming. (He didn't add that he would also have to give up the summer job he'd arranged with some difficulty as assistant to the attorney general of the state of Maine, since the job required someone who could drive.)

Ann wrote that she was sorry. She invited Muffin to come home with her instead.

"Wow," said Muffin as the chauffeur drove them up the long winding drive to the house. They spent the morning seeing over the grounds. They went to the carriage house, with the tack room filled with old sidesaddles and bridles of horses long dead, the trophy room filled floor to ceiling with dust-covered ribbons from horse shows thirty and forty years past. There were old carriages, too, heavy four-horse coaches and light open phaetons, two great sleighs with the fur robes folded and waiting on the red leather seats. In a nearby stone building, once the barn, was a collection of antique automobiles, all in mint condition, with wood and brass and chrome gleaming. Some had been owned and used by the Lacey family, others collected by Charles when he was younger.

They ran through the grape arbor to the pool, not yet filled. The pool was lined with amber tiles and bordered around the black sandstone, so porous that in the heat a child's dripping footprints soaked in and evaporated almost before he had gone. Ann and Chip had had all their birthday parties here as children. Even now in spring before the pansy beds were blooming or the table umbrellas or lawn furniture was in place, the air seemed haunted with the calls and laughter of children in Lord & Taylor swimsuits, playing blindman's buff. In one corner the white-uniformed ghost nannies dried tears and applied Band Aids and explained that swimming right after lunch would give you a cramp and you'd die. Around the diving board, facing the noon sun, brown ghost mommies in flowered bathing suits wore straw hats and gold watches; they drank gin and smoked cigarettes and squashed the butts out in the lawn beneath them for the gardener to pick up.

"Perhaps I'll have a dance out here, when I come out," said Ann.

"Not in the ballroom?"

"But wouldn't it be nicer out here? With a big marquee on the lawn? We could have supper by the pool."

"When is your date?"

"Whenever the full moon is, that September, after we graduate. Madelon booked it practically the day I was born. 'The only

parties people remember are the first and the last of the season,'
she says."

"I suppose."

They went down to look over the fox-hound kennels, now
closed, and the farm buildings. "There used to be a five-hole golf
course, supposedly, but I'm not sure where. Maude sold about
fifty acres, the part across the road, right after the war. Maybe it
was there."

"How much is still yours?"

"Two hundred acres."

"I never know how big an acre is, though."

"About one and one-third football fields, if that helps."

"Of course it doesn't help."

"Well, all I know is, it's not enough to keep those little planes
from buzzing over the house. Maude hates them. The airport's
right over there."

"No, I don't suppose you can buy acres of air rights." They
went in to lunch, and afterward played a couple of sets of tennis.

Ann's brother, Chip, arrived from New Haven at teatime.

"Do you want to work in a game of squash before dinner?" he
asked Muffin.

"I didn't know girls played squash," she said.

"You didn't? Why not?"

"I don't know. I just never heard of girls ever playing squash.
It never occurred to me."

"I hate it," said Ann. "They always used to make us play every
Saturday in the winter. All I remember is the freezing cold and
the terrible white light all around, and this booming echoing
noise the ball makes."

"Well, I'm game," said Muffin, "but don't expect much." The
squash court, like all the outbuildings, was of stone covered with
ivy. It had a good musty smell inside from the cork of the court
floor, and it did indeed retain a dank wintry chill even now in
mid-May. There were cobwebs in the high sloping corners of the
ceiling, but all the lights reflected intense white from the walls.
Muffin picked the game up quickly, as soon as she grew used to
the lightness of the racket and the deadness of the ball. She
liked it and quickly developed a forehand ricochet shot that ca-
reened from the front to the side wall, around to the back, and

dropped like a stone just where Chip couldn't pick it up without breaking his racket. As long as she could keep winning her serve, she could make every point from the forecourt. Twice she ran her score up to fourteen but stalled there, strangely unable to make game point, till Chip took the match away from her.

"That was terrific," said Chip as they walked back to the house in the fading golden light. They were dripping wet and carried towels draped around their necks, with which they mopped their faces. "You gave me a run for my money."

"In which we see the effect of years of expensive tennis lessons," said Muffin.

"Let's play again in the morning." They went in to the sun porch, a glassed-in garden room that faced the sunset, where the butler was just now bringing the cocktail tray to Maude and Ann.

"Well, it looks like you worked up a sweat," said Ann.

"Horses sweat, Ann," said Maude. "Men perspire, and ladies glow. No ice, please, Morton."

"Good evening, Grandmother." Chip kissed her. "No, nothing yet, thank you, Morton. We'll wait till we've dressed. Come on, kiddo, race you." He took off through the vast living room to the great carved mahogany stairway, with Muffin panting at his heels.

When alone, the family usually dined in the morning room, a small room walled round with arched glass doors facing east, so the room filled with sun at breakfast. It was a peaceful, delicate room, with gauzy white drapery and French corner cupboards filled with translucent Spode. The table itself, which nearly filled the room, leaving only room for the servants to pass behind the chairs, consisted of a vast sheet of dark blue glass laid over a mirror of matching size. In the evening it reflected candlelight and faces with a deep midnight glow.

"I hope you don't mind our being so casual, eating in here. We're treating you as family. We never use the dining room now, except for parties," said Madelon to Muffin. Ann had shown Muffin the dining room in the morning. It was a long room that traversed the entire house, with French windows, heavily draped, at each end and a vast fireplace brought stone by stone from a castle in Scotland. You entered by a pair of ancient oak doors studded with iron, the refectory doors of a medieval monastery. The table in the dining room seated twenty-four without any leaves being added. "We'll have a small dinner there in June when you girls come out, before one of the other girls' dances. I hope you'll be here."

"Thank you," said Muffin.

"Will you have a tea or a ball, dear?"

"Oh, both, I guess. . . ." Muffin finished her vichyssoise. "My grandmother always said that the real point of a debut was to introduce you to the ladies of society. So Mother wants me to have a tea, and Daddy wants . . ."

Madelon had stopped listening and turned her attention to Maude. Muffin looked. Maude had tucked her napkin into the pearls at her chin, picked up her soup plate, and was drinking from it, as a child might do during nursery supper to annoy its nurse. She tilted the plate up higher and higher till you could no longer see her face behind it. She finished the soup without making a sound or spilling a drop, and all eyes followed as she lowered the plate to the table again and delicately dried her lips with white linen.

Madelon turned back to Muffin. "Yes, so you'll have a tea *and* a ball. I must say, I completely agree with your mother. The ladies' tea is in many ways the . . ." Her voice faltered and her eyes were drawn back to Maude. Muffin looked. Maude's face had disappeared behind the soup plate again; it seemed possible that she was licking it.

"Maude, dear, would you like me to ring for more soup?"

"No, thank you," said Maude, replacing her plate. "I've finished. But it's not police to say *more,* you know. You ought to say, 'May I ring for *some* soup.' To say *more* sounds as if one had already had plenty."

"That's right," said Charles unexpectedly. "That's perfectly right, Mother."

The talk turned to schools. Chip belonged to the Fence Club and had just been tapped for Skull and Bones, but he couldn't say anything about what went on there.

"I've heard they guarantee you an income of twenty thousand dollars a year for the rest of your life if you need it," said Muffin.

"Yes, I've heard that, too," Chip said.

"Oh, come on, Chip, is it true?"

"Tell me, how are things at Miss Pratt's now? You must be getting ready for Tap Day, aren't you?"

They allowed the subject to be changed. Ann, Muffin, Jenny, and Lisa had all tried out for the Daisies.

"The *a cappella* singing group, Daddy. Like the Whiffenpoofs."

"Hmmm? I thought the Whiffenpoofs were men."

"Yes, well, the Daisies sing like that, too."

"Oh? Well, that sounds fine, dear."

They were on the edge of their chairs waiting to see which of them would get in.

"Now, who do you think will be head of Glee next year? A guy at Fence told me it's going to be his sister, Amy Barkenhauer."

"Oh, no!" said Muffin and Ann together. "It's got to be Jenny."

"I'm sure it will be Jenny. Everyone loves her, especially the new girls. But of course they only have half-votes. But Jenny does all the solos and everything."

"Is it true," said Chip, "that she's Jewish?"

A startled quiet fell over the table, as if a snake had slithered across the blue glass.

"What did you say?"

"That she's Jewish. I heard that from a guy in freshman Glee, I think. He said she had such a beautiful voice, it was too bad she's Jewish."

"It's impossible, Chip," said Madelon briskly. "There are no Jews at Miss Pratt's. Mrs. Umbrage is terribly careful."

"Oh, Chip, that must be a lie! I'm sure she'd have *told* me!"

"Why should she? It's nobody's business but hers. I don't see what all the fuss is about. My freshman roommate at Hill was a Jew, and he was a great guy."

"But, Chip, we all knew that Steven was Jewish. It's this sly hole-in-corner business I don't care for," Madelon said. "What would her real name be, then? Rosen? Rosenblum? If *I* were a Jew *I* wouldn't lie about it."

"I had a friend who told a lie once," said Maude suddenly. "When we were girls, before I went away to school. She started a rumor about a girl that none of us liked. But then she felt guilty and went to confession—she must have been Catholic. Yes, she was. The minister told her to take a big box and fill it with feathers and put it on the front step of the house of the girl she had lied about. Then the next day, when the wind had scattered the feathers all over the neighborhood, she was supposed to start out with the box and try to pick them all up again."

No one knew what to say after that, so Madelon rang for dessert.

Muffin, Jenny, Ann, and Lisa all got into the Daisies. This was a source of great rejoicing. They decided to try for the four-room in Green House together. It had a tiny adjoining single that Sally wanted, a room that had either been a very small dressing room or a large walk-in closet; when five girls wanted to be together, the two became a suite.

Amy Barkenhauer was tapped for head of Glee, and Sandy Gooch for second head. "Oh, what the hell," said Jenny, but they knew she was surprised and hurt. The new girls in Glee went to speak to Mrs. Umbrage about it; they had all so strongly favored Jenny they felt sure something strange had happened in the balloting. Mrs. Umbrage said they must have forgotten themselves badly if they were suggesting a recount. Think how that would hurt Amy's feelings.

The new girls wrote a farewell song to the seniors and sang it under their windows at 6:30 one morning. Two of their members accompanied them on guitar and recorder, and it was actually rather lovely. Lisa was elected to Government. So, to her surprise, was Muffin.

As a particular honor, Lisa, though a junior, was tapped to be a marshal of the Daisy Chain on graduation day. Ann, who'd felt so wild with anger at the school for so much of the past year, was amazed to find herself truly moved when the student body gathered in the sunlight all in their white piqué dresses at the bottom of the garden to march to the village green, where, in the classic New England austerity of the Congregational Church, the commencement ceremony was held. The marshals arranged the girls according to height, and then the singing began. They sat off in even, measured step, the marshals with their staffs beside them tapping the time. A long living white-and-gold ribbon of girls unwound across the green, united by shared memories and a thick chain of daisies in even garlands along 140 shoulders. Ann had several close friends in the senior class, and she smiled inwardly to realize that the ritual was doing its work, and at one or two points she began to cry. But the one whose face was saddest, whose eyes stood filled with tears from the moment she felt the daisy chain lifted against her neck, was Jenny. All through the walk to church she remembered the much lighter touch of the daisy chain John had made for her, and among the tears and cheers for the prizes and diplomas that fall to a graduating class in the normal course of events, she cried for having given up the right love, because it had come at the wrong time.

CHAPTER 12

Together and Apart

The summer before their senior year was a long, hot, slow one. John Kennedy was president and the world hadn't come to an end; perhaps Democrats were not all the low-brow incompetents they believed throughout the Eisenhower years. Of course, the Kennedys themselves were nouveau, but Papa Joe was shrewd, and Jack certainly had style. Besides, the wife—Jackie Bouvier—had gone to Farmington. Perhaps they would grow up to be first lady, too.

It was the last summer of their lives as children; by next year they would be "out," eligible for marriage and households of their own. Of course, coming out didn't mean what it once had. Few wanted or expected to secure a husband the first season out of school. Most wanted to go to college; all would at least make a feint at it. These days a husband expected a woman to have something by way of higher education, as husbands had once expected an accomplished wife to speak French, play an instrument, draw, and do needlework.

The more illustrious the college that issued her degree, the more promising the man a girl might hope to attract. The idea that the education might be of professional use to herself had not yet gathered any momentum, but certainly the experience was thought to enrich her directly. A little learning made a wife a credit as a hostess, a more lively conversationalist, and equipped her to pass the long years at home with a better class of book. Now, some of the gals would get in with an arty set at

college and develop a taste for music or looking at paintings, and
then once or twice a year you'd have to put on your monkey suit
and go sit through some damned ballet or something. But then,
they did a bang-up job raising money for the symphony or being
docents at the museum, and that was a good thing. It kept the
gals busy, and if they didn't do those dull jobs, the directors
would have had to pay someone to do them.

Once girls were out, certain debts owed by them to society
would begin to fall due. They would have to join the Junior
League, perhaps take a job for a few years, to stop being children and start having them. But for now, for this last summer,
they were free to make whatever they liked of the long bright
empty days, the golf course trim as a good wool carpet, the clean
glittering swimming pools and the light hot nights, heavy with
honeysuckle and stars with no names.

Sally planned to do nothing much. She was expected home
with her mother and Dad Humphries in Rochester. She figured
she'd get a tan, work on her golf, and try to swim at least twenty
laps a day. Maybe some of her friends would be around to play
tennis with, if they hadn't all gone to the Lakes for the summer.

June was all right. A motley group of about a dozen kids
passed the days at the club, swimming and drinking iced tea.
Some of the older boys would join them from time to time before
they all left for their summer jobs. In the evenings they went to
the flicks or played a new game called Pulling Rabbits. The
group would crouch in the dark in the hedges at both sides of a
country road. When headlights appeared, someone would reel in
a black string from his hedge, causing a stuffed white sock in the
opposite hedge to slide and jerk, rabbitwise, onto the road so
that the driver would just catch a gleam of faltering white in his
headlights. If the car stopped to avoid killing the sock, the group
would leap from the hedges, whooping, and jump on the hood,
rock the car, and make faces at the driver through the wind-
shield. It was a lot of fun.

By the Fourth of July, even this group had dissipated, yet Sally had to spend most of her days away from the house doing
something. Her stepbrother and sister would not go to camp until August, but Dad Humphries insisted she continue to share a
room with Sharon, although Pepper's room was available.

"She wakes up if I turn on a light to read at night, and she gets up at seven and wakes *me* up," said Sally.

"So get up at seven. You don't do anything all day anyway; why should you need to sleep late?"

In spite of her boredom and the griping tension of her stepfather's house, those weeks at home marked the last days of her life that she was ever happy, because in the second week of July, this happened.

It was dinnertime on a sweltering evening. Sally's mother and stepfather were quarreling about something; it had started when Sally said she was on a diet and asked to be excused from the table. "Your children have the manners of a litter of field mice!" Sally's stepfather bellowed at Clara. He put down the carving knife and leaned on the table with both fists, glaring at his wife. "They seem to expect to eat and sleep and for all I know defecate anywhere they please and anytime they please, and the rest of the time they do whatever the *hell* they want with absolutely *no* concern for the feeling of anybody else—"

"Sharon, dear, please cut smaller pieces, you'll choke," said Clara, with her hands fiddling nervously at the pearls at her throat. Whenever Harvey started to bellow, she tried to pretend it wasn't happening, so that he would see how very, very much she disapproved of his manner, and how very unused she was to this sort of thing.

"And don't you pretend you don't hear me and don't you criticize my daughter when your own is slouching there at the dinner table in her tennis clothes and . . . and *bare* feet! Who the hell ever told you you could come to the table in bare feet like some sort of Ubangi? Answer me!" Sally had lowered her eyes and was staring at her plate, her face as blank as a closed door, but inside she was filled with icy misery, wondering how it was possible for someone to hate her so much, and what she had done that even her mother never stood up for her. Across the table Sharon was eating roast beef in large greedy bites and Bunky was pouring iced tea into the sink he'd built of mashed potatoes.

"I will not be shouted at," Clara was saying in a whine.

"You will not? You *will* not?" her husband shouted. "I see, you *will not* be shouted at? Because you are Clara Kellog and your father never raised his voice to a woman? . . ." It was an old argument, and both parties had their roles more or less memorized. It was while he hurled his insults and Clara whimpered her small self-justifying replies that Sally happened to glance up and notice that something was wrong with Sharon. She was sitting very still, with her eyes closed. Her hands were in her lap, a smear of gravy from the fork she still held trailing down her blouse, and her mouth opened and closed one or twice like a fish's. Sally stared at her. She must be choking, Sally thought, very dimly, although she had seen movies and knew that a choking person thrashes about and makes grunting noises and turns purple, not this pale yellow color. I should do something, she thought, sitting very still as if her limbs were made of lead, while her stepfather snarled over her head, because every instinct of survival she'd developed in the last ten years told her that when a fight was going on, you closed up and refused to respond or attract attention until the grown-ups forgot about you and took whatever it was out on each other. It's probably nothing, she said to herself, as she sat very still and stared at Sharon as if she were very cold and small and far away, at the bottom of a well, and while she was doing that, Sharon died.

She never told anyone what she suffered in the two days before the funeral. Something clarified in her, a feeling that had hovered just beyond the conscious for years—that there was something very damaged and bad inside her that she couldn't happen to remember at the moment, but for which she must be punished. She almost thought of asking Ralph what it was, but when he got home the day the little coffin was to be buried, he just said, in a whispered moment alone with her, "Well, kid, at least you don't have to share a room with the little brat anymore. Ha ha!"

Two weeks later Clara called Sally and Bunky into her room and explained that she and Dad Humphries had decided not to be married anymore, so Bunky would be going to stay with his grandmother for the rest of the summer and Sally was going to stay with her daddy and Aunt Hester. Wasn't that nice?

Daddy had taken a new job with Owens-Corning and moved to a town called Painted Post in western New York. He and Aunt Hester lived in a glass house. Since their move was recent and they had no children with them, they had joined no clubs and met no young people. Daddy was traveling a lot and Aunt Hester played bridge with some company wives. Sometime in August it occurred to Mr. Titsworth that Sally hadn't much to occupy her, so he came home one night with a large dry aquarium with a huge snake in it.

"Fella said it's a great pet," he said. "You only have to feed it a rat about once every three months."

In the letters they got from Sally that summer, Muffin and Jenny noticed Sally never talked about Sharon's death after the first news. They were glad she wasn't upset about it, but they did think it must be tough on her to be going through another divorce.

Seen through the shifting lenses of memory, there were many scenes from that summer that came back to Muffin in later years. She went to her first deb party, a tea dance in June, although properly she oughtn't to appear in society until Christmas. She rode every day through June and July, whooping alone across parkland that had bordered on open country when she was little, now beginning to be hemmed in by housing developments or studded with rural slums, trailers on cinder blocks. She jogged along trails through glimmering green woods, the trees so thick overhead that the sun pierced to the ground only in flickering patches. She visited the back-country stream where she and Rutherford Flack used to hike in early spring, often up to the shins in mud, with brown-sugar sandwiches in their pockets for lunch. They collected tadpoles, keeping them for weeks in a scummy basin to watch their tails fall off and their legs sprout. Somehow none of them ever survived to frogdom.

One day she found again the Indian mound where they had found arrowheads. She wondered if Rutherford still had them. She still had the small fragile skull, of a raccoon or rabbit, that they had found bleached clean and half-buried in leaf mold. Rutherford had let her keep it, though he spied it first. Where was Rutherford? She never thought about him when she was at school, but alone in the fragrant woods, she missed him.

Her favorite place to ride was the old Mortpestle estate way out on the Heights. The lawns and hedges around the house were still trimmed and pruned all summer, although the mansion was closed. As children they used to love to wander around the deserted grounds, coming suddenly upon a crumbling octagonal summerhouse, paint peeling, or an empty pond with a graceful naked cherub in the middle, standing on a seashell supported by fountain fish, their dry mouths still puckered in the air. The Mortpestles opened and used the swimming pool every summer, as much for their friends and their children's friends as for themselves. Muffin remembered playing leapfrog on the long lawn that stretched from the pool to the closed house, or hide-and-seek in the boxwood maze that stretched from the pool to the woods.

The Mortpestles were gentle, generous people. Mr. Mortpestle had been born in the big house, as had his father before him. But he and his wife and their youngest son lived in the valley now, in a house more convenient to town, one that didn't require ten in live-in help, and where the snowplows could reach them in case of emergency. Their youngest son, Leslie, was a hemophiliac.

Old Mr. Mortpestle had once been master of foxhounds, and they still held hunter trials in one of the long meadows. That summer Muffin used to hack out by herself with her stopwatch in her jeans pocket and put Mistress Moon over the course, checking her habit of rushing in too close to the zigzag split-rail fences, learning to collect her pace as each barrier loomed, so she was poised at exactly the right point in her stride, at exactly the moment instinct lifted them up and over the fence.

She also that summer took charge of her younger brothers and their friends at the pool in the afternoons so her mother could play golf. Often at night she drove a carload of kids down the boulevard to Ambridge to the drive-in movies, where behind the screen in the blackness across the river you could also watch the steel-mill smokestacks belching orange smoke and blue flame. Twice in the summer they went to Westview Park to eat cotton candy and ride the roller coaster. But when she looked back on the summer, the chain of events that caught in the mind and stayed were some that hadn't impressed her more deeply than many others at the time.

By August she had grown fervently bored. One morning she

went over to the country-club stable where most of their friends boarded their horses and asked the riding pro for a job.

Mr. Chubb, who had known her all her life, managed not to laugh. "You'd have to get here at seven each morning to help take around the mash."

"That's all right."

"You'd have to muck out all the stalls in the lower barn every day. Piet hurt his back lately, and he needs some help."

"Okay."

"You have to exercise all the horses on the lunge. There's not time to be tacking and riding them."

"I know."

"I can't pay you."

"Okay."

"You'll have to have your father call me and tell me you have his permission."

"I will."

"Well," he said, because Piet actually had hurt his back and did need some help, "I'll give you a try."

"Oh, Jack!" said Annette when Muffin's father announced at dinner what he'd just told Chubb. "I am really provoked with you, both of you. Her grandmother would spin in her grave if she ever heard of such a thing."

"Why?" asked Jack, spooning up his floating island.

"Why? Why? Why can't she be a candy-striper at the hospital like all her friends? Why does she have to do *anything*?"

"Don't see why her grandmother'd rather have her cleaning bedpans than mucking out stalls. *I* wouldn't."

So Muffin went to work. The head groom under Mr. Chubb was Neddy Bascom, a surly young roustabout whose first job when he arrived from Ireland was with Muffin's father as undergroom. He was highly skilled in a dying profession, not only a handler but a journeyman farrier. No man adept at shoeing horses was going to go hungry for long in that county, since the only other blacksmith was overworked and half-blind. Neddy had quickly been taken on by Mr. Chubb, but he'd carried a grudge against the Bundles for firing him.

He set Muffin to mucking stalls and kept her at it until she was so tired she saw pinpoints of light exploding before her eyes. When all the stalls were clean, he'd send her up to the hayloft to fork down bale after bale of clean straw, and when he discovered how it made her skin crawl, he'd particularly save for her the job of climbing up to the oat bin each night for the feed grain, knowing that when she turned on the light she found the surface of the grain pile swarming with mice.

(When she was much younger, she and Rutherford had once been playing in the forbidden oat bin. A mouse ran up the tight leg of her jodhpurs. She had no words, then or later, to describe the horror of its panicked sharp claws scrambling toward her knee, she unable to push the mouse back without crushing it, unable to free it except by racing frantic fingers to unbuckle her boots, unbutton her trousers, and strip them off, by which time the mouse was dead.)

By the time her blisters had turned to calluses, hard across the palms of her hands so they clicked when they were tapped with a fingernail, she had developed a positive thirst for physical exhaustion. Working all morning alone in the dark of the lower barn, breathing the sweet warm smell of straw and manure, carrying it by great forkfuls to the wheelbarrow outside the stall, she would reach something like a trance state where her mind went blank and floated free and peaceful while her arms and back and the muscles in her thighs strained and tightened, worked and relaxed. Sometimes she would pause and follow the motes dancing thick in the slice of sunlight that cut in from the transom above the stable door, and realize, having a thought, that it was the first thought she'd had in hours.

In the afternoons she and Willem, Piet's son, would take the horses out in pairs to let them gallop in a circle at the end of the lunge ropes. Then they would walk them slowly or graze them beside the show ring until the horses were cool enough to return to their stalls.

She and Willem didn't talk much. They were about the same age, with little else in common except an easy comfort in each other's company. They'd lie in the grass sometimes while the horses grazed, watching the clouds, chewing tall haystalks, or trying to make a whistle with a blade of grass held sideways between the curve of the thumbs. Willem's hands were broad and strong and always creased with dirt. Muffin's weren't much better. One evening they walked the last two horses of the day far out to the edge of the outside jumping course. When they paused to run their hands down under the moist chests to see if the horses were cooling, Willem kissed her. A few days later, a day he'd had to work a double shift because his father's back had kept him home altogether, Willem fell asleep as they lay in the late-afternoon sun. Muffin took the lead rope from his slack hand and tended the horses. When it was time to wake Willem to lead the pair back to the barn, she kissed him.

A day or two later, when Muffin came up to the upper barn at noon to eat her bologna sandwich with Willem, she found him gone and everyone else tense with consternation. Mort Sutton had been in to exercise his new mare and, the story went, when he returned to his car he found that the wallet he left in his jacket there was missing. Someone or something gave him the idea to look for it in Piet's car, and sure enough, there was the wallet in the glove compartment. Mr. Sutton was enraged at Willem, at Piet, and at Mr. Chubb. He insisted on calling the police and having Willem arrested.

"I am not understanding," Piet kept saying over and over. "Willem good boy. I am not understanding." His puzzled old eyes darted questioningly from Chubb to Muffin to Neddy. He had clearly been crying. Neddy went on silently, sullenly, polishing Mr. Sutton's tack. Mr. Chubb tried to comfort Piet, then gave it up and stalked out. All afternoon, as she exercised the horses, brought down the grain, running at double speed to try to do Willem's work as well as her own, it seemed to Muffin that Neddy was watching her. She had never really bothered to think before of how truly and deeply Neddy disliked her, and Willem too, for her sake.

She told her father what had happened.

"Willem?" he barked. "Not possible." He called Mr. Chubb and asked for his version. Then he called the Sweetwater borough building, where the jail was.

"This is Mr. Bundle. Let me speak to Willem Van Eyck." They brought him to the phone.

"Hello, Willem, this is Mr. Bundle. D'you steal that wallet? . . . Un-huh . . . What's your father's number? . . . Oh, you don't? . . . Well, how do I get there? . . . I *know* how far Zelionople is . . . all right . . . all right. Don't worry." Then he told Annette not to wait dinner for him.

"Oh, for heaven's sake, Jack. There's cheese soufflé; it'll get all flat. Where are you going?" He said he was going to tell old Piet that Willem would be all right. "Well, can't you phone him? You'll just interrupt *his* dinner, I'm sure." Jack said the Van Eycks didn't have a phone, and went out.

After much thought, Muffin decided to call Lisa and see if she could help. Lisa was incensed and promised to talk to her father, which she did as soon as he got home that evening.

"I can't believe it," she railed at him. "I've never been so embarrassed. The Bundles have known that boy all his life . . . the mark of a gentleman is the way he treats servants, and no *gentleman* would do what you did. You know you really have no *instinct* about people, Daddy. You take the word of a shifty-eyed liar and accuse a perfectly honest boy, and all because with God knows what in the bank you still behave like a peasant when you think you might lose a few bucks. So grasping, Daddy . . . so *gauche* . . ."

That was the first and last time Mort Sutton ever raised a hand to his daughter, but the slap he delivered left a red mark on her cheek for days. And even so, for once supporting the old canard, it hurt him a good deal more than it hurt her.

Since he couldn't dissuade Mort Sutton from pressing charges ("I could choke that guy," said Jack; "what's the *matter* with him?"), he arranged to have the case heard within the week, and when the morning of the hearing arrived, into the court trooped Jack Bundle, Alida Beebe, Avery Mortpestle, Dr. Balche, and one after another Sweetwater's most prominent gentry, most redoubtable matrons, fox hunters all, all prepared one after the other to take the stand and assure Mr. Sumter that Willem Van Eyck was the straightest, most upstanding, most reliable lad of their acquaintance and a damned good hand with a horse. Willem Van Eyck was found not guilty long before the defense had been called all its character witnesses. Willem went back to the stable and back to work.

It was September by then, and Muffin had stopped working herself, so it was third-hand in a letter from Annette that she learned that Willem had left the stable after all. He got into a fistfight with Neddy. "He broke Neddy's nose, I believe your father told me." Neither would say what the fight was about, but Mr. Chubb felt that he couldn't keep them both on, so Willem had to go. Everyone would have far rather parted with Neddy, but Willem couldn't shoe horses. Willem enlisted in the army.

Muffin actually got a letter from him later that fall. It was printed in pencil, on pink stationery, for some reason. He said he liked the army. The pay was good. He'd expected to spend his two years in Texas or somewhere, but instead they were going overseas. His spelling was somewhat uncertain. He spelled it "oversees," and he spelled the place they were going "Veetnom."

It was an exciting year for Muffin, and in a short time she thought no more about Willem. It was several years later, when the name Vietnam was as much in everyone's thoughts and talk as the names of their friends and lovers that she thought of him again. When at last she remarked to her father that Willem was the first boy any of them knew to go to Vietnam, she learned that he had died there.

In midsummer, George Tyler's father died. Not as expected, of another heart attack; he was knocked down and killed by a hit-and-run driver after lunch at the HYP club. After the funeral, George and his mother were alone. She said, "There's one thing you can do for me now that I couldn't ask you before. You can promise me that you won't see Lisa Sutton for a year."

George was not particularly surprised, but he didn't take it seriously. He thought it was part of her grief, her fear of losing him, too. But she persisted. "It's not what you think. It's not the same objection your father had. What he may or may not have known to Mort Sutton's disadvantage I don't know and I don't care. But it's the girl I object to. I know you can't avoid seeing her, since you'll be at the same parties all year, but I want you to stop going around together alone. If after a year you still feel you're in love, and if she waits for you, you'll both have my blessing." George tried for several days to change her mind, but it seemed to become an *idée fixe*. So at length he agreed.

Lisa took it very quietly. "What will it be like?" she asked him. "Will we both see other people? Will we write to each other? Will we think of each other, or not?"

"I've promised not to write. I've promised that we'll pass the year as if we're both fancy free. When the time is up, then we'll be that much more sure."

"I see. Well."

"Hey, babe? Today is August 3, and it's three o'clock. I'll meet you here, on August 3 at three o'clock, one year from today. Deal?"

"Deal." She walked quickly away.

George spent the rest of August quietly. In July he and Lisa had spent most of their days at the club together and many of their nights in her father's den. Now he played a lot of golf with his mother and with friends. Once he called Muffin to see if she'd like to go to the movies, but she said she'd been mucking out stalls all day and was too tired. He thought about Lisa a lot. He took out a couple of girls he'd been seeing before Lisa, and found himself bored and restless to be explaining himself all·over again. Once Lisa had written him that she felt like his wife, and he'd been overwhelmed by contempt at how easy she had been. It was love for herself, not for him, that let her assume the rules didn't apply to her. That's what he'd thought. Now it was he who felt like a husband, far beyond games, missing her deeply. How was she? Did she miss him? It was a gloomy, restless time, particularly because of his sorrow for his father, which he felt Lisa would have known how to comfort. Not the sort of thing you discuss with a casual date, and less with one of your drinking buddies. Several of his drinking buddies called him during the month to ask if he minded if they took Lisa out.

The weekend after Labor Day, the Falling Rock Club out near Ligonier held a Junior Weekend, in which its facilities were turned over to the junior members for what amounted to a giant house party. There was a dinner dance in the shooting lodge on Friday night, golf and tennis tournaments all day Saturday, and a dance Saturday night. Candy du Pont and her friends came from Wilmington for it; prep-school roommates and romances arrived from as far east as Fishers Island and as far west as Wayzata, Minnesota. The committee, which numbered several friends of Mrs. Tyler's, pressed George to come, since the success of these parties depended on a long and attractive stagline. He went, but the moment he saw Lisa, he regretted it.

The dinner dance Friday was torture. He drank sullenly, refused to dance, was rude to his dinner partner, then in an abrupt change of mood went and apologized and insisted that she join him in the Charleston contest. He won a Swiss army knife; the girl got a gold charm for her bracelet. Lisa wore a slender black dress and a string of pearls. Her very pale lipstick set off her perfect skin in a way that tormented him. The back of her dress was cut very low. When her partner held her, his hand pressed her naked flesh, and when her smooth white-gold hair swung in a mass against her tan shoulders, George felt as if he'd go mad.

The next day he seemed to bump into her everywhere. When he came off the tennis court she was there, lean and cool in a pair of lime-green Bermuda shorts that he remembered well. He saw her foursome tee off in the afternoon. The same boy was with her as the night before; he was very good-looking and she was laughing. George's heart was like lead.

Between the roast beef and the baked apple that evening, the club hostess announced a "conversation waltz," an invention of her own. "You start out with your dinner partner and you try to talk talk talk as long as the music plays. If we catch you being silent, we will tap you with our wands and you will have to pay the committee fifty cents. When the music stops, you must switch partners with the couple nearest you and talk talk talk again. Ready?"

George invited his dinner partner to dance and wished he'd at least remembered her name.

"What's your name?" he asked as the music began.

"Mary."

"Is it Mary, or Sue?" And he began to recite the lyrics to old rock-'n'-roll songs. His partners who could remember the words would take alternate lines, and those who didn't volunteered the oowees, doowahs, and ramalamadingdongs. Twice the hostesses cried "Very good, now everybody switch!" He was in the middle of "Mr. Blue" the third time when the music stopped and he turned to find Lisa before him. "Oh, God," he said. The familiar rush of affection swelled in him as she slipped into his arms.

She gazed at him, her lips parted, but she didn't speak. They held each other, dancing slowly, feeling the wordless centrifugal warmth that drew them together. Quite soon the hostess caught up with them and fined them fifty cents.

George left the dance after dinner. He went for a walk and stayed away till late in the evening. When he found himself again at the edge of the ballroom, he paused only long enough to find her in the crowd. Then he cut in, drew her away, and danced with her out to the terrace and onto the lawn. There he kissed her. He kissed her and kissed her, his tongue deep in her mouth. Her arms were around his neck and the whole length of her arched against him. His hands slipped over the thin silk of her back from shoulder to waist. He inched his hands up the taut rib cage. When at last he held the breasts, the nipples pressed stiff against his palms, she began to cry.

Without taking his mouth from hers, he picked her up and walked with her into the darkness till they found deep shadow well out of sight of glowing windows. Stretched on the grass beside her, he stroked her breast. Her tongue moved in his mouth with the rhythm of the hand. He kissed the tears on her eyelashes, whispering, "Cry, baby, cry for me. Want me." Her hands slid between his thighs. One hand stroked, almost too light to feel, the other deftly unfastened his belt and his zipper. Both hands were next to his skin. One ran lightly the length of his penis, again and again. The other grazed the balls, gentle and loving, then slid deeper until one finger found the anus. . . .

"Jesus! Let me be inside you, please, baby, *now.*"

"I want you, darling . . . too . . . please . . ."

He tugged at her skirt.

"No," she whimpered. "Darling . . . I can't . . . I can't stand it . . . you'll leave me. . . ."

And so it transpired that at two A.M. Sunday morning in a very small town in West Virginia they were married. They completed this sacrament on the back seat of George's mother's car, and by five A.M. Lisa had managed to reenter her room in the Falling Rock Club by way of an unusually well-built rose trellis and got into bed without waking her roommate. The next morning she and her date shot skeet as if they could do no wrong, and she won the competition and returned to her mother and father's house with this trophy.

* * *

Greenwich was fairly gay that summer, though the season got off to a depressing start. One of Ann's classmates from Greenwich Country Day came home from St. Tim's six months pregnant. She'd been feeling ill all spring, had gained weight, and had lost two teeth; but no matter how often she went to the infirmary, no one could guess what might cause such symptoms. When the truth became known, no one was more astonished than the mother-to-be, who believed herself to be a virgin. (This became known through the indiscretion of the family pediatrician, who diagnosed the pregnancy, though he declined to say what she did think she'd been doing.)

Her mother retired to her house in a swoon, but her brothers insisted on lacing her into a viciously tight merry widow and staging a sad little wedding. Ann and Chip went, drank champagne, and threw rice at the bride, who was wearing the white satin gown that had been made for her debut. The brothers also produced two gross of silver matchbook covers embossed with her name and the date, September 11, 1962, of the dinner dance that had been planned for years in her honor. There were also ten dozen champagne glasses, similarly etched, which the brothers insisted upon dividing up among her friends.

The bridegroom, who was sixteen, looked flushed and rather pleased. His older brother took a shine to Ann.

"Say, what's your name?" he kept asking her. "Say, where you goinna school? Uh-huh . . . so where you wanna go to college?"

"Radcliffe," said Ann, removing his hand from her arm.

"Why, I go to Point of Woods Business College, thas right near Briarcliff, hmmm?"

"No, Radcliffe," she said, and removed the hand again.

"*Rad*cliffe?" He looked baffled. "But thassa *four*-year college."

When the bride and groom had gone away, Ann and Chip invited everyone back to their poolhouse for an "after party." The bride's brothers, sick at heart, were grateful for the gesture. The groom's brother was even more glad, though he passed out in the car on the way and missed it after all. People swam and played records and drank beer. Late in the evening Carey Compton offered to teach them all a neat new game.

"Okay, now, watch," he said, so they watched carefully. He held a broom at arm's length and spun around rapidly twenty times, counting out loud and keeping his eyes at all times fixed on the tip of the broom handle. Then he dropped the broom on the floor, attempted to jump over it, fell down, cut his lip on somebody's glass, and had to be taken to the hospital for stitches.

"Everybody got it?" said Ann as Carey. was led out, bleeding profusely. "Who wants to be next?"

Later on they threw all the lawn chairs into the pool, and then everyone went home.

This party blended into many others, planned and impromptu, that arose during the summer. Carey gave a mint-julep party on the Fourth of July, when they all drank bourbon from frosted silver mugs given him by his godmother. Someone else gave a treasure hunt with an apricot-colored poodle puppy as a prize, but the clues were too hard. For instance, one was:

When the wind is a torrent of darkness among
    the gusty trees
And the moon is a ghostly galleon, tossed upon
    cloudy seas,
When the road is a ribbon of moonlight over
    the purple moor,
He comes riding riding riding.

You were supposed to guess *The Highwayman* and drive out to the nearest highway-patrol station for the next clue. But most of them couldn't guess it, so they just drove away and never came back.

One or two events of the summer did stand out in Ann's mind. The first happened when she was driving down the main street in Greenwich on her way to get some cigarettes. She was making a left turn, properly signaled and from the left lane, when a car speeding toward her from the opposite direction ran a red light two blocks up and crashed into the tail of her car. Her car spun completely around and came to rest on the sidewalk. Ann's breath was knocked out and she was shaking all over. It was several minutes before she could master herself enough to get out; when she did, she saw that the entire right rear of her car was smashed in. Anyone riding on that side would surely have been killed.

The man who hit her was an old Negro. His decrepit Chevy had run into a lamppost, and it looked as if the engine must be crushed. A policeman had just arrived on the scene. He walked around the Negro's car and then Ann's, making note of the damage to each and recording the license plates.

"All right, anybody see what happened?" he asked.

Ann was quite sure the street had been empty, but to her surprise a woman stepped up and said, "Yes, sir, I saw it. I was in the grocery there. This girl ran through a red light and made an illegal turn right into the path of that car . . ." Ann, still shaking and fighting for breath, was so astonished that she didn't feel she could speak without crying, so she didn't speak.

"Thass right," said the old man belligerently, looking at his shoes. "She ran a light, thass just how it happened."

The officer looked at the other driver, at the witness, and at Ann. "All right, let's have your licenses." Trembling, Ann brought out her license and her mother's registration, thanking God she had her wallet with her, since she usually didn't. The man searched his pockets sullenly and brought out a tattered license. The officer examined these documents carefully. Then he said, "I'll drive you home in a minute, Miss Lacey. Unless you think you should go to the hospital. My partner can call John Herbst for you to come tow the car—your mother uses Herbst, doesn't she?" Then he told the old Negro man he was under arrest for reckless driving.

No matter how vividly she explained the outrage this event presented to her vigilant social conscience, no one else could seem to see what she felt was so wrong.

"But, dear, did Officer Brandon arrest the wrong person? Well, then. I really do not understand you."

The other event also involved the police, and it came about this way. One of Maude's pleasures was to order her car and be driven out into the country and back. She liked to look out the window. Lately this pleasure was more and more marred by the proliferation of billboards covered with advertising. "So unnecessary," she would say. "Nobody wants them, I can't see why they put them up at all." Presently a simple solution occurred to her. She ordered her chauffeur to keep a hatchet in the trunk of the Rolls, and when they passed a billboard in the course of her drive, she'd instruct him to stop and chop it down. Sometimes, he reported to cook, she would get out and help. She seemed to derive great satisfaction from this activity.

At last she was detected in the act by a county sheriff's deputy who happened to be passing as the chauffeur brought down a large board depicting a new sort of cigarette. The deputy leaped from his car with handcuffs. "Oh, it's all right, young man," called Maude, "he's following my instructions."

"Yeah, but, *lady*, he can't go round chopping down billboards!"

"No? But they block the view. Nobody wants them."

"Lady, they're private property."

"Really?"

"Yes, really."

"Oh, I see. I hadn't thought of it that way. Thank you so much. Good afternoon." And they drove off. A day or two later the sheriff appeared at the door with a court order to arrest the hatchet. It was borne away, wrapped in a towel.

Jenny and her father planned to spend the summer together, their first in a long time. He'd been working every summer since her mother died, and she'd always had to go to her grandmother in Peekskill. But this year Clif could afford to take most of the summer off, and knowing how Jenny hated Peekskill, he'd promised they could stay home together at least through the middle of August.

Clif lived in Greenwich Village in a town house on West Ninth Street. He had moved downtown when Jenny was seven, the year her mother died. It was as if he wanted to sever altogether the Upper East Side associations acquired at Harvard and to widen the breach that had begun when he chose a life in the theater and that had grown wider at his wife's death. He enrolled Jenny in the small progressive Village school near their house.

Growing up, Jenny had spent a lot of time in the cool brick

sanctuary of Jefferson Market Library and a lot of time in
Washington Square Park. She loved the park in all weathers—
in winter when it filled with snowdrifts, and bundled people
walked their dogs around and around at all hours, and in hot
summer when old men played chess in the southwest corner on
stone chess tables, the trees filled with chattering black squir-
rels and the playgrounds swarming with children.

All around the center fountain, music rang. Many brought
guitars. Some led choruses of "Michael Row the Boat Ashore";
some sang arcane blues tunes of their own composition, hoping
to be discovered by an agent from the Albert Grossman office, or
at least to have enough change tossed into their guitar cases to
get something to eat. There were also young R&B groups, come
downtown on the A train to sing in the natural echo chamber
under Washington Square Arch with their hats at their feet for
contributions. There were steel drums, Latin bongo bands, and a
trio of old men with two accordions and a fiddle who used to
show up on weekends. And there were the winos asleep in the
hot sun in their overcoats, restless junkies scratching themselves and looking to score, and others who had already done so,
nodding peacefully on the benches. These nodders didn't even
stir when the summer wind tipped the high-soaring jet from the
fountain in their direction, spattering them with cloudless rain.
Jenny and her friends instinctively failed to identify the push-
ers, though reason required they must be there, too. The police
who cruised through in their blue patrol cars seemed to obey the
same street wisdom, for in all the thousands of hours she spent
there, she never saw an arrest.

Jenny liked the active, savory mix of souls she saw in the
park. They were all, herself included, like monkeys at home in
the same concrete zoo, all exhibiting some interesting reaction
to an environment to which neither genes nor history had suited
them. No behavior seemed more or less natural than any other,
though certainly some were more dangerous than others. But
the variety alone seemed ample compensation for that. She
didn't know what to say when Mamie Mallinckrodt told her that
she, too, had been to Greenwich Village. She had visited her
grandmother, who'd lived at One Fifth Avenue at the north edge
of the park since the days when it still had the aura of Edith

Wharton and Henry James. When Grandmother judged that
Mamie was old enough to view for herself the mélange of degen-
erates that had unaccountably made themselves at home at her
doorstep, she had the doorman call a taxi, drove Mamie once
around the perimeter of the park (a distance of perhaps
three-fifths of a mile), and then returned to her door, climbed
out, and went upstairs again.

Growing up, Jenny always had a best friend or two, but they
were rarely the same more than a couple of years in a row. The
kids she grew up with all seemed to assume that they were tran-
sients in each other's lives, passing through, perhaps to be remembered, but only rarely mourned. Times changed, people
moved away, others took their places; that was the constant par-
ticulate exchange that created the city's rhythm. You expected,
years hence, to bump into one kid you'd been in grade school
with, delivering bread to your supermarket, to hear of another
running for City Council, and to read of a third indicted for tax
fraud. Most you lost track of at once and forever; that was the
city scenario. Jenny was truly astonished to find, when she came
to Miss Pratt's, that by far the greatest number of her classmates had lived in the same house from the day they were born,
gone to the same school from nursery school to ninth grade with
the same classmates, that their friends' parents were their parents' friends, and that all of them met constantly year in and
year out; and that practically all of them expected to marry and
settle in similar towns with similar people who had also known
each other all their lives until they were buried in clearly imagined similar graves. Of all the visions of human variety that had
formed part of Jenny's world, this one was utterly alien.

The most stable figure in Jenny's life apart from her father
was Malcolm, who came to live with them when Jenny was
twelve. Malcolm was an opera director and therefore perennially out of work, there being not nearly enough opera productions
to go around among even the very best of the people who wanted
to direct them. He was also a gifted cook and a raconteur of
great charm. Once he moved in, Clif was able again for the first
time since her mother died to accept roles that would take him
out of town, since Malcolm was glad to take care of Jenny.

* * *

For Jenny it was an odd, schizophrenic summer full of both passion and isolation. Her first week home she called her best friend from the Village school, Solange Feinberg, as she always did.

"Hey, it's Priscilla Prep School," said Solange. "Home to mix with the proletariat?"

"Hey, Harriet High School, how's it going?" They talked for a while and agreed to meet for coffee the next evening. Solange brought her boyfriend, Myron, who was a senior at Music and Art, already working as a fashion photographer.

"Miss Pratt's," he kept saying. "Isn't that where Jackie Kennedy went to school?"

"No."

"Sure it is. I understand the admission test is they take a transfusion to see if your blood is blue. And then when you graduate, instead of going to college you go to the DAR. Listen, I know all about it, I go to the movies."

Solange wanted to talk about ballet. It was her new passion; she was spending the summer taking classes with the Joffrey. A dancer called Rudolf Nureyev had very recently defected to the West while on tour with the famous Soviet Kirov company, and this event had galvanized her.

"It wasn't about politics, it was for *artistic* freedom. At the Kirov, you know, all they do is these Petipa ballets about elves and fairies. Here he can work with Balanchine, Jerome Robbins, maybe even Martha Graham—Christ, wouldn't that be a gas? He's so fucking *gorgeous*, they say he leaps like Nijinsky. I can't wait to see him in person."

"But are you still doing the Trots, too?" The last time Jenny saw Solange she had been an ardent Trotskyite, hardly able to work in classes around the time she spent at revolutionary meetings.

"The reason ballet is the ultimate art form is it exists in all dimensions. It exists in time, like music, and in space, like sculpture. It engages all the aesthetic senses: it's color, it's form, it's motion, it's light, it's sound. The *courage* it takes to be a dancer, you have no idea . . ."

"It isn't flat," Jenny pointed out.

"What?"

"It doesn't engage the problem of flatness. . . . It doesn't have to create an impression of depth in two dimensions."

"Hey," said Myron, "what would your headmistress say if she knew you drank coffee with Jews? Huh? What would she say if she walked in right now?"

"Look, Myron," Jenny said, "I really don't know what your problem is, but I think it's *your* problem, not mine."

"If you ain't part of the solution, baby, *you're* part of the problem," he snapped triumphantly.

"Excuse me," said Jenny, and she left them.

"Clif, I believe this heavenly child is nursing a secret grief," said Malcolm one night at dinner. Both men looked at her in the candlelight. "I'll tell you why I think so. She has a break in her lifeline—give me your hand, darling—see? A break right there, indicating a change, an event, that occurs just at the brink of adulthood. By itself it could mean a new job or a move or even a death of a close friend. But in view of certain other signs we see here, understood only by me and my Romanian grandmother, I surmise an affair of the heart. I surmise an affair of the heart that has come to an end and left behind a great aching, a sorrowful void. And how do I know this? From another sign whose meaning I learned from my old Romanian grandmother: she has eaten exactly two bites of veal piccata. Really, darling, when you were younger, at least you used to wait till my back was turned and give your dinner to the cat so my feelings wouldn't be hurt. Ah-ah-ahh!" He held up his hand. "Not a word. Remember what I always told you: never complain and never explain. You don't mind that I always told her that, do you, Clif? I had to always tell her something, and it was the first thing that came to me."

The next afternoon Malcolm came home with an instrument case, which he handed to Jenny. Inside was an extraordinary guitar. It was made of blond wood with inlays of mahogany and mother-of-pearl; it had ebony pegs and a deep, glowing tone like a human baritone voice.

"Jesus, Malcolm!" was all Jenny could say.

"They do teach you elegant turns of phrase at Miss Pratt's, don't they? Now, if you want to know where I got it, I don't feel like telling you. If you want to know *how* I got it, I pawned my watch. If you want to know why I got it, it's because I wish to impose a heavy burden of responsibility upon you. From those to whom much is given, much also is expected. Now that I've given you this, you will be obliged to learn to play it."

"But, Malcolm, your watch!"

"Did you know that it was actually my Romanian grandfather's watch? Who would have thought anything so old and ugly would turn out to be so valuable?"

Thus began Jenny's passion. Clif asked if she'd like to take guitar lessons, but Malcolm said, "No, of course she wouldn't. She's not that type at all." She already knew basic chords and several fingering styles, since they learned them at the Village school when they got bored with the recorder. But the ears and the instinct that were to set her apart were her own gift. Years later she would be known in the music business as a "natural," one who can hear and instinctively repeat the essence of a piece of music, no matter how complex the harmonies or unfamiliar the rhythm, without apparent technical difficulty. Once she mastered the guitar, she found she could express herself on piano or fiddle as well if the need arose, just as some people can absorb languages with practically no effort.

It was an exciting summer to be a musician in Greenwich Village. A new singer called Bob Dylan could be seen now and then at Gerdes Folk City; the Bitter End, the Village Vanguard, the Cafe Wha?, and the Gaslight were all thriving. Joan Baez was singing Childe ballads, Pete Seeger was singing "You Can't Spend a Dollar When You're Dead," while outside whatever club he was in pickets circled with signboards calling him "Khrushchev's Songbird." It seemed as if every hip kid in five boroughs who could play a guitar or harmonica or indeed hit two spoons together in rhythm flocked into MacDougal or Bleecker street on those hot summer evenings to drink frothy cappuccino, try to get involved with pickup bands in the park, to audition for Hootennanies Tuesday night, and to tell each other they had just met Jim Kweskin, Dave Van Ronk, Maria D'Amato, or Geoff Muldaur.

* * *

Looking back on that summer, Jenny had a strong impression of endless hours spent sitting on her bed in a pool of sunlight, practicing till her fingertips first blistered, then grew as hard as fingernails from being bitten into by the steel strings. When she could play all up and down the neck of the guitar in different keys without a capo, then she would struggle to reproduce a complex fingering heard in some club the night before, or to locate an unconventional tuning.

There was an odd, noncommittal group of devotees who found themselves hanging around the Folklore Center together that summer, haunting the clubs, tracking down esoteric recordings. Often they would come together like metal filings drawn by some magnetic accident to play for hours and talk shop and later in the summer to back each other up as three or four of them, Jenny included, began to pick up the odd paying gig and to attract a following. Certainly Jenny never imagined that the relationships forming and reforming that summer would eventually coalesce to become the nucleus of her personal and professional life for the next fifteen years. She had friends she saw nightly for weeks that she knew only as Lenny or Saul, and there was one named Bruno whom she was to run into every couple of years for a decade, each time to find that he bore an entirely new name and occupation.

Of course, that summer, as every summer, Greenwich Village became a mecca for tourists who wanted to see real beatniks or transvestites or other unconventional souls who coexisted quietly and undisturbed at other seasons. Once or twice during August there was an infestation of bikers, roaring up Sixth Avenue thirty or forty strong, wearing black goggles and denim jackets with sleeves cut off to show their death's-head tattoos. Their girlfriends sat like gun molls on the passenger seats. They would drive around and around the park looking neither to right nor left, simply circling like Indians about to put torch to a village of women and children. The combined noise of their motorcycles, made as loud as possible by illegal glas-pack mufflers, was easily above the pain threshold of any with normal hearing. Toward sunset, if left to their own devices, they would peel off into the traffic on Broadway and head down to Chinatown to eat.

Long after dark they would reappear in twos and threes and park their huge Harley Davidsons on MacDougal Street outside the Kettle of Fish. Sometimes they would stand there for hours, drinking beer and leaning against their bikes.

On one such night Jenny was walking home with Malcolm and Clif after a late set played by one of her friends. As they approached a couple sitting on their Norton passing a glass of draft beer back and forth between them, the girl said in a shrill nasal voice, "*His* mother made him a fairy." Her companion rejoined, "If I get her the wool, will she make me one?" They laughed loudly. Then the girl cried, "Motherfuck, guess who that is? That's Clifton Rose! Hey, a movie star!" "Looks more like Queen for a Day to me," said her swain. Clif and Malcolm never paused, never gave any sign that they'd heard.

Jenny realized later as she walked after them that inside she'd been screaming silently to her father: "Hit him! Please, just once, go back and hit him!"

CHAPTER 13

Seniors

$\mathcal{M}$emory is episodic. After perhaps fifteen years, isolated events emerge as clearly as if they were yesterday, but the connective tissue of days and weeks that held them together, that kept them from bobbling out of the order of time and place in which they actually occurred—that fiber is often lost, dissolved into the unanalyzable moral stuff that now composes the person.

Looking back on those first few weeks of senior year, none of them could separate one day from the next. They arranged their class schedules, got to know the new girls, they tapped for Glee Club and yearbook and all the others. They played hockey games against neighboring schools; they learned lacrosse. They sat on the steps of Pratt Hall in the sun, talking and swinging their Abercrombies. The Daisies took up their nightly rehearsal schedule. All this they knew must have happened rather than actually remembering it. The first event of the term that stuck in the minds of all, to be recalled in later years, reweighed, revalued, examined for a place in a larger pattern, was this.

In the upper classes some of the teachers would on their own recognizance lead field trips of junior and senior girls to New York or Boston to see points of interest. The biology teacher had twice in living memory taken his class to New York to the Museum of Natural History, and almost every year he took his honor students as far as West Hartford center to buy tropical fish. For this reason his course was far more popular than chemistry with Miss Barney, whose students scored high on their college boards but who never got taken anywhere. The art-history teacher always took her first-year class to the Boston Museum of Fine Arts, and her seniors had two trips, one to the Gardner in Boston and then across the river to the Fogg Museum at Harvard; then in winter they went to New York to the Metropolitan. Art history was far and away the most popular elective ever offered at Miss Pratt's, and insofar as Miss Pratt's graduates distinguished themselves at all, they usually did so in the field of visual arts.

In the fall of this senior year, the new teacher of U.S. history announced that she would lead a group of interested students to New York to see the United Nations headquarters. Every member of the senior class was interested except for the members of Glee Club and the Daisies, who had a concert with Cheshire Academy the next night and weren't allowed to go. So Muffin and Jenny and Lisa and Ann got the story second-hand from Linda Hawley.

The big attraction on field trips was lunch. Throughout the day you were considered to be at school and subject to all school rules, except for two hours at lunch, when you were allowed to vanish into the metropolis. The morning of any field trip there was a run on the housemother's closet of contraband so that everyone traveled throbbing with glad anticipation of the first possible moment when she could experience that special dizzying nausea that comes from smoking a very stale cigarette for the first time in weeks.

Sally Titsworth talked all the way down in the train about her oldest brother, Pepper, who was meeting her at noon. Because of her exile to Painted Post, she hadn't seen him all summer. Pepper picked Sally up in a limousine in front of the UN and took her to a restaurant in midtown she could never afterward remember the name of. But the waiters all wore lederhosen, the prices were astronomical, and the maitre d' was not overly fussy about requiring proof of age when the order was for Dom Perignon. Pepper also ordered this absolutely neat cheese stuff that you ate by dipping bread into it on the end of a long fork. By the end of the hour the cheese at the bottom of the pot was stiff and gummy and you kept losing your bread. But by that time, what with the second bottle of wine, a lump of bread stuck at the bottom of the pot seemed much, much funnier than getting something to eat.

Linda said that when she rejoined the group for the afternoon session Sally's eyes were glassy and her limbs appeared to be rubber. She made every movement with exaggerated caution, but if she should chance to stumble or to bump into a doorjamb, she would be overcome with a secret and silent fit of giggles. Linda and several others undertook to keep her as far from Miss Dethiers as possible, and somehow they got her through the tour.

She might in fact have been all right if Miss Dethiers had not announced as they gathered at Grand Central that she had brought with her a very absorbing book which she planned to read all the way home. So if any of the girls should happen to visit the smoking car anytime before they entered the Hartford city limits, she would be most unlikely to notice.

The entire group crowded into the smoking car.

"God, I'm glad I bought an extra pack at lunch. I'd have died if I had to smoke your Kools all the way home."

"Who's got a match? We don't want to be three on a match."

"Hey, Sally, we saved you a place. C'mon, Linda, move your buns, there's room for us all here."

"Does anyone know how to change these seats around? I get sick if I ride backwards."

By New Haven the car was in dense haze and filled with chatter, but Sally had grown very quiet. By the time they crossed the Hartford line, with a wail from the group and a choreographed stubbing out of the last butts, somebody noticed that the color had drained from her face.

"Hey, Sal? You all right?"

"My God, she's gonna take a passer."

"She's gonna blow lunch . . ."

"Hey, Sally . . ." Five faces peered intently into hers.

"'M all right," she mumbled. The train pulled into the station. They all stood up, watching Sally carefully; she was white, but it seemed she could walk. She kept swallowing and her eyes were wide as she moved stiffly down the aisle and out the door, as if trying not to jostle herself. But a few steps after gaining the platform, she threw up.

* * *

"Well, I don't think it's fair at *all*," said Linda. They were gathered in the four-room discussing the crisis. Sally was packing to go home to Painted Post. She'd been suspended for three weeks.

"I mean, half the people on the trip had a beer at lunch. Why do they have to suspend her? I thought they'd just put her on bounds like they did when Peaches drank wine at the Coachhouse."

Ann said, "What if everybody who had anything to drink all went and confessed. They can't suspend half the class, can they?" They all looked at each other.

"Look," said Linda. "I'm applying for early admissions to Smith; I'd have an incomplete grading period . . . my recommendations would be screwed . . ."

"Besides, they'd never all tell the truth. That prick Beverly Dust is already claiming she was drinking Shirley Temples."

"Oh, Jesus," said Muffin. "What's going to happen to Sally?"

When she'd finished packing Sally came in and sat down on Lisa's bed. They all stared at her, and she stared back. Lisa was the first to speak:

"Listen, I know a guy who got suspended from Princeton for taking a dump in Times Square." Sally sniffled.

"*Really.* His roommates bet him fifty dollars or something. He went to Forty-second Street wearing shoes and socks and a raincoat. He won the bet, but then he got arrested for violating the health code. He came back the next year, made Phi Beta Kappa . . . look, who cares? A year from now you won't even remember this. . . ."

The others chimed in

". . . boy I heard of got suspended from Hill for sneaking into Philadelphia and going on *American Bandstand.* A master saw him on television."

"A boy at Milton rigged the chapel bells to play 'Rock Around the Clock.' He got kicked out for the rest of the term. It was the first bad thing he'd done in his life, and his parents were delighted."

"My brother's never allowed back in the Plaza—he and his friends got drunk and threw a glass desktop out the window."

They're all all right. They all got into college. Their parents forgave them, their teachers forgot it, their girlfriends thought they were great.

Sally began to cry. "Swell," she yelled, "just *swell*. Don't you get the point? Those stories are all about boys. You can't tell me one story like that about a girl. God, I feel like such a total fuck-up!"

"Oh, no," they said. "Oh, you shouldn't, Sally!"

"It was just unfair!"

"It could have happened to anybody . . ."

"Just one mistake . . ."

"It's just rotten luck . . ."

"But it didn't happen to anybody, it happened to me! It *always* happens to me, and you know it after all that with the pig and everything."

"What pig? Come on, don't cry, it's all right."

"Come on, what pig. You *know* what pig! I killed the dumb pig; the poor thing, it screamed like a person. Oh, Christ, it was so *awful*. . . ."

"Sally, what *are* you talking about? You mean the night of Philip's accident?"

"Oh, don't be stupid. *I* was driving. You must have known that. When we heard the sirens after the crash, he changed places with me because I was drunk; he said they couldn't do as much to him as they would to me."

They were back to all looking at each other in silence.

"Shit," said Sally, and she ran out of the room. They didn't see her again until she came back just before Thanksgiving.

One hot morning in Indian summer, a message was delivered to chemistry class that Jenny Rose was wanted in Mrs. Umbrage's office. All eyes followed her solemnly as she left the room, her heart cold with fear. Either they had found out something . . . or something awful had happened.

Mrs. Umbrage met her on the porch of Pratt Hall.

"Jenny, dear," she said, in the manner she usually reserved

for heads of state, "I'm afraid there's been some bad news. Your uncle has just arrived, and we think it best you go with him now." They were at the door of her study, and inside, wearing a very expensive dark suit and serious expression, sat Malcolm.

He rose and kissed her on the cheek, taking her arm and murmuring his good-byes to Mrs. Umbrage at the same time, and in another moment they were on the sidewalk. Malcolm raised a hand, and a massive black Cadillac pulled up to the curb; the chauffeur sprang out smartly to open their door.

"Malcolm!" Jenny hissed at him.

"Uncle Malcolm to you, darling. Yes, all right, drive off, please," he said a little louder, tapping on the chauffeur's glass. "Go on, go on, go somewhere."

"*Malcolm!* God, I can see now why Mrs. Umbrage was so impressed. What is going on? Where did you get that suit? Are we rich? What the hell is this car?"

"I borrowed the suit from Tony."

"But she said bad news. Something awful has happened to Clif—"

"Of course nothing's happened to Clif, but he's in Houston and can't get here till tonight."

"All right. What is it?"

"Ah. Well. Well, the fact is the Fairmont called to say that your grandmother died in her sleep in the early hours of this morning. No pain . . . no fear . . . the very death she would have wanted. I'd like to go that way myself." Jenny was looking at him, stunned. She'd seen her grandmother the weekend before, and this news took her breath away.

Malcolm went on. "So, I thought to myself, well, I can't tell her *that* on the phone, and I certainly can't let strangers tell her. And then it occurred to me that I had some overripe Brie that wouldn't *last* another day, so then I saw the best thing would be just to come collect you and go out for a picnic."

"Oh, Malcolm." Her tears were beginning to come hot and fast.

"Do shut up, dear. What would your grandmother say? She wanted you to be happy. She still does, can't you feel her here, letting us know she's at peace, telling us not to mourn for her? *I* can." They drove around for a while, now and then stopping so

Malcolm could ask someone where the Nature was, till they found their way to the state park on the Farmington River where the school went for Field Day. It was nearly deserted. They spread a tablecloth on the grass in a spot where Malcolm could see the sweep of fiery colors that danced on the trees on the far side of the river.

Malcolm unpacked the picnic hamper. In addition to the Brie he had apparently also happened to have a pressed duck, some fresh French bread, and two pints of raspberries with crème fraîche. He served the luncheon on Wedgwood plates with their best napkins and silver and two of the crystal goblets that they usually used only at holidays. He insisted that they eat deliberately and with attention, being sure to take the utmost pleasure in the beauty of the arrangements.

"Now, *please*, darling. Remember the Japanese. Of course loss is serious, but so is pressed duck. Kindly attend to one thing at a time." Only when she was well fed and calm did he fill their glasses with the last of the rosé and propose a toast.

"To your grandmother—in honor of all the exquisite moments in *her* life." They drank. Jenny looked at him in her old way, on the verge of a smile.

Back in the car, on the way back to school, he added, "Your father and I will be back in two days for some sort of service. We'll let you know, but there will *no more tears* for you and me. Six parts out of ten, when you grieve for somebody's death, is grief for your own. But the only way to prepare for death is to accept your life and find it good. That's what your grandmother did. And if you'd just relax and let yourself feel it, I believe you'd find she's trying to tell you so." They rode the rest of the way in silence, Malcolm holding Jenny's hand. Although she felt terribly sad, she did feel, also, a kind of peace.

The cold weather closed in. The Glee Club went in a sleet storm to a concert and dance at Middlesex, but their bus got stuck at the foot of a long hill and they all had to get out and walk a mile and a half in their velvet skirts and Capezios. They didn't get home until two A.M. There was hot Wheatena for breakfast every morning. For two weeks Muffin and Lisa were assigned to the French dining table, which met in a little private room served by a dumbwaiter. Since the French teacher never came to breakfast, Muffin and Lisa didn't either. After the breakfast bell rang and their twenty-four classmates thundered by their door in their heavy shoes, grumbling, they lay in their white iron bedsteads in the big silent room filled with sunlight and reveled in illicit sleep. Jenny and Ann brought them apples from their breakfasts and later they made a good meal of the milk and biscuits the maids brought to the class buildings for elevenses.

They began composing the collection of quotes and characteristic sayings that would be published in the yearbook for all to remember them by. Ann and Jenny were convulsed with glee to learn that Beverly Dust, the pious head of the Riding Club, had chosen a quote from Dylan Thomas: "And I was green and carefree, famous among the barns." On the first day of December there arrived the engraved information on thick rag stock that their presence was requested on December 22 at a small dance in honor of Miss Lisa Chandler Sutton, at the Allegheny Country Club at eleven o'clock. All the girls who had gone to Europe together were invited, and all who had been in Sea Island. Miriam suggested that the girls come out straight from school to see Muffin and Lisa presented at the Cinderella Ball. Mort sent along a clipping from *The Wall Street Journal* about an Episcopal bishop on Long Island who formally blessed the local debutantes in a body, just as earlier in the season he blessed the foxhounds, and wished all good hunting. December 20 found Lisa, Muffin, Ann, Jenny, and Sally on the plane together to Pittsburgh, wiggling in their unaccustomed panty girdles, smoking Kents, wearing red lipstick, and trying to look grown-up.

"I've asked Philip to escort me," said Lisa, going over the list of those who'd accepted.

"Not George?"

"No, we promised not to date this year. George will take Muffin, and Ralph will take Jenny, and Sally can go with the Algonquin Twins . . . no, wait. That leaves Ann and Chip going together."

"Let the Twins take Merry Bundle, why don't you? I'd rather have a real date," said Sally.

"Oh, all right. Then you go with Chip, and Ann go with Ralph . . ." Lisa started all over again.

The Rochester contingent, Ralph and Pepper Titsworth and the Twins and Pear, were all at the gate to meet them. Lisa's brother Buddy and his girlfriend would be in in twenty minutes. The baggage-claim area was a madhouse of students hauling suitcases, ski boots, and tennis rackets and leaning over the luggage belt searching for more belongings among the guitar cases, skis, and golf clubs that emerged in an endless stream.

"Next thing'll come out of there'll be a dead body," said a sour young man in an army uniform.

"Oh, I hope so," said Ann. "I put one on in Hartford."

Jenny and Ann went home with Muffin to Sweetwater; the rest drove off in two limousines to the East End to where Miriam Sutton was waiting lambchops and watercress for eighteen for lunch.

CHAPTER 14

The Debutantes

Late the following afternoon, George Tyler was waiting in the lobby of the William Penn Hotel for his mother to finish her shopping at Kauffman's when he spotted Howard Slugg wandering disconsolately among the workmen who streamed in and out of the elevators carrying lights and glittering shoes and pumpkins with which to festoon the ballroom for the annual Cinderella Ball that evening.

"Hey, Slugg," called George, "what's the cry?"

Howard peered myopically in his direction and finally located the source of the sound.

"George," he said, crossing the lobby as quickly as his slight congenital limp allowed. "The cry is . . . is . . . the cry . . . I don't know what the cry is." He dropped into a chair by George and looked around over first his right shoulder and then his left. Since he was apparently assembled without benefit of a neck, he had to turn his plump torso from the waist to achieve this.

"What's going on, Slugg? You look jumpy."

Howard jumped. "Not at all, not at all. How are you, George? How's school? How's your family? How's your father, George? I always liked your father."

"He died this summer, Howard. You were at the funeral."

"I know he did, I know he did." Howard performed his strange over-the-shoulder exercise again. Then he turned his earnest stare to George, like a dog who's been ordered not to beg at the table.

"So, home from Rollins?" asked George.

"Oh, yes, oh, yes, home. From Rollins." Silence. "Been kicked out, actually."

"Ah," said George. "Bad acting, Howard? Too many panty raids?"

"Ha, ha, ha," laughed Howard together with George. They shared the joke of Howard the Rogue. Then his smile died away as memory returned. "I flunked out," he said. "It's very hard, Rollins. Say, George, do you think you could do me a favor?"

"What is it?"

"I wonder if you could step out and get me a bottle of, uh, rye. I'm expecting a, uh, date, and I don't want to miss her."

"I see," said George. "But why don't you just take her into the bar?"

"Underage," said Howard. "I've taken a room," he added desperately.

George whistled. "Smooth, Slugg. But are you sure she drinks rye?"

"Anything, she drinks anything. And, George, could you . . . could you slip the bottle inside a newspaper? I'll pay for it, I'll pay for the bottle *and* the newspaper, of course."

George soon returned with a bottle of very good Scotch wrapped in a copy of the Pittsburgh *Herald.*

"I'll, uh, I think I'll just take this upstairs," said Howard, seizing it and making for the elevator in his own peculiar way. Immediately two men whom George had not noticed in the room materialized at Howard's side. Howard looked up and smiled at them weakly as the three of them entered the car together and the doors slid silently shut.

Muffin had been at the William Penn all day with the other debutantes, rehearsing the promenade for the Cinderella Ball. In the evening Ann and Jenny were driven into town by Mr. and Mrs. Bundle with their dinner dresses and ball gowns on hangers in the back seat. Jack Bundle had taken rooms for them at the hotel for the night so they could dance as long as they liked and not worry about driving home in the snow. All the way, Mrs. Bundle chattered about the ball.

"It's a lovely party, a *lovely* party," she gushed, "no matter what Muffin says. The committee works so hard to make it a success, and it does so much good for the Children's Hospital. And I think the girls have *such* a good time; I know I did."

"Oh, yes," said Ann and Jenny.

"Now, this is your year, girls, so you just have the *best time.* You'll remember this year for the rest of your lives, so kick up your heels! Have a ball!"

"We will," said Ann and Jenny. Mrs. Bundle came up to their room with them to help them dress for dinner. The fathers of the debutantes had a large dressing room with valets to assist them.

"Oh, my!" she cried when she saw Ann's dinner dress. "Oh, don't you look *chic!* Why, I remember when a girl was never allowed to wear black until she'd been out for a year. You look simply lovely. Oh, let me put just a *dab* more color on your . . . cheekbones . . . there, like that. Isn't this divine? I haven't had so much fun since I was at school.

"And now, could one of you just get my darn zipper here . . . tug . . . that's right . . . now how do *I* look? Why, Jenny! Your ball gown! Oh, my, I didn't *see* this before when it was in the dress bag. I can't wait to see you in this! I never saw such lovely chiffon. *Where* did you get such a heavenly thing? I looked all fall for Muffin. There's nothing like this at Kauffman's."

"My father's friend Malcolm had it made for me. By a costume designer."

"Why, that's the sweetest thing I ever heard. He must be an absolute fairy godmother."

"Exactly," said Jenny.

They saw Muffin briefly at dinner. She'd lost weight the past summer, and now her plumpness was mostly a matter of soft roundness in the face and limbs and an outsized bust for her height. Tonight she looked flushed and very pretty. "Wish me luck," she whispered as the debutantes were herded out right after dessert to change.

"Break a leg," called Jenny after her.

"Oh, don't say that," said George. "Last year somebody did."

The ballroom was jammed to the rafters with glittering holders of tax-deductible ball tickets. Ann and Jenny were with Mrs. Bundle in her box on the first tier. George and Philip had joined them. At 11:30 the floor was cleared by a portentous drumroll and a lowering of the lights. For a moment all was blackness, and then an unctuous voice from an unseen sound booth cried, "Ladies and gentlemen, the chairman of this year's committee, Mrs. Theodore Slugg!" And she was there, on the stage in a spotlight in deep décolletage, with a rose tucked between her withered breasts. She acknowledged her applause with a queenly air, thanked all the usual people, and announced that the evening really belonged to the debutantes, who were this year, as in every previous year, truly the loveliest group of young ladies the Ball Committee had ever seen. Applause. Silence. Then the announcer flung into the trembling dark the name of the first debutante: Margaret Penn Bundle!

She appeared in the spotlight. She smiled. She descended the four stairs holding her long white skirt, the spotlight following her. Her father, dashing in white tie and tails, appeared at her side, and *his* name was announced. She placed her left hand in his for balance; she curtsied deeply and then recovered her upright position. She was wildly applauded. This went on alphabetically girl after girl until the room was lined with two double rows of daughters and fathers.

The lights came up; the orchestra played and the fathers in black whirled the daughters in white accompanied by happy cheers. Everyone was relieved that no one had fallen down. When the waltz was finished, the fathers marched off, leaving the girls in a clump on the floor. It was now the stroke of midnight.

The lights were dimmed again. In the hush there appeared from the gloom a white-draped caterer's table bearing an enormous gilt pumpkin. This was rolled to the center of the floor, and the girls, as rehearsed, took up their positions around it. Each took in her hands one of the ribbons that hung from the pumpkin.

"Ladies and gentlemen, the moment when dreams come true. Which one of these beautiful girls will be this year's . . . *Cinderella*?" The announcer's voice crackled with excitement. As the drums rolled, the girls pulled their ribbons, each one praying there was nothing on the end of it. At last a cymbal crash announced that one of them had pulled from the pumpkin a tiny clear plastic slipper. There were shrieks, there were hugs, there was untold relief as thirty-nine girls dashed off the floor and one stood buck-toothed and forlorn in the spotlight. "Ladies and gentlemen, this year's Cinderella is . . . Annie Sandra McKie!" There were waves of applause. The committee could often arrange to have the slipper fall to the girl of their choice, but one look at Mrs. Slugg gnashing her teeth showed that this year hadn't been one of them.

"Oh, Muffin will be so pleased! Annie's a darling girl," whispered Mrs. Bundle.

"And now," intoned the announcer, "the moment of supreme excitement." A red carpet was speedily unrolled from the stage to Annie. One spotlight was trained on her, and she stood gallant and resigned; another lighted the empty stage. "The moment when Cinderella will meet her . . . Prince Charming!" The orchestra crashed a triumphant chord as into the spotlight stepped . . . Howard Slugg.

"Oh, God," said George. "What have I done?"

The audience broke into mad applause. Prince Charming was always some awful grunt, but really, Howard Slugg was beyond their wildest dreams. He stood grinning happily, his head settled troll-like deep between his shoulders. Then he surpassed their most fevered expectations by falling off the platform.

More applause. Howard was crawling around in the spotlight, hitting the floor with his palms, trying to find his glasses. The orchestra struck up "The Most Beautiful Girl in the World" as if all this were exactly according to plan. Annie tripped lightly down the carpet to Howard, smiling graciously. She lifted him to his knees, lost him, got him all the way to his feet, and waltzed away with him.

The audience went mad with joy. The other debutantes flocked back onto the floor accompanied by their young escorts, who threw themselves into the waltz with an ecstatic vigor that sent their tails whirling beautifully out behind them. Billy Flack fell out of his box in the first tier onto the dance floor for the second year in a row. Backstage the two house detectives in charge of secluding Howard were being roundly and soundly fired by the joint efforts of Mrs. Slugg and the hotel manager.

Everyone agreed that it was the most heavenly Cinderella Ball they'd ever been to, and the young people danced till the orchestra went home well after four A.M.

The next day the Pittsburgh *Herald* ran a full two pages on the ball, including studio portraits of each of the debutantes and a large photograph of Prince Charming and Cinderella seated side by side on the dais. Annie smiled serenely; Howard slumped forward over one arm of the throne, completely unconscious. ". . . Prince Charming, Mr. Harold Slugg, shown here assisting Cinderella with her shoe," ran the caption. "Mr. Slugg has recently completed his studies and will join the Slugg National Bank and Trust Company next month as assistant vice-president."

"Oh, Mr. Bundle," shrieked the girls in his office as they had done every post-ball morning for twenty-five years. "Oh, don't it sound bee-u-tee-ful!"

"I'd give anything to have seen Mr. Bundle waltz with Miss Margaret. So grown-up now! So pretty!"

"Next year, when Merry comes out, I'm going to take you all," he said.

"Oh, Mr. Bundle!"

All day, snow fell lightly. The weather had turned extremely cold; there was a shiver of ice along the banks of the Allegheny River. "When I was a boy it used to freeze solid every winter," said Mr. Mortpestle sadly to his wife as they sat in their car in the cold and dark, part of a long line of cars approaching the club for Lisa Sutton's coming-out party. "We used to skate there." The line of cars inched forward.

"Yes, dear." Far along the line ahead they could see the snow dancing downward in the headlights.

"My father used to get off the train on the north side and walk across the river on the ice to his office every morning," he added after a bit.

"Yes, dear," his wife chanted fondly. It was many years since the river had frozen. The chemicals regularly added to it by Mortpestle Steel, Bundle Coke and Chemical, Jones and Laughlin, Byers Pipe, Shenango, and others had lowered the freezing point of the solution such that freezing was no longer thought likely anytime before the next ice age.

"No fish in the river anymore," he added at length. "There used to be." His thoughts seemed caught on the river tonight. The stream of cars before them inched slowly forward as all around the timeless snow folded them close between the golf course and the stark trees. "Do you sometimes feel," he asked, turning earnestly to his wife, "do you sometimes feel that everything is changing?"

At the head of the line, a half-mile before the Mortpestles, the cars pulled up one by one to the door of the club. All month rumors had flown that the Suttons had spent ten thousand dollars on decorations alone, not to mention having Meyer Davis in person! The young people were ecstatic at the theme of the party: the porte cochere, the enclosed entryway, and every room inside the club were hung with hand-blown globes of milk glass in triple clusters, and a sound system in the entryway played "There's a Pawnshop on the Corner in Pittsburgh, Pennsylvania."

"Get it?" cried Mort to his guests in the receiving line. "Get it? Pittsburgh, Pennsyl-van-ee-ah?" He was a picture of innocent rapture. Some seven hundred guests had accepted, of the one thousand invited. That was two hundred more than the social secretary predicted and two hundred more than the club could accommodate. In the last three days, workmen had built a temporary ballroom over the practice green, lined it with dark green draperies, hung it with glass balls, and installed space heaters.

"It'll ruin the lie, they'll never get that green smoothed out," voices muttered along the line. "Fella ought to be shot. Yes, good evening, Mrs. Sutton. So charming, so glad. Lovely girl you got, Sutton. Come on, Marge, I need a drink."

Upstairs in the ladies' room the debutantes were feverish. Very few had had much rest the night before; when at last the ball was over they had kissed good night whoever was handy and drifted up to their hotel rooms to find that someone—Ralph and Pepper, as it happens—had unscrewed all the numbers from the bedroom doors. Most of the girls eventually got a few giggly hours' sleep in some room or other. When they got home they spent the rest of the day bathing and doing their hair. The out-of-town boys, they had all learned at dinner, had gotten lost trying to drive from Pittsburgh to Sweetwater and spent the day at the Carnot Roller Rink.

"It was *great*," said Pepper. "Pear won a coupon to the Dairy Queen for doing the hokey-pokey."

"Yeah, we promised we'd all come back real soon. We thought we'd go back tonight."

The girls compared the dinners they had been to, exchanged lipsticks, reapplied powder, and helped pin each other's hair up.

Then they hurried down to rejoin their dates in the receiving line. Everywhere were ladies in white uniforms passing trays of champagne. "Oh, nurse . . . I'm worse," called the Algonquin Twins, snatching off glasses two at a time. "I'll take two of these and call you in the morning."

It was not thought strictly proper to eat or drink before greeting the host and hostess, but the receiving line was very long. After everyone in it had had a glass or two, most of them couldn't see that it was strictly necessary to greet the host at all, and so the line dissolved. By 12:30 the two ballrooms were jammed with dancers so tightly that they could barely clear a space for Mort's ceremonial waltz with Lisa. Those in the temporary ballroom didn't hear it at all. They were dancing to the music of the Meyer Davis Orchestra piped in from the front room, interrupted at unexplained intervals by short, static blasts of "There's a Pawnshop on the Corner in Pittsburgh, Pennsylvania," still blaring away in the gelid entryway.

Philip joined the first waltz with Mrs. Sutton. "It's being a great success," he said to her.

"I'm glad you think so, cookie; you don't know what this means to Mr. Sutton."

"I can imagine," said Philip.

"Can you?" asked Miriam Sutton. "Look, cookie, I'm too old and fat for this. Why don't you buy me a drink." He found her a seat at a nearby table and went to get her some bourbon. At the bar, as he waited to be served, he heard snatches of conversation.

"The dinner party at the Wrights' was so crowded, Marge had to set up a deuce in the powder room. . . ."

"It's damn good bubbly, I'll say that for him."

"She's a beautiful girl, though, you'll have to admit that."

"Look, there's Mrs. Spoonbill! She said she'd regretted!"

"But my point is, it seems as if everything's changing. I mean . . . do you know what I mean?"

Philip found Miriam still alone when he returned. She was watching Mort closely as he danced first with Jenny, then with Muffin. Even across such a crowded room you could hear his shrill laugh.

"You know what he wanted to do?" said Miriam to Philip, accepting her drink. "He wanted to have a big brooch made for me, with three big diamond balls . . . just for tonight." She took a long drink and shook her head. "What do you make of a man like that?"

"I don't know," said Philip.

"Don't you?"

At 1:30 supper was served in the dining room. Mort had brought in a caterer from New York.

"There's a black gushy thing in my omelet," Mr. Spoonbill complained to his wife. "See, here's another one. I told you we shouldn't have come." Petulantly he picked out his truffles while his wife signaled to the waiter.

"Dick's coming with the sweet buns, dear, and the sausage is all right," she said.

On her other side Avery Mortpestle was saying, "Nothing used to change when I was a boy. Did it? I don't think it did. I must ask Alida."

Old Mr. Sumter was eating roast beef. "When we were down in Virginia hunting, a fella put us up. Had a whole cellar full of wine. He showed me. Used to drink it every night with dinner. That's right. Every night, company or not. That's right." He signaled for more milk. Supper, he found nowadays, was the whole point of these parties. He'd come if his wife insisted, but he only stayed till he'd had supper. Supper was extra good tonight, and he was glad. He hadn't liked his dinner. On nights when he didn't like dinner or supper, he took his wife home early and would pointedly, expressively, march into the kitchen and eat a bowl of cornflakes.

Lisa was cut in on every few steps. She danced for hours till her feet were bruised and the orchestra had played "I Could Have Danced All Night" eleven times. In between they played "Everything's Coming Up Roses." Monty Byers was paying her a lot of attention, and so was Jack Heinz, but everywhere she looked it seemed she saw George watching her, and it was getting on her nerves.

It was George's mother's idea that they stop seeing each other. It was *his* idea that they keep their marriage secret till after the year was up. (Of course, she'd have suggested it if he hadn't, but he didn't know that.) So, since this whole thing was *his* idea, she wished he'd grow up a little. He couldn't expect her to sit home on a tuffet. She wasn't a *nun*.

In fact, if he wanted to be that way about it, she could always have the marriage annulled. Prosser Mellon had danced with her twice already, and she'd had a crush on him since she was twelve. George had no right to stand there like her keeper, and she wished he would go away, and after a while he did.

Merry Bundle disgraced herself by throwing up in the ladies' room. Annette was so cross that she wouldn't help at all. Ann offered to go with Mr. Bundle to take Merry home and put her to bed. Jack carried the body upstairs, and to Ann's surprise he sat on the spare bed watching while Ann struggled to get Merry out of her gown and at last put her to bed in her underwear. "Am I in bed yet?" Merry kept moaning, and at one point she sat straight up and yelled, "Who's there?"

Their eyes met once across the comatose body of Jack's half-naked daughter. Then he snapped off the light and took her arm and they hurried back down the stairs to the car, for some reason full of suppressed laughter. The long, curving driveway was slick with packed snow. Jack set off too fast, and the car fishtailed wildly, then spun into some bushes. They shared a moment of panic. Jack tried the ignition. The wheels spun. "Stuck!" He giggled. "Never mind, I've got another one." And he ran back up the drive to the garage. Soon he returned in another car and they drove off.

The Titsworth brothers had a great idea. "Gonna be just what this party needs," they said. "Gonna show Mort how much we appreciate 'm." They vanished for about an hour, and when they returned they had with them eight dozen pairs of rented roller skates. "White for the ladies, black for the gennelmen. Size painted right on 'em. If you don't know your size, take a ten, that's a good size, that's what I wear." The young people joined in with a will.

Old Alida Beebe had stayed far past her usual hour. "The girl may be all right," she was saying to Avery Mortpestle as they performed a decorous box step. "Her father's a perfect jackass with a horse, but . . . Here, what was that?" A pretty young girl in flowing chiffon with auburn hair streaming behind her streaked past them with a rumbling noise, spun around once, and disappeared into the temporary ballroom. She was followed closely by two speeding boys in dinner jackets; one negotiated the curve and disappeared after the girl. The other went straight and crashed into the orchestra stand.

"Whoopsie," he said as he clambered to his feet and headed off again after the first two.

Soon the ballroom was filled with people on roller skates dodging among the dancers, dancing with each other, zooming suddenly off toward the supper room, where they were caught up short by the edge of the carpet, and fell headlong.

"Just the sort of thing I was saying, Alida," said Mr. Mortpestle mildly. "I don't believe we ever had skates at a ball, did we? I'm sure I would have remembered."

"So would I," said Alida. "Such a good idea. I wonder if they have my size."

The band played on in much the same spirit as their brother musicians on the *Titanic* played "Nearer My God to Thee." The skaters zoomed around and around the edge of the ballroom, while the dancers plodded in the middle. There was a spirited game of Crack the Whip during which several people rocketed into the string section and crushed at least one valuable cello. When the game of Fox and Hounds began, with Jenny as the fox and Alida Beebe the huntsman in full cry, blowing "Gone Away" on an ornamental horn she'd removed from above the fireplace, Meyer Davis said he really must be going. The fox went to ground in the pantry safely, and the foxhounds came to grief in collision with the omelet table, scattering eggs and truffles and piles of cinnamon toast all over the room. They lay in a heap with their skates in the air, howling and blaming each other. "Oh, dammit," said Alida, pulling up short at the door, "the hounds have lost the scent."

They went back into the ballroom, where the last of the musicians were just packing their cases and beating a retreat. For another hour they whizzed happily round and round the floor to the loud metallic blaring of "There's a Pawnshop on the Corner in Pittsburgh, Pennsylvania."

"Always one of my favorite songs," said Alida as at last she gave up her skates. "Grand party, Mort," and she shook his hand in both of hers. "Haven't had so much fun at a party in years. Look forward to seein' you in the huntin' field." Mort had tears in his eyes when he reported this conversation to Miriam.

The caterer seemed more entertained than anything at the events of the morning. Meyer Davis eventually sued Mort for damage to the cello and his reputation, since the story had been told and retold with embellishments up and down the East Coast long before Christmas was over. And it did in the end cost Mort thousands to repair damage to the practice green and the ballroom floor, but he would have considered it cheap at the price if it hadn't been for one thing: the news that sometime after dawn a boy named Randall Carpenter had been found dead, his car crashed into a concrete abutment on the Ohio River Boulevard—the fat boy the children called the Algonquin Twins.

CHAPTER 15

The Wind on the Water

The snow was lovely, dark, and deep that winter—too deep for outdoor sports. Athletics consisted of walking the loops or of snow sculpture supervised by the field-hockey coach. Some wits in the junior class managed to build a scale model of the Kremlin large enough to crawl around inside and were preparing a hammer-and-sickle flag on the sewing machine in the domestics room when the art-history teacher recognized the architecture and the grounds crew was sent to tear the edifice down.

Ann found herself much in sympathy with the come-hither bitterness of the frigid weather that closed them all in with such killing beauty. She preferred to take her afternoon walk alone that season, and one day she wrote an avant-garde poem about the alien shroudlike quality of the ice and snow in the woods. It was inspired partly by e. e. cummings, partly by Japanese haiku.

Over and over as she walked or dreamed or slept, she saw two still images: one was the lean, handsome face of Mr. Bundle as his eyes met hers over the undressed presence of drunken Merry; the other was of a car crushed against an arch of concrete with its nose pushed in like aluminum foil. Day after day the snowy world seemed to isolate her in blinding brittle light. She sent her poem to the *Atlantic Monthly,* from which it returned promptly with a form rejection. She submitted it to Beverly Dust, who was editor of the school newspaper. It duly appeared with all the punctuation and inverted word order corrected. At dinner, Jenny complimented Beverly on the winter issue and said it was too bad she hadn't thought of including that poem that starts, "I think I know whose woods these are . . ."

The seniors were writing their term papers for English class. These were meant to be their first exercises in research and reporting and therefore did not have to deal with literary subjects. Mamie Malinckrodt was writing a history of knitting with a passion that seemed nearly unhinged. She had finally gained what so many had sought for so long: permission to knit during classes (on the grounds that she was doing research). She also knitted during study hall, during prayers and hymns, and even sometimes in the bath.

Sally was writing a paper entitled "Trucks: The Clipper Ships of the Highways." Muffin, in a mood to admire whatever was solemn and symbolical, was struggling with T. S. Eliot's *The Cocktail Party*. Its themes of trinity and madness, and particularly of the difficulty of discovering who is sane and who is mad, who lost and who saved, even who is rude and who truly polite at a party, she found obsessively interesting. The more obscure the drama became, the more she believed in it and the more she was relieved, for it gave her hope that God, like T. S. Eliot, might have a purpose for even His most ambiguous behavior.

Ann's subject came from a suggestion from Miss Barney, who stopped her on the snowy sidewalk in the early blackness of a midwinter evening as students and faculty streamed into the yellow warmth of Pratt Hall for supper. It was shortly after her poem had appeared in the school paper. Ann remembered afterward the scent of woodsmoke on the air from houses along Main Street and the fact that Miss Barney still wore an ornament made of small Christmas balls, red ribbon, and plastic holly pinned to her wool coat, and a terrible Persian-lamb hat. Did Ann read Archibald MacLeish? she wanted to know.

Of course Ann had read that "a poem must not mean, but be," and she knew by heart the sonnet "The End of the World" and found it deeply depressing. Often, when putting on her bloomers for volleyball or struggling to make conversation with Mr. Oliver at lunch, she would find herself swiftly taken by the image of the circus sideshow, the absurd participants, the absorbed audience, and then of that awful shift of perspective when the top blew off, revealing the blankness of "nothing at all." It was many years before it occurred to her that it was possible to distinguish between the haunting vividness of the metaphor and the truth of what it implied, to embrace one without the other. And in between were times when the image so perfectly accorded with her own depression that she later wondered if the poem had suited her state of mind or caused it.

At any rate, it was not the much-anthologized poems that Miss Barney spoke of, but the verse drama *JB*, about the trials of Job.

JB was a riveting choice for Ann. It afforded her (in afternoon study hall) one of those peak lifetime moments of illumination that perhaps can occur only when one is eighteen. She found the play to be about trying to reconcile the irreconcilable imperative. She found, summed up in a couplet, the simple truth she'd avoided for so long, the paradox that one had to accept because it explained everything else: If God is good, He isn't God; if He's God, He isn't good.

She got an A on her term paper, followed by a stern talking-to from Mrs. Umbrage, who had noticed that in Pisco on Sunday she no longer bowed her head when the minister prayed, or went forward to receive Communion, or stood with the rest of the congregation to recite the collects and confessions.

"It's extremely disrespectful and an embarrassment to the school," said Mrs. Umbrage. "Many of the townspeople have remarked on your behavior, and I must say I think it reflects very poorly on the way you were brought up—what would your mother say?"

"It's not disrespectful, it's just the opposite," said Ann stubbornly. "I respect other people's beliefs too much to pay lip service to them when I can't believe them myself. 'If God is good He isn't God, if He's God, He isn't good.' I respect your right to believe in Him, but you must respect mine not to."

"I'm not questioning your right to *believe* anything you like. It's your behavior I'm concerned with. I will not have the townspeople talking about us as they surely shall if this continues. As long as you are a Miss Pratt's girl, you will stand and sit and recite with the rest of us."

Only Jenny was unimpressed. "It only makes a difference if you think that God is a person," she told Ann.

"Of course He's not a person, He's a being," said Ann.

"Being, person, it's still a matter of thinking that God either loves you but isn't powerful enough to keep you safe, or that He doesn't really love you. Just like Mommy and Daddy. Those aren't the only choices, you know—it depends on God agreeing with your definition of good. Suppose God is in everything and loves everything equally, good and bad?"

"But that's impossible—what would be the point?"

"Who said there was a point?"

"There *is* a difference between good and evil!"

"I didn't say there wasn't a *difference*. I just said God may value them differently than you do."

Ann found this argument perverse and baffling and declined to discuss it further. The notion thrashed disturbingly in her mind for several days, but finding no purchase, no foothold at all in her, it soon perished, leaving no mark.

Spring vacation came and went. The Suttons took a house in Sea Island again, but only Sally Titsworth was invited to join them. Two days after they arrived, Ralph and Pepper Titsworth turned up. They had nowhere else to go because their mother was in Reno getting divorced from Dad Humphries and neither of them fancied the thought of spring in Painted Post. The Suttons welcomed them, but it was nothing like last year's house party. It seemed as if this year no one could talk of anything but college—the acceptance and rejection letters were due three weeks after the girls went back to school. Ralph kept walking around the beach club saying he was hoping to get into Simmons, but Garland and Katie Gibbs were his fallbacks.

After spring vacation the days were dominated by the looming of the event that would determine the course of their next four years—no, their whole lives.

It seemed ages ago that they had spent long autumn afternoons talking about where they hoped to go to college, meeting with the college adviser, and painstakingly printing in the long applications.

"It's a shame you did so poorly on the Boards you took last spring," Miss Withers had said to Muffin. Miss Withers had sparse blue hair and a pink scalp, and she wore a navy-blue suit with the kind of white blouse that has a sewn-on tie at the throat. "The colleges don't like to see a girl's scores go down after her practice tests—makes them think she's peaked. Well, I wouldn't advise you to try for Sarah Lawrence now, dear. Let's put you down for Bennett, shall we? If you still want to go to a four-year college when you finish, you can transfer perhaps. But a pretty thing like you will probably be married before then." She gave Muffin a hostile simper.

"Thank you so much," said Muffin, and applied to Sarah Lawrence, Penn, and Smith, with no fallback.

Miss Withers agreed that Jenny should try for Radcliffe. Her Board scores had been nearly perfect, except in math, and her grades were high, though privately Miss Withers thought her recommendations might not be. "A bit too sure of herself; inclined to be insolent," was what Miss Withers would have written. But then, they called Harvard the Kremlin on the Charles; perhaps Jenny's type was just what they wanted there.

Ann's record was just as strong as Jenny's, but for her Miss Withers was strongly pushing Bryn Mawr.

"That or Vassar, my dear. You can get in anywhere, of course, but you've spent your whole life in New England. Don't you think it would be broadening to get out and see another area?" For a girl of Ann's background, she couldn't help feeling, Bryn Mawr was just so much more *suitable* than Radcliffe.

"But, Miss Withers, I really prefer not to go to an all-women's college," Ann explained firmly. "Life is coed, and I think school should be too."

"That's such a minor concern, dear. Take my word for it, you'll find Bryn Mawr as stimulating as you could want." Ann applied to Radcliffe.

Because Lisa was an officer of the school, Miss Withers felt she could apply to any of the better middle-ranking schools, although her Boards were low and her grades just above average. "Now, Wheaton or Connecticut, they'll take you in a shot, my dear, because they're looking for the well-rounded type. They know a girl with a record of leadership at Miss Pratt's will offer them just as much as some greasy grind with straight A's from the local high school." Thinking it over, Miss Withers had concluded that from Miss Pratt's Lisa could probably even make Sarah Lawrence.

Sally was home on suspension during the weeks the seniors were making their college decision, but Miss Withers had a brief conversation with Sally's mother and that was all that she felt necessary. Of course Sally's records were poor, but admissions staffs had a language for girls like Sally. "A late bloomer," Miss Withers would write, "popular, well-rounded, a little slow to find herself academically." The admissions officer would understand her to mean that Sally was the granddaughter of Mrs. Kellog from Michigan, and, of course, a Miss Pratt's girl. Sally would go straight to one of the more social junior colleges, then marriage and four spoiled babies—no, three, Miss Withers decided; the girls were having smaller familes now. Lazy, probably. Miss Withers had seen so many girls exactly like Sally arrive as new girls, return for their tenth, their fifteenth, their twenty-fifth reunions, that it bored her think how easily she could write Sally's life story.

The week the college letters were due, the entire senior class became obsessive with anticipation. They talked of little else. Never before had they been so keenly aware of the untruth of so many lessons on which they were raised. Good things come to those who wait. Every cloud has a silver lining. The Lord helps those who help themselves. Blessed are the meek, for they shall inherit the earth. It isn't whether you win or lose, it's how you play the game.

Never before had they seen with such unnatural clarity that, past experience to the contrary, life was in fact placidly indifferent to how badly they wanted whatever they wanted, and that it would satisfy some and disappoint others with serene disregard for their view of the justice of the case. It was not only how gallantly you played the game that mattered, but also how many cards you were dealt in the first place. Among the senior class there were many faces gray with lack of sleep, taut with nervousness.

"If I don't get into Connecticut my father will kill me. He'll murder me. He says all the time what a dummy I am. He doesn't know how *hard* I try . . . oh . . . yes, thank you" (proffered tissue, muffled sobs).

"I know Miss Withers was wrong about my College Boards. I

can't get into my first choice, I can't get into my fallback. If I don't get in anywhere, I'll kill her. I might as well. I mean, what else can I do if I can't even get into Bennett? I might as well just kill her. I *knew* I should have applied to . . ."

"If I don't get into Radcliffe, I'm going to die. I don't *want* to go to Vassar, I don't *want* to go to Smith. If I have to go to school in the woods with nothing but girls, I'll never get married."

"You know, it's practically life and death, you know? I mean, it can change your whole life. Suppose the one man in the world that you're supposed to marry is at Yale or someplace, and suppose if you get into Briarcliff you'll meet him at a mixer but if you go to Hollins you never meet him? I mean, are you supposed to be an old maid your whole life just because of a letter? That's sitting over there in your dorm right this minute? I mean, may I please be excused, please, Miss Barney, I think I'm going to . . ."

Many plates of Jell-O sat uneaten at lunch as the word spread—no one knew its source—that the college letters were definitely on the mail tables back in the dorms.

Ann and Jenny both got into Radcliffe. They embraced with a shout of triumph and accepted by return mail. Muffin could tell by the fatness of her three envelopes that she'd been accepted everywhere she applied. She didn't bother to open the letters; she just sat down on her bed and wept with relief. Lisa was turned down at Sarah Lawrence and Connecticut, made the waiting list at Wheaton, and was accepted at Briarcliff. She put on a happy smile. "I never wanted to go to four-year college," she said. "Now I won't even have to fight with Big Mim about it—I can just have a two-year party!"

Sally was turned down at Bennett, Briarcliff, and Pine Manor. She came into the four-room after the bell rang for the first athletic period and threw the three short letters of rejection on Muffin's bed. "What the fuck am I going to do?" she demanded. Their euphoria froze like a palpable cloud in midair and hung there as they turned to look at Sally and then one by one at each other. She didn't get in anywhere? Didn't get in *anywhere*? They'd never heard of that happening.

"Now what the fuck am I going to *do*?" Sally repeated. No one spoke. What the fuck *was* she going to do?

What did people do? Travel? Why? Where to? Who with? Get a job? Sally? Doing what? Miss Pratt's was a *prep* school. It prepared you for college, that was what came next. What else was there to do?

Mr. Titsworth was soon on the phone to Miss Withers. He laid her out in lavender, was the delicate way she described their conversation, which apparently ranged freely over the subjects of Miss Pratt's very high tuition, the competence of the college-placement office, the school's future standing among college-preparatory schools, and what he was pleased to call "you juiceless old bluestockings."

"As far as I can tell, the only thing she's learned there in three years is how to barf in a train station," he was reported to have bellowed into the phone. "I thought the least you were going to do in return for my six thousand bucks was to get her into someplace that might teach her something useful . . . like *typing* or *cooking*."

Miss Withers was on the phone to all the junior colleges in the East who had for so many years enjoyed a symbiotic relationship with the likes of Miss Pratt's. She tried the old line that had been so effective twenty years ago, that a C from Miss Pratt's was like a B+ from a public high school. The admissions officers were unimpressed. Miss Titsworth's unexceptional interview, her academic record, and especially this suspension here—three weeks for "unseemly behavior"?—no, thank you, they could not reconsider. Competition was stiffer than ever, Miss Withers should know, it was the beginning of the postwar baby boom entering college, and there was the draft, of course. Very few youngsters took a year off as they had in the old days for fear of landing in the army. But the draft didn't apply to the girls—Miss Withers was sure. Nevertheless, as the draft loomed more insistent for the boys, even the girls' schools noted that every youngster who could sign her name seemed to seek the haven of college. Perhaps it was in sympathy for the boys, perhaps it was some sort of sporting instinct not to take advantage of the accident of sex, jaunting about Europe or something while their playmates were having their heads shaved at Fort Dix.

"Never mind," Mrs. Umbrage remarked serenely, when Miss Withers reported her failure. "*Plus ça change, plus c'est la même chose."* She laughed gaily. "Aren't they funny, how they take it all so seriously. If they don't go to one school, they'll go to another. If they don't go to any school at all, they'll do something else. What difference could it make? Chicken fricassee for supper tonight, Miss Withers. Your favorite, isn't it? There's the dingle—come along."

The last weekend in April was the last open weekend of the spring. Muffin Bundle was taking Ann with her to join her parents for the Maryland Hunt Cup. They got almost no sleep the night before they left, partly because they were so excited and partly because Beverly Dust kept the whole corridor awake by screaming into her pillow to make her voice hoarse and sexy. Beverly was going to Senior Weekend at Hotchkiss.

By six o'clock Sunday night the last of the weekenders were back. As the girls sat down to thin soup and Euphrates wafers, the school closed its doors to the outside world for the long month of tapping, exams, dates, germans, last sermons, last government papers, last farewells. "Did you have a good time?" asked the new girls at Beverly's table, breathless.

"It was a panic," said Beverly. "Just a panic. The band played 'What'd I Say' till midnight, and everyone did the nigger twist. You name it, we did it." The new girls sank into a reverie of moonlight and corsages. Beverly was still wondering what she should have done about her date's gas. I mean, was it right to just pretend she didn't notice it? Or would it have cleared the air to say, "He who smelt it dealt it" or "Silent but deadly" or hold a lighted match to the seat of his pants and pretend to wait for the explosion the way her brothers would do? Boy, she never even heard that anyone could fart nonstop for two days.

"How was it? How was it?" demanded Jenny and Lisa and Sally after supper. They were sitting in a circle on the floor in the four-room over the Sara Lee banana cake and some instant Medaglia d'Oro they'd bought illegally to celebrate Ann and Muffin's homecoming.

"Fabulous!"

"Heaven!" Ann and Muffin exclaimed simultaneously.

"The race was incredible . . . the horses were all at least seventeen hands. They were all taller than our heads at the withers. . . ."

"Oh, and we saw this jockey get trampled, his collarbone was crushed to a powder, and another horse threw his rider and kept racing with his reins and stirrups flying . . ."

"Wait a minute, wait! Where did you stay? Who did you see? What did you eat?" Those left behind and starved for outside stimulation looked forward all weekend to the pleasure of every vicarious detail. And those who had been away looked forward to the retelling, so much so that it was often hard to know, Ann thought, of the experience or the account they gave of it, which was the more vivid reality.

After spending the night with friends of the Bundles' on the Maryland shore, they'd arrived at the racetrack several hours before the race, to have a tailgate picnic and to walk the course and see the horses in the paddock. Ann was struck that three times in the first ten minutes she thought she saw someone in the crowd she knew who turned out to be someone else. Eventually she realized that virtually everyone in the crowd simply looked and dressed like the people she already knew. They ate with three or four other couples, friends of the Bundles'. With their fried chicken, Mr. Bundle gave Ann and Muffin each a chilled green bottle of beer, despite his wife's murmurs of protest. He gave Ann a wink as well, which for some reason warmed her to the core.

After lunch they walked up the sloping green fields where the course was laid out, to the paddock. Mr. Bundle explained to Ann that the Maryland was the toughest timber course in the world.

"But I thought the Grand National—"

"Not a timber course. A lot of their big fences are hedges, and a horse can skim through them. Here you jump clean or you get hurt." Ann looked with awe at the solid post and rail they were passing. Its top beam was at her eye level. It had to be five and a half feet high. "Takes a lot of heart, this race," he said.

They joined the others at the paddock, which they had permission to enter because Mr. Bundle was a master of foxhounds and an honored subscriber. Ringed around the outside were expen-

sively dressed sportsmen trying to talk their way into the paddock without the cherished pass, and without success. Inside,
Mr. Bundle pointed out to Ann an enormous black horse whose
coat had a reddish glow, almost the color of eggplant. "Gay
Abandon," he said. "My friend Burt Painter won the Huntcup on
that horse's grandsire in 1946. They've been trying to breed
another winner ever since—they think they've got him this
year. I do too. 'Scuse me—I want to have a word with Burt."

Ann and Muffin made their way off by themselves, getting as
close to the huge animals as they dared. The horses were being
walked in a wide circle to keep them calm and distracted from
one another. Some wore hoods of racing silk to prevent their
wasting nerve and energy shying or fighting. Ann and Muffin
studied the number behind each horse's saddle, then consulted
the program to see which horse was which.

"Green-and-white silks, No Trump—wait . . . No Trump's a
gray. Oh, it's Tillery's Spree—isn't that the horse you drew in
the pool? Oh, my God, look at this chestnut! Look at the head!
Lord, that's pretty!" Muffin found each horse more beautiful
than the last, but Ann's heart was firmly with Gay Abandon.

"Yes, he's truly huge," said Muffin, "and look at him dance!
Beautiful moves. Oh, here, look here, this is Sultan's War. He
won two years ago, I think. Let me look in the program . . ."
But Ann wasn't looking at Sultan's War. She was following Gay
Abandon with her eyes and thinking some stirring thoughts
about the sport of kings, and at the same time, without con-
sciously dwelling on it, registering the fact of the long black tes-
ticle sacs that swung between the horse's legs like a kind of
bird's nest. And it was that sac that made the difference between
these spirited creatures and the foolish nags she had bullied as a
girl of ten. And that was where they carried the "heart" needed
to face a test like the Maryland, and was that too where the boys
and men she knew carried their most precious qualities, their
nerve and their heart? And what a strange arrangement to carry something so precious in so exposed a location, outside the
body; it must make them nervous. And did men's sacs look like
that, and if so, where in their pants did they put them?

Mr. Bundle came up behind them and took each girl by an elbow. "What's wrong, did I startle you? It's almost time for the

riders to be up—let's go down by the thirteenth. You can't see the whole course as well as from the hill, but you see the biggest fence right under your nose."

Mr. Bundle watched the start through field glasses. Ann enjoyed how Muffin threw her whole body into helping the horses along, crouching slightly as they reached the first fence, then straightening with a spring as they flew over. Then at the third fence there was a pile-up and one rider fell. In a flashing gap between horses, Ann saw that he'd rolled or been kicked under the fence, and he lay there as the rest of the field thundered down upon him. With sick horror she pictured his view (if he was alive) of the narrow chests, the stirrups and girths, and the melon-shaped bellies as horse after horse bore down on, and over him.

As the ambulance bounced across the field toward the fallen rider, the field swept on around the first loop and back toward them, all the while Muffin excitedly taking each fence with them, and Ann very still, as if she could prevent another accident by staying frozen. There was another pile at the thirteenth fence, right in front of them. "Go, Jailer, go! . . . Oh, damn, he's down!" howled Muffin. It was the horse she'd drawn in the pool. "No, he's up—but no rider—he's going on!" The crowd began to laugh as Jailer valiantly took his place back in the lead, gamely holding to the course and leaping with the rest.

"Jerks," said Mr. Bundle. "There's nothing funny about a horse loose on the course." Just as he spoke, Jailer stepped on his own flapping reins and fell. He rolled frantically, with three feet thrashing the air, one leg dangling strangely, and from far away you could hear him shriek with terror to find his feet in the sky and the monster gravity attacking him from behind. Ann worried about him all through that night until Mr. Bundle found out for her that although his leg was broken, he'd been put in a cast and if the leg healed well, he'd be kept for stud.

Gay Abandon had been at the front of the field from the start, and when Jailer fell, he took the lead. Mr. Bundle was looking through the glasses again. "They're over the sixteenth—Gay Abandon's still in front! . . . My God, look at that pace! He can't keep that up for another mile—but *damn*, look at him move! Atta boy, Allie!" The girls strained to see, but the horses were small distant streaks without the glasses. "Come on," said Mr. Bundle, "let's run up to see the finish—that's where we'll see a horserace!" They began to run, Mr. Bundle explaining to Ann that Burt Painter's young son Allie was riding Gay Abandon and Mr. Bundle thought he was letting the horse use himself up too soon . . . but maybe Allie knew his own mount . . .

As the horses came around toward the last stretch, only six of thirty who started were still in contention. Gay Abandon was in the lead, and the crowd was going crazy. No one could believe he could set that pace for three miles. No Trump, the favorite, was closing fast on Gay Abandon, but his jockey was using the whip so hard you could see the lather splatter with each blow. Allie Painter never touched the whip, as if he knew exactly what his horse had in him, and knew he wouldn't have to ask unless there wasn't any more.

The two horses came down on the eighteenth neck and neck. The crowd was screaming, and both horses were running flat out, gulping up turf with huge pounding strides, but when they reached the fence, Gay Abandon didn't jump. He just plowed right into it, smashed through the two heavy top boards, and fell on the ground on the other side with a long splintered shaft of timber sticking out of his side.

Muffin, Ann, and Mr. Bundle walked together, speechless, to where the blood drained out onto the grass, like the contents of a punctured wineskin. Presently the track vet came with a bottle of yellow fluid hanging upside down on a portable rack. Soon this was dripping slowly down a brown rubber tube, through a fat needle gleaming under the quivering black coat, now dull with sweat.

"Anesthetic?" whispered Ann.

"No," said Mr. Bundle.

Just then Mrs. Bundle found them.

"Well, I have walked up and down that hill at least six times looking for you. Why didn't you come back to the paddock? Bunky Hillyer drew No Trump and won the pool, you know, and she's so pleased—ninety-five dollars. She's going to buy cable-knit sweaters for both her girls . . . Oh, my God!" She turned from the sight of the horse's body with her hand clapped over her mouth.

"Ann . . . Muffin!" she called brightly over her shoulder, her back to them. "Come along, girls, or we'll be late to the . . . to the . . . Did you hear that Mrs. Hillyer won the pool? She's so thrilled. They're on an awfully tight budget, you know." As Ann and Muffin walked quietly on together in the sun, they could hear her talking to Mr. Bundle, her voice rising and falling wildly behind them: ". . . your judgment sometimes, honestly, I could . . . they'll have the most *awful* nightgowns—oh, you know what I mean—nightmares . . . now, *why* did you let them stand there and gawk at that gore, will you kindly just explain? . . . oh, never mind!"

"Will the Painters still want to give a party?" Muffin asked her father when they were in the car.

"Of course," he said.

By the time they reached the Painters' farm, the stableyard was full of cars, and more were parked on the green lawn at the side of the house. Burt Painter was in the yard greeting new arrivals. He was beaming drunk, with his eyes full of tears; he embraced Jack Bundle.

"Good to see yah, good to see yah. Helluva close call, wasn't it?"

"Your boy rode a fine race," said Jack.

"I know he did. Say, these your girls? We need some pretty girls, that's just what we need, Jack. Take 'em inside and get 'em to cheer Allie up. He rode a good race, didn't he? Proud of him. 'Scuse me a minute. Hello, there, good to see yah!" And he left them to greet some new arrivals.

The little stone house was already jammed to the doorways with guests smoking and talking and edging past each other sideways from one crooked, low-ceilinged room to the next. Mr. Bundle was soon stopped by friends.

"Say, Jack, d'ya hear about Nat Baily? Got planted at the third fence, that's the fella. Doc called the hospital an hour ago, says his collarbone's crushed to a powder. Never lost consciousness, either. *He*'ll never ride again. . . ."

"Bundle! Glad you're here, been wanting to ask you . . ."

Mrs. Bundle insistently herded the girls upstairs to the powder room. "Goodness, what a relief. I've been dying to tinkle all afternoon. Mr. Bundle *rushes* so. Aren't you just dying? I can never go in those chemical toilets they have at the race. I keep thinking someone will push it over and there I'll be with my girdle around . . . oh, you don't have to? Well, I'll just be a minute. Isn't this fun to be together again, just like the Cinderella Ball . . . and Lisa's party! Oh, but the poor Carpenter boy, wasn't that sad? He turned out to be an only child, you know. The mother'd been an AA for years, but she fell off the wagon and had to be locked up . . . poor Mr. Carpenter was a beau of Aunt Coco. She was one of my bridesmaids . . . Muffin, dear, would you mind turning on the faucet for me? . . . my old nurse used to say that running water . . . perhaps if you girls want to go along downstairs after all . . ."

The girls made their way down the crowded hall into a room bare of furniture but full of guests. There were fox-hunting prints on the walls and a faint smell of hound even through the perfume and cigarette smoke. Near the door a big woman was attempting to drink from a vast silver bowl filled with crushed ice and lined with mint. Her nearest neighbors helped her to lift and tilt it and cheered as she took a good long draft. Then the bowl passed to Ann.

"Go on! Go on!" tall hands and voices urged. Ann took the bowl in both arms and tipped until icy sweet bourbon tasting something like toothpaste poured into her mouth.

"That's the stuff!" cried the tall voices. The bowl was an ancient challenge trophy engraved with rows of names of horses long dead. Ann passed to Muffin, who drank deeply. They stayed in the room for several more circuits of the bowl, or perhaps there were several bowls, saying little and drinking whenever they were offered.

"Thing I love is, without a glass, you can't tell how much you've had," they heard the big woman say. "I jus' drink till I start calling everyone awful names, and then Bill makes me go home."

"Speaking of Bill, where is Bill?"

"That's right, where is Bill? He was right here . . . is anyone standing on something squashy?"

"Ol' Bill, he might have just slipped away."

"Always underfoot."

"That's old Bill."

After half a dozen turns at the bowl, Ann's feelings about the scene began to change with lightning rapidity. She could no longer tell how long she had been standing there, how soon she might expect to leave, how long she had been feeling this shy pleasure, no, this romantic sadness, no, this cynical hilarity, no, this shock and irritation at the scene around them. In later years she would identify such feelings as stemming from nothing stranger than boredom, emotional trauma, and bourbon. But in the brightly lit tunnel of the mind at eighteen, her thoughts began to shimmer with the aura of the profound.

"'This is the way the world ends/ Not with a bang but a whimper,'" she muttered to Muffin crossly. Out on the green turf a gallant animal lay dead, and in here, gabbling, thoughtless humans soaked their brains in alcohol and exchanged inane remarks. Muffin nodded.

With great clarity and suddeness it had just come to Ann how really exhausting and sad life was. No one really understood her, did they? Not even Muffin. She fought back a hot threat of tears. And here she was, hundreds of miles from home with Mr. Bundle probably drunk as a lord somewhere by now and Mrs. Bundle upstairs in the bathroom with the water running. Feeling very indignant on her own behalf, she pushed out of the room and out the door. Muffin followed.

The world outside was heartbreakingly green. "'If God is good; He isn't God; if He's God, He isn't good.'" Ann brooded resentfully. Something was dreadfully wrong, with a world that caused her to suffer such restless misery, such . . . nausea . . . and yet, there was the killing beauty of her world . . . this world of wealth and privilege, of wastefulness, of costly pleasure . . . where a noble horse would break his own heart striving to please the vainglorious humans he trusted most . . . this world, the object of envy, but where she was seen as a "pretty girl," never as a poet . . . where she . . . thought she better sit down.

* * *

"So we tossed back some juleps," said Muffin.

"Did you really? You mean they passed it to you whenever you wanted?"

"Oh, yes, it was wonderful."

"Wonderful," Ann echoed.

"Then what?"

"Then we went out to the stable to get a little air, and we found this pile of about four dozen dead roosters."

Silence.

"You found what?"

"They have this big cockfighting tournament the night before the race. It's illegal, of course, but . . ."

"How gross."

"Oh, *Lisa!*" said Ann and Muffin together.

CHAPTER 16

Commencement

The month of May brought, not violets out of a dead land, but a cloud of oppressive heat that plodded in like a great reptile and squatted over the valley. Up and down Main Street, forsythia, azaleas, magnolias, and hyacinths force-bloomed at the same time, until the air was nearly fetid. Mrs. Umbrage canceled Field Day again, and there was the usual overwrought changing of the guard as outgoing officers of clubs and government passed their batons to the newly elected juniors. For their senior biology project, Muffin and Sally dissected a fish. They could not find its ovaries, but found it had worms instead. (Years later Sally was to have a recurrent dream, its source long forgotten, of a locked nest of long, flat, writhing tapes in the space within her where no baby ever grew.)

The seniors finished their last exams and sent out invitations to their graduation. Lisa was elected head marshal of the daisy chain, to no one's surprise. One morning a few days before graduation, the seniors were awakened at 6:30 in the morning by the sound of seventy new-girl voices, grouped on the lawn between the senior houses, singing.

Sleep-drugged faces began to appear at the windows. In the senior rooms others began removing their hair curlers and rubbing off Clearasil. "Shit, what's that racket?" said Jenny, from deep in her pillow.

By now every window was full of faces; the housemothers and a few girls had come out to the lawn in their bathrobes. The new

and old girls gazed across the bright early-morning distance
that separated them like their impending parting. Some cried
openly.

Good-bye old girls
Our old girls
And though we know you aren't gone yeeeet
On graduation day
We all will want to say
That our old girls we'll ne'er forgeeeeet!

After the last graduation practice, Sally talked Muffin into
slipping out behind the science building to study the weeds.

"This little green one is yummy stewed and served with hard-
boiled eggs, and this one here can be dried and made into tea,
and this one has special medicinal cancer-causing properties
when smoked."

"This is asinine, Sal—they can see the smoke back here from
the music-bungalow window."

"Oh, so what? If anyone comes, we'll run out screaming fire!
fire!"

"Oh . . . okay." They sat side by side in the dirt as they had
so many times before, leaning against the stone wall of the
building and looking off into the trees.

"Last time," said Muffin.

"Oh, I don't know—I could be persuaded to slip in a quick one
between daisy chain and graduation."

"You lie—you'll miss school just as much as everybody else. In
a week you'll be calling up long distance to sing 'In the Gloaming' to me over the telephone."

"Fat chance, babycakes. Mrs. Umbrage and Miss Withers can
take the gloaming and stuff it full of little green noogies."

"You lie in your teeth. Besides, they can't stuff a gloaming—
gloaming is twilight."

"Is it really? I thought it was one of those little wooden houses
with six sides that grandmothers have on their lawns. I did.
Why are you laughing at me? Quit it or I won't let you have any
matches."

"Okay, I have a serious question. Are you ready?"

"Have I really been having an affair with Mr. Oliver under his desk in study hall? Not what you'd call an affair, really, just the odd hand-job. . . ."

"Sally, what are you going to do?"

"What? You mean me? Oh, you mean, what am I going to do?"

"Right. What are you going to do?"

"I'm going to Chile in July to go skiing with Peaches, you know—her deb party on Daddy's plane?"

"Not exactly a lifetime plan, would you say? Besides, you don't even like Peaches."

"No, I know, but she wanted to invite Ralph and Pepper and she couldn't have them without me."

"Okay, but then what are you going to do, say, in September?"

"You know what, Muffin?"

"What?"

"Get off my back."

"Oh."

They smoked in silence for a while. "Besides," said Sally suddenly, "in a week I won't be calling you, I'll be at your house for your party. We could sing 'In the Gloaming' there, wouldn't that be nice? Just stop all the dancing and link arms there and sway . . . who'd you invite to escort you, by the way?"

"I haven't decided yet."

"What do you mean, you haven't decided? It's in a week! Some poor jerk's going to have to rent white tie!"

"Yeah, I know."

"So what's the problem? Hey, what about your friend Rutherford you used to catch tadpoles with?"

"Oh—it's such a once-in-a-lifetime thing, to be able to invite anyone in the world—all the people you've met all over—I didn't want it to be someone so *safe* . . ."

"Well, how about George, then? Hey, George'd be perfect. He *owns* a set of tails."

"Lisa and George are writing. They're not supposed to be, but they are."

"Really? How do you know?"

"Watch the mail table. She gets these business envelopes mailed from Richmond—he gets someone to mail them for him out of town, and I think he keeps a post-office box there for her to write him."

"God, why bother?"

"It's secret—they promised his mother. I guess she doesn't want any of us slipping up, so she's just pretending it's all off."

"I'll say. I haven't heard her mention the guy's name since Christmas, and aren't we getting quite a few letters from the Harvard Business School?"

"Don't ask me—I'm not her keeper."

There was another long silence. Muffin lit a fresh cigarette and began thoughtfully peeling the layers of paper apart at the end of the match.

"Hey, Sal?" she said, looking at the ground. "If I tell you something, will you promise never to tell anyone, ever?"

"Sure."

"I wrote to David Bell and asked him to escort me."

Sally froze. She felt a terrible chill of apprehension, and her first impulse was to get up and leave. Whatever was coming, she knew she was going to hate it.

"Uh-huh. David Bell. I thought you'd been kind of out of touch with him."

"I have."

"Did he write back?"

"No." Sally felt a deep rush of relief. Muffin said, "His wife did."

Sally looked at her. Muffin's clear wide eyes looked so baffled and hurt that Sally felt as if the pain would cut straight through to her. "Sally, what did I do to make him want to do that to me?"

Sally could see the scene: David Bell and his wife, laughing over Muffin's letter, so naive, so affectionate; she could just see them deciding how best to embarrass her. The anger ached in Sally's throat so that all she could do was shake her head. That's what happens when you try for something you're not supposed to get. That's what always happens. Sally knew it, and now Muffin knew it.

"I think I'll ask Chip Lacey to escort me."

"Chip!" cried Sally, wanting the other subject closed and shoved away and never mentioned again. "Well, all right, honey, but he's got about as much of the *je-ne-sais-quoi* as a raw carrot."

"I think I just had enough *je-ne-sais-quoi*. He's pleasant and kind and he likes me. Besides, I think Ann would like it."

"Pleasant and kind—that's a hell of a recommendation. Chip Lacey! That's like going to your coming-out party with your own brother."

"Not *your* own brother—"

"No, that's true. You could try Pepper—if you don't mind pouring him onto the dance floor—well, maybe not."

"Sally, Chip likes me, and at this point it's a welcome change."

"I guess so—but what if you marry him? Instead of babies you'll have all these little carrots—what'll they look like on horseback?"

"Christ, I didn't say I'd marry him—we're talking about one night!"

"All right, all right! Shit! Ditch the weeds! Here comes Miss Von Riehban!"

The juniors gave the farewell german, whose subject, as always, was the constancy of young hearts that have once been true to each other. (Scene: Solitary old woman on porch at twilight staring sadly at hands in lap. Year theoretically 2008, although costumes and rocking chair suggest Dust Bowl, circa 1930. Enter second old woman, stage left, gray wig slightly askew. "Excuse me, are you Mrs. Jones? They told me in town you might have a room to rent. Why . . . are you crying?"

"No, no, not at all—I've just been peeling onions—it's only that at this time of day, somehow I get to thinking about when I was a girl and the way I thought life would be."

Heavy sigh. Puts down suitcase. "I know what you mean. Goodness, it seems so long ago. But you know, something in your voice just now seemed to remind me . . . I once had a friend, ah, such a friend! How little we thought at the time what it was to have such friendship. Why, I haven't seen her in forty years, and yet I still miss her so . . . her name was Millicent."

"Millicent! But that's my name!"

After the German the whole student body linked arms and sang "In the Gloaming." They were joined by those housemothers and faculty members who had once been girls at Miss Pratt's.

* * *

In the gloaming
As we linger
You and I may shed a tear
Years from now
We'll still remember
Girlhood days we loved so dear!

Mrs. Umbrage, not an alumna, watched with Mr. O'Neill and
Mr. and Mrs. Oliver. Afterward the Daisies got up to sing for the
last time (except for the several times on graduation day when
they would sing for the guests of the school). Traditionally on
this night they sang their entire repertoire, amid an orgy of
weeping. Everyone looked forward to it very much.

The group began with a medley of Cole Porter songs, including a haunting solo by Jenny of a song called "Love for Sale,"
which, Mrs. Umbrage believed, might easily be interpreted as
having to do with the world's oldest profession. It was sand-
wiched between "You're the Top" and "Brush Up Your Shakespeare," so she let it pass. About five minutes later they sang a
jolly tune called "Who'll Bite Your Neck When I'm Gone":

Who'll put their monogram
On your little white diaphragm?
No telling how long
I'll last (be-doop-op-oooo)

Something in her stiffened. She leaned over to Beverly Dust
and asked her if she knew what a diaphragm was. "Oh, yes,"
said Beverly, who was sure it was something to do with her tum-
my. Well, Mrs. Umbrage knew, too. A diaphragm was a con-
traceptive. She stood suddenly, applauding, and announced that
the concert was over.

She would probably have taken it back if she could. In the roar
of rebellious fury that followed, she began for the first time in
her life to wonder if she should think about retiring. She didn't
think this action any more breathtakingly arbitrary than many
others. What was happening? Why were they so angry? When
had she seen girls angry in a body before? Never. Alone she
could handle them easily, as she had for decades, by manipulat-
ing their need for approval, by belittling them, by destroying

their faith in their own judgment. But in a group? What if all the girls were angry at the same time at the same thing? What if they stuck together and stood their ground? She commanded them to leave the hall at once. They did not. If anything, they drew together and moved toward her, yelling, weeping, demanding that the singing continue as it had every year. They demanded! They wept with rage instead of sentiment. God, how strange the young were—as if there were really anything left to weep for! She glared at them and they glared at her, and each saw a vision of a new future that made them tremble.

"Girls!" Miss Umbrage's voice projected above their stamping and shouting, although it seemed not to be unseemly raised. "Girls, I would remind you of the tradition that we leave this hall in silence, and that no one speak until tomorrow morning." She had no idea what she would do if their own passion to be united with the ritual subjugation of their mothers and sisters couldn't hold them. But it did. Slowly, over a period of minutes that seemed like hours, the stamping and clapping declined, the shouts were lowered to angry talking, to whispering, and then to the voiceless murmur that was the sound of 140 young women crying. Silently they returned to their dorms, and in turmoil, with all the unspoiled scrupulousness that was best in them, they observed the rule of silence until the seven A.M. bell the next morning. And by that time, of course, their passion was muted. And besides, it was graduation day.

Ralph and Pepper Titsworth came to watch them get their diplomas, but neither of Sally's parents did. Philip and George were there, along with the whole Bundle family, Mrs. and Mr. Sutton and Buddy, the Laceys with Maude and Chip, and Mr. Rose and Malcolm. The daisy chain and the graduation ceremony went off without a hitch in brilliant sunshine. Several juniors heard Ralph say to George as the daisy chain wound by, "Don't you just love to see them all in white, knowing half of them will be on their backs before midnight?"

After the buffet lunch on the lawn, the Daisies gave their last official performance, during which the entire junior class was rounded up and locked inside one of the dorms out of earshot, as reprimand for the insurrection of the night before. By midafternoon the last senior had been crammed into the last station wagon with her suitcases and skis and record player and her stuffed animals, leaving a mountain of cartons and trunks to be sent on by Railway Express.

There had been many tearful scenes of parting in the hot fragrant nights of the last week. The old girls had said good-bye to the new girls, wept and wished on their rings, and said "Be Happy!" only to meet again at breakfast. The seniors had crept into each other's rooms after the last bell and talked until the moon went down, and made pledges and promises until they were too tired to talk. By graduation day they were practically wrung out with the pain of missing each other before they were even apart. When the actual moment of leaving came, it went just as fast, with a wave and a last shout and attention already turned to the first legal cigarette, the celebratory drink, and where parents, sisters and brothers, and boyfriends would meet that night for dinner.

These would be followed by days and nights of genuine sorrow—of missing a roommate's passionate interest in the most minute details of one's comings and goings. Very few would ever again have that particular kind of closeness with anyone, and some would miss it, although it wasn't perhaps a kind of intimacy that was particularly necessary. Many missed a special friend's sense of humor, and for months—even years—after found themselves saying, "I know just how Lolly would have laughed at that!" But for the first few days no one felt anything so strongly as the elation of being free at last. And Sally, Muffin, Jenny, Ann, and Lisa were particularly spared any finality in parting, since they were going to meet on Friday in Pittsburgh for Muffin's coming-out party.

CHAPTER 17

June

$\mathcal{P}$ittsburgh had looked forward to Muffin Bundle's debut for years. There hadn't been a ball in the Bundle house since the party for Muffin's Aunt Julia, just before the Depression. (The week after she came out, Julia had broken her neck and died in the Green Hunter class at the Sewickley Valley Horse Show.) Old Mrs. Bundle refused to entertain at all during the Depression. She said it was in bad taste when so many were suffering, although toward the end of her life, when she was getting more dotty, she unbent so far as to give a birthday party for her little dog Seesue. All the hairy little guests sat on Queen Anne chairs around the dining table and were served filet mignon, and Seesue had sparkling diamond fillings implanted in her teeth.

Ann and Chip Lacey and Sally Titsworth drove out together from Greenwich. Philip Sterret was stopping in New York to bring Jenny. Ralph and Pepper Titsworth arrived a day ahead of schedule, fresh from a party on Long Island given for the famous Serena Arundel, which had ended, according to *Time* magazine, with the host's new hundred-thousand-dollar guest lodge burning to the ground. They said Pear would be along by Saturday if he got out of jail in time.

Muffin and Merry Bundle spent all day Friday driving back and forth to the airport to collect new arrivals. Between trips there were phone calls from guests driving in who said they were just off the boulevard in someplace called Alliquippa and would somebody please come lead them to where they were supposed to be.

On one trip to the Pittsburgh airport Merry ran into Mr. Sumter, the family lawyer, red-faced and furious. He'd been sent to meet his wife's grandniece, for whom he was giving a dinner dance before Muffin's ball tomorrow night.

"Never heard of such damn foolishness in my life!" he howled at Merry without preamble. "Plane's late—went to call my wife—what do you think happened? I got upstairs to the pay phones and every single one, *every* one, has a sign on it. 'Ladies.' That's what it says, like a powder room. Weren't any marked 'Men,' either. Silliest damn thing I ever saw. I ignored it. Started into one of 'em, and this fella comes over and points at the sign, says, 'This is a ladies' booth.' I said to him, 'Listen, sex has gotten a long way in this world, but it hasn't gotten to the AT&T!'

"Then, when I finished talking to my wife—she never heard of such a thing either—this other fella, bald fella, comes over grinning and he keeps tugging at my arm and saying something about a candied camera. There was a camera there, too, a huge black thing. Licorice, maybe. 'Smile!' he kept saying." Mr. Sumter imitated the deranged toothy smile. "He kept wanting me to sign some release and yelling something about the television. Know what I said? I said, 'I may be on my last legs, but I've got at least one good punch left in me, and *you're* going to get it!'"

Later, when Merry and her group left the airport, she saw Mr. Sumter, laden with niece and suitcases, running for his car with a flock of young men carrying clipboards running after him.

"Oh, please," they begged, panting. "Sir—for *Candid Camera*—just tell us your name . . ." He squealed away from the curb wearing an expression of ferocious rage, with the young men frantically writing down his license number.

At home, the young people lay in the sun around the Bundles' pool, gleaming with baby oil. Bumblebees meandered, droning, among the bordering pansy beds. Morning-glory vines covered the stone wall that banked up the pool against the slope down to the long meadow below. The bank this time of year was dense with white and gold honeysuckle, and its sweet fragrance mingled in the air with the smell of chlorine. Far down in the meadow, Mistress Moon was grazing. On the grassy terrace above,

Ralph and Pepper were fleecing Muffin's little brother in a high-stakes game of croquet.

From time to time Mrs. Bundle would appear in her tennis dress—of course, she hadn't had time to play tennis, but it was too hot to wear anything else—to report that another group of packages had been delivered by the Gift Corner. The list of gifts was by now well over three hundred. For the last two weeks Annette had had a woman in full time just unwrapping them, entering the name of the giver and the description of the gift on a numbered list in Muffin's white kid debutante book, and sticking corresponding numbers on the presents so Muffin could identify them when she came to write her thank-you notes. Then the presents had to be arranged on linen-covered tables, with the givers' cards, in the upstairs hall, where people could come and see them.

Muffin realized all too well that the gifts had almost nothing to do with her—that they were given to honor her parents and tradition itself. She had tried halfheartedly to impose her own personality on the process by suggesting that instead of gifts, contributions be sent in her name to the Watson Home for Crippled Children. But Mrs. Bundle said her grandmother would spin in her grave; it would be a dreadful affront to those who had always done things the usual way; and that was the end of it.

So now the upstairs hall was filled with rows and rows of scented satin hangers from the Women's Exchange, lace-covered sachets and traveling cases for gloves and lingerie, beaded evening purses, scarves, jewelry, at least a half-dozen gold charms engraved with a calendar, the day of her ball marked by a ruby or emerald chip. There were also belts, cashmere sweaters, lacy slips and nightgowns, monogrammed leather and silver picture frames, crystal ashtrays, antique pillboxes, perfume bottles, scented soaps and bubble bath, masses of flowers, many telegrams, and one gold yo-yo. Muffin was embarrassed and rather angry about it. She didn't want to be churlish when she was in fact nearly mad with joy at the luxury, the fun, the sense of incredible specialness that was hers because of this party her parents were giving her. But there was something about that row upon row of expensive objects that made her furious.

Her mother couldn't understand her attitude.

"But wouldn't any girl in the world be *thrilled* to have these lovely things? What good does it do for you *not* to have them, just because not everyone can? What harm can there be in your having a lovely season you'll remember all your life?"

Many years later it occurred to her that her anger at the presents may have had less to do with moral indignation than with a desire to be seen as herself. If the white linen tablecloths had been stacked with something she wanted, like new tack for her horse or finely bound books, she might have behaved quite differently. But by then, of course, it was years too late to take back the hurtful bewildering things about waste and stupidity she'd said to her mother.

The night before the ball, the girls had dinner alone together on the wide stone porch at the side of the Bundles' house overlooking the Ohio River Valley. Muffin pointed out the tall stacks across the river that belonged to the family mill, and to the Mortpestle plant. Charles Dickens had said that Pittsburgh looked to him like hell with the top taken off, but many of the stacks no longer belched smoke and flames. Decades before other cities grew alarmed, the Mellons had pushed Pittsburgh into a program of stringent air-pollution control. The great art collections of the Carnegies, the Mellons, and the Fricks that had been moved to New York and Washington for safety were now, ironically, housed in more deleterious atmosphere than Pittsburgh's. Here on the Heights the air was sweet and green as the lawns and the honeysuckle. In the twilight the girls watched a hummingbird, scarcely larger than a bumblebee, buzzing the flowering hedge beneath the porch, a tiny hovercraft. They ate rare meatcakes and scalloped potatoes and drank cold beer from monogrammed glasses. It was their first evening together not as schoolmates but as friends.

"Where will we all be fifteen years from now?" asked Jenny. There was a long, dreamy silence.

"Beverly Dust will be a housemother at Miss Pratt's," said Ann.

"And Linda Gooch and Sandy Hawley will be living together raising poodles and drinking beer in their undershirts. . . ."

"And Mamie Malinckrodt will be knitting baby booties for the Women's Exchange. . . ."

"But where will we be?"

They had finished their coffee. Their cigarette ends glowed in the dark, and they could just see each other's outline as they tapped their ashes into the glass plates streaked with lemon meringue.

"Whatever happens," said Muffin, "we'll always have each other. Well, I mean, at least you'll always have me—nothing will change the way I feel about you all."

"Me too," said Sally.

Ann took Muffin's hand silently. Jenny nodded. Lisa, who privately expected to leave her roommates in the dust as far as glamour, success, and social conquest were concerned, just as she had outstripped them in popularity at Miss Pratt's, said, "Let's make a pact. Let's swear that wherever we are, we'll all go to our fifteenth reunion."

"Swear, swear, swear, swear."

"I swear," said Sally, "that on October whatever it is, 1978, I'll meet you at the top of the mountain loop with a pack of cigs and a flask of Jack Daniel's for you all." They all laughed. "Wouldn't want to break my record," said Sally.

The dinner for Mrs. Sumter's grandniece Libby Gurley was held at Sumter Hollow, a beautiful house in a deep crevice in the hills famous for its acres of March daffodils. The daffodils were so famous, in fact, that they attracted many Sunday drivers, who wound along the long road to the house at a maddeningly slow pace, happily unaware of Mr. Sumter raging in the rhododendrons that all those damned cars on the road were scaring the horses, and he had a good mind to go get his BB gun and let 'em know what 'Private Drive' meant. "But, Harlan," Mrs. Sumter always said, "as long as they don't pick any? You can't blame them for feeling spring flowers belong to everyone."

"Can't I? Maybe my gardener's salary should belong to everyone, too." But of course the whole thing secretly pleased him very much, and he and his gardener worked extra hard to develop their new strain of pure white double-nosed jonquil with which to astound the intruders.

Libby and her aunt and uncle were receiving their guests in the sweet hot twilight on the lawn behind the house. The girls, dressed for Muffin's party, tottered about in long bright dresses, the heels of their dyed-to-match shoes sinking into the grass. Libby, a heavy cheerful girl, was dressed in yellow silk and looked rather like a jolly daffodil herself.

Her escort was Carey Compton, a boy she knew slightly because he was much admired by her Madeira roommate. Carey was well known to Ann, if not to Libby, for his remarkable toasts, and tonight at dinner he extended himself to the limits of his range and beyond. When the main course had been dispatched, he rose and tapped his glass for silence. He spoke wittily and well of the great charm and popularity of the guest of honor, how she was in part a stranger in this town and yet truly at home here, by reason of the many friends she'd made on summer visits to her aunt and uncle. He began then to speak of the Prodigal Son, who absented himself from the family bosom for such a long time and yet who was never out of the minds and hearts of all. He reminded them of the nature of the homecoming celebrations when the prodigal reappeared; he compared them, with a gracious gesture to the host and hostess, to the splendid dinner being laid on tonight. But somehow when the climactic moment arrived, when he had swept all the guests to their feet, glasses raised, ready to join him in a toast to kind, plump, round-eyed Libby, he inadvertently compared her, not to the Prodigal Son, but to the Fatted Calf.

This raised a howl of delight, accompanied by prolonged applause and clinking of silver on glassware, during which Carey blushed purple to his hairline. Libby was a terrific sport about it. Later, in a desperate attempt to recover the situation, Carey danced with great verve with Mrs. Sumter. He attempted to waltz with her out the French windows of the dining room onto the terrace, not realizing that a low stone bench blocked the way, and they fell heavily onto the flagstones outdoors, which didn't really help much. Mr. Sumter was so mad by then that he spent the rest of the party out in the driveway shooting craps with the car parkers.

Libby seemed to have a wonderful time in spite of Carey, and certainly everyone else did because of him. Muffin was sorry when she had to signal to Chip Lacey that it was time for her to go home to change from her dinner dress to her ball gown. "Nervous?" Chip asked as they drove away.

"Actually not," she said. "This afternoon I was sure I'd be sick, but I'm having a wonderful time."

"I'm still trying to sort out what Ann told me about all of you," Chip said. "Wasn't Lisa supposed to be so tight with someone called George?"

"Supposed to be. Why?"

"Because I saw her in the bushes making time with Ann's friend Philip."

"Really? Are you sure?"

"Very sure."

"That's peculiar."

"I thought so."

Muffin's old nurse had come out of retirement for the evening to act as her lady's maid. In her old white uniform she helped Muffin into the oyster silk gown that they'd spent six hundred dollars for at Saks on the grounds that she could add lace to cover the décolletage and wear it again as a wedding gown. The hardest part was getting into the long kid gloves that had to stretch smoothly to above her elbow. "I can never get them on and off by myself. Am I supposed to pee with them on?" Her nurse, who never responded to things a lady did not say, did not answer.

Just before she went downstairs, her father, looking shy and handsome, met her in the hall. From a small velvet box in his pocket he took a square-cut emerald, huge and pure and flashing with warm blue light, and hung it around her neck on a slender chain. She gazed at him, eyes welling, mute with love and amazement, and he slowly smiled. The old nurse, on the way to help Mrs. Bundle dress, passed them and gasped, and soon they were joined by Mrs. Bundle. She said only, "Jack, could I see you in the bedroom for a moment, please?" As Muffin went slowly down the stairs to join Chip, the emerald glowed with the light of the hundreds of candles that lit the hall, and her heart glowed with the adoration of Electra.

She could hear her mother's voice through the closed door "The worst taste . . . jewels that size . . . girl of eighteen . . . even *I* don't own . . ."

Downstairs there were masses of flowers on every surface, all yellow and white. The furniture had been removed from the great hall and the Aubusson carpet rolled away. A band played near the stone fireplace (which was also filled with flowers), and another, smaller group of musicians was down at the pool, where a small marquee stood for dancing, and torches were reflected on the water. There were bars, it seemed, set up everywhere: at the pool, on the terraces, two in the ballroom, and one in the billiard room below. Rapidly the house filled with people, as it had not in thirty years. Lisa and Philip came in together, and Muffin was momentarily startled to see that Chip was right: Lisa was clinging to him and he was looking at her as if he'd just gotten a present he'd given up hoping for.

Rutherford Flack came in with the rest of his family and greeted her with an elaborate bow. Ralph and Pepper arrived with Pear and Libby Gurley. The Suttons arrived with Lisa's brother, Buddy, and his new girlfriend, who had dyed half her hair blue for the occasion. George Tyler came in with Jenny, and he seemed aggressively merry. For over two hours, hundreds of people streamed in, and for hours after that, nobody left.

In the ballroom, what Ralph and Pepper called "the Lawrence Welk set" were foxtrotting with majestic pleasure. Outside, Ralph and Pepper and Pear, who'd been drinking Bloody Marys at the Suttons' all afternoon, had discovered the moon.

"Hey, look at that big white thing," said Pepper, pointing above the silvered slate rooftop. "Hey, that's a great thing. How do they get it up there?"

"I *love* it," said Pear. "A big round light, much better than the Arundels' decorations."

Ralph threw back his head and howled. "Aaaaaawhooooo! Arharharhaawoooooo!"

"What's happening? Is he blowing up?"

"Calling my mate. Sick with love. Wild animal passions unleashed at the full moon. Aaaaawhooooo!"

In the ballroom the foxtrotters smiled at the sound of the wolf howls coming from the dark lawn. Soon the howls could be heard circling the house as the wolf pack started to move, prowling the dark for Scotch and for love.

In the ballroom Lisa and Philip were dancing. Lisa had declined to let several people cut in. Philip held her now as if she were an armful of flowers, fragrant and precious. As they drifted slowly with delicious grace, the highly charged paper-thin space between their bodies opened and closed, as if they formed a single organism, delicately pulsating. She turned her face toward his; his lips were so close to hers that he could feel their warmth, but resisted the touch. Lisa could feel the tantalized impulse vibrate in him. With deliberate languor she subtly grazed her body along the length of his, feeling the hot, hard pressure of him, once again lightly withdrawing. And all the while with every nerve she could sense the furious presence of George watching every move.

Outside, the wolves had found Merry Bundle sitting cross-legged on the lawn with a circle of empty gin-and-tonic glasses around her. Her shoes were off and the straps of her gown had slipped off her shoulders. She was singing along with the music from inside and looking extremely content. Pear howled and stopped to sniff. Merry laughed happily. He dropped to his hands and knees and crawled toward her, making canine whimpering noises at her; she answered in kind. He nuzzled her bare shoulder, tearing at her strap with his teeth. The other wolves gave small howls, and Merry began to giggle again. He nuzzled, yipping enthusiastically, the loose bodice of her dress. It slipped easily, yielding her bare breast. Pear, panting and whimpering, lapped in surprise at the little nipple. The other wolves drew closer, staring and making appreciative wolf barks, and Merry laughed happily. After watching another moment or two, Ralph and Pepper, much inflamed, left Pear to it and loped off baying louder in search of a similar prize for themselves.

Over Lisa's dreaming golden head Philip could see George Tyler making his way toward them across the dance floor. George looked intent and angry. Philip felt somehow muffled by the wave on wave of desire that enveloped him. He watched George approach, felt him firmly turn Lisa from his arms, saw her silently go away from him, as if he were seeing it through the shimmering waves of heat that rise from the pavement in summer. He saw the fierce, familiar way they worked together as they began to dance, like the click of the tumbler falling when a key turns in its own lock. Neither George nor Lisa, whispering angrily at each other, once looked back at Philip, to see him standing alone on the floor for a long minute, following them with his eyes. At last he walked away to the terrace to find a place to sit down.

The moon was sailing high, and the night wearing on. The wolves, after baying and circling, hunting relentlessly and drinking a lot more Scotch, had happened onto a prize more thrilling than any they had seriously hoped for. Jenny, walking up from the pool, where she had been dancing, met them loping across the croquet lawn, panting and yapping and looking for Pear.

"Gotta tell Pear we're leaving," they explained excitedly, taking turns talking and howling their wolf call. "Gotta tell him to get another ride home. Found some babe who's so hot for it she wants to take us both on! Gonna take us to her house, aaaawhooooo! Oh, God, let's hurry!"

"She's waiting for us by the driveway. Gotta tell Pear before she changes her mind! Arh-arhwhooo!" They loped off.

Jenny walked on around the corner of the house, guessing that some smart deb had played a joke on Ralph and Pepper. She expected to see no one by the driveway, and half thought of waiting to watch the wolves' reactions. But there was indeed a buxom female figure standing patiently in the shadow of the little Japanese maple tree. Jenny went closer, curious and disgusted. The girl turned for a moment toward the moonlight, long enough for Jenny to recognize the pale, simple moon face of Nancy Flack.

Jenny found Philip sitting alone on the terrace and had him on his feet and running with her, almost before she had time to gasp out the problem. They caught up with the wolves far down the driveway, looking for their car, still howling and giggling.

"Stop! You *can't* go!" Jenny called to them. "That girl—that's Muffin's friend. She's retarded!"

"Whaddya mean?" Ralph snarled. "How do you know?" The brothers were caught off balance.

"Yeah, whaddya mean?" echoed Pepper. Both of them were drunker than Jenny had thought, and the quality of their excitement was as much hostile as sexual.

"She had an accident—she has a mental age of ten," said Philip. "I went to school with her brother," he interrupted Ralph, who was clearly going to challenge him.

Pepper had finally managed to grasp the situation and chosen his response. "Well, so the fuck what?" he yelled. "I mean, what the fuck difference does it make? She seemed just like any other stupid deb to me!"

"Yeah, how were we supposed to know? Who could tell the difference?"

"Yeah, wanna hear what she said to us?"

"No!" roared Jenny. "We want you to forget it and leave her alone!"

"Yeah? What business is it of yours, bitch?" Ralph turned on Philip. "Who's gonna stop us, the hit-and-run queen? You gonna run over us with your rent-a-car?"

And the two began clumsily running toward their car. Philip caught up with Ralph first. He caught him by both arms, picked him up, and hurled him far over the bank, so that he landed yelling with pain and rolled away in the darkness. Pepper stopped to kick viciously at Philip, and then again leaped for his car. He was halfway behind the wheel when Philip pulled him out and slammed him across the trunk. He held him down with one arm, straining but never faltering, staring into Pepper's eyes in silent challenge while Pepper struggled without success to rise. The moment Philip let him up, Pepper kicked him as hard as he could in the groin, crying now and screaming, "Fuck you, you jealous fucking faggot! You wouldn't know what to do with a cunt if it sat on your face!" Ralph loomed out of the darkness and leaped Philip from behind, and Jenny saw Pepper land a series of savage kicks before Philip shook free. With one blow of his fist he sent Pepper sprawling on the driveway, where he lay sobbing and cursing. A second blow knocked out one of Ralph's teeth and sent him over the bank again. Philip stood in the road staring at Pepper in the gravel. He seemed to be trembling slightly, but Jenny soon saw that he was in fact silently crying.

Philip and Jenny lay in the long grass in the meadow. Far up the hill they could see the lights from the ballroom, though they were too far to hear the music. Or perhaps the band had gone home. The moon was beginning to set. Philip had abandoned himself to tears for hurts so old and deep that his weeping had exhausted him. Lying in the grass beside him, Jenny held him. Later she had wiped the tears and blood from his face with his handkerchief and the warm liquid from her own mouth, once gently licking his swelling eyelid like an animal, to keep from hurting any more than necessary. Then she lay a long while very close to him, not touching him. He grew quiet and lay with his eyes closed, closed up inside himself.

Softly she reached out with her fingers again and touched the swollen eyebrow. He didn't stir or wince. After a moment she raised herself to one elbow, leaned over him, and with her lips and tongue very lightly caressed first one eye, then the other, then again, as if to heal the wounds and the tears. Around them the cool smell of grass and the low buzz of night sounded like earth's irregular heartbeat. Softly she kissed his mouth. She took a long time just to feel his lips with her lips, barely moving, before she tentatively moved to caress his lips, then teeth, then the deep warmth of his mouth with her tongue.

At last she felt his arms reach around her. Without taking her mouth from his, she unbuttoned his vest, then opened the stiff front of his shirt, and with her tongue still deep in his mouth she began to stroke his chest. She felt his nipple stiffen beneath her fingers and heard a noise in his throat, a deep sound that seemed like a question. Her hand lay still a moment, then began to caress his chest again. This time he stirred distinctly toward the hand and with the same sound in the throat began with his mouth and tongue to go beyond response to initiation.

Her hand slid down his body to the inside curve of his thigh. She felt him flinch slightly as her fingers found a bruise left by Pepper's kicks. She kept her touch so light that it was almost just a cloud of warmth gently hovering around, over, between his thighs, always moving softly until she knew by instinct the hot swelling of his groin. Only then, only once, did she let her hand slide softly around his balls. His breathing changed abruptly. Swiftly she dealt with the buttons and zipper, and when her hand freed from the cloth and then itself contained the long stiff cock, she suddenly turned her face from his kiss and looked. In another moment he felt her mouth against his chest, caressing the breast with her warm breath and then flicking the nipple stiff with her tongue; then her mouth was surrounding his cock, lips and tongue and teeth moving until it seemed that he must explode.

"Stop," he said, "let me."

She looked to his face, softly wrapping her long hair around the cock so it wouldn't be cold when she took her mouth away.

"Lonely," he whispered. "Let me." She nodded. With one motion like a spring uncoiling he had reversed their positions so that she lay beneath him, and he slid into her, looking scared for the one moment that her eyes widened as if she might scream. He froze.

"Hurt?"

She nodded, her eyes locked on his.

"Bad?"

"No—you come, please come, I want to see you come."

He looked for a moment as if he would keep still, but then he began to move inside her, stabbing irresistibly. She couldn't help the soft hurt noises that flew from her throat as she felt him strike flesh deep inside her, causing a dazzling burst of something near pain. But she could see in his face that he couldn't have stopped if he were killing her. Then he suddenly held; she could actually feel the long shaft shudder inside her. He never took his amazed wide eyes from her face.

Long after he had smoothed her long skirt down around her legs in the late-night chill and they had lain for a long time looking at the stars, he said to her, "That was my first time."

She nodded. After a long pause she said, "You have a very long, very beautiful cock."

"I was afraid there was something wrong."

She smiled, looked embarrassed, shook her head.

"Do I really?"

"Yes."

"Thank you," he whispered.

The moon was nearly setting over the Ohio when Avery Mortpestle began to think they might be getting home. He'd been standing on the terrace for nearly an hour, feeling perfectly happy. For one splendid evening everything was just as it al-

ways had been. The debutante was a sweet, pretty girl, in love
with her escort, just as she should be. There was plenty to drink,
and all of the best; and at suppertime there'd been a quiet room
for the more senior guests, where he and his wife and the Sum-
ters, all his friends, were brought their supper by the servants,
just as it would have been in old Mrs. Bundle's day. Jack had
even had out the gold plate for them; Avery hadn't seen that
since the New Year's hunt breakfasts they used to have here
when Jack's father was alive.

The children had been happy and polite, and some of the prettier girls had gone swimming in their dresses just as they ought.
He liked to see them run up the lawn, with the dripping silk
clinging to them from neck to ankle, giggling and holding their
shoes in their hands. Harlan Sumter claimed he'd won six bucks
off the car parkers—*that* was just like the old days.

Instead of the white-uniformed maid serving coffee and beef
bouillon to the departing guests in the hall, Bundle had set up
an actual nurse with an oxygen tank to revive those guests who
ought not to drive. Avery Mortpestle thought this a fine innova-
tion, and he had booked the nurse for the Child Health Ball, of
which he was chairman. Ah, but he couldn't help remembering
the parties during Prohibition, when somehow you never quite
knew if this drink might be your last. They were *all* too drunk to
drive in those days. Used to drive into things more often, but
killed themselves less, it seemed. Cars not so fast back then, he
guessed.

The house was finally empty again, but Jack Bundle didn't
want the night to be over. Never since the night his sister Julia
died had the house been so full of ghosts. The musicians had
gone home at last, and the sun would be up in an hour. He didn't
know where his wife was; in bed, he hoped. Little Merry had gotten drunk again tonight—did she do that often? It suddenly occurred to him he ought to ask somebody. Julia used to get drunk,
but that was because it was Prohibition, and because she was too
bright for a woman of her generation. God knows, brains
weren't Merry's problem. He lit a cigarette. The sky had already
begun to lighten enough that he could see the smoke drift out

from the dark terrace over the lawn. He leaned against a pillar blue with wisteria.

What could Julia have grown up to be? A country-club matron, like Annette? He couldn't picture it. Neither, he believed, could Julia. A brain surgeon? Not then; too early. A grande dame, such as their mother had been? Too late; the era had already past for that. That life ended with the Great War.

Where was Muffin, this haunted predawn hour? he wondered. Making love with her young man, if she had any sense. But knowing Muffin, he doubted it. Annette had done her work there, too. Mothers and daughters, the blind leading the blind.

Behind him, Jack heard a door open and close. He turned and saw, at the far end of the porch, a slim figure glimmering white in the lavender darkness. He watched her stand looking out over the valley. Then he lit another cigarette to let her know she wasn't alone. She saw the flare of the lighter, turned, and came over to join him.

"Can't sleep?" he asked.

Ann shook her head. Her hair was still damp from her swim.

"Boyfriend gone?"

She nodded.

He nodded, too, and absently put his arm around her. They stood together, close and peaceful, for long minutes, watching the sky lighten and the stars dissolve into the warm light of the coming sunrise. Every change of color in the sky at their backs could be read in the flat mirror ribbon of the river far below them to the west.

"Can you see the Sewickley Bridge down there, tiny little thing where the river bends?" he asked. She could. "When I was your age, I had a friend, Johnny Wigton. One night after a party he bet us all he could dive off that bridge. There was a lot of money on it, I forget how much. He collected. I'll never forget how he looked, soaring off into space ten stories above the water. He cracked a couple of ribs, I think; I know he swam to shore on his own power. God, he was a courageous little bastard."

Ann looked up at him, but he was far away, eyes on the river.

"Johnny was a little younger than I was, but I admired him. I *loved* him. But later, I don't know what happened to him—he

was around, I guess, but I never seemed to see him except now
and then on the train coming down from town. You know how
you grow up with someone and they're part of your life and you
think they always will be—but then you don't see each other and
after a while they're nothing to you anymore . . . no, you don't
know yet. Never mind.

"A long time later I heard he finally made the same bet, I
think with some guys he was drunk with down at the Sewickley
Inn, and he dived off the bridge again. But this time his head hit
the water and shattered. Like a rotten pumpkin, I picture
it . . . when my sister and I were children the chauffeur used to
take us to the bridge after Halloween with our jack-o'-lanterns
and let us drop them off to see them splatter on the river, just as
if it were pavement."

He was silent for a while. Then he added, "Tonight's the first
time I ever thought of it as all one story—my friend when he
was young, and how it ended . . ."

Ann did not trouble to speak. After a while she put her arm
around him, too, and they stood so for quite a while, very still,
fine-tuning their senses to perceive minute changes in the quality of the light, the dawn sounds of the birds, the warmth of the
air. At last, stiff and slightly restless in full daylight, they realized that though the house would soon be stirring, they didn't
care to part.

They'd had a stiff gallop through trails so thickly covered over
with new leaves of June that they seemed like bright light tun-
nels of green. Now they let the horses walk side by side, their
own legs dangling against the wet bare backs of the horses, the
reins slack on the necks. They had spoken very little, nor did
they speak now. Jack pulled up his horse in the warm corner of a
small closed meadow below the old Mortpestle house. He slipped
to the ground and tied his horse's reins to a low rail of the pas-
ture fence. Ann did the same. They walked into the meadow, to a
soft hollow, deep with wild blue vetch and meadow rue, which
held them as in the cupped hands of the earth while they made
love. It was a sweet, fervent, agonizing hour, combining the
piercing hunger of first love with a trancelike abandon to the
state when the unthinkable becomes the inevitable. Their pas-

sion was high and prolonged, brought to peak after peak of nearly unbearable tension before the final shattering release.

When at last the hour was past, the tears dried and cries qui-
eted, the deep grass around them ceased its rustling and they
lay very still, looking at the sky and at each other.

Ann was the first to speak. She whispered, "Jesus."

"Jesus what?" He waited. He felt more vulnerable at that moment than she could have imagined. She thought very carefully
of the hundred things she could say, the many things so deeply
felt as to be almost unspeakable, and chose at last, "Jesus, I'm
hungry."

Coda: October 1978

The wooded hills along the Farmington River Valley shimmered flaming reds and yellows, exactly as they had when Muffin was a new girl, when her mother was a new girl, when, for that matter, the only new girls in the region were pubescent Amerindians preparing for their own rites of passage. Loving autumn in Connecticut as she did, Muffin had deliberately chosen to drive up to Lakebury by way of country back roads where what had changed in the land was so much less obvious than what had remained the same. It was interesting how she had gradually come to feel a sense of belonging to this area, verging on a sense of ownership, just as strong as the belonging she had once felt to Sweetwater. Evidently, feeling at home was an ingrained part of her personality by now; in point of fact, she had no roots in this area, although her husband, Chip, did. As she drove, thinking about the country, she remembered with wry pleasure an anecdote she'd uncovered while researching local history for her Dessert and Discussion Club. A forebear of Chip's had once been given an enormous tract of virgin farmland that more than included the entire present town of Farmington, Connecticut, but the title had been lost because land was cheap while paper was dear, and the farmer's wife had used the deed to cover a pie and burned it up in the oven. (This sort of tale delighted Muffin, the more so because of the deep annoyance the story caused her mother-in-law.)

Even if it hadn't been for the promise her roommates had

317

made about this reunion, Muffin would have looked forward to it
intensely. She loved people and she loved to hear their stories,
and she was convinced that once you had been truly close to people, the love would always be there between you. Her mother always said that whenever she saw her old school chums they
came together as if they had never parted. Muffin believed it.
She had never been able to distinguish between loving and being loved.

Muffin had even made the effort to show up at the smaller, interim tenth reunion that had been held in 1973. When they were
in school, the interim reunions drew Antiques from the local
suburbs, the gals who could easily pop in for the day and be
home in time to put the kids to bed. Unexpectedly, the girls who
came back in 1973 were mostly those who had careers they were
proud of; if they spoke of children, it was in terms of arranging
an hour of "really high-quality time" with them each day while
maintaining a full course load at law school. They were not the
girls Muffin had known well, the girls who had been the most
successful at school. And while they all seemed glad to see her,
Muffin felt a little funny being one of the only ones who "didn't
work" and who in fact lived much as her mother had, as they
once thought they all would.

There had been a lot of talk at the tenth, about how the Miss
Pratt's of 1963 bore more resemblance to the school in 1923 than
to anything that had happened in '65 or '68 or 1970. Mrs. Umbrage had retired the year after they left, and the cheerful
young couple who replaced her had done away with most of the
restrictions Mrs. Umbrage had declared essential to the spirit of
the school. If anything, Miss Pratt's had a stronger academic
standing than ever.

"It's not to be *believed*," Muffin told Sally on the long-distance
phone after the tenth reunion. Muffin had expected Sally, of all
people, to be ecstatic about the changes at school. "They can
wear blue jeans to class, and there's a smoking room in every
dorm, and they don't have to go to meals . . . I mean, last winter the head of school went to Planned Parenthood for the weekend and had an abortion, and everyone knew it. . . ."

"Oh, fine, did they give her a ticker-tape parade?"

"But I'm serious. I mean, it might even be great to be there now. . . ."

"Oh, I'll send in my application right away. Do they serve cocktails before dinner too?"

"Hey, what are you so pissed off about?"

"Hey, what do you swear on the phone for? Don't you know they listen in? They can take away your service. That'd be fun, explaining that. Not: 'No, you can't call me, my roommate from Miss Pratt's used such foul language that the phone company cut me off.'"

"I'm sorry."

"Look, thanks for calling, it sounds great. I'm really sorry I wasn't there, but I gotta go. 'Bye!"

At the tenth reunion the class secretary had asked to be replaced. She was a sweet quiet girl whom they'd elected almost for the joke that one who knew so few of her classmates well should be in charge of all the letters and alumnae news. She was finishing up her residence in cardiology at Beth Israel now and didn't have time to do it anymore. The group unanimously elected Muffin to replace her, and Muffin decided to take the job really seriously.

So the fifteenth reunion was Muffin's baby. Almost three-fifths of the class had signed up, the biggest reunion Miss Pratt's had seen in years, and everyone agreed it was because of Muffin. She'd written special letters to everyone in the class; she'd tracked down difficult addresses and in some cases she'd even called to talk to those who didn't respond. Of course, there were some who couldn't be reached. Cindy French had died in Thailand in 1968 from eating a stew made of shellfish from a pool of stagnant water. The Peace Corps co-worker who had brought her body into Bangkok said she had known perfectly well what was in the food and what the danger was, but she was too polite to hurt the feelings of the village women who stood around her beaming as they ceremoniously presented the bowl.

Gail Stillman told Muffin on the phone that as a teacher herself now she bitterly resented the fact that Miss Pratt's had failed to "program for future use." "The point of education is to plant in your tiny mind the idea that you might grow up to *do* something or *be* something. . . . I don't think at Miss Pratt's it occurs to you that you're going to grow up at all."

"But it's changed so much," said Muffin. "And so have the rest of us—please come, you'll be surprised."

"I'll be surprised if I come, all right." Gail added that she wanted her name taken off the list of contributors to the school that was published in the bulletin each year—it was her mother who gave in Gail's name, and Gail considered it an outrage. "Oh, dear," said Muffin to Chip, "she always *was* intense."

Muffin had learned with some shock that Amy Peller had been drowned on her honeymoon, swimming in the Aegean. The parents appreciated her call, though, and agreed that perhaps there ought to be some sort of memorial to her at Miss Pratt's since she'd been so happy there. At least they assumed she was; Amy had always seemed to be happy everywhere.

Muffin hadn't been able to find Sylvia Townsend. She had left the last address the school had for her, and if she still lived in Chicago, her number was unlisted. The family had been badly harassed by the FBI because Sylvia's younger sister was on their Ten Most Wanted list. No one knew if the sister was living underground with whatever shards remained of her radical cell, or if she had been blown to unrecognizable bits in an explosion of a Greenwich Village town house in 1969.

Marietta Bourjaily was living outside Toronto with her husband; they had a belt-and-sandal shop. Her husband had declined the pardon that President Ford had extended to draft evaders, saying he couldn't be pardoned when he had not committed a wrong. Marietta told Muffin on the phone that she'd been back to the States only once in nine years—when her father was dying—and all things considered, she doubted if she'd come back again.

Muffin always said afterward that even though she'd looked forward to it for so long, she'd had bad vibrations on that reunion day from the minute it began. First of all, she was late getting off because Chip's dalmatian bitch had gone into labor at five o'clock that morning and deposited eight tiny puppies in the whelping box in the master bathroom. The last pup had been born after Muffin had dressed to leave. Muffin had had to cut the cord for the bitch, who was too tired to bite it herself or to lick the baby clean. In the car driving up, Muffin found herself fretting that the runt was so weak and small. In their first litter of dalmatians, three of the pups had been born deaf, and the local Dalmatian Club insisted indignantly that this was entirely Chip and Muffin's fault; for the purity of the breed, the pups must be destroyed. Now every new litter depressed Muffin for the first two weeks until she was sure that the pups were sound.

And then the blow about Sally. Blow—it was more of a splintering crash, followed by a more terrible silence.

Muffin went through with the reunion, of course. It was unreasonable to expect the rest of the class to feel more than a sober moment for the loss of a friend whom in truth they'd relinquished years ago. In fact, the dinner was gala and Muffin carried it off with apparent high spirits.

"Now, answer honestly," she had asked the group as she had planned to when she rose to make her announcements. "How many of you thought you'd never come to a Miss Pratt's reunion again?" Half the members raised their hands.

"And how many are glad you came?" There was a burst of genuine applause, and all hands raised.

"I'll drink to that!" yelled Mamie from the back of the room, and the jugs of Gallo red went around the tables.

"Before we get down to serious gossip, I just want to remind you that there will be breakfast with the students in the morning, followed by walks or tennis or going to classes—time to revisit all those places you've cherished in memory" (laughter). "Then there'll be lunch on the lawn here at Antique House, and any of you who have interested husbands—or interesting husbands" (laughter)—"coming to pick you up, they're welcome to join us for that.

"I have one other announcement to make, and that is that you may remember while we were here there was a certain amount of trouble with things disappearing. I lost a gold watch, I know, and Linda lost a ring—quite a few apparently lost stuff over the three years. Anyway, it's been returned." (A loud murmur buzzed the room.) "I don't know by whom—the package was sent to the alumnae office here, and they threw away the outer wrap-

ping, so I don't even know where it was mailed from. If it was
from someone who is here tonight, I want to say thank you. And
in any case, I have the things, so any of you who lost stuff, see
me after we finish up tonight."

Muffin had felt she had to stay through the Dutch-treat lunch
on Saturday to collect money from everyone for the Kentucky
Fried Chicken. Then Lisa and Ann and Jenny accepted her invitation to drive back to Greenwich for the night.

The four were sitting now on the glassed-in terrace of the
house. Madelon had come in briefly to greet them but had gone
back to her wing of the house and stayed there as she always did
now when Muffin was entertaining. Chip had gone up to bed an
hour ago; he'd heard what little they knew about Sally: found
hanging from a false beam in a poolhouse in Dayton by her four-
teen-year-old stepson. Chip realized that although there was little talk, that they needed each other's presence, and in some way
tonight they were alone together, whether he stayed in the room
or not.

Muffin was the first to cry. For the first few moments after
she'd heard Beverly's words, she'd felt as if she were looking
through a defective kaleidoscope. She'd shake it and look at the
pattern of colored stones inside and get only image after image
of her life in the years since she'd left school. Chip, their wedding, the vacations, the dogs, Maude's death, and so many dinner parties and dances and friends and things other than Sally.
But gradually in the intervening night and day her focus began
to narrow. Gradually she began to see picture after picture of
Sally, sitting on a log in the woods at school smoking a cigarette,
laughing in study hall, giggling drunk in Sea Island, crying the
night she didn't get into college, Sally as one of her bridesmaids,
hilarious postcards from Sally the summer they went to Europe,
and so many postcards and phone calls since—Sally. Perhaps a
narrow thread in the fabric of fifteen years, but always there—
never forgotten. Oh, God—poor Sally.

Lisa got up to pour herself another glass of wine. Ann and
Jenny had shared a joint; Jenny was now sitting cross-legged on
the floor with her eyes closed, rocking almost imperceptibly on
the base of her spine.

Muffin felt more tears rise suddenly in her throat. "You know,

I really love Mamie," she said aloud. The others nodded. Ten minutes later Ann said, "Remember the hat she bought in Venice?" In the silence that had fallen among them in the hours since dinner, they had sat together in the glass room, being closed in together by the light itself as the last violet streaks of sunset were replaced by the thickness of night. Sometimes they talked in elliptical codes, exchanging key words, phrases, images. Sometimes one or the other would suddenly tell a story of something that had happened to her since they parted that seemed to have a connection to the rest of them. Sometimes it turned out not to. In between, they passed around sadly whatever they had left in their minds of Sally. It didn't turn out to be much.

Muffin tried to remember every time she'd seen her since graduation. Of course Sally had been the matron of honor at Muffin's wedding. She looked great that summer, thin and chic, and she loved being the only one of them married. Sally's husband, the one she'd eloped with, was finishing up law school. He had said to Chip: "I really admire you, just taking a few years off to do what you really love to do." (Chip was at that time spending full time restoring a 1927 Bugatti and playing tournament bridge.) "I think that's what life's *for*," said Sally's husband. "You should do what you really *love* to do."

"You'll be out of school next month," Chip had said. "Why don't *you* take some time off, before you settle into the grind?"

After carefully considering, the husband said, "I never could think of anything I wanted to do that much."

Muffin hadn't thought about that in years. She really couldn't remember much about her wedding except for the wedding night. So she didn't remember much about Sally being at the reception. Or Jenny or Lisa and George. She did remember, though, one image of Ann waltzing with her father. Why that? Muffin wondered. Was it noticing that Ann and Jack looked very much like each other? They were close to the same height and they were both lean and handsome, with almost the same long narrow nose. And there was something oddly similar in the dignified, slim-hipped, slightly stiff way they moved. Or was she just so glad to see Ann, since she'd been such a stranger to them all?

* * *

For many years after she left Miss Pratt's, Ann had avoided everyone and everything that reminded her of it. She lopped it off like a diseased limb, not even keeping in touch with Jenny for the year they were both at Radcliffe. It was only in the last year or two, after finally achieving some peace in her marriage, after two solid years in a row of not a single crying jag, that she began to soften. Perhaps it was a matter of finally, belatedly, achieving some professional success, earning some approval from someone, if not from Madelon. In any case, she'd come to feel that life was too short to renounce any part of it. Perhaps also a couple of years of WASP-baiting at the hands of the urban Jews who were her friends and her husband's friends had finally worn out her feelings of guilt. If other people were entitled to accept with pride their more fashionable ethnic origins, perhaps she could forgive herself for having once been a preppy asshole. And to consider that the reluctance she had felt at the thought of renewing old ties with her classmates had less to do with false pride against Miss Pratt's than with embarrassment of their having been fifteen together.

"Remember the night we read that book that we thought was a sex manual, and tried to get drunk on Listerine?" she asked aloud.

"Oh, my God!" cried Muffin.

"Miss Van Kleek!" said Jenny.

"Was that the night Sally and Jenny got caught with the espresso maker?" asked Lisa. "I don't think I remember."

Ann was grateful that she'd let herself come back. For so long she'd spoken of her years at Miss Pratt's as one might speak of a stay in a sanatorium for an illness that has since been eliminated. In college her friends would wrangle long into the night over films whose images had filled their dreams, that had informed their sense of themselves and the world, Hollywood films that had played every town in the world from Duluth to Tripoli, art films they had seen over and over with their boyfriends on Second Avenue or upper Broadway.

"I won't go to *Casablanca*," Ann's roommate always said, when the Brattle ran its Bogart Festival at reading period. "I don't believe in Bogey; I don't believe it's possible to be callous on the outside but sensitive at heart."

Ann didn't know who Humphrey Bogart was; she'd never

heard Bob Dylan or Joan Baez. She'd never heard of *Get Smart*,
the cult television show, and she wondered when the phrase
"would you believe . . ." entered the language. It took her a
while to think where she'd been exactly when her classmates
were gathering all these stimuli, films and music and political
passions, they'd experienced in common, like tribal rites of passage.

She'd missed the Bay of Pigs. The school took in one copy each
of the Hartford *Courant* and the New York *Times*, but no one
but Jenny ever read them. A few people had transistor radios,
but no one ever heard the news. In the mornings they stayed in
bed till the scream of the second bell at 7:25 warned that they
had five minutes to dress and be in Pratt Hall for breakfast. At
the six-o'clock evening newscast there was the compulsory silence of study period, and at eleven they were in bed. Her only
strong political impression remembered from Miss Pratt's was
that the morning Jack Kennedy was elected, the hymn Mrs.
Umbrage called for in morning prayers was "Oh, God, our help
in ages past, our hope *four* years to come."

She did remember the day the first American space satellite
went into orbit, but only because Miss Barney had insisted that
her classes be allowed to watch the television coverage in her
sitting room instead of coming to class. It was junior year, but
only the seniors took chemistry; Ann's class was quite browned
off, as Sandy and Linda put it, to miss the chance of seeing television, no matter what was on.

She'd seen *The Guns of Navarone* in Lucerne, and that did
figure once in a college discussion of heroism and whether it
existed in women. She'd been to the theater, mostly musical
comedy, more than the movies, but no one she knew in college
ever showed any interest in Shirley MacLaine's performance in
Irma La Douce. Anyway, she hadn't even gotten to see the whole
play, because midway through the second act her grandmother
realized that the play was all about a French whore.

"Oh, my dear, what a joke on Madelon. But not suitable at all,
dear, we'll have to go."

Ann had protested in amazement. It was a comedy. Madelon
knew perfectly well what it was about; it was she who had ordered the tickets. Maude laughed merrily.

"Help me find my glove, dear, is it under the seat? Don't be silly, you're a schoolgirl, you can't watch a play about a tart. You're not even *out* yet. Oh, now I've dropped my cane." Ann was so annoyed that she wouldn't even speak to Maude the whole way home to Connecticut. But Maude didn't mind. She just chattered to the chauffeur.

After years, some of them years of pain, it began to strike Ann funny to trace the misunderstandings, the fears, the waste, the compulsive drives that seemed to have their source in her lost schooldays. "If God offered me three more years to live, and they were the three years between fifteen and eighteen, I'd cash in my chips," she said. "But then, would you want to be seventeen again?"

"I wouldn't touch it with a barge pole," said her husband.

"The only difference between you and me is *we* thought they were the happiest years of our lives."

"Boy, were you in the dark," said Stu. "My friends knew they were fucked up. We made a career of it. My friend Larry had three psychiatrists before he graduated from high school. And all that was the matter with any of us was, we wanted to get laid. Well, all except Larry."

"That's all that was the matter with any of us, too, but we *thought* all we wanted was to link arms and sing 'In the Gloaming' together. And then get married, walking down the aisles on our daddies' arms wearing long white gowns."

"Even you? You wanted that?"

"Oh, of course. We were never very clear about the fucking-in-the-bridal-suite part, but we had the walking-down-the-aisle-with-Daddy part nailed down."

"It's hard to tell what was just from being in a stupid place, and what was from being a stupid age."

"It is, but at least at seventeen *you* could observe a person of the opposite sex firsthand and draw a few conclusions. We believed everything they told us about sex, and we never saw a boy except in situations that were so loaded that they always blew up."

"Oh, well," he said, "no harm done." This made them both hoot with laughter.

When she got to Radcliffe, Ann—whose Miss Pratt's classmates had thought of her as all stiff spine and intellect—had plunged into an affair with a boy whose most obvious attraction was that her mother and Mrs. Umbrage would loathe him. He was brighter than Chip or Carey Compton or any of the boys she grew up with, he was rude, he had unreliable table manners, and he was black. He was also extraordinarily funny and a lover of such tireless power, such inventiveness, such passion and gentleness, that she was terrified to leave him. He was going to make a wide slashing mark in the world; that much was written all over him. Ann had not yet remotely considered that she might earn her own success. She assumed she would have to marry it. But his strongest attraction was that he appeared to hate her as much as he loved her. He might make love to her all night till she cried from the torment of his exquisite blend of rape and tenderness; he would whisper in the darkness that he loved and needed her, that no one else had ever stirred him as she did, that no one else would ever understand her as he did. But if she ever spoke of the future as if it were something they might find themselves in together, he would laugh, in public if possible, at the notion that he would ever marry an overbred ofay deb like her. Because he humiliated her so often, the rejection eventually became an obsession with her. He had created the perfect master-slave relationship.

Of course at the time she understood very little of this. It was just one long ache, the years with Rowley, of desire, anger, happiness, depression, self-loathing. It took years of thinking and reading and talking, night after night in her women's group trying to describe it, trying to tell the truth about how it had really been, before she came to understand the affair as an exorcism. Rowley had taken all her fears about herself: that she was spoiled, naive, and stupid; that it was loathsome to be rich and white when other people were not; that to be a woman was to be a terrified impotent puppet. He had sensed it in her, voiced it, beaten her with it, rammed her with her own self-hate into every orifice, and this had made her his creature. And all this had been so complicated, so hard to work out, and so fascinating when they began to understand it, that she and her friends had talked it through over and over. (The latest was that even last year, when she saw Rowley in Washington, she had found that she would have left the lunch table and made love to him in his van in the parking lot if he'd asked her to. There *was* something lasting between them after all—something akin to love—in addition to the sick stuff. Rowley was of course no longer the man who had insisted on fucking her in the ass when she had her period, or who had once made her suck his toes while he beat off. No man of sensitivity could have survived the war between men and women that began in the '70s and come away having learned nothing. Besides, Rowley had lost his wife and young son in a car crash the year before, and lost at the same instant much of his manic pride.)

Anyway, she had thought so much and talked so much about the mechanics of the relationship that she realized tonight she'd thought very little—really very little, considering—about the way the affair finally ended.

All through her junior year she'd been trying to find the strength in herself to leave Rowley. She'd stop seeing him for a couple weeks, she'd get through the black feeling of being a damaged neurotic Barbie Doll, that not even a sadistic shit like Rowley would want to marry. She'd get to feeling good, even, to enjoying going to bed alone and getting up as early as she liked without having to take any flak from Rowley or his roommates, or being expected to make breakfast. And then she'd see him somewhere. She'd run into him on line at the Brattle Theater after the libraries closed, going to the last showing of *The Seventh Seal*, or she'd come out of Lowell Lec. (from a course they had planned to take together) and pass him smoking and talking to some girl, never looking at her as she unlocked her bike and pedaled away. And it would start all over again. Then one morning, the week before exams began—it was one of her good periods, a stretch where she hadn't been with Rowley in nearly a month, and besides, felt great that she was going to ace her exams—she got up one morning and threw up in the sink in the dorm john.

When she told Rowley that she was pregnant in spite of the diaphragm, she expected him to be furious, but he wasn't. The only question he asked was whether she'd seen a doctor. She asked him to help her get the money for an abortion. Her own money was in trust for years still; she couldn't raise a cent without explaining what it was for, and she didn't own a car or stereo or anything else worth selling. Rowley did. She wanted to finish her exams first; he had a week. She didn't see him for six days. Then he took her to the Midget for coffee and asked her to marry him.

She went home with him that night and they cried in each other's arms till full day, when she had to go take a comp-lit. exam. She didn't want to marry him. She didn't know if she ever had wanted to marry him. She just needed not to be so viciously rejected as to be told over and over that he wouldn't marry her if she did want to.

He was sorry. He was sorry, he was sorry, he was sorry. He wanted the baby. He wanted to marry her and he wanted the baby. He was afraid without her. And he needed her to want him.

When her exam was over, she went back to her dorm. She looked for a scrap of paper that she had never meant to keep, but had kept, as it turned out, and she made a phone call. Just after supper the call was returned. She took it in the booth in the up-stairs hall.

"I got your message," Jack said.

"Thank you for calling back . . ."

"I told you, anytime. What can I do for you?"

She hadn't expected him to be so abrupt. With a boy her own age there would have been more preamble, more explanations for having been out of touch. But she hadn't seen him in three years, and she probably hadn't thought of him in two. Except, maybe, to remember that the last time they parted he gave her a phone number and told her that if she ever needed him, to call. It was the kind of thing she'd said herself to adolescent friends perhaps a dozen times.

She said, "I need a thousand dollars and a round-trip ticket to Puerto Rico." Then she held her breath, and the silence on the other end seemed to go on forever.

He finally said, "When do you want to go?"

"As soon as I can. Tomorrow."

"All right. The money and the flight information will be at the Western Union office in the morning. You can pick up a prepaid ticket at the airport. Is there anything else?"

"No," she said. "Yes . . . thank you."

"Anytime." And he hung up.

* * *

The next morning she checked out of the dorm, saying she was going to stay with some graduate-student friends. She stopped at the Western Union office. The money was there, with the flight number of a plane to San Juan leaving Logan Field at 11:30. She left Cambridge with a small suitcase, a raincoat, and—this always made her women's group howl when she mentioned it—a paperback copy of *Of Human Bondage*.

As she sat in the airport, she started to read, but after a few minutes decided just to cry, since that's what she was doing anyway, so she put the book away. She cried for Rowley, pictured him calling the dorm at this minute, frantic to find her, slowly realizing that she had left him. Taken their baby and really, finally, left him. She cried for the baby. She cried for herself for the loss of the baby, for the loss of Rowley, and for the very real terror she felt at the thought of the abortion. And after a while she cried just because she had never felt so ill and so exhausted in her life.

Her plane was called. The stewardess at the door of her cabin checked her boarding pass and gestured her to find a seat in the first-class section. She walked onto the plane, and there, standing in the aisle, was Jack.

She slept leaning against his shoulder through the long flight south. He took her to a hotel, and in the morning he went with her to the address of the one doctor whose name she knew. They found the office closed. She sat down on the step and stared into space while he questioned, in rapid Spanish, a couple of men lounging on the porch of the next building. (Her Spanish was rudimentary, but she could piece together the gist, which was that they don't know anything, one day the office is just closed, they think the doctor has been arrested.)

From a phone booth Jack made a string of calls to New York, and finally a local one. He got a taxi and took her to another doctor, and he waited in the anteroom of the small pink stucco building while without benefit of anesthetic the doctor swiftly and roughly scraped the contents of Ann's womb out of her, with curettes still scalding hot from the sterilizer. When he was finished, the doctor looked at Ann's face. He ordered her to put on some makeup before she left the office; if his patients walked out looking like that, he'd soon be arrested, too. She said she hadn't any. With a look of utter disgust, he insisted that she borrow from his receptionist some scarlet lipstick. Then he turned her over to Jack, who smoothed her hair, his expression indecipherable, then took her back to the hotel.

They spent one more night in San Juan. He got her everything she asked for, listened to anything she wanted to talk about, but never asked a question. She never told him anything about Rowley. About the abortion, she said only that she had not been prepared for the physical pain. But that the worst thing about it was lying awake wondering with each searing stroke deep inside her, "Was that it? Was that the moment? Was that the stroke that made the baby die?"

They parted at Kennedy Airport. All he said was, "If you ever need me, you know how to reach me." She didn't see him again until Muffin's wedding to Chip.

If it hadn't been for Sally's death, Jenny told herself, she would never have gone to see John O'Neill. Not that she didn't think of him. She found when she was touring that the closer she got to New England, the more she remembered traveling back to school after vacations, her heart in her throat with aching to see him. Sometimes she doubted she'd ever feel anything so intense again. The night she won the Grammy award, and another time or two on national television, she'd look into the camera suddenly and think: John—are *you* out there? Are you proud of me? Would you still love me? But she didn't want to see him. There were other friends and lovers she'd lost along the way that she thought of sometimes in the same way; if she thought of John with more tenderness, it would only be because your first love is like that. Anyway, he'd never tried to get in touch with her. What if he were stout and bald and bragged to newer teachers about her sight translations? Or wanted to show her snapshots of his kids and the missus?

But from the moment she heard the news that Sally was dead, she was fifteen again. The shock was disorienting, and the moments ticked by, and the years dropped off. She was just back in the same dormitory room, filled with familiar bewildering sorrow. Something is wrong—what is it? Oh, yes, Sally. Something is wrong—what is it? Something hurt . . . Something hurt Sally so much it killed her. . . . How . . . ? When . . . ? Sally . . . How much did it have to hurt before you wanted to die?

By the time she reached the classrooms where he used to teach, she'd forgotten that she ever wanted not to see him; her only thought was panic that he wouldn't be there. His room would have changed, of course; it was fifteen years. He'd have gone home to supper—did he still live in town? The corridor was deserted, and each room she passed was empty. But when she got to the doorway of the room where she had read the *Aeneid,* he was there.

He wasn't doing anything. He was just sitting with his elbows on the desk, leaning slightly forward and staring straight ahead of him at the empty room. His hair was thick and slightly graying; his attentive face was lined. He looked lost in thought, but not relaxed like a daydreamer: his body, leaner than ever, looked taut and poised for something.

He looked up and saw her before she spoke. He had scarcely turned his head, as if wanting not to overcommit himself. His smile was exactly what she remembered, the same blend of shy and unguarded. As he never had before, no matter how many times she wanted him to, he came and kissed her at the door of the classroom, and he kissed her like a man who's been in love for a long time. Feeling the slim tense lines of him against her, she suddenly felt something come into focus, the sense that though there had been men she'd loved longer and more completely than John, her hands had measured them against him; nothing again had ever felt so exactly like love as the way he felt to her.

She stayed only a few minutes. They talked standing in the doorway.

"You're too thin," was the first thing he said to her.

"So are you . . . doesn't your wife feed you?" She almost hoped he would say he didn't have one.

"Not very much. She teaches French at a day school in Hartford, and she usually gets home late and tired. . . . I do too, so I don't feed her either." He smiled. "So we're both too thin and she looks a lot like you."

"Do you have children?"

"One fat baby girl. Dierdre."

Jenny smiled. They had talked about children's names, in the short time when they let themselves pretend that he would wait for her and they would grow up to have a life together. He had been for Dierdre, she against.

"So you're just having your first baby at your great age?"

"We tried a long time for one. Dierdre's adopted, and that took a long time too, to get an infant."

"Do you have a picture?" Jenny laughed at herself that it was she who asked.

"Do you know, I almost brought one when I left for work this morning . . . but then I thought . . . you wouldn't come . . . and then I told myself I wouldn't wait to find out."

"But you did."

"Apparently. I happened to see you drive up a couple of hours ago, and I got thinking that the worst thing would be if I started to leave and we ran into each other by accident and you didn't care. I thought if you wanted to see me, you'd look for me here, so I've just been sitting here."

She told him about Sally, and he was saddened.

"Poor little Sal," he said. "I was afraid she was in trouble, but she was never the kind who knew how to ask for help."

"I'm stunned."

"I know, but you see another side of a person when you teach. When someone bright can't manage to learn, it's something she's doing to herself. I tried with her."

"I know you did—I remember it."

"With the dumb ones, special effort makes a difference. But it didn't with Sally." He put his arms around Jenny, and she held him hard. "Let her go, baby. You think you could have helped her, but I don't. I think whatever it was was already done."

"But she was so young," said Jenny, near tears.

"We were all young. We did what we could for each other." They stood holding each other in silence for another minute or two. Finally Jenny pulled away a little, far enough to put her arms around his neck and look at him. For long minutes he looked steadfastly back into her eyes. A lot of things occurred to her to say that would have been wrong, and nothing that seemed particularly right. At last they just kissed each other, long and deeply, one more time, and after that she walked away.

Remembering, Jenny hadn't spoken for a long time. Ann and Lisa had compared notes on raising children. The record they were listening to was over; Muffin got up to put on another. From her half-lotus, opening her eyes, Jenny said, "For the first time in about two years, I wish I had some cocaine."

Nobody said anything.

"Have you ever had cocaine?" she asked. Lisa shook her head

Muffin said, "I seem to have missed the drug era completely—I keep telling myself it was all a lot of sound and fury . . ."

Jenny said, "Well, I never did drugs very much. The only one I liked at all was cocaine . . . you know how you feel when you spend an evening with people you really like and you get past all the trivial bullshit—how's your work, how's your ass, how's your kid, how's your dog—and around midnight you get to feeling so close and so centered and so good about each other that everyone laughs? And all everyone wants is to make the others laugh? It seems like it should be an easy place to get to, but really, who has the time more than once or twice a year? Or the friends? The only other thing that gets me off like that is coke. Once in a while, for about twenty minutes."

"We used to laugh like that together all the time," said Muffin.

"Yeah, I know. Especially Sally. That's why I brought it up." After a while Jenny added, "I had a friend named Fred who did so much cocaine his nose was running all the time. It's not *supposed* to be addictive. The drug itself doesn't hook you, but old Fred couldn't seem to stop it. He couldn't even play a whole forty-five-minute set without dashing offstage to snort. After a while, doing it in the nose didn't even get him off anymore, and he told me he quit. But I guess he just wanted to laugh like that one more time, because one night he tried to stick a thousand dollars' worth up his behind. Well, that's what the coroner said. All I know was he was dead in his dressing room. Jesus, he was a funny guy."

None of them really knew how to talk to Jenny. From everything she said, from the way she was with them, they knew she felt just as she always had; and yet they felt they should set her apart some way, because they had read about her in *People* magazine. They all knew, for example, who Fred was. When Fred died it was front-page news on three continents. He and Jenny were supposed to have been longtime lovers, and the night he died she was opening the show for him at the Hollywood Bowl. Of course this was the first time they heard that he hadn't died of a heart attack. But since they knew all the rest of it, they didn't know what to say. So they didn't say anything.

"Do you happen to know what the word 'karma' really means?" Jenny asked. They shook their heads.

"It's the theory that life keeps bringing you around and around over the same ground, as if you were on a spiral staircase. You keep moving, going up, so you're never in exactly the same place in the same way, and yet it *does* keep bringing you back around to face certain things again and again, until you learn whatever it is you have to learn. My karma seems to be to love a lot of people who die when they've got no business to."

She closed her eyes again and began silently to chant the syllables that would slowly sink deeper and deeper into her center until they vibrated along every nerve, burning out the pain that pressed from the outside and replacing it with a blue floating peace. Om namah Shivaya, Om namah Shivaya, Om namah Shivaya, Mother, Malcolm, Fred, Sally, Mother, Malcolm, Fred, Sally.

"Are you doing TM?" she heard Muffin ask her. She shook her head.

"Well—are you allowed to say what it is? I'd like to know, if you are." Jenny thought about it, and about some other things. After a while she began to talk.

Jenny had been touring in Europe when her father called to tell her Malcolm had been murdered. For two months after that she traveled, worked, ate, fucked, and slept in anger. She cried all the time. She swore to herself she'd stop talking about it, which was just keeping her horror fresh, and then she'd be gripped, like the Ancient Mariner, and she'd find herself going through it all again, Malcolm with his eyes wide with fear, his hands tied, and his throat cut, lying on his own bed. Malcolm murdered by some vicious pervert shit he'd picked up, Malcolm dead from the danger of loving his fellow humans in an unconventional way. By the end of the tour her manager said if she didn't pull herself together he was going to cancel her contract, because Jenny was just too nuts to work with; he couldn't be bothered.

She went to a shrink in New York. He said she could only be freed by finding in herself the homicidal anger that she must surely feel, the desire to murder the man who murdered Malcolm. Her anger grew. She ran into a guy in a bar on Bleecker Street, a guy she'd first met in the Village in the early folk days who said that his spiritual name was now Gopa. "Hey, man," said Gopa, "that's not the Way. You want to be free from the pain, you got to surrender it. You got to let go of the anger. It's got nothing to do with right or wrong, man, it's just about pain and growth. You don't know why Malcolm died. Maybe he killed someone in a former life, maybe he learned all his lessons and earned the right to float off into the ozone. It's none of your business why. Surrender it. Let go. You want to get out of the pain, then you got to give up whatever you invested in wanting things to be fair and just and okay for you. Whatever Malcolm's lesson was, man, he's learned it. The guy who killed him, that's God's business. He's got lifetimes of pain in front of him, so pity him. But your lesson is to open up to the fact that you lost someone and you have to figure out what it means in your life. What are you learning by losing him? Why did God put that pain in your life?"

And that, more or less, was how she (with five hundred others) came to find herself a month later sitting in a resort hotel in the Catskills, temporarily retitled the Siddha Yoga Ashram, sitting barefoot and cross-legged on the floor of what used to be the ballroom, chanting Sanskrit at five o'clock in the morning.

It wasn't easy for her to go there. All weekend she had to fight to overcome her skepticism. It didn't help that when she emerged, stiff from her first long afternoon of prayer and meditation, she found that someone had stolen her shoes. It didn't help to calculate that although they had each already paid a fee, admittedly modest, to cover room and board for the weekend, the ashram was making hundreds of dollars selling them fresh oranges, mangoes, and pears each morning and afternoon, which they then presented one by one to the guru as their offering during darshan and which was then carried away and turned into fruit stew or salad for their next meal.

What made her stay was the presence of the guru himself, whom Gopa had called "a living saint, a totally realized being." She had first seen him when he entered the ballroom partway through the first prayer session, and the faces of his followers had glowed at his very presence, reflecting his progress through the room as sunflowers turn themselves to the sun.

He was a small brown man wearing bright orange robes and blue bedroom slippers, and he spoke in a Hindustani dialect that was simultaneously translated by a young Indian woman, but forever afterward Jenny remembered his words each time she saw him as if he had spoken in his own voice in English. He spoke and smiled like a man so brimming with glee, so utterly infused with joy at everything he heard and felt and saw, that he could scarcely keep from giggling. He was a little brown man who so loved the world, as it was, that for him there was never anger or disappointment or fear, or anything to forgive.

He told them, among many other apparently simple things, that many who were there for the first time were afraid that they would be tricked, that nothing would happen, or that something would happen to other people, but not to them.

"I guarantee you," he said, "that when the weekend is over, every single one of you will have seen God. And you will know you have done so. And when you do, you will not say, oh, mercy, oh, shooting stars, something new under the sun, something more wonderful than I ever dreamed of. No, you will say to yourself, ah, so that's it. I have felt that before. I have had it right along."

For a day and a half, during the three-hour-long sessions of chanting aloud, chanting silently, or hearing the guru, Jenny got nowhere, fought boredom, prayed that she wouldn't have to go to the bathroom. She was locked in the present, in the specific details of who and where she was, and what she was feeling at that moment and whether the people next to her were annoyed that she had to scratch her foot or whether they were faking the moans and twitches that shuddered through their bodies (supposedly caused by the kundalini force rushing along the energy paths within them, breaking through knots of tension).

Then in the darkened hall one late afternoon, surrounded by people sitting stone-still, or yipping like animals, or shaking or weeping, she slipped out of herself and floated into a dim, warm space beyond time. In a few seconds, or perhaps it was a few years, she saw reels and reels of pictures of people and places and chains of events, taking place in real time, all taking as long as they needed to take. She found that she was experiencing an event, apparently simultaneously, from the point of view of each person involved. She saw that each person was trying, each was feeling deeply, each doing what he could do, or what he had to do.

She saw her mother, a woman about the age that Jenny was now, slowly dying. For the first time in twenty years she felt, not her own sorrow and anger at losing her mother, but what her young mother felt at losing her life. She felt love and pity for her mother, she felt her mother's wrenching grief at leaving her young daughter. She felt that her mother was truly and forever dead, and seen from the deep midnight arc of inner space where God was, there was nothing to mourn ("Margaret, are you grieving/Over Goldengrove unleaving?").

She went minute by minute, again and again, through Malcolm's murder. For all these months of witnessing the scene in her mind until she wanted to scream with rage, she had never let herself experience it through Malcolm's eyes. This time she saw the murderer approach as Malcolm had, from flat on the bed. She felt what he must have felt, to have opened himself to this person, to have allowed his hands to be tied. She felt his willingness.

She saw the knife raised, felt the flesh pierced, understood the emotional betrayal as worse than the physical pain. She lived with him through stroke after searing stroke of the knife, waiting with agonized acceptance to learn which was the stroke that killed him, which of the scalding slashes actually made him die.

She understood at last, and for the first time, that Malcolm was beyond anything she could do for him. She could be free at last, not of missing Malcolm, which was her own feeling, but of her pity for him, which he no longer needed, and of the compulsive pain that came from trying to prevent his death by not accepting it. Her heart, she was aware, had opened like a fist relaxed, and the knot in her chest was now filled with a deep glowing joy that extended from her to everything that had ever been or would ever be.

The thought of Malcolm reminded her (as it had before? had it?) of John O'Neill. So many years ago, the first man she really loved. She thought of Malcolm on the bed with his hands tied, and then she thought of John—of how young he had been, how guilt-ridden, how hungry. She saw for the first time what he must have seen when he looked at her: a very young girl with a strangely adult self-possession, she had thrilled and scared him. She had wept with frustration the day in the hayloft when he first told her he wouldn't make love to her. (She saw now that it was her obstacle on the gyre, the place on the spiral that life kept bringing her back to. The love she wanted to give and couldn't. Love brimming in her, rejected. Her mother gone where love couldn't follow. John loving her but closing her out. Malcolm gone now. What was the lesson?)

Her other loves and her success had done much to arm her for life in other ways. But that had nothing to do with this pattern, this particular constellation of events that kept recurring, as other kinds of challenge or loss recurred to other people but not to her. It was breathtaking to admit the possibility that it was not malevolent coincidence—that the pattern, the recurrence, was the very fact she must accept, so she could reach beyond it to some understanding.

Remembering John.

She and John had helped each other feel less confused, less alone. She had refused to understand why he wouldn't make love to her. "You're afraid because you're a virgin," she said at her angriest. "That's true, but that's not why," he had said hopelessly. Underneath, she knew it was just his decency, his knowing that sleeping together would make it too hard to grow up to whatever had to come next, either something lasting between them, or the end of what was between them. God, it was hard to remember being fifteen, when you felt so much and knew so little! At last, in pain at being turned away, she had closed him out. She stopped meeting him and she closed herself off from the love for him she had felt. She never really let herself think about what it had done to him when she turned away, not even when, much later, he said he had been wrong. He said he needed her to love him more than he needed whatever had held him back.

She had said it was too late. In the room, around her, the chanting had begun again, and then the curtains that covered one wall were pulled back to let in the dusk. She found that her face was wet with tears and that about ten minutes had passed.

"What time is it?" asked Muffin. The record was over again, and Muffin and Ann were playing Scrabble.

"I'd like to sing," said Lisa. This surprised the others; it used to be always Lisa who refused to sing except with the whole group of Daisies. She began "How High the Moon . . ." and the others found their pitches after a bar or two and joined her, a very tentative rendering of the old arrangement.

"Well, that wasn't good," said Ann afterward.

"No," said the others. Ann began "You Go to My Head," and they got through it better. Ann thought, as they were singing, that sharing the music, working together night after night as they had through senior year, was in many ways a stronger bond among them than all the playing they'd done together. Working together. She wished they could dig Sally's grave together, it would be such a relief to be responsible for shifting all that earth. Instead of this intangible weight of time passing, of things changing, of never being able to quite see anything whole, until it was too late. They each had some sort of vision of the others' lives, but how many pieces were missing? For example, why hadn't Muffin and Chip had any children? They had set themselves up in this huge house with nothing particular to do except raise children, it would seem, but then none came. Was it because of the population explosion? Was it medical? Was it just being trapped in some permanent state of adolescence, not really wanting to give up their games and their extraordinary closeness to each other? If they were having trouble, why didn't they adopt? Muffin was always the perfect affectionate aunt to Ann's son . . . so why had she none of her own? A strange thing to not know about your friend and sister-in-law. Was it respect for her privacy that had kept her from asking Muffin? Or no longer wanting the responsibility of hearing each other's deepest feelings? Or was it just some distaste at the thought of hearing anything too intimate about her brother's sex life?

Missing pieces. For that matter, there was much they couldn't see whole about themselves. Things they had forgotten, times they'd failed to add up two and two to see the pattern forming. If they could all open their hearts tonight and pour out everything inside, without reserve, without concern for protecting themselves or each other, would they finally, for one moment, be able to understand anything useful? Or would they be dazzled into immobility by the sudden vision of how many days and words and chance happenings and distant movements were bearing on every moment of their lives? Would they be terrified to grasp, for one moment, how little it was possible to comprehend the infinite, tiny, but cumulative ways they had acted on and reacted to each other?

Muffin was thinking much the same thing, but "focus" was the word she used for it. It was interesting how much help it could be just to know the right word for the thing you were trying to think about. She'd been given the word "focus," as one might lend or recommend a new power tool, by her friend Josie one day at lunch at the club. Josie'd gotten it from her psychiatrist.

"What's analysis like?" asked Muffin. "Are you allowed to talk about it? Because if you are, I'd like to know." Josie said that mainly the doctor just listened to her and asked questions once in a while. Muffin said she wasn't sure she understood how that would help.

"Well, he can show you that you can be looking right at something and not seeing what's there, depending on how you're focusing. Like, one day I was telling him this dream I'd had about seeing my father holding a giant pretzel stick, this big"— she gestured—"and he just interrupted and said, 'How big?'"

Josie was being treated for vaginismus, an emotionally triggered condition that made intercourse painful or impossible, and this moment at the psychiatrist's had apparently led to a string of childhood memories whose discovery opened the way for her cure. "Well, at least I'm much better, most of the time."

Muffin had thought a lot about focus. She had thought especially that while much of what happened in life was beyond your control, you *could* control what part you focused on. You didn't have to lie down and wallow in things that were difficult or painful; you could focus on whatever was positive. Tonight, listening to Jenny, she had added a new interpretation to the concept. If you could focus on something from a point of view that was not centered in yourself at all, you might find that it bore a completely different meaning from what you had always thought. For instance, something might happen in your life that puzzled and hurt you as long as you kept trying to figure out why it happened to you; but if you could see it from God's point of view, maybe it would turn out not to be about you at all. Maybe its effect on you was just a by-product on the way to something else. The way the story ends shifts the meaning of everything that leads up to it. What she was particularly thinking about was this.

When Chip and Muffin became engaged, Madelon had invited her up to Greenwich one weekend when Chip was away, and after dinner, with Charles and Maude grouped around, had announced with great fanfare that Chip and Ann were adopted.

"We never saw any reason to tell them that they are not Laceys," she said. "We managed it very carefully so that almost no one could say for sure that they were not our own, and the servants who knew could be trusted. It did not seem to us to be any of their business—the children, I mean. They were much happier believing that they were ours. In any case, the decision is made and it's far too late to change it."

Muffin's first instinct was to laugh. The news itself, while startling and curious, hardly fazed her when she first heard it. What she focused on instead was the air of drama with which Madelon delivered it. "They are not *Laceys!*" Of course that was exactly the way Madelon would weight it. It was a supreme moment of Madelonism, already a private source of hilarity to Muffin. Of course, later she would have to face the secret as more complex than funny, beginning with the fact that it *was* a secret, when secrets from Chip were the last thing she had wanted.

"We feel," Madelon was saying, "that you have a right to know who your husband-to-be *really* is. He has turned out very well, of course, but blood matters—it matters very much, I believe. And as one who may someday be the mother of his children, you have a right to know his true background." With that she handed Muffin an envelope. Muffin took it upstairs with her and studied the contents that night. There were the names of the natural parents and a brief description of their circumstances, compiled by the agency that had handled the adoption. There was also a medical history of the mother's family, what little, apparently, the girl had known of such things. Muffin's principal emotion at the time was a trivial satisfaction that she happened to know the correct medical name for the disease that killed the girl's father. On the form it was colloquially described, but Muffin knew the Latin term because it was a rare trait, and according to perversely proud family tradition, the same thing had killed her maternal grandfather. There was next to nothing about Chip's father except race, religion, and occupation. In the morning Muffin returned the envelope to Madelon and said no more about it.

When Ann had announced that she was going to marry the man she'd been living with in Cambridge, Madelon told Muffin she was going to invite him to dinner. Muffin didn't believe he'd come. Stu Rosen was a highly independent and irreverent person, and he'd made very few bones about kowtowing to Ann's parents. However, he did come, on a night when Chip was away at a court-tennis tournament in Boston.

At dinner Madelon was particularly unctuous, making the point over and over and far less subtly than she could imagine, that their impeccable breeding would never allow them to express disappointment at Ann's choice of husband. The Laceys did not air their dirty linen in public. Ann had chosen the alliance that she wished to make, and the Laceys would from that day forward present a united front to the outside world of support and acceptance for their new son-in-law.

After dinner, when she and Muffin and Maude and Charles were seated with their demitasse cups in the living room, Madelon gestured Stu to a seat near the fire, and she produced a large manila envelope.

"Now that you are to be a member of the family, I have something to tell you," she began, and then she made to him much the same speech she had made to Muffin.

"We feel that you, as the father of her children, have a right to know who your wife really is. Because blood will tell, young man. Breeding counts. There may come a time when some piece of information contained in this envelope will explain a great deal to you, and that is why we feel you have a right to it." She rose and crossed the room to him and handed him the envelope. He waited until she was seated again; then, without once look- ing at the envelope, without ever taking his eyes from Madelon's face, he stretched out his hand and dropped the envelope into the fire.

"What counts, Mrs. Lacey," he said, "is talent and intelligence and a good heart." Then he rose and said his good-evenings and left. As the hall door closed behind him, Maude, smiling slight- ly, began to applaud.

Muffin never mentioned this scene to Chip or to Ann, and as far as she could tell, Stu never did either. The only real post- script had been added several years after Stu and Ann married, when Maude died (peacefully in bed at the age of ninety-three). When her will was read, Madelon was incensed to discover that Maude had left a really very sizable bequest free and clear to Stuart Rosen. "I know what it is to have no money of your own and be married to a rich person. It makes trouble in a marriage," she had written. Stu Rosen was no longer in that position. And if, as Muffin and Chip believed, Ann had grown more relaxed and at peace in the last two years than they had ever known her, and if the change had something to do with Stu, proud Stu—as how could it not?—then it appeared that Maude had guessed right.

The last Scrabble game was over, and the four agreed that they were probably tired enough to sleep. When they said good- night in the hall upstairs, Lisa kissed each one impulsively. Again they watched, a little surprised, as she closed the door to her bedroom. Muffin slipped into the master bedroom quietly, so as not to wake Chip. Alone in the hall, Ann and Jenny embraced for a long moment before they parted to find their rooms along the carpeted darkness.

In the morning Lisa was the first to leave; she really couldn't stay away any longer from Harvey and the baby. She left them as she had met them, with a bright, opaque stream of chatter. All her friends were divine, her husband was just super, she was having the best time, and she thought everyone she knew was just dear. They should give her a ring *any*time they were going to be in New York.

They knew from the alumnae magazine, not from Lisa, that her marriage to George Tyler had broken up about two years after the big wedding at St. James's in Pittsburgh that her father had been so proud to give her. (They had all been bridesmaids, and Alida Beebe had arranged to have the Sewickley huntsman dressed in his pink coat play "Gone Away" on his hunting horn as the happy couple drove away from the church.) After the divorce, Lisa moved to New York and got a job at the Frick, and after a year or two had remarried a successful lawyer, a young partner at Sullivan, Cromwell. Actually, Jenny did know one other incident that Philip had told her of, but she didn't mention it to the others.

Lisa had run into Philip at Jenny's first concert at Carnegie Hall. It was the year that Jenny was promoting the album that made her famous, so that meant it was just before Lisa remarried. Lisa seemed very subdued and self-involved, Philip said. She seemed surprised to see him there. She'd carried Philip on her books so long as being in love with her that she'd even forgotten he knew Jenny.

They went back to her apartment so she could let the sitter go home; Philip looked in to see her sleeping son, who even with his thumb in his mouth was a perfect blond miniature George Tyler.

They sat and talked and drank champagne. ("More champagne than milk," she said, opening the refrigerator, "just as things should be.") She said everything was super. George was being really a very good daddy, and the divorce was civilized. She just adored her job. It was so good for her to be independent. She had always *seemed* very sure of herself, she knew, but having a job gave her a new kind of self-confidence.

After a while, as a sort of salute to old memories, Philip kissed her. "You can't imagine how many fantasies of doing this I've had," he told her. To his surprise, she kissed him back, and kissed him and kissed him, with a strange sad heat, until they were both shaking. He unwound her arms from around his neck and gently settled her back on the couch away from him.

"Lisa," he said, "I don't do this. I'm involved with somebody else, and I want to marry her." She wouldn't believe it. Or she wouldn't believe that it made enough difference to prevent him doing something he obviously wanted to do. She cried before he left, unable to see that any principle or fresh desire could carry more power or weight than the dreams they had had when they were eighteen.

It was Muffin, of course, who had to write up the "In Memoriam" message for Sally for the alumnae bulletin. She'd called the husband (Sally's third) to see what he wanted said about the way Sally died. He seemed really terribly broken up. He told her, among other things, that in the note Sally left she said she hoped her friends would remember her stepsons as if they had been her own children.

Muffin had written to each of the boys at once, telling them things about what their stepmother had been like when she was near their age, and why her friends had loved her. She had also written to those of Sally's friends who would understand what Sally had been thinking of when she asked them to remember her boys. So she was much involved with correspondence in the few weeks after reunion. Most of it had to do with Sally, but she did get two letters that touched on other things. The first was from Linda Hawley.

Dear Muffin,

I just want to let you know once more what a dynamite job you did on the reunion.

You really got people talking to each other again, and a lot of us needed that. I wanted to tell you, too, that I'm sorry about Sally. I never was as close to her as you were, but I know that it must have been an awful shock to you. I hope you're getting through it, and that you'll let me know if I can help.

There's one more thing I want to tell you, although I know I shouldn't—but all of a sudden there's no one else I *can* tell who might understand. You remember how close Sandy and I were at Pratt's? She's Merry's godmother and we still see a lot of each other. I realize I . . . [illegible] . . . the best way to explain it is, I had a couple of rocky years with Steve, right after Merry was born, you may have heard. He'd get going on my mother and how alike we are, and then he'd start yelling at me that I never get anything straight and I only remember what I want to remember and so on, and he'd yell at me that I was crazy. I felt so terrible all the time that I'd think: That's right, I must be crazy—how would I know if I wasn't? One of the things I held on to was Sandy. I'd think: Wait a minute, I've known Sandy twice as long as I've known Steve; I even lived with her longer, and I know everything about her and she knows everything about me and she doesn't think I'm crazy. It's like a rock, even if you don't know it, that sense that there's somebody out there who just plain *knows* you, and you know them. I mean, that's the whole point of Pratt's, I always thought. The friendships.

Anyway, when I got home Saturday night after the reunion, of course the first thing I did was to call Sandy (she's in Hawaii) to give her the blow-by-blow on everything she missed. She was very sorry about Sally, and then I said, "Guess what? The famous klepto sent back all that stuff she stole while we were at school!"

And she said, "Yes, I know. It was me."

The other letter was essentially a bread-and-butter letter from Lisa. She, too, thanked Muffin again for all the work she'd done on the reunion, and said how much it had meant to them all. And she thanked her and Chip for having herself and Jenny and Ann to stay. "I don't think I could have faced just going home and saying to Harvey, 'Guess what?—my friend Sally's dead.' I mean, since he didn't ever know her or anything. Anyway, it was hard for me to say at the time, but having that time together with the three of you just to sort of decompress mattered a lot to me.

"It's hard to really stay in touch, isn't it? I mean, we all try, but when you just don't see each other from one year to the next, you can't really expect it not to make a difference.

"I wrote a paper about F. Scott Fitzgerald when I was at Briarcliff, and I came across this thing he said in a letter once to Edmund Wilson. It was when they were both in their forties, and for some reason Scott was writing about when they were in college together (during the war), and he said: 'It was fun when we all believed the same things. It was more fun to think that we were all going to die together or live together, and none of us anticipated this great loneliness. . . .'"

BETH GUTCHEON is the author of *Saying Grace, Domestic Pleasures,* and *Still Missing.* She has written several film scripts, including the Academy Award-nominated documentary *The Children of Theatre Street.*

The Modern Classics by Beth Gutcheon

Five Fortunes

A warm, witty, and hope-filled story of five unforgettable
women and the unexpected friendships forged over
a transforming week at the "Fat Chance" spa.

**"A quintessential American woman's tale . . . I loved it. [Beth
Gutcheon] has absolutely perfect pitch when it comes to capturing
the lives of these remarkable women." —Anne Rivers Siddons**
ISBN 0-06-092995-2 • $13.00/$19.00 (Can.)

Saying Grace

This "deliciously readable" (*San Francisco Chronicle*) story
focuses on Rue Shaw, a woman who has it all—a great child, a
solid marriage, and a job she loves—and wants to keep it that
way, despite the changing world around her. Funny, rich in
detail and finally stunning, *Saying Grace* is "by turns
heartwarming and heartrending" (*Boston Globe*).
ISBN 0-06-092727-5 • $13.00/$19.00 (Can.)

Still Missing

When six-year-old Alex Selky never comes home from
school one day, his mother begins a desperate vigil
that lasts for days, weeks, then months against all hope.
The basis for the feature film *Without a Trace*.

**"Haunting, harrowing, and highly effective . . . a stunning
shocker of an ending. . . . It strings out the
suspense to the almost unendurable." —*Publishers Weekly***
ISBN 0-06-097703-5 • $13.00/$19.00 (Can.)

The New Girls

A resonant, engrossing novel about five girls in prep
school during the '60s into whose protected reality
marches the Vietnam War, the woman's movement, and
the sexual revolution—and changes their lives forever.

**"Funny without sacrificing intelligence, intelligent without being
pretentious. It's all-around good reading." —*Boston Globe***
ISBN 0-06-097702-7 • $13.00/$19.00 (Can.)

Available in bookstores everywhere, or call 1-800-331-3761 to order.

Cliff Street Books
An Imprint of HarperPerennial
A Division of HarperCollinsPublishers
www.harpercollins.com